Th'
Are ...m.

'As always with Louise's novels prepare to be moved, probably to tears, but to be enriched in the process. Just as her characters learn from each other even as they trip over every obstacle, so we learn a bit more about what it is to be human as we stumble along with them ... Another beautiful book from her pen' Live Many Lives

'What an incredibly amazing talent Louise Beech is. Each and every story she comes up with is emotional, insightful and powerful ... full of love, heartbreaking and heartwarming at the same time and ultimately unforgettable' Novel Deelights

'You can literally feel Beech's empathy and understanding rising in waves from the pages ... A moving, intimate, compassionate book that will make you angry, sad, fearful and happy'
Suidi's Book Reviews

'Louise is the queen of exquisite and moving writing that has you reaching for tissues ... A beautifully moving, exquisite and powerful read' Lost in the Land of Books

'Well done Louise Beech on another wonderful book'
Maddy's Book Blog

'Incredible story and subject matter, which I thought was very brave to delve into. This book has literally broken my heart and sewn it back together' No Empty Shelves Here

'The storytelling is at its usual, beautiful best, and the sensitivity and acknowledgment of the situation ... is perfect ... Another absolute beauty to add to this author's outstanding catalogue' Karen's Reads

'This book is far more than a story of a young autistic man. It is the story of acceptance ... of love, family, understanding ... Louise Beech hasn't just created characters, she has created living people who leap out of the pages into your life ... A fabulously written story that touches the reader's heart' Condy Gurl

'A very moving story about a mother's love for her son ... makes you think what you would do in that situation'
Echoes in an Empty Room

'Achingly brilliant and totally compelling – *This Is How We Are Human* made me laugh, made me cry, challenged some of my perceptions and above all made me care deeply for the three main characters' The Book Club

'The story is sensitively written, and drew me in with every page ... you have to remind yourself that it is fiction, and I think it would make for a beautiful movie' With a Book in Our Hands

'No words can describe how beautiful this book is. I have loved every single book by Louise Beech, but this one stands out so much. I shed tears not only of sadness but also of joy, of stress about what was going to happen and of utter amazement at the beautifully written story' Me Love Books

'There are no words to describe the beauty of this book. It reached down to my soul ... The characters are incredibly lovely and one by one will worm a way into your heart only to break it ... then heal it piece by piece' Mrs Loves To Read

'This is one of the most poignant, brilliantly written and profound human-interest stories I have read!' Nicky Reviews Reads

WHAT READERS ARE SAYING...

★ ★ ★ ★ ★

'A beautiful, heart-wrenching, poignant, sensitively rendered and truthful book'

'Louise does it again. Another brilliant story'

'Wonderful, touching and heartwarming'

'Breathtakingly beautiful ... never wanted it to end'

'Beautifully and empathetically told'

'An incredibly moving portrait of love in all its forms'

'A truly breathtaking read'

'THE book you must read this year ... heartwarming, poignant and everything between!'

'The characters are so realistic, and the situation they find themselves in makes for an intriguing plot'

'Outstanding portrayal of realistic people in an extraordinary scenario'

'Fascinating and thought-provoking ... really gives an insight into life with ASD'

'Wow! What a FABULOUS BOOK! ... I might have found a new favourite author'

'A beautiful yet thought-provoking novel'

'Enchanting; it's almost as if Beech puts a spell on you'

'Pure perfection'

'A superb book ... Difficult subjects, sensitively handled'

'Very sensitively written and makes me think that the author really knows someone who is on the spectrum'

'Characters that evoke such emotional responses, I found myself laughing and crying and willing them on'

'Full of human frailty and strength ... Beech has opened up the eyes of a crowd as she explores adult autism'

'Extremely moving, sometimes very funny, extraordinarily thought-provoking'

'If you only pick up one book this year, this should be it'

'A beautifully written, sensitive book'

'An extraordinary and powerful story'

'A stunner of a book. It is moving, powerful and sensitive'

'Made me smile, cry and think a lot about loneliness, life, happiness'

'A truly beautiful book that has an incredible purity'

'A brave book and will no doubt elicit some in-depth discussions'

'The characters themselves are absolutely wonderful and they each have so many layers'

'Shows all the true complexities of love, sex and autism'

'So heartfelt and so real. I will miss Sebastian'

ABOUT THE AUTHOR

Louise Beech is a prize-winning author, whose debut novel *How To Be Brave* was a *Guardian* Readers' Choice for 2015. The follow-up, *The Mountain in My Shoe*, was shortlisted for Not the Booker Prize. Her next books, *Maria in the Moon* and *The Lion Tamer Who Lost*, were widely reviewed, critically acclaimed and number-one bestsellers on Kindle. *The Lion Tamer Who Lost* was shortlisted for the RNA Most Popular Romantic Novel Award and the Polari Prize in 2019.

Her novel *Call Me Star Girl* won *Best* magazine Book of the Year, and was followed by *I Am Dust*. Her short fiction has won the Glass Woman Prize, the Eric Hoffer Award for Prose, and the Aesthetica Creative Works competition, as well as shortlisting for the Bridport Prize twice. Louise lives with her husband on the outskirts of Hull and loves her job as a Front of House Usher at Hull Truck Theatre, where her first play was performed in 2012.

Follow Louise on Twitter @LouiseWriter and visit her website: louisebeech.co.uk.

Also by Louise Beech

How To Be Brave
The Mountain in My Shoe
Maria in the Moon
The Lion Tamer Who Lost
Call Me Star Girl
I Am Dust

This Is How We Are Human

Louise Beech

**ORENDA
BOOKS**

Orenda Books
16 Carson Road
West Dulwich
London SE21 8HU
www.orendabooks.co.uk

First published in the United Kingdom by Orenda Books, 2021
Copyright © Louise Beech, 2021

A catalogue record for this book is available from the British Library.

ISBN 978-1-913193-71-3
eISBN 978-1-913193-72-0

Typeset in Garamond by typesetter.org.uk

Printed and bound by CPI Group (UK) Ltd, Croydon CR0 4YY

For sales and distribution, please contact info@orendabooks.co.uk

'The need to be together, against all the odds, to stand side by side – whatever the grindstones of life permit – and to feel that the very stars dance in each other's eyes transcends all; love is solemn simplicity; and is inevitable'

Wolfy O'Hare

This book is dedicated to the Mills family,
and to Joanne Robertson's little Sebastian.

SEBASTIAN GETS READY TO SINK

I love it here. I love this river. It's freezing this morning though. It's seven-fifteen. Not the right time yet. The water looks colder than I am. It's bouncy and brown and moody. The sky is too. Clouds rush away from it. Even with my red coat and my leather gloves and my Hull City hat and my Puma trainers on, I shiver. I'm glad I'm not taking them off. Normally I take all my clothes off and just wear trunks and goggles when I swim. Really, it's like how you get ready to have sex. I'm going to miss sex. And swimming. But I don't want to swim here.

This morning I have come to sink.

There are two benches here. The left one was my dad's. We ate sandwiches here like this was our living room with a river going through it. We always took our shoes off too, no matter how cold it was. But today I need them on to help me sink.

It's seven-twenty now.

Not time yet.

I open my notepad at the *How To Sink* list. Number one is *The Bigger The Water The Easier It Is To Sink*. You are less likely to float if the volume of water is greater than the volume of you. Number two is *Wear Very Heavy Things*. I stand. It's seven-twenty-five.

Almost time.

I climb over the rocks to get to the water. There are gaps that try and trap me. It's a good job I must keep my shoes on. I'm out of puff when I reach the small beach. The waves lap at my Puma trainers while I catch my breath. They're ruined, which is a shame because they cost fifteen pounds fifty.

I read the rest of my *How To Sink* note. Number three is *Take A*

Vertical Position In The Water With Your Feet Pointing Down. I'll do that when I get to the middle. Number four is *Get Into A Tucked Position*. This is because objects sink in water if they take up less space. I know the rest. Just do the opposite of everything I normally do to try and float.

It's seven-thirty now. It's the right time.

It used to be my favourite time when I was with HoneyBee. Now it's my last time. So here I go.

To sink.

VERONICA GOES TO THE SEXUAL HEALTH CLINIC

Veronica is monstrously overdressed.

The pink silk scarf and delicate diamond drop earrings that she chose carefully this morning now only accentuate how different she is to the other women in the Rowan House waiting room. Most of them are less than half her age and look as though they're attending a gym or social club. A fug of cigarette smoke and celebrity perfume emanates from their young pores. Veronica muses that Sebastian, who's making himself comfortable in the corner by some books, looks far more suited to the place in his baggy grey joggers, Superman hoodie, and brand-new Puma trainers that he only wears on special days.

Perhaps it's a good sign; perhaps he is in the right place; perhaps *they* are in the right place. Perhaps someone here can help her.

Abandoning a pamphlet about sexually transmitted diseases, Sebastian returns to Veronica.

'Mum,' he says. 'That woman with big, zazzy hair looked at me like she might want to have sex with me.' His swimming goggles are wrapped around his wrist, and he still has a trace of egg yolk on his softly stubbled chin. Veronica wipes at it with the edge of her lace sleeve.

'Fucking pervert,' says the woman in question under her breath.

'Really,' sighs Veronica. 'There's no need for that. He's jus—'

'He just needs telling,' she says, her purple-mascaraed eyes glaring.

Veronica stands and strides purposefully to where the woman sits, grateful now of her armour, of her dusky Valentino coat, of her favourite scarf. Fear lights the woman's eyes, just a flicker, then it's gone. Then she scowls.

'Sebastian is autistic,' Veronica says in a low voice. 'Only stupid sees stupid. Only pervert sees pervert. I'll thank you to mind your language.'

'*Me* mind *my* language? He's the one who fu—'

'Cheryl Cooper,' calls the receptionist. 'Room three please.'

The zazzy-haired woman stands, squares up to Veronica for a second, and then tuts and heads down the corridor. Veronica returns to her son. Sebastian is flicking through *Sex Health* magazine now, his wild, wavy hair lifting at the turn of each page. How beautiful he is to her; perfect. She can behold him for hours. That's the best word to describe it – *behold*. Curled lashes that would make a model jealous, eyes the colour of ripe acorns, chubby lips perfect for kissing, cheeks she can never resist pinching.

'I thought it would be more like *Love Island*, Mum,' he says.

'It's a clinic, darling. We talked about it last night.'

'You said it was a sex house.'

'No, a *clinic*, where people *talk* about sexual issues.'

'But I don't want to talk about sex. I want to have it.'

'I know that, bu—'

'Can we go to KFC after this?'

'We'll see.'

'Veronica Murphy,' calls the receptionist. 'Room four please.'

'Can I take this?' asks Sebastian, holding up the magazine. 'There's a picture of a tiger on a woman's bottom on page thirty-four.'

'*What*?' Veronica flicks to the page. The image is of a roaring tiger tattoo on a semi-clad woman's left buttock. 'No, I think we'll leave this here, darling.'

They head along the corridor, past rooms one, two and three. Veronica knocks softly on door four and a sharp voice calls, 'Come in!'

Sebastian pushes in first, keen as always to investigate the room, to see where the books are, if there are any fish, and to pick the best seat. In the main chair at the desk sits a woman who looks like she hasn't eaten meat for a good few years. A green polo neck is one size too big and sags at her pale neck; wooden beads scream *I love all things natural and I'll judge your plastic shoes.*

'Please, take a seat.' She gestures to the chairs by the window. 'I'm Mel.'

Sebastian sits on the chair next to Mel's and says, 'I'm Sebastian James Murphy and I'm twenty years and six months and two days old.'

'Oh. Hello.' Mel seems uncomfortable having him sit so close that their knees touch. Veronica sees in her eyes the things she has seen in so many eyes over the years. Flashes of discomfort, sparks of mild repulsion, flickers of *why does he have to bother me?*

'Sebastian, remember about boundaries.' Veronica pats a seat next to her, by the window. 'Maybe you should sit with me.'

Joining his mum, he says, 'She doesn't have any fish.'

'Not everyone does.'

'Mine are called Flip and Scorpion. They're bright gold.'

Mel opens her mouth to speak but is interrupted by a soft tapping on the door. She responds in the same sharp tone she used earlier. A girl bursts into the room, out of breath, damp hair the colour of spring daffodils stuck to her forehead. Girl is the word that comes to Veronica, though she is perhaps almost thirty. The gust of air sends papers tumbling from the desk; she picks them up, apologising profusely, her white uniform with blue lapels gaping as she bends, revealing a hot-pink bra. The sexiness of the garment contrasts with the girl's youthful appearance so sharply that Veronica exhales – and realises she is staring.

'This is Isabelle,' says Mel.

'So sorry, my car was be—'

'Isabelle is a student nurse in her final year, and if you don't object, she'll be sitting in today.' Mel doesn't look at the girl, but her narrowed eyes make clear how unimpressed she is by her lack of punctuality.

'I am happy she is here,' says Sebastian.

'It's fine by me,' agrees Veronica.

Gratitude colours Isabelle's eyes. She sits next to Mel, moving the chair away slightly as she does. Veronica stifles a smile at this subtle assertion of autonomy. Isabelle crosses her legs and pulls down her skirt. Sebastian has not taken his eyes off her; she smiles at him with the warmth of a late summer evening.

'What brings you here today, Mrs Murphy?' asks Mel, all business.

'I'm here about my son.'

'That's me,' says Sebastian.

'And what seems to be the trouble?'

Veronica composes herself, makes sure her scarf is perfectly smooth. She has been here before. Been to see doctors and social workers. Been to various autism support groups. She has told her tale many times in the past few months and had it fall on unsympathetic, unhelpful, unsure, and unable-to-do-anything ears. This time, no decorating it with gentle words or holding back. She has worn her softest colours, her most elegant earrings, but she will talk hard.

'Sebastian thinks about sex *all* the time,' she says.

'Stop talking about me,' he interrupts. 'Why are you talking about me? I'm right *here*.'

'I know, darling. But this is something I have to say here, OK? If I say anything that isn't true you can tell me, can't you? Remember, I said this morning that I would be talking about you, but you'd be here, and you can comment anytime?'

'I'm just going to look at Isabelle.'

She smiles.

Veronica returns her attention to Mel. 'You see, Sebastian's sex drive is on *fire*. He's obsessed with it. And that would be fine if he were able to just go out and meet someone like other young men his age and, you know' – Veronica coughs, embarrassed – 'do the sowing the wild oats thing that they do, but he can't, can he? He's autistic, as I imagine you've realised, so this limits his ability to mix with and meet girls.'

'I see. Well, these urges are very natural in a man of twenty, no matter what special needs he has.'

'Twenty years and six months and two days,' corrects Sebastian.

'Yes, they are,' says Veronica. 'But he's a young man who has no means of ... well, of *satisfying* his needs. You understand that? His needs are just a joke to most.'

'Not to me.' Mel is a picture of professionalism.

'Maybe. But to most people he's the stuff of *The Undateables*.'

'Not here,' insists Mel.

Veronica looks Mel firmly in the eye. 'I saw how you responded when Sebastian sat so close to you earlier.'

Flustered, Mel insists she would have been the same if anyone had insisted on sitting so close, so suddenly.

Veronica catches Isabelle's eye. *She gets it*, thinks Veronica. *She didn't see Mel recoil from Sebastian, but she believes me.*

'This room would be better with fish,' says Sebastian, unwrapping his goggles from around his wrist and putting them on his forehead, flattening his wild curls and making it look like he has four eyes.

'He can't meet people easily the way any of us can,' Veronica says to Mel.

'I *can*, they're just not able to see me properly.'

Veronica nods. 'Sometimes it's hard for you to understand what young women's facial gestures mean, isn't it, darling?' To Mel, she says, 'Everyone thinks autistic people can't read faces, but there's no proof. Sebastian is an individual. Autism isn't one size fits all. He generally knows my expressions. But young girls? That's tricky.'

'Have you tried talking about it with him?'

'Of course I have. We talk about everything, don't we, darling?' Sebastian shrugs.

'Sex is everywhere. In music videos and soap operas. He loves watching *Love Island*, and of course on there they swap beds in a matter of days. So he probably thinks it's something you can have, whenever and wherever and with whomever you want.'

'Which of course you can't,' says Mel, her tone even.

'I know *that*! For God's sake, he's not a pervert.'

'What's a pervert?' asks Sebastian. 'The zazzy-haired woman said I was one.'

'Which zazzy-haired wo—' starts Mel.

'Look,' snaps Veronica, 'I just need someone to *talk* with him. Guide him. I can't find the right help. He's *not* a pervert; he's my only child. His father died when he was seven and it's been just us ever since. I don't know what to do. I'm *exhausted*. He doesn't have any close friends his own age, you know, to maybe talk to. There's just ... me.'

Sebastian grabs a leaflet on *Sexual Health, Asylum Seekers and Refugees*, pulls his goggles over his eyes, and flicks through it without pausing to read a line. He then hands it wordlessly to Isabelle, who smiles, dons some tortoiseshell glasses she finds on Mel's desk, and does exactly the same. When she is done, she shrugs. He shrugs back.

'Does Sebastian have a support worker?' asks Mel.

'No, I never felt I needed anyone ... until now. I've been to see various people about this. My doctor told me to come to a clinic like this, since you specialise in sexual matters.'

'Look, before we go on, let me ask a few questions about Sebastian so I can ascertain exactly what help we might be able to give.'

'I like eggs,' he says. 'I like swimming. I like tigers. I like Billy Ocean. And I know I would like sex if I could get it. Have you had sex, Isabelle?'

'Yes,' she says.

'Is it good?'

'It's best with someone you love.'

'OK,' says Veronica to Mel. 'Ask whatever you need to.'

'How old was Sebastian when he was diagnosed, and what led to it?'

'I suppose I always knew. A mother just does. Then he went to nursery at three and I noticed his lack of interaction. While the other kids were mixing, Sebastian was running in circles around the room, flapping his arms like a little bird. The nursery nurse suggested I talk to someone. A doctor referred us to the children's centre, and they assessed him. Said he had Autistic Spectrum Disorder.'

Veronica feels her throat tighten. She will not cry; she will *not*. Isabelle's face softens, and she leans a little further forward in her chair. Sebastian has twisted his goggles around to the back of his head so that the elastic cuts through his closed eyes.

'Sebastian calls it "autism spectrum perception"', says Veronica, sadly.

'Yep,' he says.

'Has he ever taken medication?' asks Mel.

'No, never. It was offered to us all the time, especially when he didn't sleep. But I never wanted my boy all drugged up.'

'Just to help me in how we deal with your current issue ... I can see that Sebastian is physically twenty years old, but how old is he emotionally would you say? Mentally?'

'Mentally, he's very intelligent. He reads a lot. Has opinions on everything. He's like a sponge. Emotionally, that's the tricky one. You can't give an age to something like that. If I told you he was a sixteen-year-old at times, you'd say he was a child. But he isn't. He goes to college three days a week and—'

'An everyday college, not a specialist one?' asks Mel.

'An *everyday* one.' Veronica resists verbalising her outrage. 'He's doing his level two in bricklaying – he passed level one – and he'll eventually get a level-three diploma. Last month, for example, I was ill one day and couldn't move. Our housekeeper, Tilly, was away that week. After giving me a stern chat about taking things easy, Sebastian put a wash on and changed the bedding, and went to a local shop with a list and got everything on it.'

'She *still* didn't take it easy,' says Sebastian.

'He can physically live an everyday life.

'Yep.'

'But he's vulnerable to ... *suggestion*. He'll take what you suggest literally. Change scares him. If he got off the college bus at the wrong stop he'd panic because he's out of his comfort zone. But he would know to ask someone for help.' Veronica shrugs. 'You can see how tough this is. A sexually mature body demanding what it needs, belonging to a ... well, a vulnerable adult.'

Mel nods. 'Do you just need me to talk to him, one on one, do you think?'

'I don't know,' says Veronica at the same time as Sebastian says, 'No, thanks.'

'OK,' says Mel. 'Tell me, on a day-to-day basis, what it's like with Sebastian. Is his high sex drive the only problem?'

'Yes,' says Veronica. 'No. Look, he doesn't understand boundaries, not like you and I do. He needs someone to explain consent better than I can. I've tried. I showed him that Tea and Consent thing where if you can understand when it is and isn't OK to serve tea, then you understand consent. It was on social media. I think Thames Valley Police came up with it. But all Sebastian said was "I don't like tea".'

'I don't,' he says. 'It isn't hot chocolate.'

Veronica kisses his cheek. He wipes it off and smears it on the wall. She still hasn't been as frank as she needs to be. The words are choking her. The room feels small.

'He asked me the other night why he is twenty and hasn't—' starts Veronica softly.

'Twenty years and six months and two days old,' corrects Sebastian.

'Younger men than him have had lots of experience by now.' Veronica pauses. 'I worry that he might...'

'What?' asks Mel.

'Look, he knows that women have to be eighteen. I know it's sixteen, but I felt telling him eighteen was better.' Sebastian frowns at her, opens his mouth to speak, but she quickly continues. 'He can be very ... well, forward. He is happy to tell you his thoughts. I worry...'

Veronica glances at Isabelle. She's wearing the tortoiseshell glasses upside down, mirroring how Sebastian has now positioned his goggles.

'Do you think he would ever *force* anyone?'

'God, *no*. There isn't a violent bone in his body.'

'There are two hundred and six bones in the body,' says Sebastian. 'Mine are all good bones.'

'But he could end up in trouble, yes?' Mel's brow furrows with exaggerated concern. 'If he said the wrong thing to a young girl. Remember, *she* doesn't know he has autism. And neither do her parents.'

'This is why I need help,' admits Veronica.

'Did the doctor suggest some sort of medication to supress the sex drive?'

'Yes, but I already told you, I don't want him drugged. I don't want him to think his sexuality is wrong. It isn't. It's entirely natural. I want him to know he's not strange or bad or wrong.'

'Have you suggested that he try and meet someone *similar* to him?' asks Mel.

'You can ask me, you know,' says Sebastian. 'I'm still here. I haven't disappeared into skinny air.'

'Do you want to tell them about the university dance then, darling?' asks Veronica.

'Nope.'

Veronica turns to Mel. 'I suggested going to the weekly special-needs dance, and he just said, "Will I get a girlfriend?" I said possibly. And he said, "But I don't want her to have autism. I want to breed it out of the family." Those were his exact words. But everyday girls aren't interested in him. Occasionally I see them looking at him. I know he's lovely on the eye, and they see that. But the minute they talk to him...'

Mel nods. 'Look, I can certainly refer him for something one-to-one. Would you want him on his own in a room with anyone?'

'He won't understand. I'll have to be there too.'

'I honestly don't know what else we can do then.'

Veronica imagines walking out of this stifling room, away from Mel's clunky wooden beads and fake-concern nods, away from the young student nurse who is clearly taken with Sebastian enough to give him all her attention, away from her beautiful boy, and not coming back. No. *No.* How can she want such a thing? The guilt at thinking, even for a second, that she can abandon him strangles her. She undoes her scarf and puts it on her knee. Tries not to sob.

'Isabelle,' she says, 'I wonder can you take Sebastian outside for a few minutes? I need to say something in private to Mel.'

'Are we going to have sex?' Sebastian asks, eyes shining.

'No, but I do know where there are some fish,' says Isabelle, standing.

'*Where?*'

'Come on, I'll show you.'

As Isabelle is closing the door she gives Veronica a comforting, *I'll take care of him* smile.

3

VERONICA SPITS IT OUT

Mel looks expectantly at Veronica. Veronica realises it is time to say it. To spit it out. The thing she thought of the other night – alone, in tears, in her dark kitchen – but fears saying aloud.

'They hurt him,' she says first.

'Who?' asks Mel.

'Some kids on the bus. The other week. They weren't from his college or I'd have had them expelled.' Veronica closes her eyes and recalls the moment Sebastian walked through the door, jacket ripped and cheek bruised, still singing a Billy Ocean song. She tried to touch his face, tearful, demanding what on earth had happened. Sebastian shrugged and said he was OK. 'They played a pornographic video on a phone and got him all wound up and then they laughed because he was aroused ... and beat him up.'

'That's terrible,' says Mel kindly.

'He wouldn't tell me who they were.'

'They need reprimanding.'

'It isn't the only time. Some of the boys on his course, they tease him. They know he hasn't had sex. I only know because his tutor told me. Sebastian didn't. But he...' Veronica's voice wavers. 'He denied it when I talked to him. The other night he said that if he doesn't meet a girl, he might die.' Veronica has to breathe deeply not to cry.

Now spit it out, she thinks.

'I've been thinking,' she says, 'that there is an answer. A way. I could just pack and we go to Amsterdam and I take him to a ... well, a *professional* person. You know – a woman of the night. Someone who can meet his needs.'

'How old is he again?'

'Twenty.'

'No, I mean emotionally.' Mel fiddles with her beads. 'You said he's more like a teenager, so I have to advise that this would be highly inappropriate.'

'No.' Veronica controls her voice. 'He is *not* a child.'

'But still, you're talking about going to Amsterdam and taking a vulnerable adult with special needs for a night in the red-light district?'

'It wouldn't be like that,' snaps Veronica.

'What would it be like?'

Veronica regrets sharing her idea. Faced with Sebastian's bruised face, it came to her, a seemingly simple solution. She hasn't really thought about the how. She hasn't made actual plans. Now she feels ashamed. 'I'm only *thinking* about it.'

'I don't think legally that I can advise or recommend something like that.'

'You don't understand. I feel helpless. I can't bear his distress. He hasn't shown it here, today, but I see it. Every day, asking when will he have sex. Asking why doesn't anyone like him. Can you imagine how that makes me feel? If I could just ... make him *happy*. I've always been able to do that. But this ... how can I?'

'Maybe go back to your doctor – the answer might be medication.'

'I'm *not* going back there,' cries Veronica. 'Why do I need to calm him down?'

'Maybe he's not emotionally ready to be having sex.'

'How the hell do you know what he's emotionally ready for? I'm his mother and I know exactly what he's ready for.'

'Perhaps if he *was* emotionally ready, he would have found somebody.'

Veronica is momentarily wordless. She imagines taking hold of Mel's wooden beads and wrapping them tightly about her throat until she passes out and the patronising look on her face dies.

'Have you any idea how to deal with *human* people, never mind autistic people?' she asks softly. 'Or is everything you know something you've read in a book?'

'I could refer you to somebody,' says Mel, coolly.

'Right, I think we're done here.'

Veronica stands, flicks her scarf back around her neck, and gathers her bag from the floor.

'I have to tell you,' says Mel, 'that if you do take him to a prostitute, then I'm obliged to inform the social-services team. I have to safeguard a vulnerable adult.'

'Then I'm telling you *nothing*!'

Veronica strides from the room, head high, and draws on all her strength to close the door quietly. She leans against it, clutching her lapels with trembling hands. Laughter from nearby. Sebastian and Isabelle are at the opposite end of the corridor, by a large tank full of luminous tropical fish. He has the tortoiseshell glasses on upside down and she wears his goggles. He flaps his hands, not in panic, but to mimic a large rainbow fish that swims in circles.

As Veronica approaches them, she hears him say, 'I've got two fish. In their tank, fish can see all of us and hear all of us, but they're separate.'

'We have to go now, darling,' says Veronica, gently.

'I don't want to leave, Mum.' Sebastian shakes his head. 'I like Isabelle. She likes me. We look at things with the same eyes. Look – we swapped and tried each other's on.'

'Isabelle has to work now. You said you wanted to go to KFC.'

'Yes, yes, KFC.'

Sebastian takes his goggles carefully from Isabelle's head and puts the glasses on her, then goes back towards the waiting room.

'I might just be a student,' says Isabelle, watching him tidy his hair in the reflection of a large-framed poster, 'and I don't know what I would say in your difficult circumstances, but I wouldn't say some of the things Mel did.'

'Thank you.' Veronica is moved by this young creature with skin like ivory soap and sad, sad eyes. 'You'll make a very special nurse. How long have you got until you graduate?'

'Six months.'

'Are you specialising?'

'My degree is in learning disability.'

'Wonderful,' smiles Veronica. 'Do you know what area you want to go into?'

'I'm not entirely sure yet. I think I'd like to work with children or young adults.'

'Will you look for work around here?'

'I'm not sure yet.' Isabelle isn't guarded, rather she seems unable to say the many things that flit across her face.

'I hope so,' says Veronica. 'We could do with more nurses like you.' Sebastian has disappeared around the corner. 'Look, I have to go. But thank you. And good luck in your career, wherever you go.'

Veronica heads back to the waiting area, sure she feels Isabelle's eyes following her. But when she looks back, Isabelle has gone, and the large rainbow fish is still the only one swimming in a circle. Veronica can't help but wonder if she's imagined the young nurse, and that if she were to call the clinic tomorrow, they would ask her, 'Isabelle who? We don't have anyone called Isabelle here.'

When she finds Sebastian studying a book about the Aztecs, she is back in the world where only they exist.

ISABELLE WRITES A NOTE TO THE NIGHT

Dear Night,

I dream of strangling Dr Cassanby to death with his black silk tie. All the time. He makes me choke him with it until he almost passes out sometimes, but I want to do it until he's dead.

It's weird – he looks a bit like my dad did ten years ago. He's not as heavy in the face and stomach, and he's taller, but the determined way he walks is my dad. And that only makes me hate Cassanby more because it makes me miss my dad. The old one, anyway. The one I don't have anymore.

He takes me to the Westwood Restaurant for dinner and afterwards he sucks on a cigar, which he only smokes after red wine, he says, then chews some gum. I have to smile through clenched teeth. Then he drives us back to his house (which is beautiful in a way that rarely used homes are) and asks me to unfasten that wretched shiny tie, wrap it around his limp wrists and tug on it until the skin chafes...

Isabelle puts down her pen. She shakes one of her snow globes and sets it down on the desk. While the spiralling storm within settles into calm, she closes her book, marking the page bearing the half-written note with a perfume sniffer stick. She writes her notes to the night because it's the only way of getting through the dark. They remind her of the letters she wrote to her dad when he used to go away, so it comforts.

Standing, she unclips her buttery hair. She then unfastens her white-and-blue student nurse uniform and stands, letting it fall to the floor with a whisper. It's time to discard not only her clothes and her tidy hairstyle, but her inhibitions, her pride, and her self-respect.

Within the glass dome, the flakes settle on the plastic gold-and-black New York skyline like white ash after a fire. It's her favourite snow globe. It was the first one her dad bought her. She was eight when he came home from that city with it. She clapped her hands so happily that afterwards he found her one in every city he visited. They line the desk and windowsill and bookshelves. Glancing at them now, at the silent cities, it occurs to Isabelle that right now her dad is also trapped in a bubble.

But no matter how hard she shakes him he never opens his eyes.

Isabelle takes her black stockings from the bed How she hates them. They would be as effective a strangulation device as Cassanby's tie. Instead, she must roll one up each leg, clip them on to matching suspenders, and go and tend to the doctor for two hours, for which she'll be paid four hundred pounds in crisp notes – perhaps an extra fifty tip if he climaxes twice – and a box of chocolate liqueurs that she will give to her dad's main nurse, Jean.

After a long day Isabelle is not in the mood.

Is there any day that would have her in the mood?

No.

But choice has never been an option when it comes to her night work; when it comes to the creature she transforms into as darkness falls. Who on earth would *choose* to spend hours studying Managing Complexity in Learning Disability during the day and then leave the house at seven o'clock to work all evening? Who would *choose* to end up so exhausted they fall asleep in lectures and have to work twice as hard to catch up? Who would *choose* to constantly fear the moment someone at university or in everyday life recognises them as the escort they paid to slap them with a shoe last night?

Isabelle knows something has to give – somewhere, some*how* – but being a nurse is her dream, and the escorting is a necessity, because everything is different now.

'We're not what we do, we're what we *dream* of doing,' her dad told her once. 'Never give up on your dreams, lass They're not meant to happen easily. If they were, why would we reach for them? They'd simply drop into our laps.'

Isabelle dreams of finishing university in six months and starting work as a nurse, helping youngsters with special needs. She dreams of the changes she might make to other families. Most of all, she dreams of the day her dad comes back to her.

Sliding a black stocking through her fingers, it's all she can do to not rip it apart and fall on the bed crying. What would her dad say if he knew *this* was what she was doing? But there's no other way to keep him in the place he loves, the place he worked so hard to get, the place he's now oblivious to. He need never know, Isabelle decides. When he returns to her, she'll come up with some story to explain how she took care of him; she just can't think of it now.

Now she must go out into the night.

She must put on her armour; she must paint her mouth fire-engine red and outline her eyes in smoke grey. She must step into her spike heels and spray on Chanel No 5 and go out into the cold January night and tend to Dr Cassanby.

How did it come to this?

ISABELLE LOOKS BACK ON HOW IT CAME TO THIS

Isabelle's dad owns three casinos in the region. He has always worked in the entertainment industry, previously running clubs, managing cabaret acts. Privately, she thought that casinos just cash in on the desperate, but she couldn't help but love seeing her dad so passionate about what he saw as his other three babies, so she kept her thoughts to herself.

One evening, about seven months ago, Nick – the manager of the biggest casino – came into the kitchen, where Isabelle was studying. He was there to see her dad, who had just this minute left for work, calling from the hallway that he'd see her in the morning. Nick is like an uncle to Isabelle. Many find him intimidating, with his surly attitude, shaved head, and crisp grey suits, but she knows the soft layers beneath.

'I'm worried about Charles,' he said.

'What do you mean?' Isabelle's chest felt tight.

Nick started out of the room, shaking his head. 'Sorry, I shouldn't ha—'

'You can't *not* tell me now.' Isabelle stood, spilling coffee across the laptop keyboard. 'Damn it.' She grabbed some kitchen roll. 'Nick, is he OK?'

Nick sighed and returned to the table. 'I just ... He seems extra tired, don't you think?'

It was true. A normally vibrant man, he hadn't seemed himself in recent weeks. But she realised that Nick wasn't being completely honest. 'That isn't just it, is it?' she said.

'No. It's...' Nick shook his head. 'He'll never tell you because he wants to protect you.'

'Nick, I'm twenty-nine not nine. Tell me.'

'I didn't know whether to tell you, but, yes, you do deserve to know.' He paused. 'Financially ... things aren't going well. Clientele is on the decline.' He sighed, annoyed. 'Online gambling has a lot to answer for. It's so much easier to keep a habit secret on your smartphone than to visit a venue. But Charles insists it's just a slump. I think we're in trouble though ... But, well, he's a proud man. He's always made sure you're OK...'

Guilt squeezed Isabelle's heart with a hot, sticky hand. When she started her degree, Dad insisted he would pay, not wanting her to end up with a huge student loan. He bought her a car too.

'You think I should help out more,' she said. It was a statement, something she knew to be true. But work placements on hospital wards for up to three months at a time made it impossible to find even a part-time job.

'I worry that he'll make risky business decisions.' Nick was clearly trying to be honest without being unkind. Isabelle's mum was a quiet ghost present in the room – her death when Isabelle was small was the reason Charles was extra-protective of his daughter. 'If you ... I don't know ... told him you wanted to take care of yourself from now on...'

Isabelle felt a surge of outrage – but it was only guilt. Nick was right. She was lucky that her dad had made it possible for her to do her nursing degree without financial worry. Not many students had that privilege. She felt guilty now that she had waited so long, not enrolling at university until she was twenty-six. Having a dad who kept her, who gave her 'odd jobs' so she felt she was 'contributing', had made her lazy. Money makes life easy. It means freedom. Now, she works hard for her degree, trying to prove to herself that she deserves to be doing it.

When Nick had gone, Isabelle blinked back tears. She *should* do more. But what? And how could she fit it around her studies *and* work placements?

At university the next day, she couldn't concentrate. The lecturer went on and on and on, but the words Isabelle heard were not about co-ordinating care with confidence, they were Nick's words last night. *Take care of yourself from now on.* How did the other student nurses manage? Allie, another mature student, said her debts were piling up because there simply wasn't a part-time job that paid enough and fit around the long hours she had to do in the hospital as part of the degree. Isabelle knew two girls who worked in a lap-dancing club. One of them, Erica, said she only had to work two nights to make over four hundred pounds.

Could Isabelle do that?

No. She was too shy to go on a stage. And she couldn't dance.

As she tried to take notes, and the lecturer went on and on and on, Isabelle recalled a conversation she'd overheard in the university café. She hadn't known the girls; one was telling the other about her work as an escort. 'You don't *have* to have sex,' she was insisting, clearly trying either to persuade her friend to do it too, or perhaps to justify her own choice. 'Many of the men just want company. It's easy money, and a free night out, really. I mean, think of the men we date who we wish we hadn't. With escorting, *you* choose – *and* you're getting paid for it.'

At the time, Isabelle had wondered if she was prudish for feeling repulsed at the idea of taking money for being with someone like that. Then she felt unkind, judging a woman she didn't even know. How dare she, in her lucky position of not needing to do it? Back in the lecture hall, she thought *could* she do something like that to take the pressure off her dad?

No. *No.*

In the weeks following Nick's disclosure, life seemed to continue as normal. Isabelle's dad was more like his usual self. Nick never again brought up the matter of money. How easy it was to let herself believe that all was OK, that the casinos were doing well again, that the dad who had always taken care of her still could, for now, until she qualified.

Then, three months later, came the fall.

Then, three months later, came the moment Isabelle really had to step up.

ISABELLE GETS HERSELF A NIGHT OFF

Now, Isabelle picks up a stocking, ready to go and visit Dr Cassanby.

They are more expensive than the ones she wore when she started escorting. Not only because she can afford better now, but because in finer clothes she gets a better class of clientele, and therefore meets more of the cost of her dad's care.

Slipping the sheer silk over flesh, forming a darker skin, she begins the real transition from student nurse to escort. She would far rather finish writing her note or go and talk to her dad for a while, but longing is fruitless. If she doesn't work, she won't be able to keep him at home.

As Isabelle takes the second stocking from the bed – it's snagged, too torn for last-minute disguise with clear nail polish – the phone buzzes and she answers, hoping for the hundredth time that Dr Cassanby is dead.

It's Gina, the owner of Angels Escort Services.

'Hey, girl,' she says in her always-chirpy manner. 'You've got yourself a night off.'

'Really?' Isabelle clutches the torn stocking to her chest. 'How?'

'You may be happy to hear that Dr Cassanby has explosive diarrhoea.'

Isabelle laughs. 'He *said* that?'

'Haha. No, not exactly like that. He said he has a terrible tummy bug. But that's what he meant.'

Isabelle likes that calls go through the agency; bookings are always made via Gina. It's a way to keep things professional, stops new clients harassing the girls directly, and to end things more easily if needed.

'While I've got you, I have a new client who'll be perfect for you,' says Gina. 'He's called Simon and he's a little shy, poor lad. Has quite a stammer.' Isabelle is often selected for the insecure clients; she has a reputation for being sensitive to their needs. 'He inherited a fortune from his uncle, who's big in the local cleaning industry, so he has *plenty* of cash, girl. I'd give him the GFE.'

GFE is the Girlfriend Experience; the client wants sex where both the escort and the customer engage in reciprocal sexual pleasure, where there's emotional intimacy. Isabelle has been surprised by how many men want this – even more surprised by how many believe it to be real affection, despite paying for it.

'I know you'll be nice to him,' says Gina.

Isabelle prefers clients who want their hearts massaging more than their bodies. Sometimes she wonders about setting up an agency of her own, one that's for the lonely, for the men – and occasionally women – who need a shoulder to cry on. But the Samaritans are there for that, and they're free. Who would pay hundreds of pounds to be consoled? One of Isabelle's clients – Jim, who knows she's a student – often says that she'll make a wonderful nurse.

Suddenly the young man from the clinic earlier pops into Isabelle's head.

A beautiful face. Mass of curled hair. Goggles. What was his name again?

Sebastian.

That was it. Sebastian who lent her his goggles so she could see the world through his eyes. Sebastian aged twenty years and six months and two days, as he proudly reminded them. Sebastian who asked if they were going to have sex when they went to see the fish while his mother spoke privately to Mel Cleary, the sexual-health worker.

Currently on placement for two weeks at Rowan House, Isabelle has been shadowing Mel, who she frequently thinks is in entirely the wrong job. It occurs to her now that in such a situation escorts, really, are in the best position to share advice.

She had wanted to tell Sebastian that sex wasn't all that. Sex was simply a physical action. A putting of one thing into another thing. A coming together for relief. And that she, despite her multiple experiences, was yet to have an orgasm. Was yet to feel something more than just flesh. Was yet to know the mystical experience that those who love someone with all their heart experience. She's had the odd boyfriend – one, Steve, for almost six months – but she ended things each time because she simply hadn't felt anything close to love.

'Are you free to meet Simon next Wednesday evening?' asks Gina.

'Simon?' Isabelle tries to remember their conversation.

'The guy with the stammer.'

'Oh. Yes.'

Isabelle looks in her diary. She really could do with revising that night. Her university coursework is getting intense now she's in the final year. But she can't turn down the money.

'What time?'

'Seven. I'll email the details over. Enjoy your night off.'

'I will.'

Isabelle hangs up and flops on the bed, one stocking on and the other in her hand, topless and exhausted, which she muses is odd when there isn't a client fastening his trousers nearby. Though she feels sick at losing four hundred pounds, she decides she can work extra next weekend to make it up.

How quickly she went from judgement to acceptance – from thinking she could never do something like this to realising that it was the only option. Was it fast? Not really. A month perhaps between the fall and her first client. A month in which she learned just how much it would cost to take care of her dad. A month that began with breaking down in tears while speaking to fellow student Erica about what lap dancing was like (exhausting) and ended in Gina's Angels Escorts Services office, for an interview.

It was the first time she'd ever had one in a room with leather wallpaper and boxes of dildos on an expensive-looking black desk.

Gina was Erica's aunt, and shared her forthright manner and warm smile. She wore a tailored black suit, and had smooth hair, which surprised Isabelle. What had she expected? Brassy? Brash?

'I don't even know if...' Isabelle had stammered, looking at the door, just wanting to go home.

'If you want to?' Gina spoke kindly. 'But you *need* to, yes?'

Isabelle nodded.

'Most of our clients are just lonely,' said Gina. 'It isn't always about sex – many just want someone to listen to them, and you'll make the same money lending an ear as you will doing anything else.' She insisted that enjoyment of sex was not a prerequisite for the job – nor was being good at it, though that did help – because an escort sells her time, attention and entertainment. She explained that this role was not prostitution, where only sex is given for money, but far more, and many of the women were proud of what they provided. A client might just want a dinner date or a travel companion, nothing more. 'My girls put as much passion into conversation – into listening and being there – as anything else.'

Isabelle could do that couldn't she?

Lend an ear? Listen?

Yes. She would have to.

And she *did*. That was all she had to do with her first two clients, a seventy-year-old man who craved company and talked of his days in the army, and a younger man who needed her to accompany him to an office event, and who merely thanked her when it was over.

By the time she met her third client, Dr Cassanby, Isabelle had seen the money. She had been able to pay some of her dad's care bill. She had been able to take care of him the way he had always taken care of her. And there was no going back from that.

MEET ISABELLE'S THIRD CLIENT – DR CASSANBY

The doctor was Isabelle's third client and had been the most demanding so far, despite having specified that he required only companionship, intelligent conversation and the occasional evening out.

One October evening three months ago, he opened the doors of his five-bedroom, Grade II listed home in Kirk Ella and invited Isabelle into an imposing hallway and then the lounge. Despite the simple requirements he'd given, she half expected to see cameras or chains dangling from walls, and was relieved that there were just three cream sofas and a coffee table supporting neat rows of *Capital Doctor* magazines.

Cassanby was in his late fifties or early sixties, and well groomed, with distinguished black-and-grey hair, snarled eyebrows above steely blue eyes, and the air of a man who got whatever he wanted. He certainly wasn't unattractive, and Isabelle often wondered why he needed to pay anyone. Was it the thrill? The control? Was it that he was guaranteed to get exactly what he desired?

A distinct absence of family photographs or abandoned shoes in the hallway suggested that this barren but beautiful house was occupied only by Dr Cassanby. Isabelle wondered briefly if he was divorced or just a loner. A man of his obvious wealth certainly wouldn't find it hard to pick up a gold-digging wife.

'Can I take your coat?' he asked in a husky voice that she assumed was an attempt to be seductive. This confused her. He didn't need to persuade her; he was paying. 'What's your name?'

Observing Gina's advice that it separated the escorting from everyday life, Isabelle had chosen another name, Violetta. She said it softly as he removed her coat and hung it over one of the chairs. She wondered, not for the first time, if she should have chosen something else. Violetta was an affectionate nickname her dad sometimes used. Too late. Her official profile on the Angels Escort Services website had her listed as Violetta now.

'My dad first saw my mum at the opera – it was *La Traviata*,' said Isabelle, hoping her chat would delay the things he might want to do. 'He fell madly in love with her even though she was picking her nose behind a programme. At least that's what he said. They named me Violetta, after the lead character.'

The story was true, even if the name wasn't, or the nose-picking part. In her fear, Isabelle was rambling, revealing too much and trying to hide it with made-up details.

'Do you like the opera?' Cassanby asked, regarding her with intensity.

'I suppose,' Isabelle said. 'I haven't had the chance to go recently.' Gina had said that the evening was *all* about the client, that if you pleased them mentally too, you'd end up with more clients, and therefore more money, so Isabelle quickly asked, 'Do you?'

'I don't mind it.'

'Is that one of the things you'd like us to do?'

'Maybe one of the things.' His eyes hadn't left hers. 'Would you like a drink?'

'Yes.' A drink might stop her heart hammering.

I could cross his path in a hospital ward or clinic, Isabelle thought with horror for the first of many times. What would she do? She'd have to fake some sort of illness and escape to the nearest toilets.

Dr Cassanby handed her wine in a crystal glass and said that the real Violetta Valery from *La Traviata* had died of tuberculosis, a disease that while now controlled was still one of the deadliest in the world.

In her new, slightly-too-big stockings and her classiest navy-blue dress, Isabelle wondered how she would respond if he initiated sex. He may have *said* he just wanted company, but Pam, a long-time escort she met yesterday, had warned her that some said that but wanted much more. If he wanted sex, she would have to give it. She had no choice. This was a business arrangement and she needed the money.

'We might go out later,' said Dr Cassanby, sipping wine. 'I eat later than most people do. My schedule means everything happens later.'

Isabelle wondered what kind of doctor he was but didn't ask. 'You have a lovely home,' she said instead.

'You have a lovely body, Violetta,' he said, catching her off-guard.

'Oh.'

She didn't know how to respond. Should she say he could see more of it if he wished? Was that the done thing? She felt sick. It was all she could do not to pick up her coat and run. Pam had also said she should think only of *why* she was doing it, and that one day she wouldn't have to anymore.

Pam had been doing it for ten years.

Pam looked exhausted.

Don't think about that, Isabelle thought.

'I'd like to see more of you,' said Dr Cassanby. Then, as someone might instruct a dog to fetch a stick, he told her to remove the dress and then her underwear. 'Do it slowly,' he said, voice low with urgency. 'I like this part best. Don't rush.'

Now? She wanted to ask. *Right away? No foreplay? Just here in your living room*?

But this wasn't a date.

'Now,' he added, as though hearing her internal questions.

Isabelle tried to do as he asked. She stumbled over the buttons near her chest and blushed as they revealed the lacy bra that pushed her breasts obscenely close together. Once the buttons and side zip were undone, she wriggled slowly and provocatively out of the dress, letting it fall to the ground. Not once did she look Dr Cassanby directly in the eye – his heavy breathing was enough to indicate his arousal. Self-consciously, she unhooked her bra and held the cups for a moment, not only to obey his request for slow-ness, but because this was the moment that he would see her flesh. Her fully exposed body. This was the moment she gave herself to this. The moment she surrendered every part of herself to something her heart screamed not to do.

Think of the money.

This was not a choice, but a necessity.

Not her dream, but an absolute nightmare.

She let the bra fall too, like a wispy, dark cloud. The cool air kissed her nipples. Her intake of breath at the chill echoed Cassanby's. She rolled down the stockings with patient precision and cast them aside. Finally, she slowly peeled off the simple black briefs she had bought at Marks and Spencer's for the occasion and dropped them to the floor with the other garments. She stood in just her heels. Vulnerable; at his paid mercy.

'Gorgeous,' whispered Cassanby. 'You are *gorgeous.*'

Should she respond? Move? Do anything?

'I'm going to kiss your nipples for ten minutes,' he said. 'Then I want you to have a sip of wine to cool your tongue and take me in your mouth. You don't have to move or do anything more.' He closed his eyes a moment as though imagining it.

In Isabelle's limited sexual experience, she had never met a man who verbalised his intentions in this way. She wondered if he only did it with women he paid; if it was his fetish to describe explicitly his desires. Should she say anything to let him know she would do as he had asked, or just await his approach. It was surreal. Like if she blinked, she'd awake on her bed, face stuck to revision notes and cold coffee sitting on the desk.

She didn't have to wonder for long. Cassanby crossed the room. He became active, not just a voyeur. In her heels, Isabelle was at his eye level. She looked, however, at the spot just above his forehead.

'Sit on the sofa,' he said.

She did, crossing her legs to maintain some dignity.

Cassanby knelt before her. He parted her legs and leaned closer. Every bit of Isabelle wanted to push him away, to scream for him to get his filthy hands off her, and to pick up her clothes and go home. He smelt faintly of cigar and this further repulsed her because it was a sacred odour, one associated with her dad.

This was the moment Isabelle began writing her notes to the night. They began in her head. Occasionally, she finished them later on paper. Putting one word after another got her through the things she didn't want to do.

Dear Night,
  I sometimes wonder what it might be like to just bugger off,
right now, and travel to all the cities my dad visited while I was
growing up; to see the Hong Kong skyline he described so vividly,
to see the Golden Gate Bridge appear out of mist the way he said,
to sit at the feet of Christ the Redeemer in Brazil, to walk the
cobbled streets of Prague instead of spying them through the glass
of a snow globe....

Isabelle loved the word 'note'. She and her dad always used it instead of 'letter', when he was away and they wrote to one another. Not because their missives were brief, but because she always thought the word sounded more poetic, like something a fairy would leave under a pillow.

When she was small, Isabelle's dad wrote notes to her while he was roaming the world and she was at home with the childminder, Cecilia. But he didn't only write from India or China or Russia – he penned them before departing for the airport. One for each day he was going to be absent. One for each night he couldn't tuck her in. She still has them all. The lion-embossed sheet usually opened with *Dear Isabelle,* though he sometimes wrote *Violetta*, his affectionate nickname for her. The notes all took a similar form:

Tonight, while Cecilia makes your hot chocolate and you read
the next chapter of Danny the Champion of the World, *I'll be*
in New York. It's a marvellous place – the trees are lit up even
when it's not Christmas and it seems like the shops never close.
I'll take you one day. When Cecilia turns off the lamp, look up
into the night sky and find the moon. I'll be looking at it too.

Dr Cassanby freed Isabelle from his grip and she was dragged back into the moment. The cool air hit her damp nipple. She recalled what he'd said she should do next. Hoped he had forgotten. No such luck. He held her gaze while undoing his zip and wriggling out of his trousers. Then he glanced at the wine and back at her.

Isabelle reached for it. Took a sip. Closed her eyes.

And took him in her mouth.

◻

Later that evening they went to the Westwood Restaurant. Dr Cassanby ate noisily and asked her about her life. She lied. What would a Violetta do? It turns out she would work as a hotel receptionist, live alone with a cat called Tibby and enjoy hiking.

When Isabelle drove home afterwards, she pulled over in a layby outside Swanland, and the tears she had held in check for hours finally fell. The only sounds were the occasional cars passing by, the start of rain on the roof and her wracking sobs. Never again would she cry this powerfully after a client. Not even after being strangled until she almost passed out by a businessman from London.

Not even after being raped.

8

THE LEAST ISABELLE CAN DO

For now, for tonight, Isabelle is free.

She can finish her note to the night.

No, that can wait. She can go and be with her dad. Isabelle opens the drawer and takes out a batch of notes tied with red ribbon, feeling as she unwraps them that she is opening her dad's life.

Physically, Isabelle doesn't have far to go to see her dad, but he's so far away emotionally and mentally he might as well be on the moon. She goes onto the landing. Sometimes she is sure she doesn't walk alone when she walks along this carpeted stretch. Here, in the space between her room and his, she feels a third person close by. A sense of another soul, of breath in the air, another heart beating like her own.

A sense of a ghost.

Does she even believe in such a thing?

The house is quiet, like Queen Victoria Square at 4am once Hull's nightworkers have departed and before the city's dayworkers arise, when even the birds still sleep, and the only sound is the rose-bowl fountain shedding its tears. Three doors along from Isabelle's room, past the third bathroom and the study, where, as a child, she read Roald Dahl and C.S. Lewis until dawn, is a room where her entire world lives, sleeping.

Isabelle opens the door slowly.

The ghost at her side disappears, like always.

The sound of the medical ventilator hits her first. That gasp of air followed by two beats: *gasp, thump-thump, gasp, thump-thump, gasp, thump-thump.* The repetition is both a comfort and a source of great distress. Isabelle remembers asking over and over what would happen if the machine failed, fearing her dad would die. His medical team assured her that the device is carefully designed so that no single point of failure can endanger the patient – there are back-up batteries, an alarm that alerts the local hospital and manual mechanisms that Nurse Jean knows how to work should the worst happen.

But she isn't here; she has a night off. Another nurse will cover soon. Isabelle's dad isn't left alone for long. Such round-the-clock, intensive care is what eats her earnings. Three months of escorting now, and it's barely enough, but then she'd never expected to have to pay for it herself. There was a large one-off payment from a critical-illness insurance policy, but that was consumed fast. Every medical professional warned her how expensive it would be to keep him home, said he'd be better in a hospital. But she won't have him anywhere else.

She can't. Not after what he asked of her.

It all began with a fall.

Four months ago, in the middle of September, he had been weak after a bad dose of flu. He had stubbornly insisted on continuing as normal and then fainted on some concrete steps in a carpark. He must have tumbled a long way, hitting his skull with such force that his brain collided with the bone, knocking him unconscious for days.

In the hospital, he came around for long enough to grasp Isabelle's hand, and rasp, 'I don't want to be here.'

Panicking, she thought he meant alive – in this world. That he wished to be dead. 'Don't say that,' she'd said, choking on tears. 'I want you to live, Dad.'

'No ... here...' It clearly took immense effort to speak. 'A hospital ... she...'

'Try and rest,' said Isabelle gently.

'She...' He was determined to say something. 'She ... never ... left...'

And Isabelle knew who he was talking about. Her mother. The mother she could not even remember. The mother who died when Isabelle was just a year old. Drowned off the coast of Scarborough. She'd been resuscitated on the beach and taken to the hospital, but she'd died there a day later from secondary drowning, the result of liquid remaining in her lungs. Charles had argued ever since that a delayed ambulance was to blame for his beloved wife's death; that the nurses had not done all they should; that they had failed to recognise the signs; that she could have lived.

'Bring me home,' he said, more urgently, as though knowing somehow it would be his last chance to speak. 'No matter what. There's money ... in the business ... don't leave me here...'

And then he was gone, unconscious again.

He had never asked Isabelle for anything until that moment.

When tests a few days later showed increased intracranial pressure, the specialist suggested he be put into an induced coma – possibly for up to three months – to prevent his critical functions being cut off by the immense swelling.

All Isabelle heard was *coma*.

And *three months*.

And the last words he had uttered: 'Don't leave me here.'

How could she have done?

Now, Isabelle goes further into her dad's bedroom, closing the door. It's cool, as always, the low temperature allowing his brain to fully rest and not exert itself. In a large hospital bed near French doors that open onto a small balcony, he lies, tiny within the vast space. Soft curtains sigh in the draught. She wanted to fill the place with the fresh flowers he loves but knows that harmful bacteria can grow in the water and can spread if it is spilt. Not wanting to take any chances, Isabelle paid for some exquisitely realistic lilies and orchids to be made and then put them in two large jars in opposite corners. Even if he can't see them, she knows she has kept his room as beautiful as he would want it to be. Without real flowers to dispel the subtle scent of urine, Isabelle often burns candles on the small, ornate bureau.

She approaches the bed.

The man there is a shell. He is not her dad. Not the vibrant man who used to scoop her into his arms. Not the man whose laugh filled this huge house. Not the man with the strength of an ox.

But one day he will be again.

He *has* to be.

9

VERONICA ISN'T HAPPY WITH THE SKIRTING BOARDS

Veronica isn't happy with the skirting boards.

The money she's paying to have her house cleaned and she might as well do it herself. She only keeps Tilly on out of sympathy and habit. Her husband, Pete, employed the then twenty-year-old Polish girl just before he died, to lessen Veronica's burden as she had to devote all her energy to young Sebastian. Now, Sebastian's love of everything being in order, and Veronica's free time while he's at college mean the house is always quite organised.

But the skirting boards are a disgrace. Veronica runs a finger along the one in the hallway – thick dust. Should she tell Tilly? No, the poor woman has three children and an unruly husband now, a man who isn't around as much as he should be. How can Veronica criticise her with all the worries she must have? She wishes she could find the fire that fuels her when she defends Sebastian and inject it into the other areas of her life. But no, Tilly is a good woman, and Veronica has far bigger issues than a skirting board.

'Mu-u-u-m.' Sebastian's voice floats down the stairs.

'Yes, darling?'

'Can I wear these long things in my top drawer?'

'What long things?' Veronica frowns.

'These long black things.'

'These lo—. Oh, I'm coming.' She starts up the wood-panelled stairs. 'Tilly? Where *are* you?' No answer.

She continues up the stairs and goes into Sebastian's room.

He has the largest bedroom, which fills an entire corner of the house and has two generous windows that let in light all day. As a small child, Sebastian used to follow the sunlight as it moved across the floor, saying he would one day find the pot of gold, not listening when Veronica said that was supposed to be at the end of a rainbow.

The walls are painted soft aqua blue, a colour he chose so he would feel like he was in water all the time. His bedding is the same shade, and so are the rugs. On the ceiling are rows of star-shaped lights that flash softly as he sleeps. A bubbling fish tank sits on the bureau, and inside Flip and Scorpion swim frenziedly back and forth. Lining the walls are shelves stacked neatly with books about tigers and space and the ocean, and his favourite, *A Brief History of Time* by Stephen Hawking.

Sebastian sits naked in front of his cabinet, holding up a pair of thick black tights, hair still damp from the shower. Veronica has told him that there's no point showering before he goes swimming, but he likes to 'go in clean'. His favourite album – *The Best Hits of 1985* – plays softly in the background. He has it on repeat most days and knows all the words to Pat Benatar's 'We Belong', King's 'Love and Pride' and Billy Ocean's 'Suddenly'. Veronica once asked why he liked a collection of songs from ten years before he was conceived, and Sebastian responded with a quote from a music magazine he'd read that called Ocean a poetic genius.

'I have to wear something today,' he says.

'What do you mean, darling?'

'We're doing safety skills today.'

'At swimming?'

'Yes. I'll get my fifth water rescue award.'

Veronica looks at him, her heart heavy with love. 'Sebastian, you really should put some clothes on.'

'People very rarely fall into water naked,' he says. 'So we have to wear lots of clothes today and then sink and pretend to die. This is my dying face. Look.' He squints his eyes and furrows his brow and makes a ridiculous gurgling sound. 'Then we take it in turns being the rescuer.'

Sebastian has been having lessons for nine years and is a strong swimmer. He's the oldest in his class by a long margin, but he doesn't want to stop going. Veronica has often suggested he can just swim now, whenever and wherever he wants to, but he likes the class structure, he likes the routine, and he likes getting the certificates. He has seventy-two in the drawer now.

'Would *you* rescue me?' he asks.

'Of course, I would.' Veronica pauses. 'But no, I meant you should put some clothes on *now*, darling.'

'You said it's fine when it's just you and me.'

'It is. It *was*. But ... I keep telling you you're ... older now...'

'Yep. Twenty years and six months and three days.'

'When we're older we only let ... well, our *partners* see us naked.'

'And what if we don't have one?'

'Well, then just ourselves.'

'I'll put these on then.' Sebastian stands and turns to face her.

Veronica wants to avert her eyes but cannot help taking in his beautiful body; silky skin sits on muscled arms taut from days bricklaying; his legs are sturdy, slightly bowed; the torso is rippled with youthful strength. Veronica's gaze stops there. She can't look at her son fully. Not all of him. He is a man. It takes her breath away, makes her want to cry. He is *this* body. And this body has natural needs.

Sebastian starts to wriggle his great big feet into the tights.

'No, darling.' Veronica goes to take them from him. 'These are mine. Tilly must have put them with your things. You can't wear these.'

'Why not? I like the feel of them. I'll be like a seal underneath my human clothes.'

'But they're for women.'

'I don't care.'

'*I* do. I don't want people laughing at you.'

Sebastian seems to think about this. He sighs dramatically and peels them off and gives them to Veronica. 'Stupid women's stuff,' he says.

'We have to go in twenty minutes,' Veronica reminds him.

'I know, I know.' Sebastian goes through his drawers and pulls out some shorts and socks, then sits on the floor to put them on, the way a toddler might.

A knock on the door – it's Tilly. 'You want me?' she calls.

'Hi Tillda,' calls Sebastian. He has always called her it, a mixture of her full name, Matilda, and the shortened Tilly.

REO Speedwagon starts to play. Sebastian sings 'Can't Fight This Feeling' with gusto as he wriggles into tracksuit bottoms and a T-shirt, his everyday attire. Veronica goes onto the landing. Tilly has an armful of dirty laundry. Her face is red with exertion, her black hair damp.

'You put my tights in Sebastian's drawers,' she says. 'If I hadn't seen them, he'd have gone swimming with them on under his track-suit bottoms and the kids would have laughed at him.'

The doorbell rings.

'Yes, Mrs Murphy,' says Tilly, even though Veronica has told her for years that it makes her sound like a headmistress.

Veronica goes into the hallway and sees a motionless black shape through the coloured glass window. She opens the door. It's Annabelle from across the street, her hair perfectly coiffed in waves of gold, pearls at her neck like a 1950s housewife, and lips in a tight red line. Veronica can't bear her. Annabelle's oldest girl, Siobhan, used to play with Sebastian when they were small. Since they turned twelve Annabelle has done all she can to keep them apart. Being in the same year at senior school, they shared the odd lesson, but Siobhan completely ignored him.

'Annabelle,' says Veronica.

'Veronica. I need to talk to you in private.'

'Go ahead.'

'No, not here.' Annabelle pushes past into the hallway.

'Come in, please, won't you?' Veronica closes the door after them, and points to the living room. 'Coffee?'

'This isn't a social call. This is quite serious.'

Oh good, thinks Veronica sarcastically.

'I only have fifteen minutes,' she says.

Annabelle doesn't sit. She stands in the centre of the room by the glass-topped table, sniffing the air as though the floor is running with sewage.

'It's about Sebastian.'

'Oh.'

Everything about Veronica's stance changes. How many times over the years has she heard this phrase? *It's about Sebastian.* How many times has her spine unfurled and turned into steel at those syllables? How many times has she risen out of a chair to face some fool who thinks they know what's best for him? How many times has she taken on medical professionals, people in supermarkets, teachers at school?

'What about Sebastian?' she asks.

'If he comes near my daughter again, I'll call the police.'

'I beg your pardon?'

'You heard me, Veronica.'

'Whatever Siobhan said, I'm sure—'

'This isn't about Siobhan. It's about Jennifer.' Her other daughter.

'*Jennifer*? But...'

Annabelle takes an envelope from her pocket. Veronica recognises the tiny, neat handwriting immediately.

'Your son sent this ... this *filth* to my fifteen-year-old-daughter.' Annabelle throws it on the glass table. 'I should take it to the police since he's a grown man and she's a child, but I'll give you one chance. If he comes near her again, I'll have him arrested.'

Veronica feels sick. 'Whatever is in that note, you have to understand h—'

'He is an *animal*.'

'I really don't th—'

'And I don't care if he's autistic. I don't care if he's a total *retard*, there is never an excuse for that!'

'Who are you calling a retard?' Veronica approaches Annabelle with eyes of fire and a voice of ice, and the woman steps back slightly, face now unnerved. 'Who the hell do you think you are?' She longs to say, *You think you're really something with your new*

Audio A8 and your Botoxed forehead and a husband who looks like he fell into a vat of orange juice, but holds it back. 'Get out of my house before I pick you up and throw you into the street,' she hisses instead.

'If you lay one hand on me, I'll—'

'*Out!*'

Annabelle hurries into the hallway, giving Veronica a wide berth, and dashes to the door. Ring-adorned fingers on the handle, she turns, says, 'I'll keep away from you if you keep that monster away from my family.' Then she runs – actually runs in her pastel heels – down the gravel drive before Veronica can do anything.

Veronica stands in the hallway, heart racing, breath laboured. *That so-called monster got beaten up on the college bus*, she wants to scream. *That so-called animal wouldn't hurt a soul!*

She looks back at the envelope on the glass table.

'I'm ready,' calls Sebastian

It will have to wait. She picks it up. Puts it to her heart a moment, and then hides it in her pocket.

10

VERONICA SHRUGS OFF HER FEELINGS

Sebastian comes into the hallway with his rainbow-coloured swimming bag over his shoulder and his goggles already on.

'I can't get out of the water without using the rail or the steps,' he says.

'Sorry?' Veronica is still distracted.

'I can't do it without them.'

'Why does that matter, darling?' Veronica finds her car keys, her mind on the letter burning a hole in her pocket. She will read it while Sebastian is in the water. Yes, wait until he's occupied and then open it.

'There's no rail or steps from a river or the sea,' he explains.

'But you'll never be alone in any of those places, so don't worry.'

'But I have to know *how*,' he insists, agitated. 'I won't get my fifth certificate if I can't pull myself out of the pool. I failed last time *and* the one before *and* the one before. This is totally my nemesis, Mum.'

'You can do it; I know you can.' Veronica ushers him out of the door, glancing across the street at Annabelle's house. 'Get in the car, darling, or we'll be late.'

'Can't be late, can't be late,' he says, climbing in.

They are not late; they never have been. Veronica always makes it her mission to be there – to be anywhere – at least ten minutes early. If they're not, Sebastian gets agitated. He goes into the changing area and she goes into the café upstairs, where from behind glass she can watch the pool.

Mr Keyes, the swimming instructor, gave Sebastian a private changing area some years ago. The average age in the class is just ten, so it soon became inappropriate for him to undress with them all. Mr Keyes has been a joy. When Veronica explained that the lessons were more than just about learning to swim, that they were Sebastian's world, the instructor said he could attend for as long as he wanted, and they would accommodate any needs he had as they occurred.

'I love Sebastian,' Mr Keyes once said. 'So do the other kids. These classes wouldn't be the same without him.'

Watching Sebastian line up at the edge of the pool with his classmates, almost twice the height of some of them, damp hair wild and curly, Veronica fingers the envelope in her pocket. She sips the watery coffee. Does she really want to know what's inside? Would it be better to tear it up and never see? No. She takes it out. Retrieves the letter inside.

Neat words line the seahorse notepaper Sebastian was given by his great aunt Myrtle at Christmas. Inhaling to compose herself, Veronica reads it.

Dear Jennifer,

Your sister Siobhan told me you like me. I like you too. She said I could write to you and tell you about what I would like to do and she would give it to you. She showed me this rude video and it got me really excited because it was what we could do. I know that we both have to be over eighteen and I know that you have to say yes and Siobhan said you are over eighteen and she showed me a letter where you said yes and you even underlined it. It was typed not your own writing but I don't mind. I want to kiss you first and then see you without your clothes on and then have sex. We can both shut our eyes because I saw them do that on Love Island *though I would prefer to have mine open. I want to do it more than once. I really want to do it now very very much. My body is totally ready to do it right now so soon would be good. I can't wait. Please write back to me and tell me where we can do it. My bed is big. We can do it there.*

From Sebastian

Veronica deflates.

She realises she is crying; the woman at the next table looks uncomfortable. Sebastian isn't a monster, but she can see why Annabelle is protective of her fifteen-year-old daughter. This reads, however, like Sebastian has been set up. Siobhan has clearly been teasing him. Showing him inappropriate videos like those boys did, sending him into a testosterone-fuelled frenzy. At nearly twenty, the girl should know better; a bad apple never falls far from the tree. Thinking of Annabelle calling Sebastian a monster when her daughter is the bully has Veronica scrunching the letter up in her fist.

After a while she tries to flatten it out again and puts it in her bag.

Down below, Sebastian floats on his back, fully clothed, pretending to be unconscious while two boys pull him to the edge. Veronica smiles. He remains fake-unconscious as they try to get him out of the pool, and Mr Keyes has to intervene.

It will be OK, she decides. *If I just make sure Sebastian stays away from Siobhan and her sister, it will all be OK.*

How many times has she self-comforted in this way over the years? Told herself it will all be OK if she does this or does that. Told herself that if she just gets over this one hurdle, it might be the last. She has always been all that Sebastian needs. Life was simpler when he was a child, and a good meal and their home, their simple routine, was enough. But he's older now. An adult. The world beckons. And he needs more. What if he never meets a girl? What if he gets to thirty and he is still alone? Veronica can't bear it.

When the lesson finishes, she waits for Sebastian by the drinks machine, blackcurrant Fruit Shoot already purchased to hand over to him. He bounces out of the changing area, goggles still on, takes the drink and downs it in one.

'Mr Keyes wants to see you,' he says, panting from the effort.

'Why?' The way the day has gone so far, Veronica has a sinking feeling.

'Dunno. Can we go to KFC?'

'We'll see. Wait there on that bench. Don't disappear.'

Veronica finds Mr Keyes in his small office. She studies his face, trying to gauge his reason for wanting to see her, another thing she has done many times over the years. But he shows nothing; his leathery, tanned skin is hard to read, but his eyes are warm, as always. At times, Veronica has wondered if he finds her attractive – they are possibly a similar age – and that this is why he's always been so accommodating towards Sebastian. But he's never made any sort of move. Now he leans against the edge of his desk and gestures to the chair. The cloying stench of chlorine fills the air, even in here, and the sound of splashes and excited cries reverberates from the nearby pool.

'Is everything OK?' Veronica asks.

'It's a tricky one,' Mr Keyes says kindly.

'Isn't it always,' she sighs. 'Sorry. It's just … well, it's been one of those days.' *One of those years*, she thinks. *One of those lives.*

'It's about Sebastian.'

'Of course it is,' she says, unable to hide her frustration.

'You know how fond I am of him,' he admits. 'You know I've always done all I can to ensure his enjoyment and inclusion in my lessons.' He pauses. 'But…'

'Oh, just spit it out!'

'Well, it's a bit sensitive.'

'It always is. What happened this time? Did he say something inappropriate? Is it because he can't get out of the pool without using the steps because if tha—'

'No, nothing like that.' Mr Keyes takes a deep breath. 'The thing is, as you know we gave Sebastian his own changing room because he's older than the other kids and can't get undressed where they are. But, well, yesterday he … he wandered into their area.'

'I'm sure it was an accident.'

'The thing is, he was naked. And he was…'

'Come on, Mr Keyes, we're both adults here.'

'He was semi-aroused. Now, I'm not saying he intended anyone to see, or wanted to alarm anyone, or do anything at all – I know him, he's a lovely boy. But he did scare a couple of the girls and one told her mother, and of course she isn't happy. She has said she will take it higher if he does it again.' Mr Keyes pauses. 'You can see my dilemma? I can't ever have this happen again.'

Veronica has no words. What can she say? She can understand the reactions to this, but she knows that Sebastian would have meant no ill to anyone. How fair is it that a gang of thugs got away with hurting him and yet he is the one punished now?

'It won't,' she says. 'I'll talk to him. He does still wander about naked at times and I need to make it clearer to him that it's not OK now.'

'You don't understand,' says Mr Keyes softly. 'Sebastian will have to leave. I can't take that chance. Some of the parents have said they will remove their kids from the classes.'

'Please don't.' Veronica speaks quietly, desperately. 'You have no idea what this will do to him.'

'I do. But I have no choice. I'm so sorry. I really am.'

'What am I supposed to say to him? It will destroy him.'

'I could talk to him if you like. Say something about him being so good at the lessons now that I have every faith he doesn't need them anymore.'

Veronica shakes her head and stands, straightening her soft Chanel scarf even though it hasn't moved. 'No, I'll tell him. It's fine. I'll deal with it.' *Like I always have.* She heads towards the door, pauses before opening it. 'Thank you for giving him a chance all these years. I do appreciate the huge support you've been.'

And she leaves.

Sebastian is still on the bench by the drinks machine. His goggles have steamed up in the warmth, but he hasn't taken them off.

'Was it about me not being able to get out of the water by myself?' he asks.

'Let's go,' says Veronica.

'You sound unusual.'

'I'm fine.'

She shrugs off her feelings; shakes them away like dandruff from a shoulder. She'll think of something to tell him tomorrow. Scarlett O'Hara said tomorrow was another day. So tonight, she'll cry in bed, and tomorrow she will come up with a way not to break Sebastian's heart.

'How can you *see* out of those things?' She tries to remove his goggles.

'Don't.' Sebastian moves away from her hands. 'I like how it makes the world look soft and smudgy at the edges. Do you want to see?'

'No,' she says, ushering him out into the carpark.

It might be the only way she can keep his world soft and smudgy at the edges.

'I was thinking about sex again,' he says in the car.

'Now?'

'Today. Yesterday. Last week. Always.'

'Sebastian, won't you tell me who those boys were that hurt you on the bus?' It would make Veronica feel better if she could report them to the police. That would be justice; that would ease her pain for a moment.

Sebastian ignores the question. 'Do you think there will ever be *anyone* who wants to have sex with me?'

'I...' Veronica can't speak, or she will break. 'Do you want to go to KFC?' she asks eventually.

'Yes, yes, KFC.'

Veronica makes it all the way there, all the way into the disabled toilet, before crying into her Chanel scarf, great sobs that rip through her body. When someone hammers on the door, she dries her face and leaves.

'This is a disabled toilet,' says the man on crutches, waiting.

'Not all disability is visible,' she snaps.

How much easier might it be if Sebastian's was? If he had legs or arms that didn't work? If his beautiful body had broken but his autism had mended?

But then he wouldn't be him.

He wouldn't be her beautiful, complex, challenging, difficult, wonderful boy.

11

ISABELLE READS TO HER DAD

Isabelle never wanted to kiss anyone she didn't love.

When she was fifteen and the shyest girl in 10G, she first discovered the joy of it – behind the bike sheds with Jonathon Foster. When she should have been learning her verbs in French, she whispered to him that using her tongue to kiss him was better than using it to learn a language.

Now, sitting in the chair next to her dad's bed, she smiles when she recalls her rare forwardness that afternoon. She remembers how Jonathon nodded but then told her he was leaving at the end of the month because his father was in the army and he'd been sent abroad.

But I think I might love you, Isabelle thought.

Memories flutter about her head like colourful butterflies. It's an escape to recall the past. To think of childhood moments with her dad, of joyful days when he returned from long trips and read her a bedtime story. It's a comfort to remember long-gone schooldays when she dreamt of meeting the right man and getting married and being a nurse and having children.

So far, she's on her way to achieving just one of these dreams.

Since Jonathon Foster, she has kissed only men she doesn't love. And a few she doesn't even like.

Isabelle lowers the bedrails and holds her dad's hand within hers. His palms are like cold notepaper. She rubs them warm. The *gasp thump-thump* of the ventilator continues its repetitive song, providing him with an extra breath each time so the blood vessels in his brain shrink, reducing the stress to his skull. If Isabelle wasn't a student nurse, she might be more unnerved by her dad's state, by the catheter bag half full of urine, by the EKG wires stuck to his chest, by the tube attached to the back of his head to measure the pressure there and drain the cerebrospinal fluid, by his absolute pallor. But she has seen this before; she's seen patients on wards in a vegetative state, surrounded by desperate family.

Initially, the medical team had suggested her dad might need to be in a coma for three months – that became four when he suddenly developed pneumonia a few weeks ago, due to his impaired immune responses, and almost died. He has physiotherapists and round-the-clock nurses and a team of coma specialists. Isabelle feels blessed that he knew some of the team before this – mixed with them in his many circles – and so they waive a lot of their fees. He is stable. Stable is good; just draining for Isabelle.

How can this be the man who was as vigorous at sixty as he was at forty? All she wants is for him to recover here, as he requested. It has proved hard, but she has done it. And that's despite the fact the money he told her was there to pay for his care hadn't existed.

A week after he was put into the induced coma, Isabelle used the critical-illness insurance payment to bring her dad home. Then she approached Nick to ask about money for the rest of his care.

Looking exhausted, Nick had said, 'We talked about this, Isabelle.'

'Did we?'

'I told you, we're in financial trouble.'

'But that was weeks ago,' said Isabelle. 'Dad insisted there was money in the business to pay for all this.'

'There isn't,' snapped Nick. 'We're in a lot of debt, and this house is mortgaged to the hilt. You know I love Charles, but you really should have left him in the hospital.'

The panic Isabelle felt at realising that she'd have to find a way to fulfil her dad's one wish was like nothing she had experienced before. It was like she grew up – *really* grew up – in a moment. It crossed her mind to give up the degree and care for him herself, but she didn't have the right kind of medical knowledge. Then she thought about selling the house, but she knew how much he adored it, and Nick had said it was mortgaged to the hilt, so it likely wouldn't even provide what she needed. And, anyway, where would they live? Where would she care for him at home?

Isabelle felt trapped. Bound by a situation she had created.

But she wanted to give back to the father who had always given to her. He had clearly kept this worrying financial situation to himself to protect her, and that made her feel even more guilty.

And so, she'd ended up in Gina's office for an interview.

In Cassanby's home, sipping wine and taking him in her mouth.

Now, Isabelle remembers the batch of old notes she brought from her bedroom drawer and puts them next to her dad's pillow. He doesn't move. His eyes flutter beneath their lids.

'What are you thinking, Charles?' she asks him, as she has so many times these past four months. She used to like teasing him by using his real name, loving when he shook his head and said, *I'm not your friend, I'm your dad.* 'Are you remembering the past? Is that where you go?'

For some reason, tonight Isabelle can't get Jonathon Foster out of her head; their passion behind the bike sheds. How he had promised her he would take her to the school prom before his family moved on. How he then went with Lisa Burroughs because she was more popular. When since has kissing made her body blaze like that? When has desire made her lose concentration?

Never.

If someone had predicted that one day she would kiss a seventy-nine-year-old man for three hundred pounds in mismatched notes, she may have cried. She would definitely have said she would never do such a thing, that she'd only kiss someone she loved, when passion made her unable not to.

Only reveal herself fully to the right person.

Yet various pictures of Isabelle in pink underwear, in black stockings, and in a short skirt and neat pigtails, entice clients browsing the Angels Escort Services website to read on and find out more about *Violetta*. Her profile says that she is twenty-six (really twenty-nine), that she likes the opera and shopping, that she is honey-blonde with natural breasts, has blue eyes, and that she loves champagne, Chanel perfume and Italian food.

What her profile doesn't say – but what her clients all know – is that Violetta will indulge in DFK (deep French kissing), GFE (the girlfriend experience), A (anal sex), sex in all positions, COF and COB (come on face and come on body), but not CIM (come in mouth). Agreeing to French kiss clients, Isabelle discovered, meant more business – *repeat* business – and that meant the bills were paid much sooner and she only had to work six hours a night, not eight, meeting only two clients, not more.

What she finds harder than kissing is eye contact.

After a threesome two weeks ago with an investment banker from Liverpool and her colleague, Tara – where the girls kissed and caressed one another while he bounced around on the hotel bed in his diamond-patterned socks – they shared a cab home. Tara lit a cigarette, blew smoke out of the car window and said that Isabelle had closed her eyes a lot while they were with him. As snow began to drown the world outside, Isabelle admitted that she could kiss as though she was interested, even touch as though she cared, but she could not extend the pretence to her eyes.

Now she wishes her dad would open his.

Even if he isn't fully with it, just to see them again.

'I'm *tired*, Charles' she admits, and wishes she hadn't. If he can hear, she doesn't want him worrying. 'Just a long day,' she adds quickly. 'So much to learn at university and you know how I've always struggled with revision. And Rowan House is demanding. But it'll all be worth it in July.' She tries to keep the exhaustion out of her voice. 'But tonight I'm yours. Shall I read to you?'

She often reads to him. Sometimes the notes from her child-hood. Sometimes her favourite childhood books that he once read to her. Sometimes the newspaper to keep him up to date on current events.

Now Isabelle undoes the red ribbon, opens the batch of his notes and takes out a sheet. This note is over fifteen years old and yellowed with time and touch. She opens it and softly reads aloud the words.

> *Dear Isabelle,*
>   *A city landscape is misleading from the air, you know. That's what I always think, anyway. When a plane touches down in a new place, you have no clue of its history, its culture. A new city can seem cold when you're a stranger. I miss home. I hope you'll always pretend that I'm Peter Pan or Santa Claus like you do now...*

Isabelle can't continue. She remembers looking at the New York snow globe when she was small and wishing she could see him in it. She feels the same now. The body is here, but the man is away.

Isabelle's mind drifts, the beat of the ventilator lulling her. She remembers an awful session with Cassanby. He had bitten her. When she pulled away, he said, 'If you don't want to be here, Violetta, you know where the door is. Plenty of other girls will do it.'

Her blood had run down his chin. She throbbed with pain. Her heart had screamed *NO*; but there is no such word as no when you are paid to be yes.

'Good,' he'd said, taking her silence as agreement. 'Let's play.'

Cassanby then took her hand in a cruel grip and put it over his mouth, unshaven chin scratching her hand like gorse bushes. She knew the game. They had played it before. Mouth still bloody, Cassanby wrapped his silk tie around his neck, insisting Isabelle suffocate him. Time and again she considered stopping his breath for good – stealing his air until there was no more – but he paid her double for the asphyxiation game, so he had more value alive than dead.

When she stopped, Cassanby inhaled air like a drowning man surfacing from the sea, panic and desire staining his pupils. Isabelle's hand was just inches from his mouth, like she might slap him. But he slapped her, twice, before throwing her on the bed.

Isabelle had let go then.

She had heard Dr Cassanby's ragged breath, felt his rough thrusts, but she was in New York. She thought of the one time her dad took her away with him. She saw herself running through crisp, golden leaves; saw herself turn and look into her dad's eyes, seeing the colours from above, orange flecks of sunrise, blue of sky.

Isabelle got home late that night, exhausted from Cassanby's abuse. A quick visit to say goodnight to her dad had reminded her why she endured it, why she could cope with the pain. That was when she sat at her desk and wrote a note to him, one that she will never share with him.

Dear Dad,

When we landed in New York and I was nine and you'd let me join you that one magical time (I think Cecilia was ill), I pretended all the way that you were Peter Pan and I was Wendy. So for me New York felt like Neverland. People say it can be a sordid, seedy place, but I've not been since, and I'll forever see it as sparkling lights and whizzing colour and glitzy banners.

Do you remember the lady in the fur coat in Times Square who gave me the gold-wrapped sweet and had beautiful white hands? You said she was the kind of lady who drank tea with one finger raised. But I know now what she was. Now I'm that kind of lady.

In Central Park the leaves were dying that day – they looked beautiful. You let me run free, after I begged you to let go of my hand. You were always so protective of me. 'Just this once,' I begged you. 'I won't go far,' I said.

You laughed when that dog – I think a St Bernard – barked at me, straining on its lead, the owner laughing, and I ran back to you. When I buried my face in your jacket (I can still smell the musky lining) you patted my head and said that he was just protecting his park. I asked, 'What about me?' and you said you would always protect me.

Now Isabelle is protecting *him*. But she fears him one day finding out what it took. She fears he will no longer think of her as the sweet girl he always saw her as. She's already lied to Nick. When he asked how she was managing a few weeks ago, she told him there had been a second pay-out from the insurance company and that she taken a loan, which she would worry about, he had no need to concern himself. She could tell he didn't believe her. Perhaps Nick has a sense of what she's really doing and doesn't want to judge. If so, she is happy to never talk of it.

Sometimes, Isabelle is afraid that she's losing herself, that the night work might destroy her. But what else can she do?

She pulls the sheet over his chest and tucks him in, just as he did for her long ago. In the chair, with her head on his bed, she falls asleep, briefly stirring when the rustling sheet breaks into dreams of autumn in Central Park. Dawn is coming. Her dad is waking. He is moving. His hand touches her hair. He speaks, says her name softly.

Isabelle.

No, she has imagined it.

Or is it the ghost on the landing?

It's still dark. And her dad is motionless. She dozes again. Dreams of that terrible day four months ago when she found out her dad had fallen. The day that shook her world up like the snow globes on her windowsill.

12

SEBASTIAN READS ONE OF HIS LISTS

Mum has been unusual for the last two days. For twenty-six hours to be exact. More after we left swimming yesterday. She gets like this sometimes. Mostly I never find out what it was about. Other times she tells me and it's boring, like menopause stuff or how she's worried about our neighbour's overgrown rose tree.

Today I am twenty years and six months and four days old. I know it in hours, but I feel dead old when I say it like that. Mum has been on her laptop all day. She kept shutting it when I went to talk to her earlier. She must have been reading about women's things. Today is Sunday. Yesterday was Saturday. The day before was Friday and we went to the clinic and Isabelle showed me the fish. I'm not stupid; I know my mum really wanted to talk to that Mel in private all along.

Now it's dark and she comes to my room with some hot chocolate and puts it on my shelf and walks up and down. Then she asks me to turn down *The Best Hits of 1985*, which is annoying because it's Billy Ocean. She tells me I won't be going swimming at Haltemprice anymore. When I ask why, she says it's for the best and she does that thing with her face that I don't understand.

I can recognise happiness and sadness and anger and tiredness. Lots of people think autistic people can't read emotions on faces. We can. It's the weird stuff I have trouble with. Like if Mum is smiling but saying negative things. Or frowning and saying positive things. That makes me anxious.

Tell me the real thing, I say to her now.

What do you mean? she asks me.

You're tricking me.

I'm not.

You are, I insist. *You're doing the good/bad thing.*

The what? she asks.

Like when you cried and said we were going to Florida.

She sits on my bed then, so I know she's going to be serious.

The real thing is that I know it will make you anxious not to go to Haltemprice for lessons anymore. So I'm trying to make light of it. Trying to enhance the positives. Like you will have more time to just swim. On your own. In the pool. And we can go when we want. That's good, isn't it?

They don't want me there, do they? I say.

They do, she insists.

Well, then I want to keep going.

OK, she sighs. *Mr Keyes thinks you're putting the younger ones to shame.*

What does that mean?

You're such a good swimmer now that you make them feel ... not so good.

I could swim rubbish, I say. *I'll do that.*

I get my hot chocolate now it's cooled down a bit and sip some and I'm happy that that is that. But my mum isn't done.

Sebastian, darling, you can't go. You're too old. It's... against the rules now. That's all it is. Now... tell me about Jennifer.

I don't know how my mum knows about Jennifer, but I tell her that I'm still waiting for her reply to a letter I sent and that when I get one, we are going to arrange for her to come here one night, and then Mum will have to vacate the premises so we can have sex. I don't want her there when I have sex for the first time. She can come back at midnight though and make me eggs if I'm hungry. I think I will be.

Mum looks at me for a long time.

I have no idea what she's looking for.

I don't think she finds it.

Jennifer won't be writing to you. She says it dead quietly. *And you mustn't write to her again. She isn't eighteen, Sebastian. Siobhan was messing around when she told you she is.*

Is she nearly eighteen then? I ask.

No. Mum is a bit snappy now. *Stay away from her. And Siobhan. They are trouble.*

Trouble like with the police trouble?

Mum doesn't answer.

Trouble like they're going to prison trouble?

My mum gets up again. She tells me it's getting late and I should think about going to sleep because it's college in the morning. I know this already. Then I realise I haven't fed Flip and Scorpion. I always feed them or get my mum to feed them at 3pm. I think this is the best time. It gives them something to look forward to but doesn't let them get too hungry. Poor fish. I never usually forget. I sprinkle the fish food evenly across the top of the water and realise I'm hungry too.

Can you make me some eggs? I ask.

Mum has black lines under her eyes as deep as those ridges on a car tyre. She nods and looks at me like I'm the sad ending to one of those kissy-kissy films she watches on a Saturday night while eating Maltesers. She goes downstairs. I turn the music back up again. I want to get my lists out, but she'll be back soon, so I sit on my bed and wait for my eggs. I eat them very fast. And then she says *goodnight, beautiful boy* and kisses my forehead and takes my plate away.

I've got six lists in my drawer right now. Lists organise me. They are hidden where I know my mum doesn't look, inside my Big Ben Skyline jigsaw box that is short of three pieces. I'm finished with *How To Float*. I've known how to do that for a long time. Now I won't be doing it at the class in Haltemprice anymore, so I tear it up into eighteen pieces. I put my *Best Billy Ocean Songs and Why* list aside.

Then I get out my *What I Liked about Isabelle* list.

This is my new favourite.

She was this girl at the clinic two days ago.

Number one is *I like how Isabelle looked in my goggles.*

Number two is *I like how Isabelle smelled.*

Number three is *I like how it felt when I was next to her*.

Number four is private.

My mum thinks I just want to have sex. And she's right. I do. My body needs it. My body gets ready for it every morning and all through the day and all the night too. I ache for it. I think about it all the time. I dream that I am doing it and the girl is a different one each time. Last night it was Isabelle. She felt the realest. She felt a bit like how I think love will feel.

Mum thinks that I only want sex.

But I am looking for love too.

13

VERONICA GOES ONLINE

Do you think there will ever be anyone who wants to have sex with me?

Veronica is haunted by Sebastian's question. Like a *Scooby-Doo* ghost on an endless, repetitive loop, it chased her through the dark last night, after she had tossed and turned for hours. Before this she watched a film called *Murder in the First* to try and drift off. A scene where a lawyer brought a prostitute into prison so that a young, wrongly imprisoned inmate could experience sex for the first time made her weep.

Is she really prepared to consider doing something similar?

Just after three, she got up and made some Horlicks. She looked in on Sebastian, as she often does when she's restless. His angelic, relaxed face was a comfort. He slept curled tightly in a ball, as though he was still in the womb and afraid he might be removed too soon. He didn't arrive early though, not really. He was one of those rare babies who came bang on the day he was due; 17th July 1997. Very Sebastian to be punctual.

Back in bed, Veronica sipped her drink and read again the crumpled letter he wrote to their young neighbour Jennifer.

I want to do it more than once. I really want to do it now very very much. My body is totally ready to do it right now so soon would be good. I can't wait.

She couldn't drink any more. What would have happened if they met in person and Jennifer taunted Sebastian? Made crude suggestions? Could Veronica be absolutely sure that he'd resist her with all the testosterone and longing and curiosity fuelling his body? It was too horrible to imagine how things might have ended up. She feared him getting into a situation that might make him look like

... like a monster. That dreaded, hateful word. How could she, Veronica, even use it? But there it was. And she felt a sick guilt at even considering that Sebastian might ... *No*. As he himself said, there wasn't a bad bone in his body. But there was a need.

Veronica finally fell asleep, sitting up, letter still in hand and half-empty cup on the bedside cabinet. Now she comes into the large, sunny kitchen and makes a coffee to slug away the exhaustion.

What the hell is she going to do?

What would Pete do?

She wishes every day that she could talk to her husband. He died of an unexpected heart attack thirteen years ago at barely fifty. She misses him every day; his patient, practical ways, his ability to calm any crisis or drama. He often held Sebastian snug to his body during his toddler meltdowns. No one else could soothe their boy in the same way. Veronica could, but it took much longer.

Pete and his brother Len – each in their early twenties and with hardly a school qualification between them – went from working in the family's paint firm to starting a DIY chain, Murphy Made, which grew to have twenty stores in northern England. Pete had retired early, just a year before he passed away. He and Veronica owned the house and were wealthy enough never to work again. She knows how lucky she is to be in this position. Perhaps it has contributed to her making Sebastian such a central part of her life, even now he's twenty. Who else is there? *What* else is there?

I support whatever you choose for our boy.

For a moment Veronica hears Pete's voice as though he's standing beside her in the morning light from the large windows.

You cried at that film scene last night. Do what you feel is right, no matter what society or convention says. They don't know Sebastian like you do. I trust you to make the right decision for him. To choose the right person. Don't be afraid.

Don't be afraid.

Veronica opens her laptop and starts to type her query into the search engine, but Sebastian comes into the kitchen, so she snaps it shut.

'Eggs please,' he says, sitting at the wooden table, goggles high on his forehead. 'Did you come in my room last night?'

'No,' lies Veronica, getting out the pan.

'Someone did. My door wasn't shut properly.'

'Maybe we have a ghost.'

Sebastian rolls his eyes. 'There are no ghosts.'

'You don't know that.' Veronica heats the oil. 'No one does.'

'Part of the difficulty of investigating whether ghosts exist is that there is not one single, universally agreed-upon definition of what a ghost actually is, Mum.'

Veronica smiles, knowing from the way he speaks carefully that he is quoting something he read. His memory for these things is incredible.

'OK,' she says. 'What do you want to do today?'

Usually on a Sunday morning they walk along the River Humber and rest on the bench he calls his dad's. There are two of them, wooden, placed in a V shape next to one another, looking out across the river. The one on the right is Sebastian's spot and the one on the left was where Pete always sat. They shared many an egg sandwich there. Counted the cars on the bridge and the trains passing on the tracks parallel to the path.

'I want to have sex.'

Sebastian pulls Veronica from her reverie. 'Not today,' she says.

'I want to go to my swimming lesson then.'

She flips his three eggs, not sure her voice will hold steady if she finds the words.

'I can't do *either* now, can I?' he sighs.

'You can go swimming at Albert Avenue Pool,' says Veronica after a beat.

'Don't like it there. The water isn't as watery. Don't look at me like that. It isn't. It's too chemical.'

'Shall we go for our usual walk and then—'

'Not in the mood.'

Veronica puts the eggs in front of Sebastian; three on a plate, very crispy, no sauce, nothing else.

'Are you OK?' She moves his goggles and touches his forehead, in case he's unwell, but he swipes her away.

'Why do you always think my forehead is where my problems are?' He eats messily. 'I've got my own plans for today.'

'Oh.'

'I'm going to sort my CDs into colour order.'

'OK.'

'Mum?'

'Yes?'

'You can pay for sex, you know.'

Veronica spills her coffee. Has he been reading her mind?

'Can you?' she asks, tentatively.

'Yes. God, you don't know much for a fifty-five-year-old, do you? People seem to get dead upset about it. But it's just like paying for swimming lessons. You want to learn to do it and someone who knows how to will show you for an agreed fee.'

'I don't think people pay for sex to learn how to do it,' says Veronica softly.

'I might pay. If I was rich. But I'm not. I'll just have to find someone who appreciates me before I die. I hope it's this week. I'm feeling very sexual today. Right, I'm off to do my CDs.'

When Sebastian has gone to his room, Veronica runs the tap to disguise her sobs. She can't grasp what so upsets her about their conversation. She dries her eyes on the tea towel and opens her laptop again. She feels like she should fling on her Chanel scarf, sit up straight and ready herself for combat.

She types 'high class escorts' into the search engine and braces herself. Pages and pages and pages of websites appear. Most are in London, so she types 'high class escorts East Yorkshire'. The choices are more limited. Feeling somewhat like a teenager looking up rude words in the school dictionary, she tentatively opens the first. After clicking 'yes' to being over eighteen and to understanding that the content is graphic, images of naked and partially clad young women appear. Descriptions with words like 'sweet' and 'dreams' and 'fetish' and 'angel' and 'naughty' and 'hot' race before Veronica's eyes.

She slams the laptop shut and paces the kitchen floor. Feels for a scarf that isn't there. Is this really what she wants for Sebastian? Some strange woman who takes money for sex? Veronica feels sad then. She shouldn't judge them. She has learned through Sebastian never to presume anything about anyone. Perhaps they support a family. Perhaps they come from a tough background. But to *pay* for sex? For her own son. This is the part Veronica struggles with.

Should she give in and let the doctor prescribe something that subdues him?

No.

This disgusts her far more than the thought of a professional having sex with him. Sex is natural; his urges are natural. As he himself said, Veronica paid for his swimming lessons. Is this really so different?

Reluctantly, she opens the laptop again, and clicks out of the website. Beneath it is another. Angels Escort Services. It is much more elegant than the other site; all pink, black and gold wording, with tasteful images of a mix of women in expensive-looking lingerie.

Something falls over with a sharp crack. Veronica jumps out of her seat. She goes to the windowsill. The picture of Pete playing golf is face down. She picks it up, looks around, half expecting him to be there.

She realises then that she can't do it. It isn't right. Setting her own son up with a woman she doesn't even know. Who doesn't even know him. There has to be another way.

Veronica returns to the laptop, intending to turn it off.

But there's a face. Familiar. Veronica squints and leans closer. Where does she know the girl from? The buttery hair, youthful cheeks. It can't be … It *is*. The trainee nurse from the clinic on Friday. The one who had a lot of time for Sebastian.

Isabelle.

Yes, Isabelle.

She isn't called Isabelle here though. She is Violetta. There are various pictures of her in pink underwear, in black stockings, and in a short skirt and neat pigtails. Her profile says that she is twenty-six, that she likes the opera and shopping, that she is honey-blonde with natural breasts, has blue eyes, and that she loves champagne, Chanel perfume, and Italian food. No mention of the fact that she's training to be a learning disability nurse. Veronica guesses that she's doing the escorting to pay for university.

Or maybe she has other problems?

Veronica looks at the picture of Pete.

Then back at Isabelle.

Then at Pete.

Finally, at her own refection in the black screen of her laptop.

14

ISABELLE HAS TO WORK

Three days after Isabelle's unexpected night off from Dr Cassanby, she sits at her desk, penning another note to the night and anticipating a free evening so she can revise. Like the line in the Moody Blues song playing on the radio, she has more 'letters she has written, never meaning to send' than ones she has shared.

> *Dear Night,*
> *My dad is as far away now as when I was little, and he travelled. I come home after the long nights and I bathe and bathe and bathe so that I can get warm and then I try and sleep. I always get up and write. The stuff I can't say. Stuff I may never ever tell anyone. I bet there are notes everyone writes and never shares...*

Isabelle suddenly feels so angry that her dad is in a coma. That she has this life now. That his care is her responsibility. That she worked nine hours today on her placement at Rowan House, and she'll do the same tomorrow before working all evening again. She scrunches up the note and aims it at the mesh bin near her feet, missing completely. The paper on the floor unscrunches slowly, opens, undresses. She kicks it away.

The phone on her desk vibrates. Gina's name flashes.

'Hey,' says Isabelle.

'Hey, girl,' says the ever-chirpy Gina. 'You've got yourself a night *on*.'

'What? *No*.'

'First, though, Dr Cassanby wants you tomorrow night. At nine.'

'He didn't die from his explosive diarrhoea then?'

'Sadly not.'

Isabelle smiles.

'Don't forget you've got the new guy, Simon, on Wednesday too,' says Gina.

Isabelle takes out a diary with a garish, sparkly Moulin Rouge image on the front. It is completely different to her large, black student diary; they sit side by side in her drawer, two alternate lives. How depressingly full the Moulin Rouge one is. She enters Dr Cassanby's name on Tuesday. She'll have to service him after Ethan, who's pencilled in for seven. Ethan stinks of garlic but makes every effort to conceal it with Armani aftershave. He likes to call Isabelle Tinkerbell (she wishes she could fly away) and makes her dance for him, and then takes her roughly from behind. It doesn't hurt as much as people might imagine; or perhaps she is just numb now.

'You still there?' asks Gina.

'Sure.'

Isabelle has written *Simon Sensitive Stammer GFE 7pm* on Wednesday's page.

'So are you free tonight?' asks Gina.

Isabelle's heart sinks. 'Why?'

'I had a call from a woman. Called herself Victoria but I'd bet my diamond clit ring that's not her real name. Sounded quite posh. Older. I'd say she was a bit upset too.' Gina pauses. 'She asked specifically for you.'

'Oh.'

'Yep. She thought you looked kind.'

'Kind?'

In her three months as an escort Isabelle has only seen three women. Despite not being bisexual, Isabelle has found them more enjoyable to service than the men. These women were all over fifty and pretty well educated, but unsure of their true sexuality and wanting a safe place to explore what they had denied themselves for many years. Two of them just wanted to kiss and caress without undressing, like nervous teenagers. The other – a lady called Angela

– wanted to explore Isabelle fully with her hands and mouth. Though not arousing, Isabelle found it a tender experience, one she hadn't needed to bathe vigorously after. She wished Angela would become a regular, but she never called again.

'I need to revise,' says Isabelle, though a night with a generally easier woman is tempting. 'You know I keep Mondays free.'

'She said she only needs an hour. And she'll give you three hundred.'

'An hour?' Isabelle looks at the clock. She could be back home by eight-thirty. 'Did she say what time? Where?'

'Seven o'clock at The Pipe and Glass. She's booked a table already.'

'Oh. Not her home?'

'Nope.'

'How should I dress? Is it just a meal? An hour won't give time for much else.'

'Classy, I guess. You're good at classy, girl. The Pipe and Glass is a snazzy place.'

'Did she say exactly what she wants?'

'Nope.'

'OK.' Isabelle can't turn down such quick and easy money. 'Tell her yes. I'll be there.'

'She booked the table in the name of Victoria. Later, girl.'

Isabelle hangs up and closes her diary. She has fifteen minutes to get ready. She chooses a simple black dress, the kind she wears for meals out with Dr Cassanby, and adds some pearls. Many clients have said they love the elegant look, knowing there are stockings and lacy undies waiting for them underneath. She can't imagine her underwear will matter for an hour in a restaurant – unless they drive somewhere afterwards. She pulls on silk stockings, just in case.

Before leaving, Isabelle looks in on her dad.

As she walks along the landing – past pictures of her as a child, pictures of her dad's travels, and pictures of the mum she doesn't remember but knows well from her dad's stories – she feels something isn't right. She retraces her steps, back, back, as though re-winding a clock, and her image grows younger along the wall. She stops. One of the pictures is wonky. Not slightly, but completely diagonal. It shows her mum posing on the beach in a striped bikini.

The ghost on the landing?

Chill air touches her cheek.

Now she's being silly. They always keep her dad's room cool, and that's where the draught is coming from. She straightens the picture and goes to him. The machine's noise fills the air, as always. He sleeps, as always. Nurse Jean sits in the chair reading a magazine.

'Evening, Isabelle,' she says. 'You look nice.'

'Thanks.'

Jean thinks she has a boyfriend, one who takes her out a lot and likes her to dress up. Isabelle comes to her dad's bed, touches his greying hair and kisses his chilled cheek above the mask.

'Has he been OK?'

'Yes.'

'I'll be back soon,' Isabelle says as she always does.

Occasionally, she worries that she won't be. That someone will hurt her so much that she doesn't return. Another escort, Susie, ended up in the hospital after a particularly brutal attack by a new client who it turned out had a police record. Gina can only vet a client so much – spy on their social-media profiles, quiz them, get a feel for them. Susie had her arm broken and her face cut so badly it may never heal without scars. Even if it does, the wounds inside will remain. She left the agency soon after the hospital discharged her. Gina – who loves her girls as though they're her own children – was distraught. Since then she has been wary of everyone who calls.

What would happen to Isabelle's dad if she didn't return?

She can't think of it.

She *can't*.

'I'll see you tomorrow then,' says Jean.

'Yes, tomorrow.'

Isabelle leaves to meet a woman called Victoria.

15

VERONICA DRIVES TO SOUTH DALTON

What on earth do you wear when meeting a high-class escort for the first time?

Veronica can't believe she is asking herself such a question as she looks through her wardrobe and holds various blouses and scarves against her body. Of the many dilemmas she has had about Sebastian over the years, this has to be the strangest, the most difficult, and the most morally questionable.

'*Mum.*' His voice floats along the landing.

She goes to the bedroom door. 'Yes, darling?'

'What time will you be back?'

'Erm ... hopefully by nine, or just after.'

She has told Sebastian she's meeting her friend Jayne.

'Why?' she calls.

'Private time.' He shuts his bedroom door.

Veronica returns to her clothes. What does she want them to say about her? That she means business? That she is a good mum, just trying to do her best, and doesn't usually meet with hookers to ask them to sleep with her own son? She chooses a lilac blouse and a cream scarf, and the simple, rose-quartz earrings Pete bought her in Malta.

Downstairs Tilly is finishing up for the day.

'I've done the cupboard tops,' she says. 'Oh, you look nice, Mrs Murphy. Going somewhere special?'

'Yes ... *No.*' Veronica feels as guilty as if she's having an illicit affair. And yet she wishes that's all it was. 'Tilly, will you lock up, as I have to leave now?' She goes into the hallway and calls goodbye to Sebastian. He shouts down 'private time' again, which is something he often says. Deep down, Veronica knows what he is referring to but refuses to think about it.

As she drives out to South Dalton her stomach churns. Is it too late to cancel? No. This is her only hope. She has only decided to do it because of Isabelle. Because she is a girl Sebastian has met, liked. Because of her lovely *I'll take care of him* smile at the clinic last Friday. She pictures them together at the fish tank – him with her tortoiseshell glasses on and her wearing his goggles. Isabelle might be an escort called Violetta, but she was tender with Sebastian that day.

Isn't that all that *really* matters?

She gets to the restaurant early and is given a chunky wooden table by the fire, with two fat, creamy candles flickering in the centre. She orders a bottle of Sauvignon Blanc, not even sure if Isabelle will drink, but needing one herself. She sips it, looks around, and then swigs half the glass. She tries to still her heart.

Isabelle is on time. Veronica spots her before she comes to the table. She's elegant in a tailored black dress; the antithesis of the wind-swept girl who burst into the room at the clinic. A chic woman, walking with grace. Her daffodil locks are not stuck to her head as they were then, but softly curled around her face. When she arrives at the table, confusion knits her brow for a moment, followed quickly by recognition and an open mouth.

'I know you.' She sits down. 'You were at Rowan House.'

'I wasn't sure you'd come if I gave my real name.'

'I can't remember your real name. I see a lot of people there.'

'I'm Veronica. And I know you're not Violetta.'

'Of course.' Then she adds, 'I *do* remember Sebastian though.'

This warms Veronica.

'It could be awkward knowing a client,' says Isabelle. 'But I guess we don't really know one another, do we?'

Veronica shakes her head. 'Wine?'

'Just a small glass. Thank you.'

'How does this work?' Veronica takes out her purse and starts to count the money. 'Do I give you this now?'

'Let's be more discreet please.' Isabelle looks around at the other diners.

'Of course. Sorry. This is … I've never … I don't…'

Isabelle says gently, 'With new clients, I like the money first.'

Veronica counts the notes under the table, rolls it tightly up and puts it into Isabelle's hand. Her fingers are warm. 'I'll pay for dinner too,' she says.

The waiter comes and Isabelle insists that Veronica chooses the food: she picks dressed white crab meat, cucumber pickle and sea buckthorn pureed crab stick for their starter, followed by thirty-day aged steaks.

Isabelle sips wine and looks at her, eyes shimmering in the candlelight.

'I don't know how to…' Veronica gulps. 'Well, where to start…'

'Listen, I understand.'

'Do you?' Has Isabelle read her mind?

'Yes.' Isabelle speaks slowly, holding Veronica's gaze. She guesses she is in work mode. That she is flirting as part of the job. She is mesmerising. 'I meet women who have denied what they want for many years.'

'Sorry?'

'I can help you explore your desires.'

'My what?' Veronica blushes.

'We can talk about them, which I presume is how you want to begin now, and then we can explore things more physically, if that's what you'd like. We can take it as slowly as you want. Just tell me what you fantasise about, Veronica. I'll make it a sensual experience.'

Veronica undoes her scarf and fans her face, lost for words.

'There's no need to feel nervous,' says Isabelle, as gently as if she's speaking to a child afraid to go into school for the first time. 'Many women have told me how hard it is to finally explore what they really want. Then they make love with me and they—'

The waiter arrives then with their crab starter.

'—climax for the very first time,' concludes Isabelle.

The waiter spills the cucumber pickle from one of the plates, staining the white cloth.

'I'm so sorry,' he gushes, young and nervous.

'Don't worry,' smiles Isabelle, touching his arm. Veronica notes how tenderly she does it. It isn't sexual, or flirtatious, just absolutely gentle, and the waiter calms immediately and says he hopes they enjoy their meal.

Turning back to Veronica, Isabelle says, 'There's no shame in wanting to sleep with a woman.'

'No. You don't understand.'

'So tell me,' says Isabelle seductively.

'I'm not a ... I don't want ... I'm not here about *me*.'

Isabelle nods. She has probably known all along, was maybe teasing.

'I wish I was,' sighs Veronica. 'That would be so much easier.'

'I must say, this is a first.'

'For me too.'

'I can tell.' Isabelle smiles. It lights up her face.

'No ... I...'

'Just say it. I've heard it all. I had a guy once who wanted me to pretend I was his mother. Seriously.'

Veronica laughs. Then she remembers why she's here and suddenly wants to cry.

'Just tell me,' says Isabelle kindly.

'I'm here for Sebastian.'

'I thought so. Do you want me to have a talk with him about—?'

Before she can go on Veronica asks, 'Why do you do it?'

Isabelle stops with her fork near her mouth.

'This, I mean. The ... you know, escorting.'

'I have my reasons,' she says quietly.

'University is expensive, I know that.'

'I wish it was only that,' Isabelle says, more to herself.

'I'm not judging. It's just that what I'm about to ask of you ... well, I want to know more about you. I can tell you're a kind girl. How you were at the clinic, with Sebastian. Why does a lovely girl like you have to do *this*?'

'It was either this or lap dancing.' Isabelle drinks more wine. 'That was flippant of me. My university friend, she does that. But I couldn't. Not judging. But I'm too ... shy. And I can't dance. She told me how much girls could make by escorting, especially high end and with a proper agency.'

The waiter takes their empty plates away, looking at Isabelle with adoring eyes.

'You do it for the money?' asks Veronica.

'Yes.' But Isabelle looks like she regrets the word. 'No. Sorry, that's not something we're supposed to admit. But you asked me directly.'

'I suppose some women might just like ... well, sex with lots of people.'

'Some women do enjoy their work. Why shouldn't they? They're good at it. Take pride in it. But this isn't enjoyable sex for me. If you were my client, of course I'd tell you it was. That I loved it and you were fantastic.'

'I'd believe you.' Veronica can only imagine how popular Isabelle must be. She feels comfortable in her company and is sure that men do too. 'How much money do you think you would need to stop doing this?'

She offers Isabelle more wine.

'No, thank you. I'll not be able to drive.' But she doesn't respond to Veronica's question.

Veronica says, 'There must be an amount?'

'I guess. I just ... I don't know. It isn't that simple. I have things to pay for. I mean, it won't be forever...'

'How long will it be?'

'Um ... well, a few more months ... but then he still won't be able—' Isabelle stops herself saying any more. Veronica realises this is about someone else. A partner? But surely a good partner wouldn't want her doing this.

The waiter brings their main course. Isabelle eats straight away, maybe giving herself time to think. Veronica cuts her steak. Waits. Soft murmurs of conversation simmer around them.

'It would be a lot,' Veronica says.

'How much?'

Isabelle looks directly at her. 'Two hundred thousand.'

Veronica isn't even sure what she expected the answer to be. She's not sure if she is relieved that it's so little or shocked that it's so much. Is she selling her son if she proposes such a sum in exchange for him being able to have what he needs? She feels sick. Suddenly she wants to leave, go home, make his hot chocolate and hug him like he's six again. But he isn't. He's a man now, with needs and desires. He wrote a frank and passionate letter to their fifteen-year-old neighbour. He asks every single day when he will find someone.

It all flashes through Veronica's mind, overwhelming her.

If Sebastian was here now, he would cause a stir. Say something he shouldn't. Look noisily for the fish tank and demand eggs for every course and check with Veronica which women were over eighteen. But Veronica feels sure Isabelle wouldn't care.

As though to explain the £200,000, Isabelle says, 'I can make five thousand a week. And I've been doing this since October. In that time, I've probably made around sixty thousand plus. And it isn't enough. If you're asking what it would take for me to be able to stop, that's probably an amount where I could not worry for the next few months.'

Veronica nods.

'But who the hell is going to give me that kind of money?' Isabelle puts down her knife and fork, neatly side by side.

'Me,' says Veronica.

'You?'

'Yes.'

'For what?'

For my son, thinks Veronica, and feels sick.

What kind of mother is she?

'Are you OK?' asks Isabelle.

Veronica nods. *Just go for it. Say it.* 'Remember why I came to the clinic with Sebastian?'

'About his high sex drive. You were—' Realisation dawns on

Isabelle's face. She shakes her head. 'I thought you meant for me to *talk* to Sebastian, maybe. No. I can't do that.'

'You don't know what I'm going to ask yet.'

'Of course I do.'

'What then?'

'You want me to spend a night with your son.'

'No.'

'*No*?'

'It's ... well, it's much more than that.' Veronica struggles to speak. 'I want you to spend time with him, say for the next six months. I want you to be *with* him. Yes, sexually, but more than that. Maybe a few times a week. I don't even know myself. I want to, you know, ease his ... longings.' She pauses. 'You think I'm terrible, don't you?'

'I never judge anyone. How can I?'

'Nor I.'

Silence. A piece of cutlery clatters to the floor somewhere.

'Then we are the same,' says Veronica. 'Look, I have the money. You need the money. I have a boy who desperately needs something. And you can give him it.'

'No.'

The simple word sits between them.

'I'll give you two hundred and fifty thousand,' says Veronica. 'My husband left me very comfortable when he died.' She realises, not for the first time, how lucky she is to even be able to consider doing this. But then, she would give all her money away tomorrow in exchange for Sebastian's happiness.

'It isn't the money.'

'Is it because he's autistic?' Anger heats Veronica's chest. She pushes the remains of her steak away.

'No. That's not it at all. I serviced a man in a wheelchair. The difference is *he* was the one asking me. Not someone else on his behalf. Would Sebastian know what was going on? Does he know about *this*?'

Veronica shakes her head.

'If he came to me himself, as a man of twenty, I wouldn't have a problem. But this ... it isn't right. It feels ethically wrong. I'm doing a nursing degree in learning disabilities, for God's sake!'

'It hasn't stopped you being an escort.'

Isabelle looks profoundly hurt. She starts to get up.

'I'm sorry.' Veronica reaches for her arm, aiming for the gentle way Isabelle had with the waiter earlier and instead knocking the remains of her wine over. 'I'm desperate. I don't know what else to do. And you're lovely. I feel I could trust you with him. You could ... you know ... well, *you know* with him...'

Isabelle remains in her seat, face unreadable. The waiter asks if they want dessert, to which they both vigorously shake their heads.

'I could only consider it if *he* asked me,' says Isabelle.

'I can't tell him because I want him to think you like him, not that I paid you. Someone like you would never give him the time of day – and I want him to think you would.' Veronica feels tears coming and tries desperately to hold them back.

'He'll find someone,' says Isabelle softly. 'He's lovely.'

'If you saw him socially and got talking, and he wanted to go out with you ... would you really want to?'

Isabelle doesn't respond. The waiter brings the bill, and Veronica gives him her card.

'You'll have to ask someone else.'

'I don't have anyone else.'

'I'm sorry.' Isabelle stands, knocking the table.

'*Please.*'

She starts to leave.

'If you change your mind,' cries Veronica, 'my name's Veronica Murphy and I'm in the phone book. I live in Swanland. Please call me if you do.'

'I won't,' says Isabelle kindly, looking over her shoulder. 'I hope everything works out for you and for Sebastian.'

As she sweeps away – with many of the male diners turning to watch – Veronica's phone rings. Sebastian. She pushes her chair under the table and answers.

'Mum, ask Jayne if I can go and see her fish tomorrow.'

'She's gone now, darling,' sighs Veronica. 'I'll ask next time. I'm coming home now.'

'Can you get me some KFC?'

'I don't know if it'll still be open.'

'But I feel sad,' he says.

'Oh, I'll be home soon. Why are you sad, darling?'

'The ocean is dying.'

'What?' Veronica asks.

'It was on the news that the fish are starving, and the Californian coast is turning into a desert. Can we go and feed them?'

'I'll be there in fifteen minutes, I promise.'

'With KFC?'

'I'll try.'

Veronica cries for the entire journey home.

16

SEBASTIAN WONDERS HOW HE WILL KNOW
IT'S LOVE AND NOT INDIGESTION

Mum is out.

She said she's with Jayne who I like because she has tropical fish and looks after them really well, even though her house smells like coffee you wouldn't want to drink. I don't believe Mum is with Jayne though because when she said it she did this thing she does when she makes stuff up. She gets really red cheeks. She got them when she said she hadn't eaten the rest of the Maltesers yesterday.

I wonder if Mum's meeting a man. I hope so. She needs to get some sex at her age. She's fifty-five years and four months and twenty-three days old after all. She must be dying for it. I don't think she gets any. We're the same. I want love for her too. She has nice hair and good scarves and I think she could get someone who could learn to make my eggs the way I like them.

She's on her way home now. Hopefully with KFC. I want to ask her if she really met Jayne, but I think she'll make up some dull thing she said to her so I believe her. I'll secretly know that she had a hot date and be happy for her and laugh inside when she starts watching soppy films and crying.

While Mum was out, I had private time. I need private time. I think and write and make lists and do things that make my body feel good. No one else can do any of those things for me. Today I took all my CDs off the shelf and put them back in alphabetical order instead of colour order. I have four copies of each CD just in case a hard Brexit happens. Doing this did not stop my body needing me.

Tonight it needed me again.

Then I wrote a poem about Isabelle. I can't stop thinking about her. I've written plenty of lists, but I've never written a poem. I did my research. I went to a poetry forum. Poems are usually about love, so I'm a cliché. They should rhyme but I did it my own way. I put my rhyming words at the beginning and the end and went free-style in the middle. I think it captures the essence of my existence. That's how one poet on the forum described what he had written.

How will I know it's love and not indigestion?
How will I know to declare everything I feel inside
instead of taking a Rennie after curry?
How will I know when to follow my heart
instead of following my legs straight to the toilet?
How will I know when she is the one for me
and that I haven't eaten too many onion bhajis?
How will I know it's love and not indigestion?
How will I ever know the answer to my question?

Oh, Mum is here now.
I hope she has KFC.

17

ISABELLE IS A SLAVE TO THE NIGHT

On Wednesday evening Isabelle drives to the house of her new client, Simon, listening to a classical radio station in the hope that it will soothe her anxieties. The night is ice-cold. Frosted fields on either side reflect the orange streetlights. She sighs; the melancholic music only makes her long to turn the car around and drive home and curl up under the duvet.

Not sure how to dress for a shy man with a stammer who wants the Girlfriend Experience, Isabelle was more concerned with hiding the bite marks on her shoulder, and the bruises on her upper arms and wrists. She chose plain underwear and a dress with lace sleeves, and put a gold watch on one wrist and a gold bangle on the other to hide the marks. But no matter how carefully she pulled up her bra straps, she couldn't avoid wincing, and cursed at having to go out and be a slave to the night.

Yesterday her client Ethan was more vigorous than usual. Then Dr Cassanby, straight after, was particularly brutal. His cruelty is escalating. He has always preferred Isabelle to dominate him, verbalising exactly what he wants her to do. But last night he pinned her to the ground. He didn't warn her he would be so forceful, and she had to presume it was part of his game.

What else could she do?

He is paying for it and paying well. He'll pay someone else if it isn't her. Each time there is an injury Isabelle hopes it won't be visible. She has felt the weight of other students' eyes on her bruised arms, full of pity, perhaps wondering if she has a rough boyfriend. There is some blessing in the fact that her dad won't see them.

Isabelle turns the music up and looks at the sky. No moon.

Blackness. Hospitals are renowned for being hectic when there's a full moon. Another song begins on the radio. One she recognises; it pulls her like the moon seems to pull the patients to her wards. It's an aria from *La Traviata*. One she used to hear her dad playing when he felt blue. He met Isabelle's mum at a showing of *La Traviata* in town. He spotted her on the opposite balcony, crying at the death scene.

The music soars.

Isabelle pulls over, making the car behind honk. She puts her forehead against the wheel. Is the song a sign that she should stop the escorting now? Didn't the Violetta in *La Traviata* die?

It's been a hard day. The hours were endless at Rowan House, and Isabelle barely had a moment to start her next big dissertation for the Meeting the Complex Needs of People with Learning Disabilities core. Each time she thinks of it, Veronica's distraught face comes to her, followed by Sebastian's grin in her tortoiseshell glasses. Veronica's words at the restaurant are haunting her:

Someone like you would never give him the time of day – and I want him to think you would.

How easy it would be to go into the arms of that beautiful young man instead of into the bed of the intolerable Cassanby. How much safer it would be taking money from Veronica and giving Sebastian a beautiful experience with genuinely good in-tention.

No.

Because that beautiful experience would be built on secrets.

On deceit. Lies. Money.

But Sebastian's own mother – a woman who clearly adores him with every atom in her body – thinks it's OK to propose such a thing. And who is Isabelle to judge? Who is she to say what she'd do in the same circumstances? What else might Veronica do now that she has said no?

It isn't Isabelle's problem. She's studying the developmental, health and social issues of people with learning disabilities, and is sure that at no stage in her degree will a tutor open a lecture by asking how many of them would sleep with a sexually frustrated autistic man for a quarter of a million pounds.

The song fades. She switches the radio off.

Simon is waiting with whatever demands he harbours. She drives. As she approaches his address, Isabelle thinks about the meeting with her dad's care team earlier. New CT scans say the swelling on his brain has improved, and a ventilation scan suggests his lungs have recovered from pneumonia. Dr Sharp mentioned the possibility of waking Charles from the coma. Next week. Words Isabelle longed to hear, yet she couldn't take them in. She tried to concentrate when Dr Sharp said that if they woke Charles, he would still need the ventilator, as well as his medication, in smaller doses, and round-the-clock care for weeks. After that it would take further weeks, even months, to build his strength and get back to a normal life.

Isabelle would have her dad again.

But she would still have to pay for his care.

Still have to work the nights.

If anything, he'll need her more. He will be conscious and want to see her whenever she isn't at university. How will she explain where she goes most nights until late? How will she explain where the money for his care is coming from?

Isabelle continues past icy fields. Simon's house is a large, grey place, surrounded by pine trees. She knows Gina will have checked that the address was real before letting her come. She does it for all clients who want to be serviced in their own home. Isabelle rings the bell and waits. Nothing. After a few minutes she begins to think she might escape. Then the door opens. Against the light, Simon appears as a black bulk, blocking most of the doorway.

'I'm Violetta,' says Isabelle, assuming her professional and friendly persona. She still feels sick with nerves, even after three months. 'You must be Simon?'

'Y-yes.' His voice is small. He doesn't move.

'Would you like me to come in, Simon?'

'Um, y-yes.'

He stands back, and Isabelle sees him fully; maybe thirty, with blonde, sweaty hair, ruddy cheeks, small eyes surrounded by puffiness and a white shirt that is tight under the arms and over the tummy. She moves past him. Her heels are sharp on the wooden floor.

'I made us l-l-lasagne,' he stammers.

'Smells good, Simon,' she lies.

She removes her coat and gives it to him. He wants the Girlfriend Experience and that's what she would do upon arriving at a new boyfriend's home. He keeps hold of it and doesn't seem to know what to do.

'You have a lovely home, Simon. Shall we maybe go into the dining room if you have cooked for us?'

'Y-yes.'

She follows him down the hallway. His back is damp with sweat. She glances into the bare rooms, wondering if he just moved here. In a vast kitchen diner, a silver table is set with cheap cutlery and a pathetic candle almost burnt to the bottom. She still can't smell lasagne.

'Looks lovely,' she smiles, unsure what else to say. 'Have you lived here long?'

'N-no.'

No matter how annoying, it's so much easier when a client is chatty.

'Before we eat,' ventures Isabelle, 'and have a wonderful evening together, there is the small matter of the money.'

'I d-d-don't have any in the house.'

Simon stands in the middle of the room, studying her. It's unnerving. Despite the shyness, his gaze is intense. This is awkward. She can't stay if there is no money. If a client doesn't have it ready, they probably don't intend to pay. Some say they'll go to a cashpoint and get it, and this is a sign to leave immediately. They may come back with someone else. Two or more someone elses. Someone elses with bad intentions.

'Simon, we'll have to arrange another time if you don't have the money.' Isabelle speaks kindly. 'Did Gina explain that you need to give it upfront?'

'D-d-don't you want to *be* with me?'

'Yes. But—'

'You want to leave, d-d-don't you?'

'Simon, I have to.'

'Well, you can't.'

The stammer is gone. His gaze hasn't faltered. Was it all a pretence? Isabelle's chest feels tight. She glances at the kitchen door and back at Simon. He's still holding her coat.

'I have to,' she says. This time it is her voice that breaks.

She takes one step back. Despite his size, Simon is fast. He dashes to the door and stands between it and her.

'You sh-sh-should stay.' The stammer is back; now it sounds menacing.

'Simon, Gina knows I'm here. She'll check up on me.'

'Not for two hours,' he says.

He is right. She can see that he is aware of her realisation. He is shy but not stupid. It dawns on her that this house is detached. A good distance from any others. On a quiet road. Along with the many other things carried in her roomy bag on an evening like this – a tiny vibrator, condoms in all sizes, small jars of oils, and a fully charged phone with a sensual playlist on it – Isabelle has a petite, red rape alarm.

But who would hear it?

'I have to go.' Isabelle speaks assertively and strides past Simon, towards the door.

18

ISABELLE DOESN'T THINK *STOP*

The next thing Isabelle knows, she is coming around.

Her head throbs. Where is she? Her back hurts. The floor is hard. Cold. Why? She is naked. Shit, she is *naked*. Except for her shoes. How? And then she realises that someone is inside her. Someone is breathing heavily against her cheek. Simon. It's shy, stammering Simon. She tries to speak but his hand is over her mouth. He's naked too. Heavy. Hurting her. Inside her. They are on his kitchen floor. The pain is no worse than what Dr Cassanby causes her. But he has never knocked her out; he has never done anything when she's made it clear she doesn't want to.

But still Isabelle doesn't think *no*.

She still doesn't think *stop*.

She thinks, *let him finish and then you can escape.*

And then, in her head, she begins a new note to the night.

Dear Night,

I think there's a ghost on our landing. Sometimes I'm not sure I walk alone when I go from my room to my dad's. I sense this other soul, breathe in the air, another heart beating like my own. Do I even believe in such a thing? I don't know. But someone is there who wasn't there before he went into the coma. I'm sure of it. And she – I didn't realise I thought it was a she but I guess she is – wants to catch me if I ever fall the way he did...

Later Isabelle will realise what escorting has done to her. It has stripped away the belief that is she worthy of not being raped.

Destroyed her ability to feel natural responses to unnatural violations. Deadened her instinctive fight.

Now she surrenders.

Lets him pant and push and pound. Lets him spit and sweat and stammer obscenities. When he's done, Simon rolls away. Lies on his back, panting and groaning. Maybe he'll have a heart attack. She won't call an ambulance. Isabelle knows this is her moment. She doesn't even consider her clothes, which out of the corner of her eye she sees are folded neatly on the table next to the cheap cutlery and almost finished candle. She reaches for her bag, wraps a hand around the strap. Then leaps to her feet.

Simon is fast again. But not fast enough.

He tries to grab her ankle; she kicks him in the face.

'F-f-fucking bitch,' he cries.

Isabelle races into the corridor, her heels clacking and scraping. Thank God the front door isn't locked. She hears Simon lumbering behind her. But she's out. Away. Free. She jumps into her car, hardly aware of the icy chill and her absence of clothes. She locks the doors. Simon comes to his front door, stands in its gap, a great black shadow of everything against the light. Isabelle can't see if he's watching her. He doesn't approach the car. She starts it up, briefly wondering if she has a spare coat in the back. There's nothing. Thank God it's dark. She has to hope she'll get into the house without being seen by curtain-twitching neighbours. She must be in shock; she still isn't cold, though she cranks up the car heater.

Simon is still there. Watching. Not moving.

Isabelle pulls away, puts her foot down and doesn't look back.

She waits for the tears. Waits for the screaming. Waits for the anger to rip through her. It doesn't happen. Instead she whispers two of the lines she wrote earlier in her head, over and over and over.

I think there's a ghost on our landing. And she wants to catch me if I ever fall the way he did...

19

VERONICA GOES OUTSIDE LOOKING A STATE

'I want my eggs.'

The words pull Veronica from a hot and troubled sleep; from dreams where she was searching the streets for Isabelle and found only garish, overly painted women who scratched and clawed at her face. She's glad to be awake.

'Why aren't you up, Mum? This isn't good behaviour.' It's Sebastian. He's wearing his *I AM HUMAN TOO* T-shirt; his swimming goggles are snug around his neck; his arms are crossed like a gossiping neighbour. Veronica almost smiles at this thought, but her face aches with exhaustion. 'Are you in love?' he demands.

'*What*?'

What time is it? How long has she slept?

'It's the second time you've done this, Mum. It's a good job this morning is my free period. This new behaviour leads me to think you have fallen in love. I'm happy for you, but you can't forsake my eggs.'

Veronica pushes the duvet back and grabs her silk dressing gown. It's ten-fifteen. How on *earth*? She never sleeps this late. Yesterday it was quarter to nine and she got Sebastian to college in the nick of time, though he flapped and grumbled all the way there. Each of the last two nights she was so restless that she got up to wander the house, opening doors and looking in rooms, over and over and over, not sure what she was looking for. She then sat alone in the kitchen.

'In love?' Veronica laughs harshly. 'Of course, I'm not.'

'You object with unusual mannerisms. Is it the man you met the other night?'

'What man?'

She heads for her bathroom. Sebastian follows, his arms still crossed. She sits on the toilet; he stands in front of her and continues talking while looking at the ceiling, a thing she taught him from being small when he insisted on following her in here. It's time to stop this altogether.

'You said you were with Jayne, but I think you had a date. I think you have fallen quickly in love because you are fifty-five years and four months and twenty-six days old, and it's been a long time. I don't like the peach walls in here. We need to decorate. If you have sex in our home will you do it on Friday, please? I'll be cleaning my fish tank then. Flip and Scorpion can't go on living in filth. Does your lover have a daughter that I can have sex with sometime before Tuesday?'

'No,' snaps Veronica.

'So he does exist.'

'No, he doesn't. And neither does his daughter.' She pauses. 'Why before Tuesday?'

Sebastian ignores her.

Veronica flushes the toilet.

'Sebastian,' she sighs. 'Can I get a moment of privacy?'

'You're angry. This is not normal for love.'

'What would you know?' she snaps. The moment the words are out of her mouth, Veronica is overcome with regret. 'I didn't mean that, my darling.'

'But you are right.' There is no self-pity in his words.

'Do you want your eggs?'

'Of course I do. I wanted them two hours ago. A person can die of hunger in three weeks, you know. I read that in *The World's Worst Deaths*.'

'Come on, let's get you fed.'

Wearily, Veronica leads the way downstairs. She catches her reflection in the ornate, gold mirror. Her hair is tangled and her face tight with dark lines. Tilly will be here in an hour, so she must get herself together. She can't be seen in such a state. In the kitchen she puts her coffee on, gets the eggs from the fridge and warms oil in the frying pan. Sebastian sits at the table and watches as he always does, giving hearty instructions.

'I need extra-good eggs today because I have an important thing to say, Mum.'

'Do you, darling?' Veronica flips the three eggs over.

'Yes.'

'Well?'

'I need my eggs first. I've waited over two hours for them.'

Once they are perfectly crispy, she puts them on a plate in a triangle shape and places them in front of him. She watches him savage them. Maybe it's best that Isabelle said no to her suggestion. Maybe things will settle down. Maybe he is over the worst and his hormones will begin to calm, balanced by his maturity increasing. So many maybes; she has never been lucky with maybes.

'I'm leaving,' says Sebastian, pushing his empty plate away.

'What?'

'Are your ears closed? I'm leaving.'

'But ... to go *where*?' Veronica sits opposite him at the table.

'Latvia.'

'*Latvia*?'

'Yes.' Sebastian sits stiffly in his chair to show how serious he is.

'I don't understand.'

'It's the number one country where women far outnumber men. I read it on the BBC website. Therefore, once all the men have got a lady, there will be plenty left over, and they'll be as desperate as I am. We will be the same.'

'Sebastian.' Veronica reaches for his hand. 'You don't need to leave. How about I come with you to a nightclub again. I won't sit near you. The right girl might be there this time.'

'She won't be.'

'When on earth did you think of Latvia?'

'Yesterday,' says Sebastian.

'*Yesterday*? You should think it over some more, darling.'

'I've booked my flight. This month and next are the cheapest times so I had to.'

'What? How?'

'On the internet. At Cheapflights. I fly from Manchester to Riga. It stops in Brussels and takes four hours and fifty-five minutes. I go on Tuesday.'

'Tuesday?' Veronica's head swims. This can't be happening. She can't let him go. She gets up and paces the floor, wringing her hands.

'Please don't be distressed, Mum. You're upsetting me.' Sebastian's ripe-acorn eyes pale. He pounds his hands on the table. 'You should be happy. You should respect my decision. I'll get to have sex. I have my savings. I have my passport. You can't stop me. I'm twenty years and six months and eight days old. This place is not for me anymore. I can't swim where I want to. You'll have to feed Flip and Scorpion for me. I want to keep them nice and fat.'

'Stop it.' Veronica pulls the chair from the table and sits back down, her voice firm. 'This is ridiculous. You can't just go to another country. You don't know anyone. Where will you stay?'

'At the Bellevue Park Hotel for only fifty pounds a night including breakfast.'

'What?'

'I booked it online. Good reviews. Firm mattresses.'

'No!' Veronica shakes her head. 'You'll have to cancel it.'

'Why are you crushing my dreams?' Sebastian raises his voice too.

'Because this is stupid.'

'You mean *I'm* stupid,' roars Sebastian.

'Right now, yes.'

Sebastian leaps up. He kicks the chair and runs out of the room with his head in his hands.

'Come back,' cries Veronica. 'I didn't mean that.'

He ignores her. She hears him thudding up the stairs. Along the landing. His door slams. Then Billy Ocean sings 'Suddenly' full blast. The kitchen door opens again, and Tilly comes in. She glances back at the stairs and then at Veronica.

'Everything OK, Mrs Murphy?'

What a state she must look. No wonder Tilly's mouth hangs open.

'Just a ... a little tiff.' Veronica tightens her gown and tries to fluff her hair into some kind of style. 'I need to dress. Can you start in the dining room today?'

On the stairs, she trips at the first step. Puts a fist to her mouth to stem the sob. How she longs to be the one to walk out of the door and get on a flight and never come back. She never would though. It's only a longing, one that immediately dissolves when she thinks of Sebastian, like Alka-Seltzer in water.

If he goes, what will she have?

Who will she be?

What will be the point?

She must work it out with him. The phone rings on the hallway table.

'I'll get it,' she calls to Tilly.

It rarely rings. Those robots and foreign salesmen call her mobile now. Veronica fluffs her hair again, as though the caller might see her, and picks it up.

'It's Isabelle.' Her voice is almost inaudible.

'Isabelle?' Veronica's heart contracts.

'I'm outside your house. In my car.' She hangs up.

Veronica puts the phone down, feeling sordid, guilty, bad. Why? This is something she set in motion. This is what she wants. It's something that might now stop her beautiful boy fleeing the country.

Not necessarily. She shouldn't be so quick to presume that Isabelle has changed her mind. But why else is she here?

'I'm just going out to, um, to the bins,' she calls to Tilly. She realises that Sebastian mustn't come out and see them both. His bedroom looks onto the back garden, so she is safe if he stays there. 'Tell Sebastian I've popped to the shop if he looks for me.'

Then she opens the front door. Never in her life has she stepped outside in her night attire. Never has she stepped out without at least a smudge of blusher on her cheeks or a flick of mascara on her eyelashes. Never has she exposed herself in such a way. All she needs now is to see the hideous Annabelle or one of her contemptable daughters.

There goes the neighbourhood, Veronica thinks with a smirk.

And feels momentarily empowered.

Bugger them all. Them and their judgemental thoughts about Sebastian.

At the end of the gravel drive is a black Clio. She quickly opens the door and gets in. It's warm after the January air and smells of lemon. When she turns to Isabelle, Veronica is shocked. This is not the breezy woman who burst into the room at Rowan House. This is not the elegant, composed woman who ate opposite her at The Piper and Glass. This is a girl with dirty, scraped-back hair, a pale face devoid of make-up or life, wearing only a grey hoodie and faded jeans.

They are plain together. Stripped. Raw. Uncensored.

'I have a condition,' says Isabelle, softly.

'So...' Veronica swallows and tries again. 'So you'll do it?'

'I didn't say that.'

There are small bruises at the base of Isabelle's neck and two near her ear. Veronica wants to reach out and touch them. Her motherly instinct kicks in, hard. This girl could be her daughter. Who's watching out for her? Who hurt her?

'What's the condition?'

'I'm not saying whether I'll do it until I chat to Sebastian myself. Just me and him.' She glances at Veronica. 'Unpaid.'

'Oh. But ... *oh.*'

'We can go somewhere he likes to be and talk.'

'The river,' says Veronica.

'OK. You can tell him that I liked him when I met him at Rowan House. That I want to know more about his fish, or something. Whatever you think best. You know him.'

'What is it you hope to find out?'

'Nothing specific.' Isabelle pauses. 'I'll just know if I can go ahead when I spend some time with him. This is so ... so ... It goes against what I do—'

'Don't you think it goes against *my* beliefs?' Veronica snaps.

'I wasn't judging. We have to get that clear here. If we are to proceed.'

Veronica nods.

'No judgement,' says Isabelle.

'No judgement,' repeats Veronica.

'When shall I take him out?'

'It needs to be soon.'

'Why?'

'He's...' Veronica can't finish. She is embarrassed to find that tears have pooled in her eyes and threaten to spill over. 'Tomorrow?'

'I can pick him up in my lunch break. Say twelve-thirty?'

'He has college, but I'll keep him home for once. He hates to miss anything but if I tell him you'd like to see him, I don't think he'll care.' Veronica fiddles with her dressing gown belt. 'Don't...'

'What?'

'Don't hurt my boy, will you?'

Isabelle looks upset and Veronica regrets the words immediately. 'That was cruel. I don't think that. I just mean...'

'I know. He's your son.'

Veronica nods. 'I just want him to be happy.'

'I know.'

'Please...'

'Yes?'

'Don't tell him, you know, that you're an ... that it would be for...'

'An escort? For money?' Isabelle's voice is flat. 'I won't.'

They sit in silence. Grey clouds part, and a weak winter sun breaks through. The postman takes a batch of letters up to the house. A ginger cat leaps from wall to hedge to wall. Everyday life goes on while they decide the fate of a twenty-year-old autistic man.

'What made you change your mind?' asks Veronica.

'I haven't changed my mind.' Isabelle stares straight ahead.

'But you were an adamant no. Now you're going to meet him.'

'I should go.'

'Yes.' Veronica starts to open the door, letting chill air in. 'Thank you,' she adds.

'If I agree,' says Isabelle, 'it will be on my terms.'

'Yes.'

'I'll be here at twelve-thirty tomorrow.'

'Sebastian will be waiting.'

Veronica stands on the kerb and watches the car until it rounds the corner. Then she remembers she is in the street in her dressing gown and hurries back up the gravel drive, back into the house, back to Tilly with an armful of laundry and a face full of pity.

SEBASTIAN IS LONELY

Mum doesn't understand how lonely I am.

I'm so lonely that it sometimes feels like I'd be better off dead. I can't get a date, which means I can't get a kiss. I would like to kiss. It looks like the nicest part of sex. I would keep my eyes open. I'd like to see her and know if I'm doing it right. But when a girl loves me, she won't mind if I do it wrong. She'll show me how to do it right.

Girls avoid me. They look at first because I am conventionally attractive – that means having a good body and nice hair and handsome face. But then they talk to me and I see their expressions change. Everyone thinks autistic people can't understand expressions, but we have to look at the strangest ones anyone can make, and then work out what they mean. That is called irony, you know.

And people call us stupid. Mum just did. I know she didn't mean it, but it's the worst word she could say to me. I know I'm not stupid. I am interesting and clever and funny. I might not be exactly like other people, but if they spent some time with me they might learn something new *and* have a good time sexually. But they have made me ashamed of my autism. I'm scared to bring it up with new people. I hate it. I wish I wasn't me.

Isabelle's expression stayed happy though the whole time she talked to me.

I would love to kiss her most of all.

But she deserves better than me.

So I will go to Latvia to find what I need.

21

ISABELLE AND SEBASTIAN SPEND TIME AT THE RIVER

The river is wild. An icy January wind whips and whirls the water, thrashing the sandbanks and tricking birds into thinking it will carry them one way and then tossing them carelessly the other. Isabelle is glad she wore her padded coat, but even more relieved that Sebastian is dressed warmly too.

When she picked him up at twelve-thirty ('You're two minutes late,' he said, showing her a flashing digital watch) he told her he had given up a day at college for her and he hoped she knew this could affect his career, but he didn't mind if she was here with good intentions.

'Would you like to walk along the river?' she asked him.

'That is a *very* good intention,' he said, fastening his seatbelt.

She had wanted to ask what his mum had told him this was – a date, a day out, a casual walk – but hadn't.

Now they are halfway along the chalky path that goes from Hessle Foreshore to North Ferriby, with the river angry on the left and the train track quiet on the right. He's wearing a strawberry-coloured jacket, leather gloves and a Hull City hat with his goggles over the top like a 1920s aviator. He hasn't said much, even when she asked about his bricklaying course and his fish.

Eventually they reach two concrete and wood benches in a V-shape overlooking the water.

'That's my dad's chair,' says Sebastian, motioning to the one on the left.

'You mean he built it?' Isabelle stops.

'No. We always sat here together. It's dedicated to him.'

Isabelle leans in to see an inscription, but there isn't one.

'Where's his name?' she asks.

'You need to wear these to see it.'

Isabelle takes his goggles and puts them on. She pretends to read something on the top slat. She tries to look very serious.

'I'm joking,' he says.

'Oh, OK. Do you want to sit here for a bit?'

'Of course. You've got to take your shoes off.'

'Do I?'

'We always did. Then we felt like we were at home except with a very dangerous river in our living room.'

Isabelle slips off her trainers and puts them on the gravel. Sebastian places his much larger Puma trainers – not as clean as they were in Mel's office now – symmetrically next to hers. They sit opposite one another, him on his dad's chair and her on the other.

'Do you miss your dad?' asks Isabelle, shivering.

Sebastian shrugs.

'I never knew my mum enough to miss her,' she says. 'She drowned when I was one, you see. She swam too far out at Scarborough. The current caught her by surprise. I wish I had been old enough to rescue her.' Maybe she shouldn't be telling Sebastian such things, but something about him makes it easy to speak. Something about him is as calming as a warm bath after three clients. 'Now I'm scared of water.'

'You must respect the water,' says Sebastian, back straight, not looking at her. His cheeks are bright pink in the chill. 'If you find yourself unexpectedly in the river you must fight your instinct, not the water. You must float.'

'I'll remember that.'

'Lions don't like water.'

'I'll remember that too.'

'You should. Do you want to have sex with me?'

Isabelle hides her smile. After Rowan House and meeting Veronica, she is prepared for the question. She has never been asked it quite like this. Not so earnestly. Not with such vulnerability. For the last three months no one has asked her. The men – and some women – have known they will get it. They have paid for it. Taken it. This is refreshing. She wants to cry. She wants to leave now, not hurt this sweet young man.

But she leaves her trainers next to his.

'Isn't that why we're here?' asks Sebastian.

'What did your mum tell you?'

'She didn't say. She can be very mysterious. You can't be here for my brain.'

'Why can't it be for your brain?'

'Because that isn't as conventionally handsome as my body,' says Sebastian, slightly exasperated, as though this is obvious.

Again, Isabelle doesn't know if she can do this. She almost didn't come. Gina rang earlier to see how she was after new guy Simon because she hadn't been in touch with the agency. Isabelle quietly said she was fine. That he had been awkward and not paid, so she had left, but she would obviously pay the percentage she owed Gina. Isabelle can't bear the thought of him hurting anyone else so she told Gina she sensed something very bad about him. Gina assured her she would remove him from the client list altogether.

She has tried not to think about that night. But her bruised inner thighs and the lump on her head insist that she does every time she bathes or does her hair. Isabelle just grits her teeth and whispers, *Bruises heal, bruises heal, bruises heal.*

Sebastian is looking at her.

No one ever looks at her that way.

Those warm, brown eyes make her stay.

'The thing is,' says Isabelle. 'I like to get to know someone before I have sex with them, and I don't really know you, do I?'

'You do know me. My name's Sebastian James Murphy. And you know where I live and how old I am and who my mum is.'

'But what about the things you enjoy...'

'I told you some of the things I like.' Sebastian sighs like she's a child. 'I like this river and swimming and tigers and my fish and the great artist Billy Ocean. I know your name and you know my name. You are definitely older than eighteen because you have lots of wisdom in your eyes and you talk well. So we are ready for sex.'

Isabelle smiles. 'But I like to go on a date with someone first. You know, like where you go out in the evening, maybe have a meal, and candles...'

'We're out together now.'

She can't argue with that. 'I suppose we are.'

'And why do you need candles to have sex?'

'It puts you in the mood, Sebastian.'

'I'm in the mood now.' He nods vigorously.

'Yes, but I need to be too.'

'Are you in a mood with me?' His brow furrows with confusion. 'My mum always is when I go on about sex.'

'No.' Isabelle huddles against a sudden onslaught of freezing wind. Her feet are blue, but she doesn't want to put her trainers on and ruin Sebastian's ritual. 'I enjoy talking to you. I mean that I have to be in a sexual mood to have sex.'

'I'm in a sexual mood now.'

'Both people have to be. You'd have to wait for me to be in a sexual mood too.'

'What time will you be in a sexual mood?'

'What time?'

'Yes. I like to know times.'

Isabelle then realises that this is how she thinks of her escorting, and this is how she should think about the job she's doing for Veronica: as a transaction, something she does at a set time. Veronica will be paying her for a service that Sebastian desperately needs. He just wants sex. Probably with rules. And he would clearly be happy with sex at a pre-arranged time. What harm is there then? He would clearly feel safer knowing there was a schedule. That's how she does things too. They are perfectly suited. If she was his escort, she could answer him now and say, 'At eight o'clock tonight I'll be in a sexual mood.'

But it is the lie. Him not knowing she is being paid. This nags at her way more than her bruised thighs and head.

'You don't want to have sex with me because I'm autistic,' says Sebastian, arms crossed.

'That has nothing to do with it.' This is the only full truth that sits between them.

'And that's discrimination.'

'It's not that,' insists Isabelle.

'You're like everyone else,' he says sadly. 'Everyone says to me "oh, you're really nice" or "oh, I have a boyfriend" or "oh, I'm not in the mood". It's because they don't fancy me. You're a discriminator too. Why can't I be your boyfriend? I'm not a child you know.'

'I know that. You're twenty.'

'Yes, twenty years and six months and nine days. Don't you fancy me?'

'I like you a lot.'

'Do you love me already?' asks Sebastian.

'I don't know you well enough.'

'Well, I don't love you already either.' Sebastian pulls his goggles over his eyes and then moves them back to his hat. 'But I do fancy you.'

He seems to like it when things are direct, so Isabelle asks, 'Do you just want to have sex, Sebastian?'

'Yes.'

'And you're not bothered if you love me?'

'No.'

'Are you even bothered if you like me?'

'Well, I do like you. Can you cook eggs?'

'I'm good at eggs,' smiles Isabelle. 'I could do them any way you want.'

'This sounds like my best kind of time.' Sebastian jiggles with excitement in his seat. 'Sex and then eggs.'

Isabelle smiles.

'How many times can you do it in one time?' he asks.

'As a woman, I can have it lots of times. That's how it works for me. But you might need a little rest in between.'

'You're not a slut, are you?'

'What do you mean by slut?' Isabelle's heart tightens.

'A woman who has sex all the time. I want to have sex all the time, but I'm a man.'

'I'm not allowed to then?'

'No, you're a woman.'

'Is that something you read or what you actually think?' Isabelle pauses. 'Do you know the difference?'

'I'm not stupid. Think is in my head, read is in a book. I didn't think it or read it. I saw it on telly. On *Love Island*. No one wants a slut.'

'No,' says Isabelle softly. 'No, they don't.'

'But I don't think you are. You have eyes that say nice girl to me.'

She longs to cry; she's afraid that she will have to get up and walk away, barefoot, leaving her trainers forever next to his. She closes her eyes. Sees Simon. Huge. Panting. On top of her. She opens them again and watches the choppy waves. She might be afraid of the water but here with Sebastian she finds it calms her.

He doesn't speak. She glances at him and he's also looking at the water, quietly counting something, the goggles on his hat like two eyes looking heavenward. Maybe he won't find out she's being paid to be with him. Isabelle knows Veronica would never want it to come out, so would never speak of it, and would hide any evidence.

Can Isabelle do this if she knows with absolute certainty that Sebastian will only ever think of it as a brief fling, his first love affair?

Maybe.

Maybe.

After a while she speaks. 'Say that you and I did have sex, Sebastian, which we could if you'd really like to, would you feel happier if we arranged set times? Like, say, we had sex at seven o'clock and then eggs at eight o'clock and maybe sex again at nine. And it's just sex. And it's just eggs. That's all.'

'I prefer seven-thirty.'

'OK.' Isabelle pauses. 'But what if you fell in love with me? That might make things tricky. You don't love me now but if you did, would that mean you'd want to carry on for a long time having sex with me? What if I didn't want to?'

'How many eggs have you got?'

'Oh, um – a dozen.'

'Will you make eggs *every* time we have sex?'

'I could.'

'I can promise you a good time,' says Sebastian. 'I have this book you see.'

Isabelle smiles. 'Tell me about the book.'

'It's called the *Kama Sutra*. I found it in my mum's room. Don't tell her, will you? She'll get embarrassed. She hates talking about this kind of thing. I know you'll understand. There're these pictures – there's tigers in there too but they're not having sex – but there're these Indian people and they look like royalty and they can do these twisty moves. They have the best sex ever. Guaranteed. It really is. There's a sticker on the cover that says *Satisfaction Guaranteed, £4.99* so it must be.'

'You like the idea of guaranteed?'

'Yes.' Sebastian nods vigorously.

Isabelle rubs her frozen feet. 'If I said I guarantee you can have sex and then eggs, say three times a week with me, what days would you pick?'

'My favourite day is Monday because it's the start of week, so good things go first. Then Wednesday is the middle of the week so that could keep me going. Then Friday is the end of the week, so it would be something to look forward to.'

Isabelle nods slowly to show she's taking it all in. 'If I guaranteed that on Monday, Wednesday and Friday of every week we would have sex and eggs, is that what you would like?'

'Yes. I'd like you to write it down too, so you don't change your mind. Have you got a pen?'

'If we could do that, you would like to?'

'Of course.'

'And you understand this is *your* idea?' Isabelle feels slightly better if Sebastian thinks *he* chose this. She just needs to try not to think, ever, that he didn't.

'Yes.'

'*You* thought of it?'

'It's my idea.' He speaks with pride.

'Do you think your mum will mind?'

'I don't care. Stop talking to me like I'm a child.'

'Me and you are making this decision?'

'Yes.' He sounds irritated now. 'I'm a man. You're a woman. And my mum is my mum.'

'We'll sign something then, if that's what you want, Sebastian.'

'Good.' He thinks for a moment. 'I'll even cancel Latvia.'

'You're going to Latvia?' Veronica never mentioned that.

'I was. I won't now. What do you want from this then? It can't be just me. I've got lots of tiger books. You know about my goldfish Flip and Scorpion. I can give you Scorpion. Or I can get you a present. I do have money...'

'I don't want your money,' Isabelle says quietly.

Should she do this without payment? The thought comes to her, in a flash. Should she take Sebastian out on dates and have sex with him without it being this transaction. Treat him like she would any other decent, innocent, young man.

But she will have to continue escorting. And since Simon, she doesn't think she can. Last night she cancelled a regular called Adam, saying she had a tummy bug. And she knows she'll cancel whoever she has tonight. Where will the money come from?

Sebastian interrupts her thoughts. 'I can't give you one of my fish. Flip will be lonely if I give you Scorpion. And Scorpion will be lonely if I give you Flip.'

Isabelle remembers counting the tropical fish at the clinic last Friday. He said that they looked at things with the same eyes. Do they though? He sees life in simple terms. She knows how cruel it can be. Is that unfair? She has no idea how he sees the world.

'OK,' she says. 'You keep your fish.'

'You can have one of my tiger books.'

'OK. Shall we go back?'

They stand at the same time. Sebastian passes Isabelle her trainers before putting his back on, tying the laces neatly. The wind has died a little and the river calms. They walk back towards the foreshore.

'Are we going to have sex now?' he asks.

'Let's start on Monday, shall we?'

'At seven-thirty. At your house?'

It occurs to Isabelle that once her dad is awake this might be tricky. And what if it is next week when they begin the process of bringing him out of a coma? He may be bedridden for a few weeks, and she may be able to sneak Sebastian in, so she'll cross that bridge when it comes.

'You can come to my house,' she says. 'I'll pick you up at seven.'

'Do you like jokes,' he asks.

'Yes.'

'Knock, knock.'

'Who's there?' she asks.

'Isabelle.'

She smiles. 'Isabelle who?'

'Isabelle necessary on a bicycle?'

She laughs. 'Knock, knock,' she says back.

'Who's there?' he asks.

'HoneyBee.'

'HoneyBee who?'

'HoneyBee a dear and please open the door.'

Sebastian giggles and it's the most enchanting sound. 'That's you,' he says.

'What is?'

'HoneyBee. I'll call you HoneyBee.'

'Why?'

'You are sweet to me, HoneyBee.'

Am I though? Isabelle asks herself as they reach the Humber Bridge.

Isn't she Violetta? The *La Traviata* courtesan? The woman who fucks for money. Sebastian was right. No one wants a slut. And she is a worthless slut.

22

VERONICA HAS A FEW REGRETS

A familiar melody pulls Veronica from a restless sleep. It's not her phone alarm though. When she looks at the time it's 6.30am. The room's dark; shadows rest unwoken, grey over TV, mirror and wardrobe. On goes the song. She knows it, every word. 'Suddenly' by Billy Ocean. A track on Sebastian's *Best Hits of 1985* album. It ends and starts again, slightly louder.

Veronica sits up. Sebastian is a prompt riser, even on a Saturday, but he's thoughtful at the weekend and doesn't start his music until he knows she's up too. Now he begins to sing along with gusto, belting out lines about love having new meaning and holding hands along the shore. He doesn't sing 'suddenly' though. Veronica frowns. It sounds like 'honey bee'. She can imagine him bouncing along in his room.

He was bouncy last night, bounding around the house with a huge smile.

Ever since he got back from the river with Isabelle.

Veronica asked him about the meeting over their evening meal. He grinned and said that his Mondays, Wednesdays and Fridays were going to be the best days ever now, and he didn't care about not being able to swim at Haltemprice anymore. That was all she could get out of him; that it was seventy-three and a half hours until he would be meeting Isabelle to have sex.

'You're not going to Latvia then?' Veronica asked.

'Nope,' he said. 'Don't worry, Mum. I took out cancellation insurance. It has to be specific, provable perils like illness, death or jury service, but I'm autistic and they won't argue with that. I'll get my money back.'

'It isn't about the money, darling,' she said, realising that this was the biggest lie she'd ever told him.

It is *all* about the money now. His whole life for the next few months. And he has no idea. She'd had to pretend she felt ill and went to lie in her already-dark bedroom, trying to keep her tears quiet. Sebastian crept in after an hour. She faked sleep. He gently kissed her forehead and whispered, 'Don't worry, Mum, I still love you more than anyone in the world and you make the best eggs.'

Veronica's throat hurts thinking about it. She grabs her robe and goes to Sebastian's room. Outside his door the music is so loud she's grateful they live in a detached house, and that it's January so the windows are closed. She knocks. Then louder.

'Come in,' he yells above the racket.

Sebastian is sitting in the middle of his room, wearing his yellow smiley-face pyjamas, flicking through Stephen Hawking's *A Brief History of Time,* while singing. The ceiling stars flash silver. Flip and Scorpion – perhaps disturbed by the volume – swim in frenzied circles.

'Can you turn it down?' cries Veronica.

With a dramatic huff, he does.

'They go together,' he says.

'Who do?'

'Hawking and Ocean. Am I the only one who sees this?'

'I'd have to say yes.' Veronica is snappy; she can't help it. She's hardly slept. Over and over she thought, *What have I set in motion*? *What kind of mother am I*? Now this rude wake-up call is the last thing she needs.

'You should open your eyes then,' says Sebastian.

His goggles are hanging from the bedpost, where he leaves them at bedtime.

'I was asleep,' sighs Veronica.

'I thought because you went to bed so early, you'd be up earlier. I just felt happy and wanted my music on loud.'

Veronica sits on his bed, plays with the goggles.

'You're happy about Isabelle?'

'Yes.' Sebastian nods vigorously.

'If you change your mind, you don't have to see her.'

'Why would I do that? You told me she liked me and wanted to meet me. So we met. And we talked. And she likes me. And she wants to have sex with me. Don't be sad about it, Mum. I know you might be jealous because you're not getting sex on Monday, but you don't need to be. You can have your pick of men.' He studies her, his acorn-brown eyes wide. 'I don't understand your face today, Mum. It's not the kind of unusual I've seen before. This is a new unusual. Tell me what this one means.'

Veronica is afraid that if she speaks, she will sob. She lets go of his goggles and takes a breath. 'I don't want you to...'

'To be happy?'

'No! That's all I want, darling. I don't want you to get hurt.'

'I won't,' cries Sebastian. 'You don't get it. Isabelle is amazing. She can make eggs. She doesn't want my money or my fish, though I'm going to give her that very small book about tigers that Uncle Jim gave me.'

'She's older than you,' says Veronica. 'She may not want a proper relationship, you know, *forever*, with someone...'

'Like me?'

'No, with someone much younger.'

'I know that,' he sighs. 'She said she might not want sex forever with me and that she doesn't love me because she doesn't know me enough. Not that it's any of your business.'

'She said that?' Veronica can't decide if she is angry at Isabelle's bluntness with her son, or relieved that the honesty may protect him.

'I'm not telling you any more. It's private.' Sebastian slams his book shut. 'What does a man have to do to get some eggs around here?'

Veronica can't help but smile. 'What do you want to do today then?'

'I just want to be with me.'

'Oh. You don't want to go to Albert Avenue baths for a swim?'

'Nope.'

'OK.'

'Can you make my eggs then?' he asks.

When Veronica makes her way down their wide, polished stairs and Sebastian doesn't follow she waits at the bottom step. Still he doesn't come. She feels completely alone. Like her beautiful boy's body is in the house but the inside has flown away. She makes his eggs and just as she's putting them in a triangle on the plate, he enters the kitchen.

'Thanks,' he says, and takes them upstairs.

Veronica stares at the door after he has gone. Usually they sit together while he eats. She carefully washes the pan and puts it away, looks around at her immaculate, sterile kitchen. No Tilly today either. No plans. The day looms ahead, vacant, empty.

She goes to her room and chooses her clothes: a silky cream blouse that ties at the neck with her favourite grey trousers. She applies her make-up carefully, covering her lines and shadows with concealer, and teases her hair into soft waves. Then she stares at herself in the mirror, wonders what the point was in making herself look good. Who will even be looking at her? Her whole life is Sebastian and now she's set something in motion that might take him away from her.

What has she done?

The phone rings downstairs. Veronica dashes into the hallway.

'It's Isabelle,' comes the soft voice.

'I know.' Veronica doesn't know what else to say. 'I guess you've agreed to do it,' she adds eventually, realising she's being brusque.

'Yes.'

'What changed your mind?' Veronica can't help but wish she hadn't.

'Because Sebastian seems to know *his* mind. He's a lovely young man.'

'I know.' Veronica realises she sounds like a huffy teenager. She needs to get a grip. She did this. She sent her boy to meet an escort. She offered the woman £250,000 to service him three times a week.

She pulls her necktie undone and can't fasten it again with the phone in her hand.

'Because, aside from the money, I feel he knows what he's getting into.' Isabelle pauses. 'Because we mutually agree to have sex. On days that he prefers.'

'But that isn't all, is it?'

'No,' says Isabelle. 'He doesn't know about...'

'No.' Veronica sighs.

'What is it?'

'I'm...'

'What?' Isabelle asks.

'I'm...' Veronica tries again.

'You're regretting it?'

'I don't know.' Veronica tugs on her necktie, chafing her neck. 'No. Yes. I'm ... God, have I done the right thing?'

'It's begun now,' says Isabelle.

'I know. And if I change my mind and you don't see him, he'll be heartbroken. I didn't think this through. I just wanted to give him what he needed, what he went on and on about. I wanted to stop him doing or saying the wrong thing to a girl and getting in serious trouble. I wanted to stop him thinking he wasn't worthy of a girl who isn't autistic, because he *is*.'

'You wanted the best for him,' says Isabelle kindly. 'I'll take care of him.' She pauses and then hurries to add, 'I didn't mean that crudely, as in, you know ... I mean in a protective way.'

Veronica can't say that it isn't just about whether Isabelle will hurt him or not. She can't admit her sudden fears are also selfish. They have surprised her. Of course she's worried about Sebastian. But she's also ... she can't bear the word: jealous. She's jealous of Isabelle. That she's going to take him away from her.

'Veronica?'

She jumps. 'Yes.'

'We should talk about, you know ... the money. I feel so awful even saying that but if I'm to give up my other work, I need to talk about it. I want to hand my notice in. I need to know that I can.'

'Of course.' It occurs to Veronica that this is easier to talk about. This she can pretend is simply an outstanding bill. 'I trust you, but you have to understand I just can't hand over that kind of money before you do ... what I'm paying you for.' She feels queasy. Haggling over money with an escort. What the hell would Pete think?

Then she remembers that day in the kitchen when she first looked up escorts on the laptop and the picture of Pete fell over. If anyone knows her heart, he did.

'I understand,' says Isabelle. 'Do you want to divide it up? You suggested at the restaurant that I should see him for six months? Is that how you see this working?'

Veronica realises yet again that she hasn't fully thought it through. What will they tell Sebastian in six months? That Isabelle is no longer interested? That she has changed her mind altogether? How is that going to affect him?

'Are you still there?' asks Isabelle.

'I'm just trying to think how to do this for the best. For him I mean.'

'Do you want to do it on a month-by-month basis? I mean, Sebastian might be the one who wants out sooner.'

'I don't think he will,' says Veronica. 'I'll pay you the full amount we agreed on regardless of how long you do this. Until we know how it goes, I'll give you £50,000 a month, and if Sebastian wants out sooner, I'll pay you the outstanding balance in full. Does that sound OK?'

'Yes.' Isabelle's voice is almost inaudible, unsure.

'You're not happy with that?'

'I am. It's just ... I'm not some money-grabbing whore.' She sounds desperately sad. 'I have my reasons for needing to do this.'

'No judgement, remember,' says Veronica.

'No judgement.'

'I need your bank details. For the transfer.'

'Just a moment.' After a while Isabelle returns and gives her them.

'So how will it happen?' asks Veronica, glancing up the stairs to check that Sebastian hasn't crept up on her as he sometimes does. Billy Ocean is playing in his room, not as loud but still on repeat. She polishes the hallway mirror with her sleeve. 'When?'

'I said I'd pick him up at seven.' Isabelle pauses. 'Do you really want to know?'

'I think so...'

'He wants sex at seven-thirty.'

Veronica isn't surprised he chose an exact time.

'I'll play the rest by ear,' says Isabelle. 'I'll be...'

'What?'

'I'll be gentle. I'll be safe.'

Veronica wipes a tear she wasn't even aware has fallen.

'I'll bring him safely home afterwards,' continues Isabelle.

'Where are you taking him?' asks Veronica, suddenly concerned this encounter will occur in the back of a car or against a pub wall.

'Here. My home.'

'Do you always do that with your clients?'

'Never. It might only be this week that I can bring him here. I can't talk about it, but if I can't bring him here, I'll think of somewhere else that's perfect.'

'You and I should meet every other week too,' says Veronica, suddenly thinking of it. 'Talk about how it's going. That feels like the right thing to do. We're both feeling our way here, after all. This is ... God, so strange.'

'Yes, we can do that. I should go, Veronica.'

'OK.'

'I know this must be difficult for you,' says Isabelle. 'Sebastian is really special, and I'll look after him.'

After they hang up, Veronica ties her neck bow neatly and checks it in the mirror.

For the rest of the day she wanders the vast house, doing little jobs that don't even need doing, and clearing out drawers that are already barely full. At teatime Sebastian finally joins her, and they eat chicken and pasta at the kitchen table. There's a beautiful oak table in the large dining room, but they have always preferred the kitchen.

'Did you enjoy your me time?' asks Veronica.

'Knock, knock,' says Sebastian.

'Who's there?' she asks.

'HoneyBee.'

'HoneyBee who?'

'HoneyBee a dear and please open the door.' Sebastian giggles as he says it.

Veronica smiles. She can't think of a joke to respond with.

'Well?' asks Sebastian.

'I'm tired. I can't think of one.' She pauses. 'Are you ready for Monday night?'

'I've picked my clothes out and hung them in the window to get some sun and moon air on them. I'm going to wear my lucky socks with the clovers on, my smart wedding trousers that have never been to a wedding and my Hull City shirt. Do you think that will be OK for my first sexual experience?'

'It will be perfect.' Veronica's voice is a dry croak. What will be truly perfect is if Sebastian says he has changed his mind and he's going to wait for a girl his own age.

'Right, I'm done,' he says. 'I'm going to polish my good shoes now.'

'Will you wear your goggles on Monday?' Veronica asks as he heads for the door. He isn't wearing them now, which is unusual.

'I don't think I'll need them,' he says, and the door closes softly after him.

Veronica sits and stares at their empty plates for an hour without moving, before finally picking them up and washing them and putting them away.

23

ISABELLE DOES THE THING SHE'S WANTED TO DO FOR THREE MONTHS

Isabelle hears the words as though she's underwater and the doctor's voice is coming from the surface. She is her mother; she is drowning. Dr Sharp is an out-of-focus, dark shape, far away. His lips are moving. Then they stop, and he gently touches Isabelle's arm, dragging her suddenly to the surface again. She's in the dining room, at the walnut table, sitting opposite the doctor.

'Are you OK?' he asks. 'I know it's a lot to take in.'

She nods. She knows most of this kind of language; she hears it every day. She sits in on hospital patients and their families receiving good news, bad news, news they don't quite understand. 'I guess I zoned out. Sorry. I'm tired.'

It's Saturday. Though she hasn't been out escorting since Wednesday – since Simon, but she won't think about that – she is more tired than if she had been. She has two essays to complete but no heart to do it.

'So,' says Dr Sharp, 'I explained the other day that the CT scan showed the swelling on your dad's brain is much improved and that his lungs have recovered from the pneumonia. We've decided that on Thursday we'll begin the process of waking him from the coma.'

'This Thursday?'

'Yes.'

'That's ... great. It is. Just a bit of a shock. I feel...' Isabelle doesn't quite know how she feels. She glances towards the stairs as though she might see her dad there, as he was, vibrant, laughing loudly, eyes crinkling at the corners. He's coming back. He's coming home again.

But she is not the daughter he left behind four months ago.

She is not the kind of daughter he would love if he knew her now.

'It's a natural reaction,' says Dr Sharp. 'You've lived in limbo, managing your dad's care, managing your own life at the same time, grieving and yet not. In some ways, having him at home must have been harder than seeing him in a hospital.'

'I'd never have let him go anywhere else,' says Isabelle, more harshly than she intends. 'How will it happen then?'

'It's not a process you can compare to, say, switching on a light. It won't be immediate. The longer a person has been in a coma – and your father's has been much longer than most – the more likely it is there will be a delay in waking up.'

Isabelle's heart sinks.

'We'll start weaning your father off his sedative drugs and pain medication. He should slowly come around – within twenty-four hours, perhaps on Friday. We won't be taking him off the ventilator straight away. That won't be possible until the drugs are entirely out of his system.'

Isabelle nods along. She feels bad that her mind is drifting to Sebastian at this crucial moment; to their agreement to do Monday, Wednesday and Friday evenings. But if her dad is conscious on Friday, how can she bring the poor young man here then? He's not likely to be a quiet guest. Where else will they go? He deserves more than a hotel room or the back of her car. Isabelle tries to concentrate.

'It can take time,' continues Dr Sharp, 'to wean him off this medication, because with a longer-acting sedative the likelihood of the patient being addicted to it is high. Therefore, your father may have some extra challenges, such as withdrawal symptoms, which we will of course manage. But this all takes time.'

'So how long until he's ... well, the *old* him? You know, fully recovered?'

Dr Sharp holds Isabelle's gaze, his eyes kind. 'He may never be himself again. You need to prepare for that. It will be days before he'll feel comfortable sitting up, possibly much longer before he walks. He'll start with a walking frame and then perhaps use crutches, and physiotherapy will help. He'll take his medication in smaller doses, and he'll still need round-the-clock care for weeks. It could take months to build his strength up and get back to any sort of normal life.' Dr Sharp pauses. 'He may never make it back to the full health he had before his fall.'

Isabelle doesn't want to accept it. Last night she read an article online about F1 world champion Michael Schumacher, who had been in a six-month medically induced coma after hitting his head back in 2013. Though he is now out of the coma, his family are very private about his recovery.

'You'll get support all the way,' Dr Sharp assures her.

'I'm not worried about me,' she says softly.

'We are. Your health matters as much as his.'

'I'll be fine.'

Dr Sharp doesn't look convinced. 'Anything else you'd like to ask?'

'I can't think of anything.'

'Well, you know you can call me anytime.'

When the doctor has gone, Isabelle goes to her dad's room. On the landing she pauses at the picture of her mum in the striped bikini. Unlike the other day, the frame is straight. Did she imagine it wonky? Has she imagined sensing another presence here, in the space between her room and her dad's? No. It is here now. Isabelle closes her eyes. Feels a draught around her ankles as though a door is open somewhere.

'*Mum?*' she whispers.

But it's gone. The draught, the feeling.

Isabelle looks in on her dad. Jean is away on a lunch break. The eternally chilled room sends a ripple of goosebumps along Isabelle's arms. She sits on the chair by the bed where her sleeping beauty slumbers.

'I'll be back later, Charles,' she says, squeezing his arm.

Isabelle goes to her bedroom desk. There she calls Veronica to discuss when she will see Sebastian. While they talk, she suddenly sees her trainers and Sebastian's much bigger ones side by side next to the river. After they hang up, she can't get the image out of her head. She distracts herself by doing the thing she has wanted to do for three months. She dials the Angels Escort Services number.

'Hi Gina, it's Isabelle.'

'Hey, girl, what's up?' A pause. 'You sound a bit blue.'

'It's been a long day.'

'It's only noon,' laughs Gina. 'That's a hell of a morning.'

Isabelle smiles in spite of herself. 'Gina, I need to hand my notice in. Kind of immediately. I know we're supposed to give a month, so I'll pay you what I might have earned for you in that time to cover it.'

'Oh God, I'm not bothered about that. I'm concerned that you're OK?' Gina is always about the girls before anything else. Isabelle realises she will miss her. That she has been a mother figure during the most difficult circumstances of her life. That no one else calls her 'girl' so affectionately.

'I'm fine,' lies Isabelle. 'I don't need to do it anymore. I found out this morning that they're going to bring my dad out of his coma next week. I need to concentrate on him.'

'Oh, wow, that's great news.' Gina pauses again. 'But won't you still need to pay for his care? I know you said once that he'd probably need it even when he's conscious again. If you want to see fewer clients, that's fine you know. You're one of my most popular girls. I'll fit around you, girl.'

'I don't need the wage now. My financial situation has … changed. And that's all it ever was for me – the money.' How many times did Isabelle get herself through those long, dark nights whispering, *think of the money*?

'Gina?'

'Yes?'

'Please tell Dr Cassanby to go to another agency. Don't let any of the other girls take him on, will you?' She braces herself. 'And you definitely got rid of that Simon, didn't you?'

'What really happened with him?' Gina's kind voice has Isabelle dangerously close to tears.

'Nothing. I just ... he felt very bad. They're both ... animals.'

'Simon is gone, and Cassanby will be gone too.'

'Thank you,' says Isabelle.

'For what?'

'For being kind to me. I can't lie and say I'll miss the job, but I'll miss you.'

'I'll miss you too,' says Gina. 'Me wanting to keep you is selfish. You're my best girl. Me letting you go is me being happy you won't be doing this anymore.'

But isn't Isabelle only leaving to do something far less honest, something where the hurt could be emotional rather than merely physical?

'Will you remove my page from the website today?' Isabelle thinks of her dad being conscious and seeing it, not that removing the images will make a difference. Everything is eternal on the web. History can't easily be erased. Her fellow escort, Pam, once said, 'If you want to find it, it'll be gone; if you want it to disappear, it'll stick around forever.'

'Of course,' says Gina. 'And listen, you know where I am if you need me, eh?'

'Thank you.'

After hanging up, Isabelle sits for a moment, trying to savour the fact that her three months as an escort are done. It is over. She doesn't have to paint her face and clothe her body in sexy lingerie and go out into the cold night and sleep with any more strangers. No one can do as they wish with her exhausted body.

Yet she feels nothing. She is tempted to pinch herself. Have the awful nights stripped her ability to feel everyday emotions? She glances at the Paris snow globe her dad bought when she was ten, at its glitzy Eiffel Tower, and shakes it vigorously.

Then she takes her garish, sparkly Moulin Rouge diary from the desk. She scribbles out *Simon Sensitive Stammer GFE 7pm* on Wednesday's page, until the paper tears. Then she flicks through the pages and does the same to all the previous Cassanby entries. Finally, she throws it in the bin, and kicks the bin to the other side of the room.

As soon as it's dark Isabelle tries to sleep. But she can't. The house creaks and settles, seemingly as restless as she is. Eventually she surrenders, and dreams. She is suffocating. Not drowning, not underwater, but struggling to breathe beneath a great, dead weight. Beneath a man. He grows bigger and bigger, until he fills the room, and she continues to be crushed.

A sound rescues her. A crash.

She sits bolt upright, heart hammering.

Has her dad fallen? Again?

Isabelle races onto the landing, into his room. He's sleeping peacefully, the machine measuring his heartbeat. The ventilator's gasp of air followed by two beats – *gasp, thump-thump, gasp, thump-thump, gasp, thump-thump* – is a rhythm she needs to hear. She counts the repetition a few times before heading back to her room.

On the landing, she sees it now, in the dimness of light from the downstairs porch. A fallen picture. Isabelle knows from the gap on the wall which one it is – her mum in a bikini. She checks if it's cracked; the glass is broken, though the frame remains intact. She carefully removes the sharp pieces and bins them, and hangs the picture back up.

I think there's a ghost on our landing. And she wants to catch me if I ever fall the way he did...

It's too late, thinks Isabelle. I've already fallen. I'm broken.

24

SEBASTIAN FINDS HIS REAL EYES

Mum keeps asking me about my goggles. She is very bothered about my goggles. She was bothered when I didn't wear them for college today and bothered that I haven't put them on tonight. She never used to be bothered. She never really mentioned them. Now I take them off and it's all goggles, goggles, goggles. I told her earlier if she's that bothered, *she* should wear them.

I think it's something more than the goggles, but I can't work out what. I wish she would just say it. She knows I hate to be confused. I feel stupid then. And today is a good day. It's going to be the best day I've had so far in my life since I used to go to the river with my dad. So good I can look at it with my real eyes, not my water eyes.

Real eyes sounds like realise, I say to my mum at six-fifty-one, when it's only nine minutes until Isabelle picks me up.

I'm sitting on the stairs with my small book about tigers that Uncle Jim got me, and she's polishing the mirror in the hallway even though I saw Tillda do it earlier. She's wearing a purple spotted scarf that I haven't seen before. She has too many scarves. I've no idea what I'll do with them all when she dies.

Beg your pardon? She stops polishing.

I said real eyes sounds like realise.

I suppose it does. She puts down the rag and comes and sits next to me on the step. *Are you ready, darling? Are you really sure you want to go tonight? We can go for a walk instead if you—*

A walk? I laugh. *Mum, it's dark and it's freezing.*

We could watch a film then.

I want to see Isabelle. I say it carefully. She doesn't know I call her HoneyBee now. She doesn't need to know. Some things are private.

OK. Mum pauses for a while. I count the seconds. She's wasting my life. *I'll wait up for you. What time do you think…? No, you won't know. I'll ask Isabelle.*

No, you won't, I tell her. *You don't need to see her. This is my life, Mum. I know you care about me, but I was going to go to Latvia on my own, so I can definitely go and have sex on my own.* I look at the hallway clock. It's six-fifty-four. *Right. I'm going outside to wait for her.*

I get my big coat from the cupboard. I know my mum is watching me. I'm twenty years and six months and twelve days old and I'm finally going to have sex and she needs to get with the programme. I've got my new poem in my trouser pocket, but I don't know yet if I'll show Isabelle. I like having it with me though.

My mum follows me to the door. Her face is easy to read now – it's sad.

Don't be sad, I say.

I can't help it, darling. She kisses my cheek. *I want you to know that I'm always here if you need me.*

I know that because you haven't booked any holidays recently.

I don't always make the right choices, Sebastian, but I love you.

I frown. *Did you get me the wrong hot chocolate again?*

No, I mean … It doesn't matter. You take care. Call me if you need me.

I open the door. The icy air steals all the warmth away from us. I walk down the drive. Mum is still in the doorway. She should go inside, or she'll catch pneumonia. There's a small car at the end of our drive and I don't need my goggles to know that it's Isabelle. My Isabelle. My HoneyBee.

I get in the car and smile at her because she looks so pretty. Her hair is down around her face like two yellow velvet curtains. I don't think she's got make-up on because her eyebrows are thin and her cheeks are pink, and her eyes stand out more than her eyelashes do.

I hand her my tiger book.

I promised you could have it, I say. *Will you look after it?*

Of course. She turns it over and looks inside. *I'll treasure it.*

I underlined my favourite words. Look – 'Panthera tigris' and 'apex predator'.

I have something for you too.

She hands me a piece of paper.

I open it and read it aloud. *This note promises that I will have sex with Sebastian every Monday, Wednesday and Friday, and make him eggs too, for as long as he would like to.*

I do promise, she says softly.

Can we go and do it now? I really want to.

Isabelle drives to her house. She asks about how my day was and stuff like that, but I can't think of anything except the sex we will have. Her house is big like ours but a different shape. Ours is symmetrical and hers is all higgledy-piggledy with a sticking-out bit at one side and one half of the roof higher than the other. She parks on the drive. The front lawn is lit up by rows of fairy lights and it looks like it didn't have a good final cut last autumn. I sometimes mow our grass, though my mum reminds me that we have a gardener. It's good to get rid of the uneven blades.

Isabelle looks at me. It's dark but I can see it's a serious face. *In the house, you should stay with me,* she says.

Oh, I will. I want to.

No, I mean, you can't wander off and explore. Is that OK?

That's OK, I tell her. *Mum has drawers in her bedroom that I've been told not to go in. I think she keeps that* Kama Sutra *book in there. I only read it because it was in the bathroom. I would never go in the drawers she told me not to.*

Isabelle smiles. And she gets out of the car. I do too. My legs are a bit shaky when I follow her into the higgledy-piggledy house. The hallway is square like ours, but I don't think they have a Tillda here because the mirror is dusty. I follow Isabelle up the stairs, and I keep quiet because she is. At the top is a long landing. She looks right, towards the one door that's closed, and then takes me to the left.

We go into her bedroom. It's gold and cream. There's a desk in the corner and loads of those globes you shake to make snow. If I wasn't thinking about sex so much I reckon I'd like to look at what's inside them. Another time I will. When she has shut the door, Isabelle sits on the cream sofa and asks if I would like a drink.

What time is it? I ask. *You said we'd have sex at seven-thirty.*

She looks at her phone. *It's seven-twenty-four.*

Can we start in six minutes then?

She nods. *Sit next to me, Sebastian.*

I'm fine here. Now, HoneyBee, I don't want to get you pregnant. I am capable. My penis makes lots of sperm. I don't want babies yet. I have fish. They are enough.

We won't have babies, says Isabelle.

Why? Are you faulty?

She smiles. *No. I just have an injection that stops that happening.*

Will I still make sperm?

Hopefully, yes. Shall I put some music on?

Have you got The Best Hits of 1985?

Sorry, no, she says. *Do you like Lana Del Rey?*

No. I jiggle about on the spot. *What time is it now?*

Isabelle gets up and goes and sits on her huge bed. It's cream too with tiny gold stars all over it. She pats the spot next to her, so I go and sit there. It must be seven-thirty. I don't even check. I trust her. She smells so nice. Like she's made of lemon drizzle cake. My heart is doing all this jumping around and I don't know if I'll be able to speak if she wants me to. Luckily, speaking is not what I'm thinking about now.

Would you like me to kiss you? she asks.

I nod because my yes is stuck.

Isabelle leans towards me. I stay still. Then she slowly opens my mouth with hers. I've seen people kiss like this in the films my mum watches but not so much in the videos I've seen on the internet. Her tongue touches mine. It's so soft. But even though it's soft I feel it everywhere, in my tummy, in my chest, and in my penis. There the most. I say *mmmmm* because I can't help it, and I shiver, again and again and again, like when I first get into cold water, except I'm getting into something warm.

She stops and asks me, *Are you OK, Sebastian?*

Yes, yes, I say. *Don't stop.*

If you want to at any point, just tell me.

I never want to stop, I say.

Isabelle kisses me again. I copy what she does, a bit like when Flip and Scorpion swim in unison. It's so easy. So nice. I wonder if I should only copy what she does because I actually want to put my hands on her face and in her hair and maybe on her breasts if I dare. In the end, I sit on my hands, but I can't help kissing her faster. She's the one that sighs this time. I love hearing her sigh.

HoneyBee, I say into her mouth.

I can tell she is smiling again.

Then she stops and pulls my Hull City shirt off over my head. She stares at my chest and I know she likes what she sees. At swimming lessons, the older girls in the other groups used to stare at me in my shorts. Sometimes they would giggle together. Sometimes one of them would come over and I'd get dead excited. But they always lost that glow in their eyes when they spoke to me. Isabelle has that glow now. Maybe if I don't speak for a while it will stay.

She kisses my chest. It tingles there. And in my penis too.

I don't know if I can wait any longer.

Isabelle must know all about this, maybe because she's older and knows about men, because then she pulls off her top too. She has a pink bra on that's lacy and makes her breasts look really big. I can't help staring and staring at them.

You can touch me if you like, Sebastian, she says.

Can I? I jump because I didn't expect her to speak.

You can touch me anywhere. She pauses. *I'd really like it too, you know. I like to be touched.*

Then she undoes her bra and takes it off. I put a hand on one breast. It fits perfectly. I must be made for her. Isabelle sighs so I move both hands over them, dead gentle. They are so warm and soft and heavy. She kisses me while I do it and this time it's more like the way they kiss in the videos I've seen online. She's all breathy and fast. It excites me so much. I go fast too. And she goes faster.

Then Isabelle pushes me back so I'm lying on the bed. She doesn't have stars on her ceiling like I do, only the tiny ones on the duvet cover. But I can see them anyway. In front of my real eyes. I feel a bit dizzy. Real eyes take some getting used to.

Realise, real eyes, I whisper.

What's that? she asks.

Real eyes, I say.

She pulls down my smart wedding trousers that have never been to a wedding, and then my shorts. I close my eyes for a minute but that makes me feel even more dizzy. When I open them, Isabelle is naked too. I giggle. She sits on top of me and her vagina is right near my penis. I've never seen one in real life before. She doesn't have much hair down there. Not like I do.

She kisses me hard and puts her hand around my penis and suddenly it is somewhere tight and nice and warm, and I gasp. I grab Isabelle hard and pull her tightly to my body and tug on her hair and bite her shoulder, and then I say, *I'm sorry, I didn't mean to hurt you, HoneyBee.*

You're not, she whispers in my ear.

She looks like an angel above me with her yellow hair all messy. Her chest is red. Her eyes are half closed. She moves slowly against me and she moans, and I never want it to end, but it happens so fast and my penis dies, like it's gone to heaven.

And I'm there too.

In a warm and lovely heaven.

Sebastian, she whispers against my cheek.

HoneyBee, I whisper against hers.

We lay together for a bit. I grin. Can't help it. I feel like I'm floating. I can't believe I've had sex. I've actually had sex. And it was even better than the way I imagined it would be.

I start to tremble, and Isabelle hugs me. I don't always like hugs They usually make me feel suffocated, like I can't breathe. Mum tells me I stand like an ironing board. But I don't mind this one. Is it because I'm starting to love Isabelle? But I love Mum and don't always want her hugs. I wish I knew. How will I know? What makes you know?

Can I read you my poem? I ask her after a bit.

You wrote a poem?

Yes.

Well, of course then, she says.

I lean across her and get the paper from my smart wedding trousers that have never been to a wedding. Then I read it out, with a pause between each line to let her digest them.

How will I know it's love and not indigestion?
How will I know to declare everything I feel inside
instead of taking a Rennie after curry?
How will I know when to follow my heart
instead of following my legs straight to the toilet?
How will I know when she is the one for me
and that I haven't eaten too many onion bhajis?
How will I know it's love and not indigestion?
How will I ever know the answer to my question?'

Isabelle is studying me. I try hard to read her face. I think she's sad. I didn't want to make her sad. Maybe she just thinks it's crap.

When you have the answer, Sebastian, she says dead softly, *make sure you tell me as well. Because I have no idea either.*

I am shocked. She has wise eyes. I would have thought she'd know all about love.

But you're so good at sex, I say.

That doesn't mean I know about love, Sebastian.

I feel even more confused than ever.

Can we do it again yet? I ask.

She laughs. *Are you ready again? Didn't you say you wanted eggs in between?*

I'm ready, I say. *We can have eggs later.*

We do have eggs later. Her kitchen is not as clean as ours. I like it though. She follows all of my instructions and uses the same type of pan as my mum and puts the eggs in a triangle on the plate like she does, but they don't look or taste as good. I don't say anything though. I care about her feelings.

She is very good at sex.

That, I do tell her.

25

VERONICA CAN'T STOP THINKING ABOUT EGGS

Veronica can't stop thinking about eggs.

She first made Sebastian three eggs – crisply done and flipped over, in a triangle on the plate, with no ketchup – one Christmas Day. He was seven and Pete had died two months before. Sebastian had not let her put the tree up because his dad always did it. He wouldn't eat his turkey because Pete wasn't in the chair at the end of the table. He didn't eat anything all day – not his favourite KP Dry Roasted Nuts, not brandy trifle, not even a chocolate bar from his selection box.

In the middle of the night he woke Veronica and declared that he was *very* hungry.

'No wonder,' she said. 'What would you like, darling?'

'I want something I never had with Dad.' His voice was small in the darkness.

Veronica tried very hard to think. Sebastian had always had a hearty appetite so trying to think of something he'd never in his seven years eaten proved hard.

'Eggs,' she said eventually.

'You know I don't li—' Sebastian started to say.

'But you've never had them.' Veronica switched on the lamp.

'They look like eyeballs without any irises.'

'They're delicious fried.'

'I shall decide that,' he said.

Veronica took him downstairs and warmed the fat in the pan. She cracked two eggs.

'Three,' snapped Sebastian. 'My tummy says three.'

Veronica added another. When they were done, still sloppy so he could dip bread in, she put them messily onto a plate. Sebastian threw them in the bin, saying they were soggy eyeballs. Veronica made three more slightly crispier eggs and they too were disposed of. She then flipped three more over so that they were almost burnt and put them neatly in a triangle on the plate. She reached for the ketchup.

'No sauce,' said Sebastian, and he took them carefully to the table and wolfed them down. 'Very good,' he said. 'I will have more of these tomorrow. Only you will ever make me them. OK?'

Now Veronica waits with the eggs in the kitchen. The underfloor heating warms her feet. It's six-thirty and dark outside. Sebastian will be up for college in fifteen minutes. For thirteen years she has made his eggs every day, in exactly the same way. Is he going to want them this morning? Now their pact has been broken, will this ritual end?

Last night she waited up for him, sitting on the stairs where he had perched earlier before going with Isabelle. He got home at eleven and bounced through the door. His clothes were dishevelled as though they had been thrown on in haste. She couldn't bear to think of it. Of him being naked. With a woman. With Isabelle. And yet it was exactly what she had put into action and wanted for him.

'Are you OK, darling?' she asked, stroking his messy fringe away from his face.

'I'm fine.' He pushed her hand away. She didn't mind at all. That meant he was the same Sebastian. Still her beautiful, innocent, complex boy.

'How was ... what did...?' Veronica wasn't even sure of the question.

'We had eggs,' said Sebastian happily, and disappeared upstairs.

They had eggs. Isabelle had made him eggs. He *let* her. This occupied Veronica's thoughts more than images of Sebastian writhing naked with Isabelle, crying out in ecstasy, both glistening with sweat, over and over. More than knowing her boy is no longer a virgin. It haunted her as she tried desperately to sleep.

Movement upstairs now. Sebastian clomping around his room, the same as any other morning. Veronica waits for his music: Billy Ocean's voice drifts down the stairs. After five minutes Sebastian comes into the kitchen in his red Ho Ho Ho Christmas pyjamas. Again, no sign of his goggles. He's still bouncy. He sits at the table but jiggles in his chair.

'Have we got cornflakes?' he asks.

'You don't want eggs?' Veronica feels sick.

'I fancy a change.'

'Is this because ... because...'

'Because I had sex?' he grins.

'No.' Veronica cringes. 'Because Isabelle will make your eggs now?'

'Her eggs were crap. But it's in our contract so I have to honour that. I pretended they were OK, but it's put me off eggs. It's time for new things.'

'We've got cornflakes,' says Veronica sadly.

She pours some into a bowl and adds milk and sugar. She watches for a moment as Sebastian devours them and then goes to get dressed. Halfway through tying a silk scarf around her neck, she pulls it off and throws it on the floor.

26

ISABELLE'S FACE IS MORE READABLE
THAN JIM CARREY'S

Dear Night,
This is how I've coped for four months, in notes, like when I was small and my dad was away. It's been harder though because, unlike then, I've had nothing to respond to. The night does not write back. At times I've left a blank line so I could imagine what you, the night, might have written in between my words. I've been sitting with my dad in the middle of the night, trying to read his mind. Soon he should be able to tell me...

As Isabelle's dad begins to wake, she goes and sits with him and reads aloud. Jean and new round-the-clock nurse Sue come and go, checking him, putting a hand on Isabelle's shoulder, rousing her when she has fallen asleep to insist she goes to bed. As her dad battles to surface from his coma, Isabelle feels herself being pulled under by her three-month hell. This period might be ending now – her dad's unconsciousness and her nights as an escort – but neither experience is about to release its victim easily.

Early on Thursday the waking began with what seemed like an endless stream of doctors and procedures and monitoring; such a flurry of activity that Isabelle had felt sure it would result in an animated dad within hours. Now, on Friday afternoon, she wonders if he'll remain forever unconscious – if she has lost him altogether. Sue assures her it can be days before a patient responds to anyone. It doesn't help that the ventilator will be over his face for another day or two.

Isabelle watches his eyes. The eyelids flicker and lift occasionally.

But with no light. No electric blue. In the moments they open, she imagines seeing her own reflection in them. Will he look at her and know all that she has done? Will he see the filth she feels crawling over her skin? Will he see the dents where so many men's hands have pressed and probed and pushed?

'Go and have a cup of tea,' suggests Sue, making Isabelle jump. 'You were with him most of the night. I know you haven't eaten yet. We'll call you if there's a change.'

'I can't,' says Isabelle, though her head hurts and her throat is parched.

'*Go*. I mean it. You'll be no good to him when he's fully awake if you don't look after yourself.'

Reluctantly, Isabelle goes downstairs and makes tea for her and Sue. She missed two lectures at university yesterday to be home, and she should be at Rowan House for her final placement day today, but what can she do? Knowing how much she'll have to catch up on makes her head spin, but she can't be everywhere.

One place she must be is at Sebastian's for seven. She must be attentive to him, even with all of this going on. She'll have to tell him they must be super quiet and get him into her room somehow without Sue or Jean seeing. Where will she take him next week, though, if her dad is mobile again? What if he wakes tonight when Sebastian is here? Who should she be with?

The thoughts whirl around her head as the kettle boils. Isabelle carries the two cups of tea upstairs. Halfway up the steps, she stumbles. The brown liquid splashes like old blood on the pale carpet. She half kneels, her heart hammering. In a panic, she feels like she's coming around. From what? She's awake. Her head throbs. Where is she? *You're at home, safe.* Her back hurts. The floor is hard. Cold. *No, it isn't.* Why? She is naked. Shit, she is naked. Except for her shoes. How?

No, she isn't.

No, she isn't.

Isabelle looks wildly around, expecting someone else to be there. Expecting shy and stammering Simon. He breathes heavily against her cheek. *No.* She tries to get up again, but he pulls at her. *No.* He is naked too. *No, he isn't here; you're at home, safe.*

A flashback. So real.

Push it away.

Back on her feet, trembling, Isabelle counts to ten.

It's just her. No one else.

She carries the two half-empty cups to her dad's room.

'What happened?' asks Sue, with a kind smile, looking at the measly amount of tea.

'I tripped. I'm just ... worn out...'

'Why don't you go and get an hour's sleep?'

'I can't.'

'Why?'

'He might...' Isabelle looks at her dad.

'And if he does, I'll get you.'

Walking along the landing, past the memories on the wall, she stops at the picture of her mum in the striped bikini. She hasn't replaced the glass, so the picture is matt without its overlay. 'I fell,' she whispers, 'and you didn't catch me.'

In her room, Isabelle is surprised that she drops easily into a deep sleep. When she opens her eyes, darkness has suffocated the room. She panics, but it's only six o'clock. She has a quick shower, puts on her leggings and a comfortable sweatshirt, and goes to her dad's room. No change. Sue shakes her head at the unasked question.

'I have to go out,' Isabelle tells her. 'I won't be long.' She pauses. Decides it is best to address Sebastian's imminent visit. 'When I come back, I'll have a young man with me. He's autistic and I'm ... tutoring him. His mum is a friend of mine; she's paying me to help with his college work. We'll just be in my room, working, so knock if you need me.'

Isabelle expects Sue to see through the lie, to see her for the whore she is. But she just smiles pleasantly and says she will.

Sebastian is waiting on the kerb outside his house, wearing his big red coat, his leather gloves and Hull City hat. He opens the car door and says, 'You're late, HoneyBee.'

Isabelle looks at the clock: 19.02.

'Sorry, Sebastian.'

He gets in the car. This is their third time together. Isabelle is surprised to find that she's happy; so surprised that she frowns at her reflection in the mirror, seeing a light in her eyes, a relaxation of frown lines. The emotion is one she hasn't experienced in so long. Not in this pure and natural form. Happiness is right here in the car beside her, uncomplicated, warm-eyed, and fastening a seatbelt.

'There's nothing on your face,' says Sebastian, when she looks again in the mirror. 'I'd tell you if there was because I wouldn't want anyone laughing.'

'That's good to know.'

Isabelle drives to her house.

'You're very smiley today,' he says.

'Am I?'

She thinks of earlier, of her panic on the stairs.

'Yes.' He studies her. 'Actually, I'd say you are three parts happy and one part sad. That's how you make brick mortar, you know – three parts sand and one part masonry cement. I can read your face more than any face I've seen in my life, except for Jim Carrey in *Ace Ventura: Pet Detective*. Botox is not helpful in reading faces, you know. Don't ever get Botox. You are nice as you are.'

Isabelle laughs. 'I won't.'

At the house, she reminds him that they must be quiet. 'There are some nurses here tonight,' she explains.

'Is someone ill?' Sebastian's eyes are wide with curiosity.

'No. Well, yes. My dad. They're ve—'

'What's wrong? Is it Ebola? I saw that on the news.'

'No, nothing like that. He's been in a coma, and soon he won't be. Anyway, the nurses are very busy, and we don't want to bother them. And they don't know about ... you know, about *us*...'

'I can do the sex quietly tonight. Our contract doesn't say quiet, but I am happy to add any amendments we need to make.'

Isabelle smiles. Their second evening together, on Wednesday,

Sebastian had been much noisier, crying out her name and grunt-ing. He had seemed a little agitated when she picked him up. She asked if he was OK and he nodded his head vigorously. But he wasn't as chatty as usual, and she wondered what his life was really like. Wondered what it must be like to see the world so differently to other people, and to have them view you so differently. Negatively at times.

'Sex can be nice when you're very quiet,' she smiles, leading him inside.

In her bedroom, Sebastian says, 'It's seven-twenty-five. We don't have long.'

On Wednesday he had stood in the middle of her bedroom floor for three minutes until it was the right time, telling her he needed to prepare, and could she not speak. He had counted the stars on her duvet cover, his mouth moving quietly over the numbers. He had picked up each of her snow globes, shaken them vigorously, and then set them down again.

Now he just shakes the New York snow globe.

'I like it best,' he says.

Then he sits on the edge of the bed and waits. Isabelle sits next to him.

'Shall I light some candles?' she asks.

'No. You asked that last time.'

'It can set the mood.'

'I don't need you to set the mood,' says Sebastian. 'I can set my own.'

At exactly seven-thirty he turns and looks at her. Isabelle leans in and kisses him. He has the most beautiful lips, fat and soft. His tongue is tremulous against hers, his sigh a warm rush of pleasure. Kissing was the part she hated most as an escort. It's the most inti-mate thing a couple can do so it was the hardest thing to give. With Sebastian, it is bliss. If the ugly lump of money didn't sit between them, she might let go. She might hold his face and whisper that she has just realised that she was looking forward to seeing him tonight.

But this is just sex, just physical; it is for him, not her, for money not love, and she must not mislead or hurt him.

'Can you go on top this time?' he asks.

'Whatever you like best.'

'That was how we did it first and I like it the most.'

She takes off his top and then her own. She shivers.

'Do you want to put your top back on?'

'It's OK, Seb, I'm not cold.'

'But you—'

She silences him with another kiss. Another mashing of their hungry mouths. He is so young and eager. His warm hands explore her body, more confidently than they did the first time, and she can't help but respond. Her skin tingles under his touch. She pushes him back onto the bed and wriggles out of her leggings and sits astride him.

'Remember, we can't be too noisy,' she whispers.

Sebastian opens his mouth to speak and then clamps it shut and puts his finger to his lips, the way children do when a teacher tells them to be quiet. He is two halves: a boy above the waist, sweet, earnest; a man below, urgent, pressed against her. He grips Isabelle's thighs as she guides him into her. She leans down to him as she moves, so they are eye to eye, no words, silent. Sebastian puts his finger to her lips. For a moment nothing else exists; not the room where her comatose dad sleeps, not flashbacks of a cold floor, not an obscene sum of money.

27

ISABELLE IS NOT HER OWN GHOST

Afterwards, they lie side by side.

'Would you laugh if I told you something?' Isabelle asks him.

'Only if it was funny,' says Sebastian. 'Is it a joke? I've got one ... Knock, knock.'

'Who's there?'

'Wooden shoe.'

'Wooden shoe who?'

'Wooden shoe like to hear another joke?'

Isabelle smiles, then says, 'No, I meant would you laugh if I told you something spooky?'

'No, I'd go OooOoooh.' He mimics a ghost sound.

'I think I have a ghost on my landing.'

'Why do you think that?' asks Sebastian, seriously.

'When I walk from here to the room where my dad is, I feel like there's someone there with me. Someone ghostly. Another heartbeat. Breath. *Something.*'

'HoneyBee.' Sebastian studies her and speaks as though he's the adult and she's the child. 'We are us. There is nothing outside of us. We are what we see and hear. We are our own ghosts.'

'Did you read that somewhere?'

'Nope. That is what I think.'

'We are our own ghosts.' Isabelle repeats the words softly.

'Yes. You are the ghost. My mum thought we had a ghost, just because my door wasn't shut properly. That was human error.'

'But what about all the unexplained stuff?'

'What is your definition of a ghost, HoneyBee?'

'What do you mean?' She frowns.

'What is a ghost?'

'Well, I suppose ... it's something that lingers...'

'Like a bad smell?'

She laughs. 'No. Like, when people have gone ... it's what's left afterwards...'

Sebastian shakes his head. 'If ghosts existed and could be scientifically detected or recorded, then there would be hard evidence of them, and there isn't. I *did* read that. We want there to be ghosts because it feels good to think there is something more. That, I think. But it's just you. Well, you and me, right now.'

Isabelle sits up suddenly, shakes her head.

'What's wrong?' asks Sebastian, face confused.

She wants to end it. To tell him. To give Veronica the money back. She can't deceive him this way.

'Seb ... I—'

A soft knock on the bedroom door interrupts her.

'Hang on!' Isabelle jumps up, pulls on her top and leggings. 'Hang on.'

She opens the door a crack. It's Sue. Smiling. 'He opened his eyes,' she says.

Isabelle almost asks who, and then realises. She looks back at Sebastian on the bed.

'Oh. Oh. I'll come. Give me ... I'll come...'

She closes the door and goes and sits with Sebastian again.

'I have to go and see my dad,' she says. 'I told you he was ill. Will you stay here? I know we usually have eggs now and then sex again, and I can do that soon, I promise. Would that be OK?' She pauses. 'If it isn't, I'll stay. I'll go and see him later.'

'If my dad was here, I would go with him over anyone else,' says Sebastian. 'I will wait here. Can I have some music on? I know you don't have *The Best Hits of 1985*, but do you have any Billy Ocean?'

Isabelle grabs her phone, goes into her music app, and finds his greatest hits. She plugs her headphones in and hands it to Sebastian. When she leaves, she looks back. He is swaying his head and mouthing the words.

Isabelle walks along the landing. She pauses. Listens. Senses that other soul, that breath in the air, a heart beating like her own. Does she still believe?

She opens the door to her dad's room. Everything is the same; the room is cool, as always, the large hospital bed dominates the space near the French doors, and the exquisitely realistic lilies and orchids sit in two large jars in opposite corners.

Except her dad's eyes are open.

Electric blue.

He is back.

But everything is different now.

28

VERONICA FINDS HER PREJUDICE

Veronica studies her tired face in the hallway mirror. The light through the front door's coloured glass turns the dust on it into glitter particles. She starts to wipe them with a sleeve, cursing Tilly under her breath, and thinks better of it. She looks better in those gentle hues. Not creased with jealousy of the young woman Sebastian has been singing love songs about since 6am on a Saturday.

Not tortured by what she has started.

The telephone rings. It's Isabelle. She incites so many feelings in Veronica now, including a big dose of guilt for having all the negative ones.

'Can we meet today?' she asks.

'Is everything OK?' Veronica panics. 'Has Sebastian been OK?'

'Yes, he's fine. I just need to ... well, you said we should meet up occasionally and discuss everything. I need to ... talk ... now...'

'It will have to be somewhere other than here.' Veronica glances up the stairs. 'Obviously Sebastian can't know we're...' She thinks of the word 'friends' but isn't sure it's the right one for their situation. 'He can't know we're acquainted,' she finishes.

'How about that little farm café just outside Willerby? You know the one?'

'Yes.'

'In an hour?' asks Isabelle. 'I only have thirty minutes though.'

'OK. I'll see you there.'

They hang up.

Has Isabelle changed her mind?

The thought stops Veronica halfway up the stairs. Has she

decided she wants out after all? Despite what it might do to Sebastian, Veronica can't help but hope she has. She doesn't care about the £50,000 already transferred. She will pay the rest without a thought because imagining Sebastian being all hers again – even with his longings, and even with them being back to square one – makes her heart sing. She realises now that the idea of something is entirely different to the reality of it. She thought that if she satisfied Sebastian, then their life would settle down.

But she is a wild churning of emotions; of jealousy, guilt, and sadness.

She stops outside Sebastian's room. Usually on a Saturday he would be at the pool. How she wishes for the days when swimming was his passion. When he listed how many lengths he could swim and had his goggles permanently attached to his head or wrist. Now they dangle from his bed post. He hasn't nagged to go swimming since he met Isabelle. Billy Ocean blasts from the speakers. Veronica knocks on the door.

'Wait a minute,' he calls. 'I'm in a state of undress.'

Even though it's only two weeks ago that he sat naked in front of her, asking if he could wear her tights, it feels a lifetime. She told him then that when we are older we only let our partners see us naked. He is changing. Too fast. She wants the boy back who doesn't mind his nudity, who follows her to the toilet and looks at the ceiling while talking to her.

You wanted this, she thinks. *You started this*.

'Come in,' he calls briskly.

He's sitting on the bed, wearing his *I'M WITH STUPID* T-shirt and grey jogging bottoms, hair damp from showering. Is his skin glowing? Does he look older? Does he smell different? She wants to lean in and sniff his cheek like she used to, see if the essence of her boy is still there, but fears it has gone.

'I have to go out, darling,' she says.

'Oh.' Sebastian studies her. 'Are you seeing your lover who doesn't exist with the daughter who doesn't exist either?'

'What? *No.*'

'I don't know why you have to be coy, Mum. Sex is very natural. You should go on top. It is good for women that way. I like t—'

'Sebastian!' Veronica holds her face, horrified. 'I'm happy that you are … you have … but, I'm not … I don't have a … I'm meeting Jayne.' She pauses. He waits. 'When I come back would you like to walk down by the river or something?'

'I'm meeting a friend.'

'A friend?' Veronica frowns. 'Who?'

'A friend from college.'

'You never said.'

'I did. Four seconds ago. Are you deaf, Mum?'

'Who is it? Where are you going?' Usually, when Sebastian meets one of the rare college friends who want to hang out with him, he asks her to take him and wait in the car.

'A friend,' he repeats. 'We're going to KFC.'

'Will you be OK getting the bus? You know you don't like going places on your—'

'Mum,' sighs Sebastian, 'I'm twenty years and six months and seventeen days old, and I'm no longer a virgin, so I think it's time I went on a bus on my own. I downloaded the bus times for a Saturday and selected the ones I prefer.'

'OK.' Veronica doesn't know what else to say. After a moment she asks, 'When are you going? Do you need any money? How long will you be?'

'I'll be leaving at eleven-twenty-four and I have thirty-two pounds and fifty-three pence and I don't know, but I'll be fine.'

'Good.' There isn't much else to add. 'If you need me, you have your phone. OK, darling?'

Sebastian nods dismissively. Veronica leaves the room, looking back briefly; her beautiful boy sings along to his music again, utterly unaware of her turmoil.

☐

Veronica arrives at the farm café early. Christmas lights still hang from the spiky trees along the path. A playful, icy wind tugs the silver Gucci scarf from her neck, taking it across one of the fields, Veronica in pursuit. Once caught, she ties it more firmly. When she returns to the car, out of breath and flushed, Isabelle is standing next to it, smiling, obviously having seen the clumsy chase. Veronica is momentarily angry at her amusement – or is it at her youth and ability to captivate her son?

'It's bitterly cold today, isn't it?' says Isabelle.

'I'm ready for spring,' admits Veronica gruffly. 'Shall we?'

They go into the warm, brightly lit café, which smells of strong coffee and cinnamon, and take a table by a window looking over the frosted fields. Veronica studies Isabelle; the lovely skin ruined by tired lines beneath the eyes, the golden hair in a loose ponytail, the two holes in each ear where previously diamond earrings hung. She blushes, remembering when they first met, and how Isabelle thought she wanted sex with her. She also remembers them sitting in Isabelle's car outside the house, plain together. Stripped.

Veronica's anger dissipates. This girl is vulnerable. Nervous.

The waitress takes their order – two lattes. Veronica wants to ask about Sebastian. What did they do, what has he been like? But Isabelle speaks first.

'I need to be honest with you,' she says.

'OK.'

'This won't work otherwise.'

'Won't work? You haven't...'

'What?' asks Isabelle.

'Changed your mind?'

'No.' Isabelle shakes her head vigorously. 'But I have to tell you about my situation. I suppose this has been very one-sided. I know your life. Your difficulty. But I could never talk about my reasons for doing what I do ... what I did. It was no part of this ... deal. But now ... now it is.'

Isabelle pauses when the drinks arrive.

'The thing is...'

Veronica waits, hoping her silence will give Isabelle the time she needs.

'My dad's been very ill.' Isabelle sips the milky coffee. 'He fell, hit his head, and they put him in a coma to recover. But I didn't want him in a hospital. He begged me not to leave him there ... they were his last words...' Isabelle holds Veronica's gaze. Veronica sees pain in her eyes. Lifelong pain. Recent pain. Pain that is still bleeding. 'Since I was tiny, he's taken care of me. Now I've been taking care of him, at home, and that costs. I had to find the money, somehow, and well, you know how...'

Veronica nods, feeling sad for the young woman.

'Your money isn't for me,' says Isabelle. 'It's for him. But now...'

'Now what?' asks Veronica kindly.

'Now he's back. Well, not back like he was before.' Isabelle inhales as though bracing herself. 'They started bringing him out of the coma on Thursday, and last night – while Sebastian was with me – he opened his eyes. It wasn't for long, and he's only opened them for ten minutes at a time since, but he's coming around.'

'That's wonderful,' smiles Veronica.

'It is.' Isabelle deflates before Veronica's eyes, looking exhausted. 'He has a long road ahead of him, so I still need to support him, financially. And as he recovers, he's going to want to know where all this money came from, and I have no idea what I'll say. I can't tell him I was a...' she whispers '...you know...'

Veronica nods.

'I wondered if...'

'If what?'

'If you would mind if I told him you were paying me to *tutor* Sebastian.'

Veronica wants to say that *is* what she's paying for.

'In his college work,' adds Isabelle, as though hearing Veronica's thoughts.

'He's doing bricklaying.'

'Shit. Of course.'

They look at one another. Isabelle laughs first – it's a lovely sound, deep and free. Veronica joins her, unable not to. They stop and look at one another and laugh again. The man at the next table looks at them with raised eyebrows. Veronica doesn't care. She needs this. She can't remember when she laughed so hard.

'Do you know anything about cement?' Veronica manages to ask.

Isabelle puts her head back and laughs again. 'I have a small trowel in a drawer somewhere.'

After a while she says, 'But seriously, I need to explain all the money I have. And the other thing is...'

'Yes?'

'Even if I say that you're paying me to tutor Sebastian in some way – maybe in life skills, that kind of thing, or as a trainee disability nurse to get experience – it's going to be hard to bring him home all the time once my dad's up and about. Even if we say I'm tutoring him, he'll wonder why we go to my bedroom.'

'Your dad would never believe you were dating Sebastian,' laughs Veronica.

Isabelle looks at her with arched eyebrows, and Veronica realises she has found her own prejudice. She's as bad as those she has berated over the years. She feels sick.

'I don't mean it like...' She doesn't even know what she means.

'I don't think Sebastian deserves a hotel room,' says Isabelle, kindly, ignoring Veronica's discomfort. 'Or the back seat of a car.'

'No.' Veronica shakes her head vigorously as though to free such an image from her head.

'Do you think we could come to your house once or twice a week? Say, Monday and Friday at yours, and Wednesday at mine?'

Veronica's immediate feeling is disgust. She can't help it. The idea of her own son and an ex-prostitute having sex in her home is abhorrent. *A prostitute you sought out*, she thinks, *who has already done God knows what with him three times this week.*

'I just don't know.' Veronica finishes her latte.

'Maybe you could go out?'

'I won't be dismissed from my own home. If I permit this, I'll be staying, thank you.' As soon as the words are out, Veronica regrets her sharp tone.

'Of course.'

Neither of them speaks. The ball is in Veronica's court. Would it be so bad?

'If it means my boy isn't going to some seedy hotel, I suppose it will be fine. I guess you can go to his room. It just feels so...'

'I understand,' says Isabelle. 'No mother wants their child having sex where they are.' She pauses. 'Do you want to ask me anything?'

'Like what?'

'About Sebastian. How he's ... well, getting on.'

'I don't need any details.'

'Of course. If it makes this any easier, he seems very happy. He's a natural. It might seem an odd thing to say, but he is.'

'God.' Veronica puts her head in her hands.

'What?'

'A natural. Happy. And I paid for it.'

'He'll never know that,' says Isabelle. She pauses. 'I realised the other day that a natural conclusion to this can be when I qualify, if I move away.'

'He'll be broken, won't he?'

Isabelle doesn't respond.

'It's going to destroy him,' says Veronica.

'He's stronger than you think,' insists Isabelle. She looks at her phone. 'I have to go. I can't leave my dad for long in case anything major happens.' She reaches out as though she'll touch Veronica's hand across the table, then doesn't seem to know what to do and runs her fingers through her hair. 'I can't imagine what you're going through,' she says, 'but your son will come to no harm with me. He's the loveliest boy. Man,' she corrects herself. 'I can't promise he won't be hurt when this is over, but I promise he won't be hurt while I'm with him.'

'I feel like I'm losing him,' says Veronica softly.

'You'll never lose him. He'll always know what you've done for him.'

'Yes – I paid an escort to fuck him.' Veronica gasps at her

language. 'Sorry,' she says quickly. 'I just – if he ever found out, he'd never forgive me.'

'Perhaps you don't know him as well as you think.'

'And you do?' Veronica spits.

'I didn't mean it that way. I think that he knows you're incapable of doing anything that doesn't come from the heart.'

'I'm sorry.' Veronica feels terrible for her outbursts.

'Can I tell my dad I'm tutoring Sebastian in some kind of life skills then?' asks Isabelle.

'But your dad isn't stupid – fifty thousand a month isn't the going rate for that kind of thing, is it?'

'I know. You're right. I've no idea what else to say?'

Veronica thinks. 'Look, I could tell your dad that I'm very wealthy, that we met when you were doing your placement at Rowan House and you confided in me about your difficult financial situation. I'll say I liked you – and more importantly Sebastian did. And that it may seem a lot of money, but you had a natural ... well, a natural way with him.'

'Thank you.' Isabelle looks relieved.

Veronica stands, pats her scarf. 'I'll get the coffees,' she says.

'So, Monday?'

'Monday?'

'Shall I come to your house and see Sebastian?'

'I suppose,' sighs Veronica.

'I'll be there bang on seven because Sebastian always likes to ... sorry, no details.'

They go back into the icy world, to their cars separated by an evergreen bush. They reach Isabelle's black Clio first.

'What *is* the word for us?' Veronica asks, the question suddenly coming to her.

'What do you mean?'

'Earlier. On the phone. I said Sebastian can't know that we're ... and I couldn't finish the sentence. Are we friends?'

Isabelle thinks about it. 'No judgement,' she says softly. 'That's what we are.'

Veronica suddenly wants to hug her.

But she doesn't.

'No judgement,' she agrees, and they each go their own way.

29

SEBASTIAN WANTS TO FIND ONE HUNDRED PERCENT

Isabelle is in my room.

Mum told me last night that she would be coming here today instead of me going to her house. She said it's because Isabelle would like to see where I live for a change. I had lots of questions. I wanted to ask Isabelle them, but I don't have her number. She has never given me it and I don't like to ask in case she gives me a made-up one like Emma Clarke from college did twice.

I had to ask my mum.

I asked: 1) Will Isabelle still make my eggs? 2) Will you go out or be nosy and hang around? 3) Is this going to be a regular occurrence? 4) Do I have any say in the matter? 5) Does this mean that Isabelle now wants more than just sex and would like companionship and more? 6) Does my room smell awful?

Mum said she could only answer 2), 4) and 6). She said she will be staying home but won't bother us. She said I always have a say in everything. (This might have been a bit of a lie because neither of them asked me.) And she said as long as I put my socks straight in the wash basket instead of leaving them on my bed, my room will smell nice.

Now Isabelle is in my room, filling it with perfume and hairspray, but my feelings are very mixed up. I tidied up straight after college. I got rid of all my socks and cleaned the fish tank and made sure my CDs were in order. But even doing all that didn't stop me feeling anxious.

Isabelle is wearing nicer clothes than usual – a sparkly top and tight trousers. I can't figure out if this is because she wants to

impress me or if it's because she has come to my house for the first
time. Her hair is half up and half down like she couldn't decide
what style she prefers. Her face is a bit sad I think, even though she
keeps smiling hard. Her stretched lips are shiny pink. I'm looking
forward to kissing her. This will be our seventh time having sex
because we have done it twice each time. It's only seven-fifteen so
we have a while yet though.

But I'm still feeling mixed up now.

I like your room. She smiles at me.

I do too, HoneyBee, I say. *Would you like to sit on the bed*? She
always asks me that in her room, so I think it's the right thing to do.

No, I'm fine. Is it OK if I look around?

I'm glad I tidied up. She looks at my books and at Scorpion and
Flip swimming fast in their tank.

I feed them at 3pm each day, I tell her. *If I'm not here, my mum
does it.*

Mum let Isabelle in earlier. I wanted to answer the door, but she
got there first. I was annoyed. Now she's watching *Emmerdale* and
eating Maltesers.

Would you like to have Scorpion? I ask Isabelle.

Oh, no, he's yours. And wouldn't he miss Flip?

Yes. But... I don't know what my but is.

I just feel like I want to make sure Isabelle is OK. I think she is
sad inside. She looks at the clock. It's seven-twenty-two. Eight
minutes to go. My tummy tingles. I love sex. All day, while I was
learning about thin-joint masonry, I thought about Isabelle undressing me and then being inside her.

Do you wish autism was celebrated more? she asks out of the blue.

You mean autism spectrum perception.

Do I?

That's what I call it. I think about it. *No. I wish it was curable. I
wish I didn't have it.*

But then you wouldn't be you. She is looking at me like she wants
to see inside my brain.

No, I'd be the other Sebastian.

The other one? She frowns.

Yes. The better one. The average human one.

Isabelle comes closer then and kisses me.

It's not seven-thirty yet, I say.

The other Sebastian wouldn't care about that, she smiles.

He doesn't exist. I say it angrily and then feel bad. *Sorry, HoneyBee.*

Nothing to be sorry for. She plays with my hair. My tummy somersaults. Her hands make me shiver, no matter where they are on my body. *Why don't we do something unusual?*

Like what? I ask.

Like we have sex now, at seven-twenty-six?

I think about it. But I don't like it.

Tell me why it has to be seven-thirty? she asks, kissing my ear.

You'll laugh.

Never.

I have an impaired sense of time.

How so?

My perception of it is different to yours. For me it's longer. It goes on forever if I don't check the clock. If I run my life by the time that humans have invented, I fit in with everyone else and get everywhere I'm supposed to be.

Let's do this on your time then, she whispers in my ear. *Let's do this Sebastian Time.*

But we might never stop, ever.

She kisses me again. I'm all mixed up. It is seven-twenty-eight. She pulls my sweatshirt over my head and puts it on the bed. She kisses my chest. I want sex. Straight away. My body has its own time zone. But I'm all mixed up. She kisses my mouth and our tongues touch, hot and needy. I can't resist her. My head resists, but my body is sure. It's seven-twenty-nine. She takes me to my bed. Mum washed the duvet covers today so it smells of Comfort. I lie back, and Isabelle slides her trousers down and takes off her top. Then she sits astride me. Above her are the stars on my ceiling. She is one of them.

At seven-thirty she guides me inside her, and I can relax.

It happens very fast. The first time usually does. There's this strange look on Isabelle's face. It's not disappointment and it's not sadness but a bit of each, plus something else. She shakes it away as soon as I have seen it. She smiles. Her pink lipstick is gone.

We lie side by side, like we always do for a bit. A bit is five minutes from when we begin lying there to the end, but I never tell Isabelle this – I just keep my eye on the clock.

How is your dad? I enquire.

Oh. She seems surprised that I have asked.

It still isn't Ebola?

No. He's getting better, thanks Sebastian. Slowly. But he is.

But you still seem a bit sad, I say.

Do you understand about consent? she asks me. Is this to do with her being sad or does she want to talk about word meanings now?

I know that consent means giving permission for something to happen.

Let's say we were about to have sex.

Are we? I smile and turn to face her.

No, but let's say we were … and I changed my mind and didn't want to. What would you do?

I think about this because it's a big question. *I'd want to know why you changed your mind*, I say. *You said you wanted to and now you don't, so what happened to change your mind?*

What if I said that my mood has changed, and I don't fancy it anymore?

I'd say, well I do. I'm annoyed. She doesn't want to have sex now. That is what she is going to say.

Do you think I should still have sex just because you *want to have it?* Isabelle studies me, and I wish I could know what she is looking for because whatever it is, I'd like her to see it.

But you did want to have it, I say. My head is hurting. *You said you wanted to have it. You took your clothes off.*

Can I not change my mind and put my clothes back on? Isabelle pauses. *Would you want to continue doing it if you knew I was unhappy?*

Well, I suppose I wouldn't, no. But I'd be quite cross, I think.

Cross? Isabelle looks the way my mum looked when I said I wanted cornflakes instead of eggs.

Yes. Because you've confused me. You said you want it, but you don't want it!

When you say cross ... you wouldn't hurt me, would you, Sebastian?

No, I'd never hurt you, I cry. Does she really think that? My hands are not made that way. They could not do anything but be gentle to her.

Do you understand that if a woman says no and a man continues, he has forced her? Isabelle shakes her head, and I wonder if she is as confused as I am. *OK,* she goes on, *let's say your mum has made your eggs and they're perfect and they're on the plate and she spent a lot of time doing them. Then you're not hungry. Do you have to eat them?*

I'm always hungry.

But this time you're not. You're ill. Would you?

Yes, I say, *to keep my mum happy.*

But you don't have to. You have a choice. Isabelle sighs and sits up with her back to me. I don't like her back. It's even harder to read than her face. *I'm not saying this very well, am I?*

You agreed to have sex though, I remind her. *We wrote it down.*

But if I didn't want to, just one time? It's just a what-if.

I'd get upset. I pat her back gently. *I'd cry. But I wouldn't. And I wouldn't ever hurt you, HoneyBee.*

Isabelle turns and looks at me. This face says we are equals. *How would you feel about a man who forced a woman to have sex? If he was cruel and rough and he made her do it?*

That's very bad, I say, serious. *I don't like that.*

How would you feel if someone had done that to me, Sebastian?

My heart feels very tight. *I'd want to hurt them,* I cry. *I'd kill them!*

You are lovely, Sebastian. She kisses my forehead.

Can we have eggs now? I ask her.

Will your mum be OK about me using her kitchen? Shouldn't she make them? HoneyBee looks thoughtful. *I reckon it would make her happy to be the one to make your eggs. Don't you?*

I suppose. I get up from the bed. *I can ask her. Do you want any? No, thank you.*

I find my mum downstairs. *Emmerdale* has finished and she's watching something about paedophiles living next door on Netflix. When I ask if she'll make me some eggs, I can read her face like a large-print book; she is delighted. I watch her do them like the old times. That's how it feels. Like we haven't done it in forever. Then I take them back to my bedroom and eat them sitting at my desk. Isabelle hasn't put her clothes back on, but she is under my duvet.

The second time we have sex I ask her if she is very, very sure she wants to, because I'm good at listening and learning – my teachers always told me that. She nods and suggests we play some music. I think of playing Billy Ocean for her – I've been singing 'Suddenly' all week, replacing the word with HoneyBee. I put REO Speedwagon on instead.

But I'm still feeling all mixed up.

The thing is, I don't know exactly what true love is yet. I'm thinking about what's in this room. There's me and HoneyBee and excellent sex and very good kissing and my heart feeling big towards her and trying to understand her. Maybe I love HoneyBee. But I'm not sure I'm in love with her. *In* love is different, I think. Sex doesn't mean love. I know that now. Even very good sex. I love having it with her, but it's like ninety percent of me enjoys it and ten percent is waiting for something else.

I have a new friend. We went out on Saturday.

But I think I want them to be more than a friend.

I'm confused.

It feels different to HoneyBee. I'd never hurt her. But I've had sex eight times now and it has been ninety percent something and ten percent not.

I would like to find happiness. My full hundred percent.

I'm all mixed up.

Also, my *Best Hits of 1985* CD is broken. I have three other copies still but that isn't the point. I don't like that it broke.

30

ISABELLE DOESN'T WANT TO BE CALLED VIOLETTA

Isabelle wakes gasping from a nightmare where someone is suffocating her with oversized hands. No, not someone; some*thing*. Something heavy and faceless and black. As black as a bottomless void, and thick and gluey and filling her lungs. She sits up, claws at her throat to try and dislodge the invasion.

But there's nothing there.

It's early. The house is quiet. *Dad*. The word comes to her like a hug, quashing the remnants of her dream. Isabelle says it aloud, adding to its power. He's back. She gets out of bed, pulls on her dressing gown, and – without turning any of the lights on – she heads along the landing.

Halfway, she stops by the picture of her mum in the striped bikini. In the dimness, she can't see her face. She waits. Nothing. No sense of that other soul, that breath in the air, that heart beating like her own. No ghost. Was Sebastian right? Did she imagine it all? She feels sad. But there's no need.

She has her dad now.

Isabelle pauses at his door, one hand on the cool surface, afraid to enter in case time has spun back and he's gone again. She thinks about the last eight days and him waking fully. Finally, he has a good Glasgow Coma Score. She studied this briefly in a module last term; a fully conscious patient has a score of fifteen, a person in a deep coma a score of three. There is no lower reading. It has taken her dad a week to get to fifteen.

But being fully conscious is far from the end of the battle.

He might be with her again, but all week he has swung between agitation, joy, and confusion. The occupational therapist, Allan, said this is normal, all part of the process. Charles cried while Isabelle told him upbeat stories about her day and laughed when she confessed to having felt lost sometimes. Allan said he was just getting used to a sudden influx of emotions that he hasn't consciously accessed for four months. He's been helping him with all aspects of daily life and getting back to normal – walking, eating, swallowing, talking, and loosening tight joints. Isabelle found it hard to see her once physically powerful dad shuffle around like a man thirty years older.

One of his first physical movements was reaching for Isabelle's hand and missing it entirely as though he were seeing two of them and had grabbed the second. She ignored this – she knew enough to know it was normal. Instead she let him find his own way there, to the place she had so often sought when small. To guide him would not help either of them.

Now Isabelle puts her forehead against his door.

Then she goes into his room. It's like his presence has changed the air around them. The temperature is higher now that he's conscious, but that's not what it is. It's as though his existence has altered the molecules and atoms. As though they were stagnant before and now have life. She approaches the bed. He's awake. She's glad. They might have a moment alone before the team arrive to continue his care.

'Charles,' she says softly, sitting on the bed.

All the noisy equipment has gone; the room is as quiet as though it is covered in snow. The bedrail has been removed and soon the ugly hospital bed will be replaced with his own. It suddenly occurs to Isabelle that since her dad's fall she too has been in beds she didn't want to occupy. Now they will both only know their own.

'I'm your dad, not your friend,' he smiles weakly.

His voice has seventy percent of its original strength, if she had to give an estimate.

'Dad,' she smiles back.

'Isabelle,' he says.

He always uses her full name, has never shortened it. He sometimes gave her nicknames, the most frequent, in his notes from other lands, being Violetta. She wonders again why on earth she used it when escorting. Why would she sully his special moniker like that? Was it so she would still feel like she was his; that she didn't belong to Cassanby or Simon?

At the thought of the name Simon she gags and has to pretend to cough.

'Are you OK?' He pulls himself up with great difficulty.

'Yes,' she insists, 'don't exert yourself.'

'I'm bloody fine for God's sake.' That's the old Dad.

'Do you want a cup of tea?' she asks him.

'Not yet. Stay there, lass. Don't go. Better yet, I'll make it.'

'No, you won't.' She puts a hand on his arm. It's thin beneath the sleeve.

'I'm supposed to be walking around the house now.'

'Yes, when Allan's here.'

'I can't be doing with fuss.'

Ignoring him, Isabelle asks, 'Did you hear me reading?'

'Last night? No, I slept well.'

'No, I mean while you were ... you know, in the coma?'

He pauses without looking at her. She can tell he doesn't recall hearing her but doesn't want to admit it.

'It doesn't matter either way,' she says quickly.

'What did you read?'

'Our notes. The ones from when I was small.'

The scent of the orchids in the vase is tart. Yesterday she binned the fake flowers and went out and bought fresh. All is real now.

'I can't believe you brought me home,' he says.

'Of course I did,' she cries. 'You asked me to. To not leave you in the hospital. You mentioned my mum ... I couldn't not...'

'Did I?' He looks confused.

'They were your last words to me,' she insists. 'You said there was money in the business to pay for it, and I should keep you at home.'

'I ... I'm sorry. If I said that, I don't remember. Don't upset yourself. What's done is done.'

Should she have let him remain in the hospital after all? Ignored that final plea? God, how much easier it would have been.

'So you used the money in the account?' he says. 'To pay for all this I mean.'

'Dad, there isn't any money,' says Isabelle, sadly. 'Let's not talk about it now. It'll tire you out.'

'Of course there's money.'

'There isn't.' She tries to temper her angry tone but is suddenly exhausted by it all. 'I went to Nick. He told me about the difficulties. The casinos making a loss. The house being mortgaged to the hilt.'

'I know there's no bloody money in the business. But I fenced some off in another account over a year ago, when things started to get rocky. Nick doesn't know about that. I guess in my delirium after the fall I presumed you knew. But why the hell would you?' He sighs, sinks back into the pillows. 'Isabelle, there's about eighty grand in there.'

'What?' She feels sick.

With that kind of money, everything could have been different.

Her dad frowns. 'Did you take out loans?'

'No.' She should have lied and said yes. But he'll ask to see proof, so he can pay it off. And she can't tell him the truth. She can't. She may as well lie a little more. 'Well, just a small one.'

'How did you manage?' he asks.

'What do you mean?'

Isabelle feels sick. Does he know? And which is the thing he knows? That the young man she told him on Wednesday is an autistic patient she's being paid to school in general life skills isn't really here for that? That she's an ex-escort? A whore?

'Keeping me here, at home, without that money?'

'It wasn't so bad. Your critical-illness insurance covered most of it, and I've been doing my tutoring, and—'

'What about university? You haven't let that slide, have you?'

'No. I...' She has to think. 'I borrowed from friends.'

'Isabelle, I know what this kind of care must have cost. You're a wonder to have done it. Don't look so worried. We can pay off your loan.'

'It's not that simple.'

'It's always that simple.'

God. If she had known about that account, everything would have been different. No Dr Cassanby. No Simon. Then a little voice whispers, *But no Sebastian*.

'How have *you* been?' Isabelle's dad grabs her hand without having to search hard for it.

'OK.'

'Don't bullshit your old dad now. It must have been hard.'

'I did what I had to.' Isabelle is close to tears.

'You've changed, Violetta,' he says gently.

'Don't call me that!'

'I'm sorry, I—'

There's a tap on the door. Allan.

'Come in,' calls Isabelle, relieved.

Allan enters, all efficiency and cheer. Isabelle says she'll make them all some tea. As she leaves, she looks back; her dad studies her, his blue eyes sad. He could always read her. When she was little, he knew her every mood. He grew up in a big working-class family and had to fight to be heard. He also learned fast how to see through bullshit. It's how he became such a successful businessman.

Now, she is afraid he will see right through her.

31

ISABELLE'S GHOST HAS GONE

Later, driving to Veronica's house down frosted country lanes, Isabelle suddenly has to pull over. She gets out, needing icy air on her face. Cars fly past, splashing water up her jeans. She vomits into the road. Over and over. She must get it out of her system fast because she can't be late for Sebastian. She must expel the bile before she sees him because she doesn't want her experience – that's all she can call it, not the other word – with Simon to be in the room with her and Sebastian.

It is not welcome there.

When Isabelle tried to discuss what consent is with Sebastian the other night, he got agitated. She knows him enough now to know that it was simply caused by his confusion. He hates anyone thinking he's stupid.

She gets back in the car and makes it to the shadowy house by seven-twenty-five. She parks outside and knocks on the door. How is it only two weeks since she and Sebastian first met and walked by the river? It feels like he's been part of her life for much longer already. It feels like—

The door opens. Sebastian, in jogging bottoms and his Hull City T-shirt.

'It's seven-twenty-six,' he says, agitated. 'It will take one minute to get upstairs and another one minute to—'

'It's OK, Sebby,' says Isabelle, coming in quickly. 'We'll make it, I promise.'

Veronica appears behind him in the hallway. 'Are you...?'

'Mum,' he cries, 'go and watch your soaps, we're on a schedule here.'

Looking hurt, she goes back into the living room and closes the door. Isabelle wanted to catch her eye, to somehow show she hasn't forgotten their 'no judgement' connection at the weekend. She also wants to berate Sebastian for being blunt with his mum but isn't sure it's her place to.

Instead she follows him up the stairs and into his bedroom. In his wake, the smell of something flowery and familiar wafts from his clothes. He shuts the door. She loves his room, prefers it to being in her own. They have always had time to chat first, and then she usually undresses them both, but now he takes off his top, that floral scent overpowering again.

'Seven-twenty-nine,' he says, highly agitated now.

'It's OK.' Isabelle kisses him softly. 'We'll get on Sebastian Time.'

'No,' he snaps, 'that troubles me. We'll stick with human time.'

She nods, takes her top off, and leads him to his bed, where he eagerly shuffles out of his trousers and lies back. He's ready for her. His youth and readiness thrill her. She climbs astride him, hot skin to hot skin, bristle against smooth.

'Seven-thirty,' he whispers urgently. 'Do you *definitely* want to?'

'I do,' she says, knowing why he's asking, and touched by it.

And then he is inside her. She wants to let go. To surrender. To forget their contract. The money. Money she need never have had to find.

But then it is over.

As they lie side by side after, Isabelle watches Sebastian checking the clock regularly. She knows he's counting a certain length of time until he has his eggs. She figures it's five minutes. A neat number. She notices so much about him. How he walks as though he's on a mission, even in his own home. How he smacks his lips when he finishes his eggs. How he's never afraid to look her in the eye without faltering for a second.

When he leaves to ask Veronica – at Isabelle's insistence – to make his eggs, she pulls the duvet over her naked body and closes her eyes for a second. Perhaps it's the exhaustion of recent weeks that drags her into sudden oblivion. In that void, her barriers tumble. Suddenly a cold floor hits her back; a kitchen floor.

You sh-sh-should stay.

Who said that?

She is naked except for her shoes. There's a hand over her face. A fat, sweaty hand that forces salt into her mouth, and black, gooey evil into her throat and lungs. He is heavy; so heavy. The floor so cold.

Let him finish and you can escape, she thinks.

'You don't need to escape, HoneyBee.'

Don't call me that, you fucking monster!

'I'm not your fucking monster, I'm your Sebastian.'

Isabelle opens her eyes; gasps like she's surfacing from the sea. She claws at her throat. The room comes into focus; Sebastian's face above her, so close his eyes blur into one.

'Were you dreaming?'

He comes into focus. He has a tiny bit of egg in the corner of his mouth. He looks half concerned and half afraid. Isabelle is wildly angry. Not at him – never at him – but because this is their time. This is a sacred and good place. Simon can haunt her dreams and chase her up her own stairs at home, but he isn't welcome here.

'Yes,' whispers Isabelle, heart still pounding. 'It was a nightmare.'

'Dreams are the brain's effort to clean up the mind. They are a means by which the head processes emotions, stimuli, memories, and information that's been absorbed throughout waking life. I read that in *The Dream Dictionary*. You were exploring what you can't while you're awake.'

'I wish I hadn't.'

'Do you need a hug?' asks Sebastian. 'I don't need one and I don't like them, but my mum once told me they reduce the harmful physical effects of stress, including reducing the blood pressure and heart rate.'

Isabelle smiles. 'Only hug me if you want to.'

Sebastian looks unsure.

'Is this about consent again?'

'I suppose it is.'

He pats her arm and moves her hair away from her face.

'My ghost has gone, Sebby,' she says, sadly. 'It isn't on my landing anymore.'

'It was never there.' Sebastian speaks patiently as though she is five. 'It was you, HoneyBee.'

'It was there,' she says. 'It *was*.'

Sebastian considers her with his ripe-acorn eyes. She loves being under his studious and serious gaze. She is safe here. She can never predict what he'll say, but she knows how it will make her feel.

'I have told you my thoughts on this matter. I can see that you would rather they were different ones, but I can only be this Sebastian. You know that; we discussed it. My *Best Hits of 1985* is broken. I could blame a ghost. But I know I was probably rough with it, and it was old and tired.' He pauses. 'Can you smell that?'

'What?' Isabelle is excited for a moment that he means something supernatural.

'Comfort?'

'The fabric softener?'

'Yes. I put a wash on for Mum yesterday because she was tired and Tillda didn't come. I didn't like to ask about how much Comfort to use so I put it all in. I wanted to be sure we were meadow fresh.'

'You definitely are that.'

'Good.'

Isabelle can't let her ghost go. 'I think it was my mum. And she's gone because my dad's well again.'

'If you believe that, then it makes you happy, and this is good.'

'I wish you believed it though,' she says.

'Why does it matter that I do?'

Isabelle touches Sebastian's soft cheek. Her palm rests on the bristles of his chin.

'My razor's broken,' he says.

'So am I.' The words come out before she can stop them.

Sebastian looks her up and down. 'You don't look like you are.'

'Inside.'

'How can you be fixed then?'

'I don't know.'

'I think that's for psychiatrists to do.' Sebastian puts his hand over hers. 'Eggs always fix me inside. And swimming. Let me take you swimming some time.' He looks concerned. 'We'd have to add it to our agreement though, wouldn't we?'

'Do you ever think about just cancelling our agreement?' Isabelle asks.

'No. I like it. Sex and eggs. And maybe swimming.' He frowns. 'Why? Do you want to cancel it?'

'No.'

'Good. Can we have sex again?'

They can. And they do. She keeps her eyes open so that all she sees is Sebastian. When it is over, he reaches for the bedpost and gets the goggles that have been there each time she has visited.

'You have them,' he says.

'Why?'

'I like how you look in them, HoneyBee.'

She takes them from him.

'Knock, Knock...'

'Who's there?' smiles Isabelle.

'Boo!'

'So you're a ghost now.'

'Go on,' says Sebastian.

'Okay – Boo who?'

'Don't cry ... you're with Sebastian!'

But Isabelle wants desperately to cry.

32

VERONICA DOESN'T WANT A MAN

Veronica is sure there was some fabric softener left. Sometimes she thinks there's a ghost in the house, what with imagining Pete is close all the time and things going missing like this. The other day her Maltesers were gone and she knows she didn't eat them all. Maybe it's Tilly; Tilly is the Murphy household ghost, eating all the chocolates, and using too much Comfort when she does laundry.

Veronica puts a wash on without any Comfort, knowing Sebastian will grumble that his clothes aren't super-soft like clouds. She can't believe it's Saturday again. Weekdays are a blur of Sebastian's adventures while she sits on the sidelines. She wanted his happiness but didn't think it would mean losing him.

Is she still the woman who threatened to throw her snobby neighbour Annabelle into the street? Still the woman who wanted to strangle the sexual-health counsellor Mel with her awful wooden beads? The fire inside has died. Even her faithful mantra – *it will be OK, it will be OK* – has deserted her.

Veronica finds Sebastian in his bedroom, music blaring, clothes scattered across the floor while he studies them, still wearing his *Star Wars* pyjamas. Foreigner's 'I Want To Know What Love Is' has replaced Billy Ocean. His goggles are missing from the bedpost.

'Did you lose them?' Veronica asks, heart heavy with something she can't define.

He follows her gaze to the bed. 'Isabelle has them.'

'Why?'

'That's private stuff, Mum. I don't ask about your private life.'

I don't have one, she thinks sadly.

'But you love your goggles, darling.'

'Mum, they're just goggles.'

Veronica remembers when he picked them. When he chose them for their wide and comfortable strap, for the thin eye parts, so he looked like a 'slightly evil water superhero'. Until he met Isabelle – *no, he didn't meet her*, Veronica thinks, *you forced them together* – he always had them wrapped around his wrist or forehead.

'Mum, don't look like that. All unsure. Isabelle needs them more than I do at the moment. Anyway, I'm twenty years and six months and twenty-four days old so I think I can decide what I do with my own things.'

Veronica has to accept it. 'Do you want to do something today then?'

'I already am.'

'Are you?'

'Yes,' he says.

'What are you doing?'

'Meeting a friend.' Sebastian picks up his dark-blue jeans with the deep pockets that she likes, and pairs them with his striped shirt. A sedate combination compared to some of his others. She smiles remembering his Christmas jumper by a pool in Majorca and the attention he got.

'Not Isabelle?'

'No. We only have sex on Mondays, Wednesdays and Fridays. You know that.'

'Is it the college friend you saw last weekend?'

'Yes.'

'That's nice, darling.' Veronica is delighted he has made a friend. 'Do you want me to take you and wait?'

'No, I shall get the bus again. It takes thirty-five minutes approximately, allowing for traffic and unforeseeable things like a death. I'm getting the bus at eleven-ten and will get one back at four-twenty, so I'd like my tea at five.'

'Who's your friend then? Does he want to come here sometime?'

'I'd like to get ready now, Mum.'

'Do you ever miss swimming?' Veronica is still bothered by the goggles being gone.

'I get sex now, which is better. But I did tell Isabelle I might take her one time.'

'Meet her outside of your arranged days you mean? But I thought you—'

'We'd have to rewrite our agreement.' Sebastian sighs. 'I'm going to find you a man, Mum.'

'What? I don't need a man.'

'I think now that I have Honey— ... Isabelle, you are bereft. You are in the early autumn years of your life now, Mum, and it has been a long time since you had a man in your bed. I know exactly where we can find you someone who will cheer you up.' Sebastian puts his jeans and shirt on the bed and pulls out his laptop. 'I found a website where you can meet a man.'

'Sebastian, there's no—'

'Wait until you see.' He opens a site that he has already bookmarked. 'Look at this. Look at all the choices. Look at him – he has nice hair and would suit you perfectly. Your purple scarf would bring out his eyes. You would look like a Hollywood couple together.'

Veronica looks at the screen. At the top in gold script against black it says *Gentlemen For You*, and below is a black-and-white picture of a sultry boy (to Veronica he is only a boy) topless against a window. At the bottom of the page it says: 'We are the UK's premier male escort company. For ten years, we have made thousands of women very happy.'

'Remember that day in the kitchen when we were talking,' says Sebastian, 'and I said you didn't know much for a fifty-five-year-old and that you can pay for sex just like paying for swimming lessons even though people seem to get upset about it.'

'Yes, darling,' sighs Veronica. 'And *I* said that, unlike with swimming, people pay for sex for different reasons to wanting to learn how to do it. Can you turn that laptop off please – I don't want a male escort.'

'But look.'

Sebastian clicks on a link and rows of pictures appear. Young men, older men. Black-haired, bald, bearded, greying, sullen, smiling, pouting, clothed and semi-naked.

'Matthew looks nice,' he says, clicking on a picture of a boy in a white shirt and black dickie-bow tie. 'I know he's only twenty-two, but you have a young outlook on life and his shirt is ironed and he has kind eyes.'

Sad eyes, thinks Isabelle. *Poor boy. Just a kid and having to do this.*

What's his story? Why does she feel sadder looking at his image than she did when she first saw Isabelle? Is it because she has a son and the thought of him having to escort to make money destroys her?

'Look,' says Sebastian. 'His phone number is there. He says he will travel anywhere, and he is discrete, and he will do gigs and parties and dinners and shopping and activities too. I bet he would walk along the river with you.'

'Sebastian. I'm not paying for a man. It's disgusting and sleazy.' She takes the laptop from him and slams it shut.

'Is it?' he asks seriously.

'Yes.'

'How?'

'Just the...' Veronica realises her own hypocrisy. She feels sick. How can she of all people judge?

Sebastian frowns. 'If two people decide to exchange five pounds because one of them wants sex and the other one needs five pounds, what is wrong with that?'

'I think it costs more than five pounds,' says Veronica softly.

'Does it? Is that why you won't do it? I have money in my bank account, Mum.'

'Sebastian, it isn't happening. When I want a man, I'll find my own. OK? How would you feel if I tried to...?' Veronica lets the sentence die.

Sebastian looks thoughtful. How she adores his thinking face. How his fat lips hang open and his eyes narrow.

'You would never do that, Mum,' he says. 'Because you respect my wishes and you talk to me about everything and we decide together.' He nods, decisively. 'You're right – I should let you pick your own man. Do you want the links to the other websites I found?'

Veronica can't look at him. At the beautiful boy whose trust she has betrayed. Who is far wiser than she's ever given him credit for. Whose life she had no right to control.

She leaves him choosing which socks to wear.

He can choose his clothes.

He can choose his friends.

She should have let him choose his life too.

33

ISABELLE HAS A TOUGH DAY

Isabelle puts Sebastian's goggles in her bag with some sandwiches.

It's Monday, early, dawn just the softest promise of gold. She must be at the hospital in an hour for her new two-week placement on a general ward. Only a handful of placements have been related to her learning-disabilities degree but at least being on a ward means Isabelle can do what she loves: meet patients and feel like she's making a difference. Reading and writing essays is necessary for the degree – she knows that – but nothing beats the actual experience of the job.

Isabelle looks in on her dad before she leaves. He's sleeping in the oak canopy bed she always teased was too ostentatious, snoring like a horse. How good the sound is. How she missed it when a ventilator breathed for him. Allan will be here at nine for more rounds of physio. Her dad isn't a good patient. Isabelle knows she'd curse him if he were hers. He argues against taking things slowly, expecting to be able to resume his life as though he's merely been away travelling, like in the old days.

Isabelle closes the door softly. On the landing, she pauses a moment, knowing not to expect anything but hopeful anyway. Nothing. She goes into her bag, takes out Sebastian's goggles, and pulls them over her head, catching her hair. They smudge the blunt edges; make everything appear spectral.

Is she hoping to see some sort of ghost through them?

Feeling stupid, she tugs them off and puts them back in her bag.

She arrives at the hospital ward with the sun and meets Shelby – her mentor for the next fortnight – who promptly disappears until mid-morning. It's common with NHS cuts and staff shortages that student nurses end up fending for themselves. Isabelle tags along with some auxiliaries, helping with bed baths and chatting to patients, and then familiarises herself with assessment documents. She sits with a scrap of a ginger-haired boy, who arrived in the middle of the night with breathing difficulties, which is one of the most common reasons for admittance in youngsters.

'My mum went home,' he says. 'She's got to work. I've got six brothers.'

Isabelle thinks of her quiet, single-child life. 'Wow. That's a busy house. At least you'll feel at home on this noisy ward, eh?'

Mid-morning, Shelby finds Isabelle changing beds and asks her to join them on the ward round. This daily procedure is led by a doctor and is a crucial part of a patient's care. Nurses have a vital role in ensuring the patient is fully involved in decisions. A small crowd of medical professionals stand around an elderly lady's bed, discussing her blood results and possible early discharge date. Isabelle hangs back to observe, though – depending on the attitude of the doctor leading the round, student nurses are encouraged to ask questions and comment.

There's a voice that she recognises.

'Why is Mrs Simpson still with us?' it says.

It rises above the others, like when a slightly louder TV advert wakes Isabelle just as she drops off at night. She wants to be sick. She suddenly feels as though she's naked. She puts a hand on her chest and the other on her stomach. Shelby asks if she's OK; Isabelle nods vigorously, afraid if she speaks, she'll cry. Why are the wards so fucking warm? Doesn't heat breed germs? That's basic training.

'You sure?' asks Shelby, clearly concerned.

The voice goes on, monotone, professional, nausea-inducing.

'I'm fine,' lies Isabelle.

They are done with the elderly lady and move on. The small crowd breaks up and reassembles by the next bed. That's when Isabelle sees him. Dr Cassanby. Talking to the team the way he often spoke to her; with a complete lack of emotion, commanding, like he's instructing a dog to fetch a stick. They move on again. He talks about a little girl with her arm in plaster, but Isabelle can't hear his words. All she sees are his thin lips moving, his pink tongue glistening inside his black mouth. It moves snakelike over his top teeth. She looks into steely eyes. They return her gaze, unrelenting, recognising, surprise buried, perhaps a flicker of concern, then seeing discomfort and enjoying it. Snarled eyebrows frame the ugly picture. He should be more shocked; she never told him she was a trainee nurse. But he isn't. He's a cold monster.

Isabelle should have known this day would come.

How fucking *dare* he look at her like that?

Nausea gives way to rage, white hot, savage.

They move to the next bed. He's wearing his silky black tie. The one he had her wrap tightly around his neck. The one she longed to tug on until he died.

'I'm going to kiss your nipples,' Cassanby says to Isabelle. It's just the two of them. It's like she's wearing Sebastian's goggles, and the edges are smudged. Blood drips down Cassanby's chin the way it did the night he bit her and threw her on the bed.

Then he is stammering Simon, his hand grabbing her ankle as she runs.

Isabelle closes her eyes. Someone touches her arm, and she pulls away roughly.

It's just Shelby.

'You look terrible,' she whispers in her ear. 'Do you need to take a breather?'

She doesn't want a breather. She wants to grab hold of that silky black tie and squeeze it until Cassanby falls at her feet, gagging and gasping.

Then there is another voice, not Shelby's or Cassanby's.

I'm not on the landing. I'm here to catch you if you fall. Don't fall now, Isabelle. Don't fall because of someone who isn't worth your rage. Don't do it...

The white-hot rage in Isabelle's gut simmers.

'I ... am ... yes, I feel sick,' she admits. 'I wasn't right this morning.'

'Why don't you go home and come back tomorrow?' suggests Shelby.

Grateful to escape, Isabelle nods. If she surrenders to this rage and attacks Cassanby, only she will suffer. It could end her chances of being a nurse. She walks away, her pumps soft on the tiles, not the clacking and scraping heels that escaped Simon. Passing a stock room, she slips inside and gets a suture removal kit. Putting it into her bag, she checks no one saw, and continues on her way.

Outside, she leans against a wall and frees her trapped breath. Thank God for the cold. If she smoked, she'd have five cigarettes, one after the other. Where did she park the car? On a side street five minutes' walk away. She needs to stay. Watch the main doors. Wait. The chill is good. It steadies her. She opens the suture kit and takes out the foil-wrapped package; a tiny scalpel. It fits neatly inside her fist.

After an hour, she sees him.

Cassanby.

She follows him.

He gets into a black Audi; she gets in the passenger side.

'What the hell?' He stops fastening his seatbelt. His fingernails are neat, cut short. She sees everything in such sharp detail. Adrenaline? Maybe.

'I knew it was you.' He lowers his voice. 'Your boss said you left. Said she didn't want me to call them again. I've had t—'

'Stop talking,' hisses Isabelle.

'You're not coming back to me then, Violetta?'

How can he be so arrogant? Shouldn't he be embarrassed? Worried about his dirty little secret being discovered here at work?

'Don't call me that.'

'It's not your name then?'

'No.'

'Clearly you're not a hotel receptionist either.'

'Shut up.' Isabelle shows Cassanby what she has hidden in her hand. He looks at it and then her, his face not as assured as it was earlier. 'Don't even think about drawing any attention to us. Now ... you're going to say sorry to me.'

'Get out of my car. This is outrageous. Who do you think you are, you little whore?'

The goggles in Isabelle's bag catch her eye, but she ignores them. All she hears is Cassanby's word: 'whore'. She puts the silver blade against his bristled cheek. A sharp gasp, like the first time she undressed for him. That he gasps in fear this time is intensely satisfying.

'You don't have the nerve,' he says, eyes bright with panic.

Still, no shame. He's a monster.

'Don't I?'

Isabelle presses harder, nicking his skin. She watches the crimson trickle and feels relief, the way a self-harmer must. Lets it flow the way hers did from his mouth. Lets it stain his cream shirt and sully his silk tie.

This is *self-harm*, whispers the voice. *Only you will pay for this, not him.*

'You'll never get a job as a nurse. I'll make sure of it.'

'If you move again, I'll cut your neck open.'

He doesn't move an inch.

'What do you want?' He tries to sound authoritative, but the power in his voice is gone. 'More money? Didn't I pay you enough? Christ, take it. My wallet's in m—'

'You think this is about money?'

'It's always about money.'

'This is about men like you.'

'I'm a doctor.'

'Men who think they can just...'

'Just what?'

'I need you to say sorry. Admit what you did.'

'What did I do?'

'You raped me,' she says, voice breaking.

'How dare you. I didn't – I paid you.'

'You knocked me out and I came to and you were on top of me.'

'You're deluded,' he cries. 'I did no such thing. You knew my tastes and I paid you. We had a contract the minute you agreed to be with me. I'm no rapist.'

That wasn't him, whispers the voice.

Isabelle realises she is confusing Cassanby with Simon. But Cassanby still hurt her. Humiliated her. Bit her. Can she complain though, if he paid her and she never said no? How was Simon different? Isabelle didn't even think *no* when he was on top of her. She didn't think *stop*. She thought *let him finish and then you can escape*. They were clients. Confusion loosens her grip on the scalpel. She sees herself as though from above, red-faced, weapon in hand.

And the anger abates.

Cassanby must sense this and grabs her hand so tightly that she drops the scalpel.

'I'm going to report you,' he says.

'I don't think so.' Isabelle is suddenly exhausted.

He opens his door and starts to get out. 'You don't think so?'

'No.' He stops. She holds his gaze now. 'If you tell anyone about this, I'll tell them you visit escorts. I'll tell them what you're into. What you do to women. I can get proof any time. My boss kept records. Your number will be stored in her phone.'

He sits back down 'You don't deserve to wear a nurse's uniform.'

'You're a sadist who can only get it up when you hurt women.' Isabelle feels nauseous and wants to escape. 'You're going to do two things now.'

'Am I?'

'Yes. I'm here for another two weeks so you're going to ring in sick from tomorrow. I don't want to see your face again.'

'I can't just ring in sick for a fortnight.'

'You will. Because if I see you, I'll tell everyone what I know about you.'

Cassanby doesn't speak.

'Now you're going to say sorry to me.'

'Sorry? You should be apologising to me for holding me captive and threatening me with—'

'Shut up!' cries Isabelle. She knows now; she is taking her deepest rage out on the wrong person. But still, she needs the apology. She *needs* it. 'Say you're sorry.'

He shakes his head slowly.

'Say it.' Isabelle picks up the scalpel.

'I don't understand what I'm say—'

'For hurting me.' Isabelle's words are barely audible.

Cassanby shakes his head. 'I'm...'

Isabelle waits, scalpel glinting in the weak winter sunlight.

'I'm sorry for hurting you.'

She opens her door. She gets out. Cassanby watches her.

Just before she closes the door he says, 'Don't forget you're a whore though.'

How can she? She never will. Because he's right. She makes it to her car and sobs against the steering wheel. Even if she never has to see Cassanby again physically, she will never forget those steely eyes, that voice, and that black silk tie.

34

ISABELLE REALISES

When she gets home, Isabelle doesn't want to see her dad, sure that all the shame and anger will show in her eyes. Only an hour until she sees Sebastian, something that makes her feel calm. She's grateful that it's a Monday, one of his nights. Allan finds her in the kitchen and says her dad has had a hard day. Isabelle decides to take him a cup of tea. He's sitting on the edge of his ostentatious oak bed, head in hands. Isabelle puts the mug on the bedside table and sits next to him.

'Are you OK, Charles?'

He starts. Looks at her with weary eyes. 'Just tired, lass. I'm trapped.'

'What do you mean?'

'I'm the same me except I'm inside this useless body, and it frustrates me to buggery.'

'It's gonna take time, Dad.'

'I know, I know. That's what Allan tells me. But I want to get back to work. I used to live for it.'

'I know,' she sighs, 'but you'll set yourself back if you push it. Nick's taking care of everything, you know that.'

'I suppose. So how was your day?'

'Fine.' Isabelle changes the subject quickly. 'I have to go out. That young man I'm tutoring.'

'I hope you're being well paid for it,' he says. 'How do you tutor an autistic?'

'He's not *an autistic*,' she snaps. 'He *has* autism.'

'Thought it couldn't be cured?'

'It can't. I'm not curing him. I'm ... helping him get ready for an independent life after college.'

'I want you to take some of the money,' says Charles.

'What money?' Isabelle is distracted.

'In my account.' Of course. The money that could have stopped her escorting if she had known it was there. 'Then you don't have to tutor that boy and can concentrate on your studies.'

'It's fine, Dad.'

'Please, take what you need,' he says, as persistent as ever.

'I said it's fine. I have to get ready to go out. Drink your tea. Do you want to watch the big TV downstairs? I can walk y—'

'I'm not a bloody cripple, lass. If I want to go down my own stairs, I'll do it myself.'

Isabelle stands. Some of the orchids are dying. She can no longer smell them. She must replace them.

'I'll look in on you when I come back, Charles.'

'I might have buggered off to Vegas,' he says with a wry laugh.

◊

Isabelle arrives at the house earlier than usual. Veronica answers the door; the smell of casserole, perhaps beef with some sort of spicy herb, wafts from the kitchen, taking Isabelle back to Cecilia's home cooking when she was little and her dad was away travelling. She longs suddenly for the simplicity of childhood. For simple decisions: a summer dress or jeans; hopscotch or kiss chase; liquorice allsorts or jelly babies.

'Are you OK?' asks Veronica.

'Yes, why?' Isabelle feels defensive.

'Well, it's only six-forty-five.'

'Is it? Oh. Sorry, I can wait in the car.'

'Don't be silly, I didn't mean that.' She opens the door wider. 'Come in. Sebastian is ... I don't know actually. Probably getting ready.'

Isabelle steps into the hallway. She feels light-headed.

'Are you sure you're OK?' Veronica frowns, looks her up and down.

Isabelle realises she's still wearing her student-nurse uniform. She didn't even change. It's creased and has a tea stain by the collar. She knows her hair must be tangled because she hasn't brushed it since this morning. She didn't even look in a mirror before she left home half an hour ago.

'Tough day,' she admits.

'Are you sure you should be here tonight?' asks Veronica, kindly.

'I won't let Sebby down.' But Isabelle realises that she needs *him*. That she longs for the simple happiness of being with him.

As though hearing his name, Sebastian appears on the stairs. He looks different to when she first saw him in Mel's office wearing baggy grey joggers, a Superman hoodie, and brand-new-not-scuffed-yet Puma trainers. She spots them, abandoned by the door, dirty and broken in now. Tonight, his hair is damp, the curls fighting to resume their natural chaos. He wears the jeans she likes him in and a plain red T-shirt.

But is it Isabelle who has changed? Is she seeing him now through different eyes and not the goggles she wore back then, when they swapped eyewear and looked at the tropical fish together?

'It isn't seven o'clock,' says Sebastian, flustered.

'She can have a cup of tea down here, if it bothers you?' Veronica suggests.

'I'm not ready. I was even going to light some candles. You always go on about them.'

'Shall I sit with your mum a bit then?'

'No.' he sighs. 'I can do this.'

'Do what?' asks Veronica.

'Be a regular human.'

'You are a regular human, darling,' says Veronica.

'Come up then.' Sebastian shakes his head as though the two women are unruly children he must tolerate.

Isabelle follows him up the stairs. She looks back at Veronica and realises how odd the whole situation is. They are like teenagers sneaking off together, except with a consenting mother – and with two hundred and fifty thousand pounds exchanging hands. Isabelle grabs the banister, dizzy again. She sees the cash, dirty, blood-covered, and can't get the image out of her head. Dr Cassanby is right. She's a whore.

'Come on, slow coach,' calls Sebastian from his bedroom.

She goes inside. Closes the door. Lets it envelope her, this safe place, with a softly bubbling fish tank and stars on the ceiling and tidy shelves.

'You're the same as when I first saw you,' says Sebastian.

She smiles. 'I was actually just thinking how different *you* are.'

'You were wearing that at the clinic.' He points to her uniform. 'It was cleaner then though. You are a bit of a disgrace today to be honest, HoneyBee.'

'I know,' she says softly.

She cries. She can't help it or hide it. Sebastian looks distressed and she doesn't want him to be.

'I'm sorry.' She wipes her face. 'I shouldn't have come tonight. I don't want to alarm you. I'll be OK in a minute. I just had a tough day.'

Sebby pats her arm twice and then resumes his position a few feet away.

'I had a tough day last week. My mortar wouldn't set. I did the right ratio and it was still soft and crumbly after forty-eight hours. Then I came home and Mum had run out of hot chocolate *and* eaten all the Maltesers. But then I had sex with you and felt better.'

Isabelle moves closer to him. He stands as rigid as a statue.

'Let's make us both feel better now then,' she says.

He looks at the time. It's six-fifty-five. She knows how hard it is for him to deviate from the schedule, from their agreement.

'Why don't we see what happens?' she suggests.

Sebastian looks anxious but doesn't say no. She kisses him softly. Her body responds at once to the feel of his muscular frame against hers. He's so tall and strong. He smells of Comfort and she smiles. She wants his hands on her, inside her. She wants *him*. But at first, he doesn't kiss her back, and she knows he is looking at the clock.

Then the softness gives way to urgency, to passion, like it always does; the intensity sends electricity through her body. Sebastian grows rigid against her. He kisses her in a way he never has before, holding her face with both hands.

Isabelle gasps and pulls away, causing him to frown.

She puts her hands over her eyes.

She sees.

She realises.

She realises so hard it makes her breath shallow. So hard her knees almost buckle. She is kissing a man she loves. She loves Sebastian. Seven times together – eight if you include their first walk along the river, nine if you include the clinic – and she loves him. Not even quite three weeks of seeing him, and she loves him. She takes her hands away from her eyes.

He is looking at her, serious.

'I know what it is, HoneyBee,' he says.

'Do you?' She smiles.

'It isn't seven-thirty. You want to wait, don't you? You have become me. This is how we are human. We learn from one another. What an interesting night this is.'

'I can wait until seven-thirty,' says Isabelle. 'Will you hug me until then?'

'That's not really my bag, but if we must.' Sebastian puts his arms around her and holds her in an awkward embrace, his face turned to the left, forehead furrowed with effort. 'Are you OK?' he asks.

'Yes,' she says into his chest.

For now, she is. She could stay here forever.

'I really want sex though,' he says, and she can tell. 'You got me all tingly. Those were extra-nice kisses.'

'They were,' whispers Isabelle.

'Knock, knock,' he says.

She smiles. 'Who's there?'

'Robin.'

'Robin who?'

'Robin you – now give me the cash!'

Sebastian giggles. Isabelle doesn't. At the mention of cash, she feels light-headed. She thinks of the fifty thousand already in her account, transferred by Veronica, of the other two hundred thousand still left to come. And she realises she can't accept it. She can't keep what she has already taken. Everything is different now.

She loves him.

'I can make an exception,' says Sebastian.

'What do you mean?'

'It's only seven-oh-nine but my body is longing for it to be seven-thirty. So I would like to have sex now. Maybe I will go on top. Is that OK, HoneyBee?'

Isabelle shivers.

'I'll do it any way you like,' she sighs.

Because I love you.

35

SEBASTIAN TRIES NOT TO TALK ABOUT...

Today is Valentine's Day. I've written three cards this year and I feel bad. I usually write one for my mum and that always felt good. She doesn't get any otherwise. This year I got her one with a picture of a piece of melon on it. The words *You're One in a Melon* are at the top. She *is* one in a melon.

The second card is for HoneyBee. I love her ninety percent. I was going to write that inside it, but then I decided that might be unkind. I got her one with a fishbowl on the front and it says *You're My Favourite Fish in the Sea.* The first thing we looked at together was the fish tank at the clinic, so I thought it fit us very well.

The third one is for my friend who I hope is going to be more than a friend.

I'm itching to talk about her now.

OK, I will.

Her name is Norma Jean. I know – it's an unusual name. I asked her where it came from. She said her mum is a Marilyn Monroe fan (that is the blonde lady who sang 'Happy Birthday' in a whispery voice) and Norma Jean was Marilyn's name before she became a big star.

OK, I don't want to talk about Norma Jean now.

I like to keep her inside my head. I read that it's tempting fate if you speak about something before it has happened. There is no logic to this statement, but it worries me all the same.

I will say this though: I got Norma Jean a card with two rabbits on the front and the words *Hey Friend! Happy Valentine's Day!* at the top because she is still just my friend. She goes to my college, but she doesn't do bricklaying. She does animal management. She's nice. She likes all animals, even the ugly ones. That's how we got talking. Because of tigers. I asked her if she liked them and she does.

Look – I'm talking about her again. I should wait and see if she likes my card before I say any more. This is why I haven't told Mum that I like Norma Jean more than as a friend. She might be cross that I have sex with Isabelle but I'm thinking about another girl. I would like to maybe have sex where there is no written agreement and where we see what happens.

But I don't want to make Isabelle sad.

And I think it will.

I won't tell her about Norma Jean until there is something to tell. Then I'll have to because I can't tell fibs. I'll see Norma Jean at college tomorrow. My heart does somersaults at her red hair and red freckles.

Today is Wednesday so I'm going to Isabelle's house. I'll hide her Valentine card inside my jacket until we are in her bedroom. She parks the car on her drive and looks at me. I have learned to look back at her and wait and see what she says. It's a nice bit of time, that waiting.

She says, *My dad may be around now, Sebby.*

Or a square – haha!

Isabelle doesn't laugh. *If he is, he doesn't know that you and I have sex. OK?*

I nod. *OK. Well, that's fine. It's not his business.*

The thing is...

The thing is what?

My dad thinks I'm helping you.

What do you mean? I ask.

I told him I'm tutoring you, she says. *Just so that he doesn't ask all kinds of probing questions. I don't want him to have a lot on his mind when he's supposed to be getting better. And other complicated reasons that you don't need to know.*

I don't like that she says I don't need to know. Like I'm stupid or something. Like I won't understand. But I don't say it. I'm learning that too – not to say aloud every single thing that comes into my head.

Should I call you miss then? I ask.

What?

Miss. Like a teacher.

No, just Isabelle. Not HoneyBee or anything. OK?

I say OK, but I don't like it. I'm happy that what we do is private, but I don't like to lie. Lies make my throat tight. I already feel like a bit of a liar for not telling Isabelle about Norma Jean.

We go inside. Isabelle looks tense, like the woman in the film last night who was breaking into someone's house. Then this man comes out of the kitchen. He walks very slowly as though he needs the toilet and is trying to hold it in. He looks a bit like Isabelle with his super-blue eyes, except he is more rugged and hairy, and a bit scary-looking. I felt like he might bark instead of speaking.

I didn't even know you'd gone out, lass, he says. I'm right – he's barky. Then he sees me and stares. *Oh. You must be...?*

This is Sebastian, says Isabelle. *The young man I'm tutoring.*

If you ever want any advice on opening your own casino, he says to me, *I'm your man.*

I build walls, I say. *I could build a very good casino.*

He stares at me again.

A brickie, eh? That's a fine trade to be in.

Yes, I say. *I'm in a fine trade. Is a casino like a nightclub?*

I guess.

Nightclubs have never made me happy.

Oh. That's a shame. Why not?

Sebastian, let's— Isabelle starts to say but I interrupt.

Because they never play Billy Ocean.

We'll be in my room, Dad. Isabelle nudges me to go up the stairs. *Our work is on my laptop. Do you want anything before we get started, Sebastian?*

No, just eggs halfway through.

Isabelle looks again like that woman in the film who was breaking into a house. Her dad watches us climb the stairs. I look back at him and can't read his face. Not because of autism but because he keeps his features regular. His eyes are bright though.

We go into Isabelle's room and she leans on the door. It's seven-twenty-one. Last time we didn't stick to the agreement. Lots was different last time. We had sex a minute earlier than usual. I went on top. And it was good. I don't know if that's why Isabelle seemed different. I think it was good different but I'm not sure. I would still rather wait until seven-thirty. It's hard to let go of my time.

I shake all of Isabelle's snow globes, the New York one last. I love watching the snow settle, though it makes me want to shake them again, over and over. Then I sit on the bed. My goggles are on the bedside table next to the lamp and a diary. Isabelle sits next to me. She's quiet tonight.

Your dad is quite scary, I say.

Is he? Yes, I suppose he could seem that way if you don't know him. He's had to be that way to get where he did in life. He's a softie really though.

And where did he get in life, HoneyBee?

The top of his game, you could say. He went away quite a lot when I was little. I don't really know what he did then, in truth. Probably the same as now.

My dad was always home, I say. *And then suddenly he was never home again.*

Oh, Sebby. How horrible for you.

Isabelle touches my face. I let her. I don't mind it too much. It's better than when she wants to hug. I let her but it's my least favourite part of what we do, like when we had to hold our breath under water during swimming lessons.

It's seven-twenty-six now. I decide to give her my card before we have sex. I pass the envelope to her.

What's this? She looks at me.

A Valentine's card.

Oh. Of course. I didn't get you one, Sebby. Shit. I'm so sorry.

We do not give to receive. It's something my mum says, and it sounds right for this moment.

This is so thoughtful. She starts to open it.

No, save it for when I'm gone and then you still have a bit of me.

Isabelle looks serious. *I'll cherish this.* Suddenly she jumps up and gets the New York snow globe from her desk. *Have this*, she says. *You said it's your favourite.*

Really? I clap my hands and shake it straight away and think about where I can put it in my room. I know it's special to her because she once told me about a holiday with her dad in New York.

I shake it until seven-thirty and then tell her the time and ask if she is definitely sure she wants to have sex. I like to check since we talked about consent. She nods. We kiss. I know her kisses well now. How she tastes and how she moves. She feels different when I'm inside her this time. Her body seems to do different things. I want to ask what it is, but she told me we have to be quiet. I don't like different when I don't know what it means. I don't really like it when I *do*, but at least it's easier to cope with. Isabelle looks happy. Her face is pink and glowing.

While she's making my eggs I think about Norma Jean.

I can't help it.

I feel bad.

I feel all mixed up.

Should I tell Isabelle about her after all? No. There is nothing to tell except that I have thoughts. Except that we have gone to KFC twice. Both times Norma Jean couldn't finish her chicken, so I did, even though she had ruined it with loads of barbecue sauce. We have talked four times in the college canteen, about animals and bricks and swimming. I have waited for her after last period and walked her to her bus stop.

I think it will hurt Isabelle to know about this. Last week she told me she was broken, inside. I don't want to break her any more, outside or in.

And there's this...

Norma Jean isn't autistic. I can tell. And yet it doesn't matter after all. I would like her whatever. I have Isabelle to thank for this.

Because she has shown me that I *do* deserve absolutely anyone. She has shown me that I am as beautiful inside as I am outside, which is very much. I would never have asked Norma Jean to come to KFC with me if Isabelle hadn't liked me enough to create our agreement and have great sex with me. If she hadn't wanted to be with me for nothing except the pleasure of my company, I would never have found the courage to get on the bus without my mum and meet Norma Jean.

No one has been kinder or more honest with me.

For this she will always be my HoneyBee.

When she comes back, I eat my eggs and smile lots at her.

Am I misleading her though?

I don't know.

I don't know.

I don't know.

Knock, knock, Isabelle says, and I feel better.

Who's there?

Avenue, she says.

Avenue who?

Avenue knocked on this door before?

I laugh.

But I'm still all mixed up.

36

VERONICA ASKS '*WHAT* IS SEBASTIAN?'

Another Saturday morning. Another weekend, following another blur of a week with days that alternated Sebastian being with her and Sebastian being with Isabelle. Veronica has seen more of Tilly than her own son, and at times she has been grateful of the company of her cleaner.

Now she makes a pot of coffee in her silent, clean kitchen and listens to it softly bubbling, unable to compete with the wild wind and lashing rain outside. Isabelle called last night. She wants to see her again, in the country café where they met last time. At noon. She gave nothing more away. Perhaps it's just a catch-up. To let her know how Sebastian is. They agreed that they would meet every so often, but it's only been two weeks since last time. Then Isabelle asked if she could come to the house with Sebastian now that her dad was up and about. What can it be now?

Veronica pours a large cup of coffee and sips it at the window.

'Why aren't my wedding trousers washed?'

She jumps, spilling hot liquid on her arm. Sebastian. In his now-too-tight *X Factor* pyjamas, with hair as wild as if he has been out in the storm.

'If they don't go in the linen basket, they don't get washed,' she sighs as she has many times over the years. 'Where are they?'

He ignores her. Swings the kitchen door roughly back and forth.

'Why do you want them?' She dabs her arm with a cold cloth.

'I'm going out.'

'Where?'

'KFC.'

'Who with?'

'What am I, Answers.com?' Sebastian kicks the door.

'Well?'

'I am well, yes, Mum, very well.'

'Sebastian, stop it. And stop playing with the door. Who are you meeting?'

'My friend.' He continues swinging the door.

'From college?' she asks.

'Yes.'

'That's nice. You can bring him here, you know.'

'I know. But I prefer KFC. Anyway, I have to get myself ready.'

'Do you want a lift? I'm meeting—' Veronica manages to stop herself just before she says Isabelle. 'I'm meeting Jayne. I can drop you in town.'

'Nope. I enjoy public transport now. Though the buses do not always arrive on time, they are many and the late one from previously becomes an early one for me.'

He disappears.

He leaves before she does, wearing his torn jeans, bright-red coat and Hull City hat, Lynx spray choking her in his wake. On her way to the car, Veronica goes out into the street to pull the emptied wheelie bin back onto her driveway. On the opposite path with her own bin is Annabelle. Veronica is glad she is wearing her silver Gucci scarf and plenty of lipstick. She feels more able to battle in her warpaint.

But Annabelle doesn't look like her normal self. Her usually coiffed golden waves are a choppy sea today, and it clearly isn't from the angry wind that downed most of the wheelie bins. Her tight lips aren't painted, her clothes are creased, and the customary pastel heels have been replaced with beige slippers.

'Veronica,' she says briskly as acknowledgment.

They haven't seen one another since Annabelle called Sebastian a monster. But any rage Veronica still has over that, and her daughters' cruel treatment of him, abates when she sees how ill her neighbour looks. Black rings circle her eyes.

'You look terrible,' she can't help but say. 'Is everything OK?'

Annabelle shakes her head wearily. 'I'm ill, Veronica,' she says. 'You probably heard that my husband left me?'

'No, I didn't. I'm sorry.'

'That's kind of you, but you don't have to be. I haven't been … well, I haven't been the most neighbourly person, have I?'

'Still, I wouldn't wish ill on you.'

Veronica is about to turn and go to her car, but Annabelle says, 'He had been seeing prostitutes.' She whispers the last word. 'My Gerald. Seeing women of the night. For years. It's so humiliating.'

Veronica wonders absentmindedly if Isabelle could have been one of them; if in some curious twist she contributed to Gerald leaving her hateful neighbour. He and Veronica have something in common: they both hired an escort.

'He should be ashamed, not you.' Veronica doesn't know what else to say.

'But he isn't. What on earth do I tell my girls?'

Though Veronica feels sad for the woman, she doesn't want to stand around chatting about the girls who cruelly tricked her son.

'I have to go,' she says.

On the drive to the café, with rain lashing at the windscreen and slowing her journey, she feels sad. Sad for herself. Sad for Isabelle. But not for Sebastian.

Isabelle is already at the café, sitting at the same table as last time, overlooking the now stormy fields. As Veronica approaches, she finds herself glad to see her. She suddenly wonders what will happen when this strange situation ends? Will they remain friends – no, not friends. *No judgement*. That's what Isabelle called them last time. That's what they are.

Veronica sits opposite Isabelle.

'How are you?' she asks.

'Good,' smiles Isabelle. 'You?'

'Good too. Have you ordered?' When Isabelle shakes her head, Veronica calls the waitress and orders them both lattes, remembering last time.

'Is this just a catch-up?' she asks.

'I have something to tell you.'

'Oh.'

'It may come as a bit of a surprise.'

'OK.' Veronica's tummy turns over.

The waitress brings the drinks, and the two women smile uneasily at one another, Isabelle's face full of something, and Veronica feeling nervous. They sip from their chunky mugs at the same time.

'I'm going to give you the fifty thousand back,' says Isabelle.

'Oh.' It isn't what Veronica expected, though she isn't sure what she did. She never is when they meet up.

'I don't want the rest of the money either.'

'You don't ... but I don't understand.'

'I don't need it now. My dad's getting better, and there's money I never knew about.' Isabelle looks a sad for a moment. 'If I had known I would never have needed to ... well, you know.'

'Are you sure you don't want any of it? But does that mean...?'

Is Isabelle going to end the agreement too and break Sebastian's heart? A small part of Veronica still wants that – not her boy destroyed but things going back to how they were before all this, before Sebastian grew up and wanted sex. But nothing is going to take her back to then.

'I'm sure,' says Isabelle. 'But even if Dad wasn't out of the coma, I can't take the money now.'

'Why? What's wrong? Is Sebastian OK? Has something happened?'

'No. Yes. Not to Sebastian. Nothing bad, I mean...'

'Then what?' Veronica demands, knocking her mug over and spilling milky coffee everywhere. 'Damn!' The waitress appears and mops it up with a handful of napkins.

'Would you like another, madam?'

'No. Yes. Sorry.' Veronica is hot and loosens her scarf. 'Why can't you take the money?' she asks Isabelle.

Isabelle inhales. 'I love him,' she says.

Isabelle has met someone new and is ending what she and

Sebastian share. Veronica can't help but smile. It isn't about the money, she can easily part with that. It's about maybe having Sebastian back, undoing what she has done.

'It's Sebastian,' adds Isabelle.

'*What* is Sebastian?' forms on Veronica's foolish lips until she realises.

'I love him,' repeats Isabelle, as though she can't get enough of saying it.

And it dawns on Veronica how happy she looks. She didn't notice until now how the haunted look in Isabelle's eyes has dimmed, how her cheeks glow, how a shy smile plays on her lips.

'You love...' Veronica can't finish. She isn't sure how she feels about it.

'Yes. I love Sebastian.'

It's that simple. Three words.

'But you ... but he...'

'I know,' smiles Isabelle. 'I've questioned and analysed it. But it's true. It's there. It's real. I do. I've never felt anything like this. It caught me by surprise the other night. It was the total cliché of taking my breath away.'

'How can you?' The question jumps out of Veronica, and she realises how cruel it is. 'I don't mean that,' she backtracks. 'I mean ... I don't know what I mean. But, well, you're so much older than he is, for a start.'

'I'm only nine years older,' says Isabelle.

'Not really.' Veronica is saying all the things she has always argued against. 'You know he isn't twenty how other people are.'

'I do. He isn't anything like how anyone is. Are any of us?'

Veronica doesn't know what to say.

'I know this must be hard for you,' says Isabelle. 'I never expected it.'

A question comes suddenly to Veronica. 'Have you told *him* this?' she asks.

'No.' Isabelle fiddles with a stray strand of hair, the way Veronica has noticed she does when she's uncertain. 'It doesn't feel right to.

I don't want to ... overwhelm him. Make him think he has to feel the same way.'

'What are you going to do then?'

'What do you mean?'

'Will you just carry on seeing him three days a week like you do?'

'I guess so. I love being with him. And he never knew about the money, so now we're the thing he always thought we were. It's just him and me meeting three times a week, to his requirements.'

'Except you love him.'

'Yes.'

Veronica lifts the cup to her mouth even though it's empty. The waitress brings another and puts it on the table.

'When I first met Sebby, by the river,' Isabelle says, 'I told him that if he fell in love with me it might make things tricky because he'd want to carry on having sex and I might not want to. Remember when we talked about how he might be broken if I ended things after six months?' Isabelle shakes her head. 'We presumed *he'd* fall in love with *me*. How arrogant of us. We didn't consider that I might fall for him. We never planned what we'd do then. We're as bad as the people who laugh at *The Undateables*. We thought we were doing our best for him and never considered he might know that himself.'

'You mean I'm bad.' Veronica feels sick. 'That's what you're saying. He isn't your son. You just got roped into this because of me.'

'I don't mean that,' says Isabelle kindly. 'Everything you've done for him is with your heart. I mean that, well, maybe we should have just asked him.'

'I wanted him to think someone like you would want him – unpaid and without any coercion or influence from me.'

'And someone like me does,' smiles Isabelle.

Veronica lets this sink in. Really sink in. This should be what she wants. Isabelle is a lovely girl, one whom she has grown rather fond of. But there's still that niggling word she can't help thinking: escort. Yet she's no better. She employed one. For her son.

'You don't want him with someone like me, do you?' Isabelle isn't stupid.

'I haven't said that.'

'Your silence does.'

'I don't think that.'

'I was good enough to be paid, but you don't really want me with him, do you?'

Veronica still can't say that she's happy with it. She isn't unhappy. It has just taken her by surprise; she needs time to digest it.

Isabelle shakes her head and abruptly stands, turning her chair over. It tumbles to the ground, inviting the eyes of the other customers. She picks it up with a noisy scrape. 'You just made me feel more like a whore than any of my clients ever did,' she hisses, her eyes teary.

'No,' cries Veronica. 'Stay. Finish your latte. I don't think that. This is all so ... I just never expected it.'

'You said no judgement.' Isabelle looks her in the eye. 'I said no judgement too. But you are full of judgement.' She turns and leaves.

'No, wait.' Veronica gathers her things together and leaves the money for the bill.

By the time she gets outside Isabelle is almost at her car.

'Wait,' cries Veronica. 'Please.'

Isabelle turns. Icy wind whips her hair violently about her face. She looks beautiful in the storm – wild and raw. They were raw, unstripped and uncensored together in her car that day. This time Isabelle is. But Veronica is bound by her prejudices.

'I'll pick Sebastian up on Monday as usual,' says Isabelle. 'I'll take him somewhere else, so you don't have to have me under your roof anymore. Then I'll take him to mine on Wednesday.'

'You don't have to go somewhere else.'

'I do.'

Something occurs to Veronica, and she asks before she can think. 'Have you told your dad?'

'What do you mean?' Isabelle stops fishing in her bag for her car keys.

'That you love Sebastian.'

'Not yet.'

'Why not?'

'What's that got to do with you?'

'You love Sebastian, so why aren't you as quick to tell him as you are to tell me?'

'Fuck you.'

Veronica is shocked. But why? She's the one behaving terribly.

'Don't bring my dad into this.' Isabelle moves a step closer, her face aflame. 'You got me into this. You got in touch with me and asked me to see Sebastian. So don't you fucking judge me!' She opens the car door.

'I'm sorry,' cries Veronica. 'Please, don't go like this. I'm sorry.'

Isabelle pauses but won't look at her.

'Keep the money,' says Veronica. She realises too late it sounds cruel, but she doesn't mean it be. 'What I mean is that you earned it. You deserve it. I don't mean that you're a … you know. Just that it's yours. You looked after my boy. I won't give you any more.'

'I don't want it. It's dirty to me now.'

'It isn't.'

'It is. You just made it that way.'

As Isabelle gets into the car something falls from her bag and splashes in the muddy slush. Veronica reaches for it – Sebastian's goggles. She rubs them on her scarf to clean them, but doesn't want to hand them over. Isabelle holds out her hand, wordless. Veronica drops them into it. He gave them to her – she has to. Isabelle slams the car door. Veronica watches as she drives away. She wants to cry; wishes she could. But tears won't come. If they did, she's sure she might feel better. Release the pressure in her head and heart. But she's left standing on a wintry path lined with spike-like trees, as cold inside as the wind is on her face.

37

ISABELLE DOESN'T WANT TO CHANGE THE AGREEMENT

Isabelle and Sebastian stand side by side at the edge of the pool. It's not busy at this late hour so the water gently laps at the pale-blue tiles. Sebastian stands so close to the edge that his toes curl over the side and are already wet; Isabelle stands a little further back, still dry, and afraid. She feels more self-conscious here in a pink bikini than she did when wearing lingerie for clients. She feels like a child. Scared and exposed. Looking at Sebastian in his red shorts warms her though. His body is a wondrous sight, even in the harsh, fluorescent lights; every detail of his taut stomach and muscled arms is lit. She longs to kiss him, to feel him against her.

But they are here to swim.

It's a Friday. They should be at Sebastian's house. On Monday – despite her fallout with Veronica at the weekend – Isabelle turned up at the house. Veronica looked surprised, then immediately pleased, and opened the door wide. Isabelle couldn't help but be cool after their heated exchange, but she was relieved Veronica let her in. There was no opportunity to talk because Sebastian came straight downstairs. She was glad. In his room, the first thing Isabelle noticed was the New York snow globe sitting next to his fish tank. She smiled when he shook it eight times.

When she left later, she asked Veronica for her bank details so she could return the £50,000, and Veronica gave them without argument.

'No judgement,' she said softly.

Isabelle didn't feel like reciprocating. She simply nodded.

On Wednesday Sebastian came to Isabelle's as usual and it was while he was eating his eggs that he suggested they deviate from the usual schedule and go swimming next time. Isabelle's heart had sunk. It was the last thing she wanted to do. But for him, she would. For him, anything. He looked so excited when he announced that he felt good about changing the agreement. That he was surprised at himself.

And here they are – to swim.

But Isabelle can't jump in. She can't move. It has been a long week. She's on edge. After confronting Dr Cassanby in his car last week, he hasn't come into the hospital. She heard that he'd taken compassionate leave over something. The irony; it is her who needs that kind of time off. Every day this week she has dreaded him suddenly turning up. Every door that opened on the ward corridors, she felt sick. Now she's finished there. She'll be back at university on Monday. But still she's agitated about it, and even more scared than usual of the water.

'Come on,' urges Sebastian, clearly ready to go. 'I'll count to three.'

She wishes he would hold her hand but knows he won't.

'I can't,' she says.

'It's not that deep. Only three metres.'

'I can't,' she repeats.

'It's because you don't have the goggles on.'

They are wrapped around her wrist.

'Neither do you,' she says.

'No, but I'm an expert swimmer. Put the goggles on. Then you'll be ready.'

'I won't. I'm a lion,' she says softly.

'No, you're not.' Sebastian frowns at her.

'You said lions don't like the water.'

'They don't.'

'Neither do I.' Isabelle starts to tremble. 'Remember, I told you my mum drowned.'

'You did.' Sebastian turns to face her, his arms crossed, eyes serious. 'She went out swimming too far at Scarborough, you said.

The current caught her by surprise, you said. And I said that you must respect the water. I said that if you find yourself unexpectedly in a river you must fight your instinct, not the water. You must float. But this isn't Scarborough. This isn't a river. This is a pool, and this is Sebastian. You're safe with me. I've had nine years of swimming lessons and I have four Water Rescue Awards. I only didn't get my fifth because I couldn't pull myself out of the water without using the railing or steps. I know the water, HoneyBee. You taught me sex and I'll teach you swimming. Don't you trust me?'

'I do,' she smiles.

I love you.

'Then jump with me.'

'Will you hold my hand?' she asks, hopeful.

'No, I won't, because that's dangerous. But I'll be next to you.'

Will you catch me if I fall?

'I can resuscitate you if you do drown,' he adds.

'That doesn't make me feel any better,' laughs Isabelle.

'Come on. I'm going in, you big cowardly custard.'

'OK, wait!'

She inhales.

'Ready?' he asks.

She nods.

They jump. The water swallows Isabelle down in a great, greedy gulp, dragging her to the bottom of the pool. It must be deeper than three metres. No, Sebby would never lie. She waits to surface but it doesn't happen. What did he say? You must float. But she isn't. Is Sebby? Bubbles fizz past her open eyes. She should have worn his goggles and then she'd be able to see more clearly. Where *is* he?

Then someone grabs her arm. Isabelle panics. Starts to swallow water and thrash. Is it Dr Cassanby? Simon? No. They're not here. The hand pulls her to the surface. She emerges with a gasp. Sebastian is at her side.

'Where were you?' he asks.

'At the bottom. I couldn't float.'

'You big lump,' he laughs, and swims away.

Isabelle can't help but laugh too. She kicks her legs to stay afloat. There is still a fear of being at the bottom of the pool, of drowning, but when she looks at Sebastian it dissolves. She lets herself enjoy the water. It is warm. It is cleansing. She is clean. She is not being paid to be with Sebastian. She is returning the money to Veronica. She is here because she wants to be. He is too.

He always was, she just had to get there.

In the water, they dance. Sebastian circles her, laughing. He tags her and swims away, and she reciprocates. His joy is pure here in this liquid heaven. He dives under the surface and tickles her tummy and then swims away again. She chases him, graceful despite her lack of ability, lifted by the water and by her happiness. Is she imagining that it's just the two of them? She looks around. No – the pool is empty. It's all theirs. Together they are weightless, neither of them heavier or lighter or bigger or smaller.

Equal.

Why was she so afraid? She's swimming with a natural. With the man she loves. She smiles. How could anyone *not* love him? Sebastian is so many things: strong and kind and angry and trusting and passionate and childlike and interesting and funny. In a relationship with him there wouldn't be complications, only honesty. No hurt, no force, no cruelty.

Isabelle is clean. This is a baptism. All the filth she was coated in after being an escort rinses away. Violetta dies. She is born again. Isabelle. HoneyBee.

'Let's kiss,' she says to Sebastian.

'No heavy petting allowed in the pool,' he says.

'But it's just us.'

'One kiss,' he sighs, as though she's a demanding child.

For Isabelle it's almost impossible to stop with one kiss. Their mouths are warm and wet. She presses to him. Wraps her legs around his waist and lets the undulating water carry them both, as one. She feels him respond to her, his youthful, instantaneous reaction a thrill.

'Don't make me want sex,' he says, 'not when we can't.'

He looks around at the tiled walls.

'It's past seven-thirty,' she smiles, knowing he was seeking a clock.

'We can't,' he says, serious. Gently, he unwraps her legs. Pats her head. 'I am very ready, but we can't, HoneyBee. Not here. It wouldn't be appropriate.'

She relents. After all, she taught him about consent. She has to respect his no too.

'OK, Sebby.'

She watches him swim back and forth, fast and smooth, an expert.

'I love you,' she whispers.

One day she will tell him. But not yet. It's too soon.

'I can swim on my back too,' he cries, and shows her.

She wishes she had a picture of him, so she could look when she's at home alone in her room. She should take one, of both of them.

After a while, Isabelle starts to shiver.

'You're cold,' Sebastian says. 'You should get out. It's dangerous to let yourself get too cold in the water.'

'Are you coming too?'

'In a minute. I have missed the water. I will be out soon.'

Isabelle dries off and changes back into her jogging bottoms and sweatshirt. She waits in the foyer. Sebastian joins her after half an hour, glugging a carton of juice, hair dripping onto his jacket.

They get into her car, shivering in the cruel February wind.

'Let's get a selfie,' she says, before fastening her seatbelt.

'I don't like photographs,' he says. 'How can I be sure what you'll use it for?'

'This is just for me,' says Isabelle.

'These humans – I call them that with sarcasm, HoneyBee – at college took some pictures of me once and drew rude things on them and posted them everywhere.'

'Oh, Sebby, that's awful. I'd never do anything like that. This is just so I've got something of you to have when you're not with me.'

'OK.' He looks thoughtful. 'I don't want to look at the camera.'

'Well, where will you look?'

'Have you got a book?'

'A book?' Isabelle searches around the car. 'All I've got is this.' It's a small book about the best hotels in London. She can't even recall where it came from.

'I will look at this.' Sebastian opens it and scowls at a page inside.

Isabelle finds her phone. While she leans towards Sebastian, smiling into the lens, he continues to glare at the book. The resulting picture is comical. But she loves it. She might get it printed and put in one of those snow globes you can pop photographs inside. She'll buy one for Sebby too. He can put it next to his New York snow globe, and she can put hers with the many others.

She starts the car up.

'Do you still want to have sex tonight?' she asks him.

'We did swimming.' Sebastian fiddles with his seatbelt, clearly not happy that it's twisted. 'That has satisfied me. Maybe we should do that from now on?'

'Instead of sex?' Isabelle leans over and sorts out his belt. Her face is right near his. Should she just kiss him?

'Yes,' he says. 'I think we should just go swimming three times a week instead of having sex.'

She doesn't kiss him; her heart contracts.

'Not ... have sex?' she repeats softly. She can smell him; the Comfort on his clothes, the Lynx body spray, the remnants of chlorine. How can she be with him and not kiss him, not touch him, not have him?

'We can rewrite the agreement if you like,' he says. 'Can I put the radio on?'

'I'm happy with things the way they are. Aren't you? Maybe we could go swimming once a week and have sex the other two days?'

'I think I liked doing this with you even more.'

'Did you?'

'I never did swimming with a girl. How do I get this radio to work?'

'Oh.' Isabelle pulls over.

'You look sad.' Sebastian studies her, his brow furrowed. 'It makes me feel anxious.' He touches his chest. 'You were very good, HoneyBee, and you gave me very good sex that I needed. I bet I'll never have sex that good in my lifetime because no one will ever be my first like you have been.'

'But ... our agreement?'

Sebastian searches in his pockets and pulls out the piece of paper she gave him almost a month ago. It's folded neatly. He opens it and reads it carefully aloud. 'This note promises that I will have sex with Sebastian every Monday, Wednesday and Friday, and make him eggs too, for as long as he would like to.' He looks at Isabelle, adds, 'Now I don't want to. You can have this back if you like.'

Isabelle can't take it.

'What about what *I* want?' she asks when she composes herself.

'We didn't write an agreement for that.'

'I guess we didn't. You keep that one anyway.'

'Do you want to do a new one just for you?' he asks, putting it away again.

No, she wants to say. *I just want there to be no agreement, no money, no schedule.*

Slowly she shakes her head.

'I might write one anyway,' he says. 'I'll give it to you next week. Can we go now?' He fidgets. 'I'm hungry. Are you coming back to my house to make me eggs?'

Isabelle starts the car up, her fingers clumsy. 'I bet your mum will make them.' The words choke her. 'You said she does them better than I do. I'll drop you off and go home.'

'Are you mad with me?' Sebastian studies her, his eyes serious.

'How could I ever be mad with you?'

'Quite easily. My mum finds it easy to be. So does Mr Evans.'

'Who's Mr Evans?'

'One of my tutors.'

'Oh.'

'Put the radio on for me, would you, HoneyBee?'

She does.

As they drive down the dark country lanes, Sebastian chats quite happily about college and bricklaying. When they arrive at his house, he jumps out of the car and heads inside. Halfway along the gravel drive, he stops and comes back. Isabelle smiles. Has he changed his mind? She opens the car window.

'Knock, knock,' he says.

'Who's there?' she asks quietly.

'Boo.'

'Boo who?'

'No need to cry, Sebastian will see you on Monday for swimming!'

When he has gone, she cries.

38

ISABELLE STILL HAS HER DAD'S SHOULDER

Still teary, Isabelle opens her front door and is greeted by a familiar tune – 'Sempre Libera', Violetta's great aria of freedom from *La Traviata*. The song takes Isabelle back to things she can't recall; she knows it must be because her mum and dad listened to it when she was a baby, maybe even in the womb. The Italian lyrics mean little, but they make Isabelle long for something she can't name.

'Dad?' she calls.

She follows the music and finds him in the living room, in the comfy and worn plaid chair that he always favoured, a mug of something on the coffee table. He looks tired. Old. His eyes are still bright though, despite the dark shadows beneath. A real fire flickers in the hearth, her flames like crimson dancers in a club.

'You're up late,' Isabelle says.

'Am I?' He cries over the music. He looks at the clock: it's ten-fifteen. 'This never used to be late for me,' he laughs. 'My night would just be starting now, lass.'

So would mine, thinks Isabelle sadly.

'You have to rest, Charles,' she says. 'You can't rush things. I know it's three weeks since you woke up, but that isn't long, not really.'

'Bugger that. I'm sick of being told to take it easy. Allan told me today that I should have a nap. A *nap*? In the afternoon? Pah!'

'Can I turn the music down a bit?'

He shrugs.

'Why are you listening to this?' She sits on the sofa opposite him.

'I'm feeling melancholic. Thinking of your mum. We met at this opera; you know that, don't you?' He smiles, remembering. 'Karen had on this gorgeous green dress and told me afterwards that she'd borrowed it from a friend as she'd had nothing decent to wear. She was sitting in the balcony opposite mine and kept sobbing, which tickled me no end. I chatted to her in the interval and got her number at the end. She told me that *La Traviata* means 'The Fallen Woman', and I thought she was hinting at her own past.' He laughs heartily. 'Nothing could have been further from the truth.'

Isabelle can't help but think of her mum's picture falling off the landing wall.

'Karen made me see it again on our first date, and that's when she explained the full story to me,' continues her dad. 'It's very tragic. About Violetta, who life cruelly leads astray, and who becomes a courtesan – a high-class prostitute. Then she finds true love, and of course that all ends in tears too. Karen adored it.'

I was Violetta. You called me Violetta too.

'I wish I could remember her,' Isabelle admits, sadly.

'She was a very special woman. Made me love the opera. At first, I thought it was all a bit gloomy, but she made me appreciate the tragedy, and of course the music. Now, when I listen to it, well, it's like she never left us.' He studies Isabelle. 'You look like her.'

'Do I?' Isabelle pauses, unsure. 'I...'

'What?' asks her dad.

'I think she was *here*.'

The fire spits and hisses in the brief silence following the words.

'What do you mean?' he asks after a few beats.

'While you were in the coma, I *sensed* her sometimes ... on the landing...'

'Come on, lass, you know I don't buy any of that spiritual crap.'

'Yeah,' sighs Isabelle, 'you'd also think that I'm my own ghost.'

'Your own ghost?' He frowns.

'Sebastian said it,' Isabelle says more to herself.

'Is that who you were with tonight?'

'Yes.' Isabelle fiddles with a cushion tassel.

'Are those goggles?' Her dad points to her wrist.

She hadn't realised she was still wearing them. 'We went swimming.'

'Is that part of your tutoring?'

'Yes, Dad. We do all sorts.'

'He's a curious one, isn't he?' he muses, eyes narrowed.

'Is he?' Isabelle feels defensive. 'How so?'

'How much does his mum pay you to tutor him?'

'I think that's *my* business, don't you?'

'Just checking you get enough. You spend a lot of time with him, and I wouldn't want anyone taking advantage. You're like your mum in that way. Too nice sometimes.'

'I don't mind ... I...'

'You what, lass?' he asks.

'I'm fond of him.'

Isabelle can't look her dad in the eye, afraid he'll see the truth. But Sebastian doesn't want sex now, only to go swimming. Does that mean he doesn't care? She tries not to think about it; she looks into the fire to distract herself. Maybe it means he *does* care? Swimming means so much that she should be happy he let her into his watery world. Maybe next time they're together she should tell him how she feels. If he knows that, he might admit he cares too.

'You OK, Isabelle?' Her dad's studying her.

'Yes. Long day.' She pauses. 'Dad...'

'Yes?'

'It was hard when you were in a coma.' There. She has said it. The thing she never wanted to burden him with.

'I'm here now,' he says. 'And I paid Allan today, and Jean. You don't have to think about that now.' He pauses. Is he going to ask how she really found the money? Has he worked out that the insurance pay-out can't possibly have covered all of his earlier care bills? 'You just think about your nursing.'

Suddenly she longs to tell him everything. To spill the ugliness into his lap. To vomit the vile words. To unburden herself. If the pool cleansed her body, shouldn't she have the strength to speak it aloud? To say, *Dad, I was raped.* Because it was rape. Simon raped her. Despite feeling clean after her swim, she can still feel his heavy body on top of her. Still feel Dr Cassanby biting her. Still feel Simon grabbing clumsily for her ankle. Still feel Cassanby throwing her onto a bed.

She did *not* deserve it. She was *not* paid to be treated that way.

But will her dad still love her?

Will Sebastian?

'Are you sure you're OK?' her dad asks again.

There's no avoiding his scrutiny – his bullshit-detecting gaze.

'No,' she admits. But she can't say it. Doesn't want to expose her shame.

With obvious effort, he pulls himself out of the chair and comes to the sofa. He sits next to her, and she puts her head on his now bony shoulder.

'It may not quite be the shoulder it was,' he says, 'but it's still yours.'

Isabelle closes her eyes. To the flicker of fire and the familiar smell of her father, she drifts off.

When she wakes later, the fire has almost died, her dad has gone, and there is a duvet on top of her. The goggles are digging into her wrist, so she pulls them off and puts them on the sofa arm. It's past midnight. She should move up to her own bed, but it's warm here. The simmering embers are hypnotic, and they relight a fire in her tummy; a fire Sebastian sparked when they had sex last week. She puts a hand over her stomach. Smiles.

Remembers.

Upstairs, in silence, with him, she climaxed for the first time in her life.

Isabelle had told Sebastian he could have the New York snow globe he loves, and he had shaken it excitedly and then put it on her bedside table so he could join her in bed. As the snowflakes settled on the skyscrapers, and he moved inside her – neither able to speak in case her dad heard – Isabelle's body surrendered to the exquisite pleasure of being with him. Her muscles contracted one after the other, a sweet spiral of sensual spasms. She gasped and buried her face in his neck.

'Is your breath OK?' he whispered. 'David at college had an asthma attack while he was digging. He sounded like that.'

'It's fine,' she smiled.

Afterwards, Isabelle looked at the skyline in the snow globe and saw herself running through crisp, golden leaves in Central Park with her dad on that rare childhood trip together. She had seen all the colours from above in his eyes that day – orange flecks of sunrise, blue of sky. She turned to Sebastian with his wild hair and damp lips, and saw those shades in his eyes too.

But what did he see in hers?

Because now he only wants to swim with her.

39

SEBASTIAN KNOWS WHAT LOVE IS

I shake Isabelle's New York snow globe for the tenth time and put it back next to Flip and Scorpion. I always shake it an even number of times. Even better if that even number ends in zero. Zero is neat. Perfect. Symmetrical. Life isn't. I know that. That's what I have learned by living. But I'm attempting to make it more symmetrical for everyone involved.

In fifteen minutes, I'm leaving to meet Norma Jean.

I can't sit still. I keep walking around my room and then back again, in perfect circles like zero times ten, twenty, thirty, forty. We're not going to KFC this time, even though it's Saturday. Yesterday I asked if she wanted to come and see my dad's bench on the river, and she said yes, without thinking for long. Mum's dropping me off and then picking me up after an hour and forty-five minutes. I think that will be a sufficient amount of time to tell Norma Jean how I'm feeling and give her my new poem.

Last night I updated my *How Will I Know It's Love and Not Indigestion?* poem.

I read it aloud again to see if it sounds right.

How will I know it's love and not indigestion?
How will I know to declare everything I feel inside
instead of taking a Rennie after curry?
How will I know when to follow my heart
instead of following my legs straight to the toilet?
How will I know when she is the one for me
and that I haven't eaten too many onion bhajis?
How will I know it's love and not indigestion?

How will I ever know the answer to my question?
I know now I know Norma Jean.
She has made me see
that the three Cornettos I ate in ten minutes
are not the reason my tummy is churning
like the washing machine just before it finishes.
Now I know it's love and not indigestion.
Now I know Norma Jean,
I have seen.

It does sound right. I hope Norma Jean likes it. I've written it inside a nice card that I nicked from my mum's drawer. I'll put it in the inside pocket of my coat. Eight minutes until we leave. I shake the snow globe again, ten times, put it back down, and then walk ten times around my room.

Sebastian, calls my mum from downstairs.

What?

Five minutes. Are you ready to go?

Yup.

I head down. Mum is already in her coat and has on a gold scarf I've never seen her wear before. Like she needs another. She has loads of questions in her face. It's a face she often has these days. She has been very quiet with her mouth though, not talking as much as she usually does. I'm worried about her.

I can see you have questions, I say, putting my trainers on. *On the way you can ask me six. OK?*

She smiles. *OK, darling.*

The car doesn't start straight away. When it finally does, she drives slowly because of the ice. I put the radio on and sing along to Beyoncé even though I'm annoyed that most DJs only play chart songs and not the great classics of the 1980s.

Go on then, I say after a bit.

What? she asks.

Questions.

OK. Who is your friend?

Question one. It's time she knew. *My friend is Norma Jean.*

She frowns, taking her eyes off the frosty road for too long. *Norma Jean. But that's a girl's name.*

Yes. She's a girl.

You never said.

No, I say, *you presumed she was a boy, Mum. Presumption is the road to error.*

Is she just a friend ... or is she more?

Question two.

At the moment, a friend. I turn the radio down because this is important. *But I intend to make my true feelings clear today.*

And what are your feelings, darling?

Question three.

I think I love her, I admit. *I'm going to be brave and tell her.*

Is Norma Jean...? My mum doesn't finish.

Question four.

Autistic? I say.

No, a nice girl, she says, annoyed. *That's what I was going to say.*

Yes, she's a nice girl, though I don't really know what that means. Isabelle is a nice girl too, but Norma Jean is a nice girl that I love. She likes animals, Mum. She never laughs when she shouldn't.

When she shouldn't?

Only at my jokes, not at my serious.

Ah. Mum pauses. *Don't you love Isabelle then?*

Question five if I ignore the previous one.

I do. But not the way you love girls. It's a bit like the way I love you except of course that's weird cos we have had sex. We're not going to now though. I have decided I can't now that I love Norma Jean. It would not be decent.

Mum studies me and I tell her to keep her eyes on the road.

Does Isabelle know that you don't love her? she asks.

Question six.

No, I say. *It's not what you blurt out, is it? I do know that.*

But what if she...?

Another question, but I can let it go.

What if she what? I ask.

We have arrived on Hessle Foreshore. Mum parks near a wooden bench and the rock with the acorn carved into it. The river is still. The beach is empty, which isn't surprising on a cold February day.

What if she what? I ask again.

Nothing, darling. What are you going to say to Norma Jean?

Mum, that is too many questions. And that stuff is private.

Yes, you're right. Are you sure…? I mean … I don't want you to end up hurt. What if…?

Another question. I'm agitated now. I know what her *what if* is.

What if she doesn't like me too? You think she couldn't, don't you?

No, she cries. *Not at all!*

I don't mind. I have prepared half of my brain for her saying that she just likes me as a friend. I would rather be more than friends, but I can be a friend if it means seeing her.

But what about Isabelle? Mum says again.

What about Isabelle? I snap. *She is special to me. She will be happy for me.*

My mum doesn't look like she thinks this.

Who knows Isabelle better? You or me. I know everything about her. You don't. Did she give you a snow globe? No. Did she take a photo of you both? No.

Mum looks sad.

I feel bad so I say, *You can ask one more question before I go.*

She strokes her scarf. *You know that I love you, don't you, darling?*

That's a waste of a question. You know the answer.

I don't have any other questions, she says. *It's nice that you are going to see your dad's bench with her though.*

OK. I have to go. It's eleven-twenty-six and Norma Jean is meeting me near the mill at eleven-thirty.

Will you be OK? Do you know where you're going?

No more questions, I cry, banging the dashboard and making her jump. *I'm twenty years and … do you know what? I don't need to say my full age. I'm a man, not a boy. That is all.* I open the door and the cold takes my breath away. *Can you pick me up here at one-fifteen?*

Yes. Have you got your phone in case?
In case what?
I don't know. In case she doesn't turn up or something.
She'll turn up, I snap.

I get out of the car and slam the door and head along the fore-shore path, towards the mill.

Norma Jean is already there.

I smile. I knew she would be. How cute she looks against the sun. Red hair like one of my mum's posh candles. Boots with different coloured laces in each one. Wearing her denim jacket that I always say she must be cold in. I'll let her wear my coat if she needs it. I smile. And she smiles back.

☐

I'm not going to share everything about my time with Norma Jean. It is my private business. I will say this though. She loved my poem. She read it really slowly in her head and then she looked at me and then she read it again out loud. Then I said that I loved her. She did not say if she loved me, but I don't mind. You don't give to receive. Anyway, she is going to come out for a meal with me. I will have to think where we could go and see if my mum will take us. I can work that out when I'm in bed tonight. I think Norma Jean is on her way to loving me or else she'd have run away when I said I loved her. We held hands when we sat on my dad's bench. I told her about him. I don't believe in ghosts, but I admit I did pretend he was there watching me.

You don't have to be autistic to like me sexually.

You just have to be human.

☐

I get into bed at exactly eleven o'clock, but I can't switch off. I toss and turn. I'm happy but I have so much to think about. I realise I need to write something before I can get to sleep. I get out my jigsaw box and find the agreement that Isabelle gave me. I read it again.

This note promises that I will have sex with Sebastian every Monday, Wednesday and Friday, and make him eggs too, for as long as he would like to.

Even though it is invalid now, I think I'll keep it because HoneyBee *is* very special. I can't have sex with her now that I have told Norma Jean how I feel about her. It wouldn't be fair to either of them. I go back in the jigsaw box and get out my *What I Liked About Isabelle* list.

I like how Isabelle looked in my goggles.
I like how Isabelle smelled.
I like how it felt when I was next to her.
I like how my penis feels when I think of her.

I used the word *like* a lot but I don't think you need to make list when you love someone. I *do* love HoneyBee. I'm just not *in* love with her. And I can't be Norma Jean's boyfriend – not fully committed – until I tell Isabelle this. Until we have a new agreement.

I get my pen and pad out and have a think. Then I write.

This note promises that I will always go swimming with HoneyBee when she wants to, as long as it fits around my schedule and the pool is open. I will never let her sink or get too cold.

I think she will be happy with this.
Now I can sleep.

40

VERONICA SPEAKS TO THE WIND

Veronica wakes on Sunday morning, her duvet on the floor after a restless night and her make-up still on after finishing a bottle of wine with her late supper. Sitting up makes her head thump; her pale, mascara-streaked face in the mirror opposite is a horror. She rarely drinks; now she remembers why. What was she thinking? She wasn't. Or at least she was trying not to.

Until yesterday, when Sebastian revealed his love for another girl, Veronica had begun to accept that Isabelle loved her son; she'd begun to imagine the two of them as a couple. Isabelle and Sebastian, together. She began to imagine days out. Christmas. Holidays. A family. The future. Real life.

But that won't happen now.

Veronica gets up, the effort making her dizzy. The house is silent, as though someone wrapped it in cotton wool. It's just after nine and usually Sebastian would be moving around. Concerned, she steals along the landing and carefully opens his bedroom door. From beneath a mound of duvet and two throws gentle snoring emanates, barely rivalling the bubble of the fish tank. Veronica smiles and closes the door. She is happy that Sebastian has found what he was looking for. She hopes everything went well for him yesterday, but then feels sad knowing it will mean pain for Isabelle.

In the kitchen she makes strong coffee and drinks it black.

After ten minutes Sebastian comes in, topless, his muscular chest in direct contrast to the Disney pyjama bottoms.

'I'm hot,' he says. 'Have you put the heating on too high? A man could die of heatstroke here.'

'It must be mild outside, darling,' she says. 'The heating is the same temperature as it always is. And you *were* sleeping under a duvet and two throws.'

'Have you been spying on me, Mum?'

'You weren't up, and I was worried.'

'You need to pick your worries, Mum. Brexit is bigger. Tigers becoming extinct is bigger. The pet shop changing their brand of fish food is bigger. Me sleeping in for once is minor.'

Veronica smiles. After a moment she asks, 'How did it go? You know, with Norma Jean?'

A large grin cuts his face in two; the kind that she hasn't really seen since he was small, and he would run around the room clapping his hands with sudden joy. Her heart melts.

'Though it is my private business, I will tell you I'm hopeful that Norma Jean and I have a future together, in which form I don't know yet, but we have a connection and it is more than just friends. We're meeting for lunch at college on Monday, and I might invite her here for an afternoon next weekend if that's OK?'

'That's wonderful, and of course it's OK.'

'Good. My eggs?'

'Your eggs,' says Veronica, delighted he wants them.

When he has devoured them and is about to disappear upstairs, Veronica says, 'You said yesterday that Isabelle will be happy for you and Norma Jean. Are you going to tell her?'

'Honesty is always the best policy.'

Her heart contracts. 'When will you tell her?'

'Do you mean what time?'

'No, just loosely.'

'I've decided that this isn't the kind of honesty that should have an exact time.' He sighs. 'I *know*, that isn't like me. I'll do it when it feels right.'

Veronica stares at the empty doorway long after he has gone. *When it feels right.* She can't argue with that. Washing his plate, she starts to worry about how he'll tell Isabelle. Will he do it in a way that cushions the blow? Should she warn Isabelle first, in gentle words? No. She should have more faith in Sebastian.

She puts the plate away

Maybe she should arrange to meet Isabelle and have a chat. Not to tell her but to see how she is. She wants to clear the air fully after her cruel words the last time they met. She calls her on the hallway phone, speaking quietly in case Sebastian reappears.

'Can we meet?' she asks. 'In an hour? The usual café?'

Isabelle pauses, perhaps unsure. 'What do we have to say to one another now?'

Veronica understands her reluctance. Last time they were together Isabelle admitted her love for Sebastian, and she treated her unkindly. 'I'd really like to see you. I feel bad ... you know, for last time...'

Isabelle doesn't respond.

'Are you still there?'

'OK. See you there in an hour.'

Isabelle is already at their usual window table, two steaming lattes in front of her, when Veronica arrives. Isabelle looks exhausted. Her hair is dirty and scraped back into a messy knot. She smiles at Veronica, but it seems an effort.

'First,' says Veronica, sitting down, 'I want to apologise. I was cruel last time. I said a lot of things I shouldn't have, things I don't think.'

Isabelle sips her drink.

'I'm sorry,' says Veronica.

Isabelle continues sipping. 'Sebby doesn't want to have sex now,' she says after a moment.

It isn't what Veronica expects to hear, though it makes sense with what she now knows.

'He just wants to swim. He said he likes doing that more with me.' Isabelle speaks with forced joviality. Veronica sees sadness in her eyes. 'I'm fine with it. I have to remember that Sebastian is a complex young man and maybe next week or month he *will*. This is all different for me now, you know, I don't need the money anymore, but he doesn't know that. It's just as it always was to him.'

This could be Veronica's chance to gently warn her; to say her son could be pulling away like this to save her feelings. But she can't speak.

'The fifty thousand will be back in your account tomorrow.'

'Oh.' After a beat Veronica leans forward and says softly, 'I wish you'd keep it. It's yours. You earned it.'

'But you don't get it – I didn't.'

'I don't mean that in a derogatory way.'

'I know you don't.' Isabelle holds her gaze for the first time. 'It's not because I see it as dirty. I know I said that last time. It's just that being with Sebby wasn't work. It was the most natural thing in the world. Work was being with the foul, sleazy men I had to endure.' She pauses. 'Not all of them were like that. That isn't fair really. A lot of the men I ... *had* ... were just lonely.'

Like my darling boy, Veronica wants to say.

'But some were...'

'Some were what?' asks Veronica.

Isabelle shakes her head. Veronica can see she's struggling not to cry.

'You can talk to me,' she says kindly.

'I can't ... say it...'

'Say what?'

Isabelle shakes her head again, more violently, face set.

'Say what?' repeats Veronica, putting a hand over Isabelle's.

A long pause.

Then, 'There was a man...'

'Yes.'

'He...'

Veronica waits, her hand still over Isabelle's.

'He... I ... didn't consent... He...'

Veronica feels sick. 'You mean he...?'

They look at one another again.

This isn't the kind of honesty that should have an exact time. That's what Sebastian said earlier.

The moment is timeless

Then Isabelle stands, slowly, as though it takes great effort and she doesn't want to draw any sort of attention to herself. The poor girl is probably exhausted from having been ogled and pawed and penetrated. And now it seems this wasn't always part of the deal. That even though Isabelle willingly gave every part of her body in order to pay for everything, some men *still* had to abuse that.

Veronica is so angry she can barely stay in her seat. The fire is back; the flames that flared when she had to face unhelpful professional after unhelpful professional about Sebastian, when she had to face teacher after teacher, when she had to face judging eyes after judging eyes, are hotter than ever. She rearranges her gold scarf with vigour.

Then she stands too, united with Isabelle.

'Let's go to the car,' she says softly. 'It's more private there.'

They pay, and Isabelle lets herself be guided to Veronica's car. Once inside, they sit in silence for a moment. Then Isabelle begins to cry; wracking, gaspy, agonising, ugly sobs that echo in the small space. Veronica leans over and holds her, tightly, the way she often did Sebastian when he had his breakdowns as a young child. Isabelle cries for a long time, until the sobs lessen into little gasps, and finally into nothing. In their wake, the quiet is deafening. The wind rattles the car as though wanting to join them.

'That needed to be out,' says Veronica kindly.

Isabelle nods, her face red.

'You're a very brave girl, Isabelle. For carrying that around. For doing all that you have.' She pauses. 'Was there no one you could talk to? A friend at university?'

'I didn't want to say it out loud. I thought I could bury it. Ignore it.'

'That never works.'

'No. And in some ways, I didn't have time for it. I've had too much to deal with. I bottled it up so I could care for my dad and do my coursework.' Isabelle plays with something around her wrist, and Veronica realises they are Sebastian's goggles. 'I don't have that many really close friends, you know. I'm not sure why I find it hard to get close to women. I often wonder if it's because I never had my mother. I never really ... well, learned *how* to be with females. Isn't that sad?' She looks at Veronica. 'In a way you're my only friend.'

'So we *are* friends.'

'I guess we are.'

'Well, as your friend, I apologise again. I didn't mean to make you feel like a ... you know, whore ... like you said last time. You can't imagine how sorry I am about that.'

Isabelle nods. 'It's fine. That's all me. How I feel. Worthless.'

'You're not worthless.'

'It's going to take me a long time not to feel that way.'

'Your value can't be measured in money, darling. You're brave and kind. Everything you've done has been because you love your dad.'

'Thank you.'

A robin redbreast lands on the front of the car for a moment. They watch him peck at his feathers and look around at the world until he flies off again.

'I love your son.' Isabelle turns to Veronica. 'I always will.'

'I know you do.' Veronica feels sick. *But my son doesn't love you*, she thinks. *Not in that way. I wish he did. And now he wants to tell you this...* Is it her place to tell Isabelle of Sebastian's feelings so that she can deal with it sooner, prepare for the impact of him saying it to her?

This is all Veronica's fault. She started it. She thought she knew what was best for Sebastian without consulting him. Even if she hadn't sought out Isabelle for him, he would have probably met Norma Jean anyway, and then Isabelle would have been spared this new hurt.

Oh God.

'I might tell him,' says Isabelle, almost to herself.

'What?'

She seems to remember Veronica is there. 'Nothing.'

'Tell me?'

'If I tell him I love him, then it's out and he might feel the same.'

He might not, Veronica longs to say.

'I think I will.'

'When will you do it?'

This isn't the kind of honesty that should have an exact time.

'Next time I see him,' says Isabelle. 'Tomorrow. I thought it might be too much for Sebby, but haven't we underestimated him already? He isn't a child.'

'No, he isn't.'

'We're supposed to go swimming tomorrow, but when you get back can you tell him I'll pick him up at the usual time and take him to mine instead because I'd like to talk with him?'

'Are you sure?' asks Veronica.

'I am.'

'Why don't you...?'

'What?'

Veronica wants to warn her. Could she delay them meeting? Surprise Sebastian with a day out tomorrow? But what would be the point? Hasn't she interfered in his life enough? She should let it go. Let happen what will. Sebastian's life isn't hers. This is what she's been fighting for all along. That he be seen as an individual. Someone with certain needs, but who knows his own mind, who isn't some *idiot savant* or fool. She has pushed for acceptance and equality for him her entire life yet managed to set limitations for him herself.

'Nothing,' says Veronica. 'You should do what you need to.'

Isabelle plays again with the goggles. 'I should go.'

'How's your dad?' asks Veronica.

'Getting back to normal – or as normal as can be after what he's been through.'

'Isn't that the only normal any of us can hope for?'

'It is.' Isabelle starts to open the door. 'I don't know when we'll see each other now. It depends on whether Sebastian and I remain together, doesn't it?'

'It doesn't have to depend on that.' Veronica realises she is sad at the thought of not seeing her. 'You can still call me. I'd like that.'

'Me too.' Isabelle smiles. It's weak, not quite reaching her eyes, but there.

'No judgement,' whispers Veronica.

'No judgement.'

'Friends?'

'Friends,' says Isabelle. She gets out of the car.

Veronica sits for a while, listening to the wind and wishing hard that Sebastian loved Isabelle back. But he doesn't. And she must let his life play out as it has to, not how she wishes it would.

'I love you, my beautiful boy,' Veronica says to the wind.

41

ISABELLE IS MEASURED BY A PERCENTAGE

On Sunday, after meeting Veronica, Isabelle went into town and found one of those snow globes that have a space for your own photograph. The only one she liked had a silver base, shimmering star-shaped flakes inside, and was made of glass, not the thick plastic of the cheaper ones.

But it was cracked.

The line was at the back, barely visible. Would she think only of its flaw? The others were flaw-free but lacked its beautiful finish. Isabelle didn't like them. With her thumb over the crack, she shook it a few times. This was definitely the one. She bought it and then went to Boots and had the picture of her and Sebastian printed, twice.

One for her, one for him.

At home in her bedroom later, she pushed one of the photos inside the snow globe and spent five minutes shaking it and watching the starry flakes settle around them. She smiled at the picture – at Sebby studying the Best London Hotels book intently, hair still damp from their swim, while she leans every part of her body towards him and smiles. It relaxed Isabelle to watch the silver whirlpool blur their faces for a moment before they re-emerged. She'd felt her dad was trapped in a bubble like this while in the coma.

She and Sebby are not trapped, only joined.

Maybe she should have bought a snow globe for her picture too and put it next to the others. Put her and Sebby alongside those exotic cities. The two of them are the centre of her world now.

Isabelle fell asleep with it in her hand.

Now it's Monday. Now she leaves to pick Sebby up, hoping

Veronica has told him they are coming to her house instead of going swimming. He's waiting on the path outside his house, scowling at the cold, as always. It feels like she's been doing this since the start of time, yet it's been five weeks. He gets into the car, filling it with Lynx spray and Comfort; and also comfort without the capital C. She'll never again smell these things without thinking of him.

'What do you want to talk about?' he asks straight away.

Veronica has told him then.

'Well, it's—'

'Because I have talking to do too,' he interrupts.

Isabelle's heart swells. 'You do? OK. We can do talking all evening then.' *And maybe do more than that,* she hopes. 'You don't mind not going swimming?'

'We can go swimming next time. Swimming is always there. Let's not decide a time tonight.'

'A time?'

'To talk,' he says. 'We had sex at seven-thirty. I liked that.' Isabelle's tummy contracts at the thought of their bodies together. 'But this isn't the kind of honesty that should have an exact time. We should listen to music and let it happen when it wants to.'

'We'll do that then.'

At Isabelle's house, she starts to go up the stairs and realises Sebby isn't behind her. He's standing in the hallway, red coat in hand, expression unreadable.

'Can we be different?' he asks.

'What do you mean?'

'I'd like to sit in your kitchen this time. See a different bit of you. Me and Mum often sit in ours.'

Isabelle isn't sure she likes the idea. She just wants to take Sebby upstairs and find a way to kiss him and feel his heated body against hers again. But she wants him to be happy too, so she says, 'You go in then and I'll say hi to my dad and join you.' She points towards the kitchen door and watches him disappear.

Then she finds her dad in the living room, asleep in the usual worn plaid chair, a mug of something on the coffee table. A real fire flickers gently in the hearth. She hasn't the heart to wake him, but she doesn't want him intruding on her and Sebby when she doesn't know what they might be talking about. She scribbles on a scrap of paper – *I'm tutoring Sebastian in the kitchen, I'll come and see you after* – and leaves it on the table, where he'll see it. Then she goes to her bedroom and gets the snow globe.

In the kitchen, Sebby has made himself comfortable at the walnut table. He has put the different placemats into a neat square. Isabelle sits opposite him. She wants to tell him how she feels. It fills her throat and mouth. She looks into his ripe-acorn eyes, wills him to know that she loves him and to feel the same. The fridge hums. Sebastian dismantles his placemat square.

'Can we have music on?' he asks.

'There isn't a radio in here.'

'OK.'

After a beat, Isabelle hands him the snow globe.

'Is this for me?' he asks, holding it carefully like his gorgeous, large hands might shatter it.

'Yes, for you.'

He shakes it vigorously and grins, any fear over its fragility gone. 'I like this more than the New York one. This is my new favourite. Look at us! I look scholarly, don't I? And you are beautiful, as you always are.'

'Am I?' The words catch in Isabelle's throat.

'Of course. You must know that – I'm not giving you new information.'

'I don't.'

'You are in the ways that matter. I remember you once said you were broken inside but...' He pauses, having seen the fine crack on the back of the snow globe. 'I still love it,' he says, after a moment.

And I still love you, she imagines him saying.

Isabelle wraps her arms around herself and feels for the first time in months like she actually might be beautiful. She wishes they were upstairs, in her bed. That's where she is the most beautiful of all.

'What did you want to talk about?' he asks

'I ... well ... oh...'

'Shall I go first?'

No, I should go first, thinks Isabelle, suddenly, urgently. But she lets Sebastian speak.

He puts the snow globe down on the table. The flakes settle. 'You have given me courage,' he says, solemn.

'Have I?' She smiles. 'Well, that's good.'

'Yes. Do you remember the poem I read you?'

'The indigestion one?'

'Yes.'

'Of course. It was wonderful.'

'I have finally realised when it's love and not just indigestion.'

'Have you?' Isabelle puts a hand to her chest.

'It's because of you,' he says. 'You gave me the courage.'

'I'm so happy.' She is.

'I *do* love you, maybe ninety percent.'

'Sorry?'

The fridge clicks and stops humming. In the silence, the sentence seems to have an echo: *Ninety percent, ninety percent.* The word 'love' made her soar, but Sebastian's emphasis on the word 'do' and his measurement of ninety percent stings. Ninety percent?

'I've been waiting for my hundred percent,' he explains. 'Now I've found it.'

'You have?' Isabelle is confused and yet senses the picture that will emerge when the starry flakes settle, when she lets him speak, won't be one she wants to see. The fridge hums again. Sebastian plays with one of the placemats.

'I've found Norma Jean,' he says.

Another woman's name pierces Isabelle.

'I am in love with her. A hundred percent.'

She lets it sink in. Feels sick. Sad. Desperately sad.

'Why are you telling *me*?' she asks, each word agony.

'Honesty is the best policy. I've realised that I can no longer have sex with you if I hope to have sex with Norma Jean. That is disloyal.

And I hope to one day know Norma Jean in this way. I understand this might hurt you because we have shared a lot, but luckily you don't love me a hundred percent either so we can still see each other and go swimming.'

Isabelle can't speak.

I do love you a hundred percent, her mind whispers.

'Do you want to know more about Norma Jean? I don't mind telling you. It's private but I'll always share these things with you.'

'Can you tell me another time?' she manages to say.

'What did you want to talk to me about then?' asks Sebastian.

'I ... oh ... it's gone...'

'Can't have been important then. That's what my mum always says.'

Isabelle gets up and goes to the kettle, just to do something. He doesn't love her. *He doesn't love her.* Yes, he does. Ninety percent. But that might as well be not at all. She flicks the kettle on just to create more noise.

'What do you want to do now?' Sebastian asks. 'We could still go swimming since we got the talking done.'

'I don't think I'm in the mood,' she says.

'Are you scared still?'

'What do you mean?'

'Of the water.'

'No,' she sighs. 'You made me feel safe there again.'

'Good. We can keep going.'

'You still want to see me then?' she asks Sebastian softly.

'Of course. Do you still want to see me?'

She nods. The kettle boils. She makes coffee she doesn't want.

'You haven't called me HoneyBee tonight,' she says without turning to face him.

'Haven't I, HoneyBee?

'Not until then.' She can't help but smile despite feeling sick.

'I didn't mean not to. You *are* my HoneyBee. You always will be.'

Isabelle closes her eyes. Then she takes her coffee to the table and sits again. She watches Sebastian shake the snow globe and peer closely at the falling flakes, face aglow. This is what she deserves. She lied to him. This is what she deserves. Veronica said her value could not be measured in money, but it has been measured in a percentage. And she deserves it.

But oh, she loves him.

'I have something for you too,' he says suddenly.

'You do?'

'Don't open it until I'm gone. I think you'll like it. You gave me one five weeks ago and then you did all you promised in it.' Sebastian goes into his pocket and takes out a small envelope, which he gives to Isabelle. She looks at it and puts it aside on the table, part of her afraid of what is inside.

'Shall we listen to music on my phone?' he asks.

Much as she adores him, she needs to be alone, to process what he's told her.

'I'm suddenly tired, Sebby,' she says. 'Can I take you home? Would that be OK? We can go swimming on Wednesday if you want.'

'Yes.' He leaps up. 'I will find a good spot for my new snow globe. And I have an assignment about health, safety and welfare in construction that will occupy at least two hours of my attention.'

Isabelle realises she has essays to write too, but no heart to do it.

'Can we listen to the radio on the way home?' he asks.

They do. Isabelle is glad of the distraction, of the random hits from the eighties, of the songs that Sebastian easily names and states the exact month and year of release. When they arrive at his house, he jumps out of the car with a quick goodbye and hurries up the gravel drive, turning to wave briefly before going inside. No knock, knock joke. After a moment, suppressing a sob, Isabelle pulls away. Then she sees him on the path in the rear-view mirror and stops with a screech of brakes.

He comes to the window. 'I was all mixed up,' he says. 'I didn't want to hurt you. I'm glad I didn't. My time of being all mixed up is over. Thank you.'

Isabelle doesn't know what to say.

'Knock, knock.'

'Who's there?' she asks.

'Isabelle.'

She smiles. 'Isabelle who?'

'Isabelle my great friend.'

And he disappears.

When Isabelle gets home, her dad is still sleeping in the chair. She sits on the sofa opposite him and quietly opens Sebastian's envelope. The writing inside is careful and neat. The fire spits and sparks. She reads the words three times over. Then she cries without making a sound so that she can be near her dad while she hurts so much, and yet not burden him either.

This note promises that I will always go swimming with HoneyBee when she wants to, as long as it fits around my schedule and the pool is open. I will never let her sink or get too cold.

42

ISABELLE'S CHILDHOOD IS RUINED

'I was waiting for you, lass.'

Isabelle starts. She has fallen asleep on the sofa, Sebastian's note still clutched in her hand. Her dad is standing over her, some emotion she can't decipher creasing the skin around his blue eyes. The room is cooler; the fire has almost died.

'I woke up and there you were,' he says.

He sits next to her, the sofa sinking so they slip towards each other.

'Where did you go earlier?'

'I was tutoring Sebastian.' Saying his name hurts now.

I do love you, maybe ninety percent.

Her dad studies her, and Isabelle can't read the look. She rubs her eyes and sits more upright. She feels queasy. Exhausted. She just wants to go to her room and get her head around the evening. But her dad is watching her, and she doesn't want to know why.

'I need to talk to you.' He moves a stray hair away from her cheek.

'You as well?' she snaps.

'What do you mean?'

'Nothing.' She sighs; the last thing she wants is more talking. 'Can we chat tomorrow, Dad? I have an assignment to do and it's late.'

'I'm sure it can wait.' He speaks firmly but not unkindly, the way he did when she was small and had broken the swing in the garden by being too rough or had stayed up later than she should reading *Peter Pan.* Thinking of their favourite book, she recalls all the notes he wrote to her while he was travelling the world, words that also kept her going while she lost him to the coma. 'Nick told me about something,' he continues. 'Something he's seen.'

'Seen?' She starts to get up. 'Can't this wait?'

'No, lass.' He takes hold of her hand, stopping her escape. She always loved how much larger it was than hers, how safe she felt when hers was inside his. He exhales. 'I love you, you know that.'

A hundred percent? she wants to ask.

'Of course I know it.'

'You can talk to me anytime, about anything, you know that, don't you?'

'Yes.' She wants silence now though. Her head hurts. Her heart hurts.

'Why didn't you tell me?'

'Tell you what?'

'Nick saw something online.'

'Online? I don't...'

She should see it coming but the picture is blurred by the whirl of silver flakes, ones she creates in her mind so she doesn't have to look.

'You, Isabelle. He saw you online. Pictures of you on a website. Offering your ... services.'

And the silver flakes settle in her mind. The embers in the hearth die a little more. Pictures of her on a website. There is only one website where her images have been. She remembers asking Gina to remove her page, knowing it would be futile, that online history can't be erased. Pam once said, 'If you want to find it, it'll be gone; if you want it to disappear, it'll stick around forever.'

Her dad knows.

Nick. Why didn't he come to her first, talk to her? How could he go straight to her dad? How did he even find her page? Gina took it down. Or did he see it before, and only now for some reason decided to tell Charles? Isabelle's mind throbs.

She can't look at her dad. All those nights. All those months. All that hiding. All that pain. All that blood. All those injuries. All the money she counted. He *knows*.

'I know what you've been doing.'

'What I've been...?' She plays for time.

'The escorting.' He squeezes her hand.

Isabelle shakes her head. Won't look at him. Shame is the most sordid of emotions; it slithers across the skin like filthy flies; it's a silencing hand over the mouth.

'I'm so sad, Isabelle. Not angry or disgusted. Sad.'

Still she is mute.

'I never wanted something like this for you. It must have been awful. I can't bear to think of it. *Why*? No. Don't answer that. I know why. God, I'm fully responsible ... that damned promise I forced you to make...'

Finally, Isabelle breaks her silence. 'You couldn't help being in a coma.'

'I know but I still feel terrible.'

'Please don't.'

'I do.' He pauses. 'But it isn't just that...'

He lets go of her hand and she remembers the park in New York when she was small, and he let go of it so she could run through the leaves.

'You don't understand,' says Charles now. 'I know this industry...'

'Casinos aren't quite the same thing.'

'It wasn't always casinos.'

'What do you mean?'

'Remember when I travelled sometimes? When Cecilia was here and stayed with you those weeks?'

'Of course I remember. I have all your notes.'

'I was visiting strip clubs,' he admits.

'You?'

'Not as a customer,' he adds quickly. 'As a businessman.'

'A businessman?'

'Yes. Checking them out. Then, for a while, I owned a handful of my own.'

Isabelle is stunned. And yet it isn't a surprise either. Didn't she always know on some level?

'You owned strip clubs?'

'Only for a year or two. I started out because the money meant I could look after you and keep this house that we love – that your mum loved so much. I saved most of it because I ... well, I knew I'd stop after so long.' He pauses, shakes his head. 'Because I couldn't. I hated seeing those young girls having to dance like that for old men. It was a seedy world. Girls trying to support families or paying for an education.' He looks at Isabelle. She looks away, ashamed. 'Some of them did more than dance to make good money. I grew up poor; you know that, lass. My parents could barely feed us all. So, I made sure these girls were well paid for dancing, so they'd not have to, you know, do extra ... but I could only do so much. It was out of my hands.'

'Out of your hands?' Isabelle feels sick. 'You chose to do it.'

'Sometimes we have little choice ... but it wasn't for me...'

Doesn't she know this as well as anyone?

'You're ruining the magic.' She jumps from the sofa and turns to glare at him.

'What do you mean?' Charles looks pained.

'You're ruining my childhood. All those places you evoked for me in your notes ... the lights, the streets ... saying you were like Santa Claus or Peter Pan. It isn't true, is it? They weren't magical trips.' She thinks of all the cities inside her snow globes – Hong Kong, Paris, New York, Tokyo, Berlin. 'What were you doing there?'

'I was scouting for girls ... to come and work for me. There weren't *that* many trips. I didn't do it for long. I'm sorry, Isabelle, I really am.'

'It felt like forever to me,' cries Isabelle. She backs away from him, banging her leg on the coffee table and spilling his now cold drink.

'I only did it to take care of you.' He leans forward and looks at her pleadingly. 'I did it to make sure there would always be enough money for whatever you needed. I had to be your mother *and* your father. I'm only telling you now to try and lessen the shame you must be feeling.'

'You've destroyed our trip to New York. That's one of my most cherished memories. Please tell me you weren't—'

'No. That was just us. A holiday. I'm sorry.'

'I'm going to bed. I just can't...'

Charles stands too, approaches her. 'God, I wish you'd known about the money in that account. I've done my best to take care of you and I've failed. You need never have been an ... escort.'

Isabelle wants to agree but realises she would never have met Sebastian. Even if he doesn't love her a hundred percent, she can't imagine being in a world without him in it.

'Please tell me no one hurt you?' asks her dad, desperately.

She sees Dr Cassanby, black tie shiny, eyes hard, hands cruel.

She sees Simon.

She closes her eyes.

Then she lies.

'Not really. I switched off. It wasn't so bad.'

'Why did you call yourself Violetta?' he asks sadly. Nick must have told him. 'That was my name for you.'

'It helped me endure it,' she admits. 'It was wrong of you to make my pet name a hooker from an opera. I was a child. It's like you tarred me with it ... and now look at my life...'

'It was just because the opera reminded me of your mum,' he says sadly.

'I guess I've ruined the lead character in *La Traviata* for you just like you've ruined New York for me. I guess we're even.'

'Oh, Isabelle.' He reaches out for her, but she can't let go and fall into his arms. 'Are you still doing it? You don't need to now. I'm here.'

'No,' she says softly.

'Are you sure?'

She nods. Turns away from him. She needs space. The night has been intense. Sebastian, and now this. She can barely breathe. 'I just need a moment, please, let me be.'

'OK, I will, lass.'

She starts to walk away.

'I still love you,' he says. 'Remember – we're not what we do, we're what we dream of doing.'

'Are we?' Isabelle stops near the door. 'I'm not sure anymore. I'm not even sure what I dream of now.' She opens the door to the hallway.

'I'm not stupid, you know,' he adds softly.

She pauses, halfway through the door.

'You're not just tutoring that Sebastian, are you? He's a client, isn't he? Why? I'm here now, you don't need...'

Isabelle shakes her head vigorously. 'Do *not* bring Sebastian into this,' she cries, turning to face him. 'I am *not* an escort anymore, I told you.'

'Come on,' her dad says gently. 'It would have to be for money for you to have sex with an autistic.'

'How dare you?'

'I didn't mean that quite how it sounded, lass. I just ... well, the poor kid probably has no other option. He seems like a lovely lad, but it must be more than just tutoring. I thought it was odd all along that he comes here and you both go into your bedroom.' He cocks his head. 'How come you're still seeing him if you don't do it anymore?'

'Shut the fuck up.'

Her rage flares at his crude dismissal of Sebastian. She enjoys how good it feels to yell at him. He recoils at the words. She has never spoken to her dad this way.

'And don't call him *an* autistic. It isn't a thing, and neither is he.'

'No, I didn't mea—'

'OK ... yes, it was for money. But just at first.'

Charles nods, calm, but this infuriates her more.

'You have no fucking idea about it, so don't nod patronisingly at me. If you really want to know, it was for a quarter of a million pounds.'

She enjoys the surprise on his face.

'Yes. Let that shock you, Dad. Know that about your sweet daughter. Two hundred and fifty thousand pounds. You were in a fucking coma, what choice did I have? When his mum came to me and offered me all that money to see her son three times a week and give him what he needed, what could I do? It meant I didn't have to fuck all those vile men. It meant I got to be with a sweet, sincere young man and pay for *your* care. So yes, Sebastian was a client, and his mum paid me a shit ton of money to sleep with him but now...'

A sound behind Isabelle makes her turn around.

It's Sebastian, shuffling from one foot to the other, his red plastic coat chafing.

Sebastian.

In the hallway.

No.

How?

No.

Sebastian: wind-swept, cheeks pink, mouth open, hands holding the snow globe with their picture inside, the air around him thick with Comfort and Lynx spray. His face. Oh God, his face. Isabelle gasps.

'Your doorbell doesn't work,' he says, eyes downcast now.

'It doesn't. What are you doing here, Sebby?' She goes to him. How much did he hear? Maybe nothing. Maybe he doesn't understand.

'Did my mum pay you to give me sex?' he asks, eyes still everywhere but hers.

She can't lie. Not to him.

You already did.

'Yes, but I gave it back,' she says in a gush. 'I gave it back as soon as I realised I...'

Her dad joins them in the hallway, slippers scraping the tiled floor.

'Go away,' Isabelle tells him in a low voice, and he stops in his tracks.

'My mum paid you to give me sex.' Sebastian states the words one after the other.

'She was only doing her best for you, because of how much you wanted to have sex with someone.'

'But she didn't *tell* me.'

'I know, but God, she loves you, Sebby,' gushes Isabelle. 'And you have to know that when I agreed to do it, I didn't know you like I do now. And then I got to know you ... and then I couldn't do it. I couldn't take the money and I gave it back ... because ... because I love you, Sebastian.'

She goes up to him and touches his gorgeous face. Carefully he takes her hand away and puts it on her own face.

'I love you,' she repeats.

'I brought this for you,' he says, monotone, his ripe-acorn eyes dim. He holds out the snow globe. 'You seemed sad when you drove away. I thought I'd hurt you. I was all mixed up again. I thought this would cheer you up.'

'How did you get here, Sebby?'

'I rang a taxi. Don't look at me like that. I know that look. You're thinking *how did he book a taxi? He's never done that before.*'

'I don't think that at all, Sebby.' Isabelle's hand is still on her own cheek. She has never seen him with such a blank look on his face, such despair in his eyes; never heard his voice so small. 'Does your mum know you're here?'

He doesn't answer.

Then he hurls the snow globe at the floor with a grunt. Isabelle jumps back, crashing into her dad. It smashes; shards of glass and star-shaped flakes scatter like fluffy seeds flying away from a blown dandelion. The photograph of them both lands on top of the carnage. To her horror, Sebastian begins punching himself in the face and wailing.

'Please don't!' She tries desperately to stop him.

Sebastian pushes her away so roughly that Isabelle's dad steps in, saying, 'Come on now, there's no need for this, lad, not in my house.'

'Leave him alone,' cries Isabelle, pulling her dad away. 'He's distressed.' To Sebastian she says calmly, 'Come upstairs with me, Sebby, it's OK, we can play music and talk.'

'No! I want my goggles back! I want my tiger book back!'

'I'll get you them if you just stop, *please*.'

But he starts wildly thrashing around the hallway, still hitting himself and wailing, the broken glass crunching beneath his feet. Isabelle can't bear it, but she doesn't know what to do. Should she try and hold him? Let him get it out of his system? She should call Veronica. Yes. She'll know what to do.

'I'm ringing your mum,' she says.

'No!' he cries, still punching himself. 'I don't want to see her! I don't want to see her! I don't want to see her!'

'OK, I won't,' says Isabelle. 'Please stop. You'll hurt yourself.'

'Come on now, lad,' tries her dad. 'There's no need for this.'

Sebastian screams, '*No!*' and turns and runs out of the front door. Isabelle follows. Is the taxi he came in still waiting for him? No – the drive is empty apart from her car and her dad's jeep, which hasn't moved for months. He disappears into the blackness beyond the string of lights along the lawn and Isabelle begins to follow.

'Sebby!' she cries.

'Let him go,' says her dad, holding her arm.

'Let *me* go. I need to make sure he's OK.'

He grips harder as she resists. 'He needs to let off steam, lass. Once he calms down, I'm sure he'll go back home, and maybe then you can talk to him.' He closes the front door as Isabelle surrenders.

She paces the hallway. Poor Sebastian. He must be heartbroken. In agony. She can't bear it. Her own hurt is fine, but his is too much to cope with. What should she do?

'Is it true that he didn't know about the arrangement you had with his mum?' asks her dad.

'I don't want to talk about it.'

'Why didn't she just tell him? I don't understand.' He pauses. 'Do you really love him?'

'Yes. Is that so fucking hard to believe?'

Isabelle gets her coat from the peg.

'Now where are you going?'

'To Veronica's,' she says.

'Is that his mum?'

'Yes.'

'When will you—'

She shuts the front door on his question and runs to her car. She has a flashback to that other moment of escaping to her car in the dark, naked then except for her heels, outside Simon's house. His hulking frame appears in the doorway again. No. Just her dad. Watching her, face sad.

Just like that night, Isabelle pulls away, puts her foot down, and doesn't look back. Just like that night, she waits for the tears. But this time they are for Sebby. She waits for the physical hurt over her dad to kick in. It doesn't happen. Just like that night, she whispers two of the lines she once wrote, over and over and over.

I think there's a ghost on our landing. And she wants to catch me if I ever fall the way he did...

But the ghost has gone.

And now Sebby has gone.

43

SEBASTIAN RUNS AND RUNS AND RUNS

I run and run and run.

It is cold. I am mad. Mad, mad, mad. It heats me up. I'm on fire. I keep running and running and running. It's like swimming, just less wet and I don't need goggles. I don't know where I'm going though. I run until the road ends and then go down another and run until that one ends and then go down another and run until that one ends too. I have to run or else the sadness will catch me. I don't want to be sad. That's the hardest. Stay mad. Stay hot. Stay running.

So much to think about.

Think of one thing at a time.

Yes. Yes. *Yes*.

Isabelle said she loves me.

I smile.

No, Isabelle lied. That first.

Isabelle lied before she loved me. Isabelle's love does not mean I should ignore that. She never told me that she got money to be with me. She never wrote that in her agreement. The small print tells us all the things we don't really want to know, the things we should know. I always read the small print. When I was going to Latvia, I read forty-two pages of small print about my booking and my insurance package. Isabelle should have written *in exchange for two hundred and fifty thousand pounds* after *This note promises that I will have sex with Sebastian every Monday, Wednesday and Friday, and make him eggs too, for as long as he would like to*. Then I could have made an informed choice.

I was not informed.

I run and run and run some more.

All I can hear is my panting and my Puma trainers pounding the ground. All I can see is my breath and the streetlights blurring past. All the things I never knew bang around in my head, bumping into each other.

Isabelle loves me.

That again.

She *loves* me.

I remember when I wanted her to love me so much. Now she does and I want her not to again. I don't want her to get hurt. But she must be. Because I love Norma Jean and I've told Isabelle. I should be even madder with her because she lied to me about two hundred and fifty thousand pounds. I can't even picture that kind of money. Maybe if I do – maybe if I visualise each note in a pile and start counting them one after the other – then I'll feel better.

But it doesn't work.

I keep hearing what Isabelle said to her dad when I was in the hallway. *When his mum came to me and offered me all that money to see her son three times a week and give him what he needed, what could I do?* I don't want to hear it, but it won't stop. *It meant I didn't have to fuck all those vile men. It meant I got to be with a sweet and sincere young man and pay for all your care too. So yes, Sebastian was a client, and his mum paid me a shit ton of money to sleep with him but now...*

And then Isabelle turned and saw me. Her face went white. People say that phrase all the time but hers really did. I should be even madder at her, but she isn't the one making me have to run and run and run.

I look at the time on my phone.

Twelve-thirty-two.

There are ten missed calls and a voice message from my mum. I don't care. Glad it's on silent. She rings again, but I click the red icon. Has she realised I'm not at home and she's worried about where I've gone? Or has Isabelle gone there and told her I know what they did? I don't care. Let her worry. Let her hurt.

Twelve-thirty-three now.

How can it be so late? I've never been outside my house at this time. I'm in a world I have never seen before. Is it blacker at this time of night? I look around but it's hard to see while I'm running. I stop for a minute. Exactly a minute. No. I have seen the night like this. I have not hurt like this before though.

I start running again.

Sweat drips down my back.

My forehead is damp.

I remember being small and thrashing around and hitting myself when things confused or angered me. Back then Mum would hold me tightly and quietly for a long time, and even though I didn't like it at first, it did something. My breathing would slow down and everything I had been mad or confused about wouldn't seem as important anymore. Now I never want to see her again.

I run and run and run.

One-twenty-two now.

Five more missed calls and another voice message too.

I'm still mad.

Part of me doesn't believe it. Could HoneyBee be lying? But that doesn't make sense. Why would she tell her dad something like that when he's just relaxing in his slippers? Judge Judy once said that if it doesn't make sense then it usually isn't true.

How could my mum do this to me?

I run and run and run.

It isn't about the money. I don't mind so much about that. Money is for buying things. Mum paid for me to have swimming lessons. She paid for me to go horse riding once, but I didn't like the saddle and it made me sneeze. She paid for me to go on school trips to Berlin and Whitby. There's nothing wrong with paying someone for sex either. I might have done that, but I only have £316.45 in my account and obviously Isabelle is more expensive than that.

It's because Mum didn't tell me her plan.

She didn't ask me if it was OK to give Isabelle money to be with me. One thing I've always liked about my mum is that she asks me. Do I want to go for a walk? Do I want to watch a movie? Do I want to have eggs? I don't always like her choice of scarves, but she has always included me in her important decisions.

How dare she try and tell me about sex?

How dare she tell me girls should be over eighteen?

How dare she tell me to always get permission?

When did she ask for mine?

I run and run and run.

It's a good job I'm fit from swimming or I think my heart would explode. I'd like to go to Norma Jean, but I've never been there. I know the street, but not which house is hers, and it's rude to go to a house in the middle of the night unless someone has died.

Eventually I'm so tired I have to slow down.

It's two-forty-five.

No more missed calls.

Now the sadness comes.

I don't want it.

I want my mum, but I don't want her.

I want to be mad but it's fading.

My heart slows too.

I sit on a bench by a pond. I have no idea where I am. It looks like a small village. It's quiet. I like it here, in the dark. I like no one knowing where I am, even myself. It's as though I don't exist. I don't know if I want to exist anymore. I shiver. I'm glad I have my Hull City hat and my leather gloves on now I've stopped running. Sad is hard. Sad is heavy. I'd do anything not to feel like this. It's overwhelming. I think of Norma Jean. Of how happy I feel when I'm with her. But it doesn't work. Even love that's the full hundred percent isn't enough right now.

I suddenly wish I could swim. Be back in the water like I used to be.

No.

I wish I could sink.

Sink to the bottom of the sea and never come up again.

I cry.

I sob and sob and sob.

I am swimming in my own tears.

When I stop, I get out my notepad. It's small and always in my pocket with a pen. I start to write. I make a list. A *How To Sink* list, recalling all the things I know you have to do to not stay afloat. I am sinking already. I might as well sink in the water. I promised I would never let HoneyBee sink or get cold, but I never promised anyone I wouldn't let myself sink or get cold.

Will they care?

When I've written my list, I turn my phone off for good and curl up on the bench. I'm surprised that I fall asleep. I only know that I have when I wake up, and the sun is coming up over the trees like a big orange sponge. I have to admit I'm scared now. I don't know where I am.

But I do know where I want to go.

The river.

My benches.

To sink.

I have a card in my pocket that the taxi driver gave me earlier when he took me to Isabelle's house. He was nice. He was called Bob Fracklehurst and he liked singing to all the eighties hits like me. He was a bit sad too because his wife just died. I turn my phone back on and call the number.

Hello, Pete's Taxis.

Hello, this is Sebastian James Murphy, I say.

He laughs. *Great. You want a taxi?*

Yes, please.

When? he asks

Now.

Where are you?

I don't know.

You don't know? He laughs again.

I'm in a village. There's a pond. I look around. *There's a pub called The Green Dragon.*

Ah, you're in Welton. Where do you want to go?

The river, I say. *Hessle Foreshore.*

I'll send you one now.

He hangs up and I turn my phone off.

It's six-thirty-eight.

That's it then. I'm going to the river. I'm going to my benches. My dad's bench. My favourite place. To sink. I don't want anyone to rescue me.

Mum always called me her beautiful boy.

But she treated me like her beautiful idiot.

Now I'll be her beautiful sinking Sebastian.

44

VERONICA DEALS WITH HER SCARVES

Veronica turns the lights off and heads upstairs.

When Sebastian went to Isabelle's earlier, she sat in the kitchen, anxious about what was happening there, and tempted to open a bottle of wine again. Remembering her ruined face the other morning when she'd had too much, she resisted and instead went through her scarves. Sebastian says she has far too many, that there are people in the world who don't even have shoes.

When he came home – much sooner than usual – he was subdued. She asked if he wanted eggs and he said no. She longed to ask if Isabelle had told him anything in particular but resisted. Surely he would tell her if anything had happened? Maybe not. He doesn't tell her everything anymore. She should be glad. He has matured so much recently, been more settled. Even Tilly commented upon it the other day, saying how happy it made her to see him contented.

As Veronica climbs the stairs it hits her how different Sebastian is now from just a few months ago. She stops for a moment and savours the thought; remembers his desperate sex drive, those horrible boys hurting him on the bus, that awful meeting with the sex-clinic worker, Mel.

Those days feel like a distant memory.

Veronica knocks and opens his bedroom door to say goodnight, a habit she has never been able to stop, despite his age. It takes a few seconds for her to register that he isn't there.

'Sebastian?' she says, despite it being obvious the room is empty. '*Sebastian*?' She looks under the bed – which is ridiculous because he's too big to squeeze under there – and flings the wardrobe doors open. Nothing.

Running onto the landing, she calls his name again. Perhaps he stole back downstairs without her knowing? She searches the shadowy rooms, feeling sick when each one is empty too. At a sudden hammering on the front door, she spins around. Sebastian? But why would he knock?

She runs to the hallway and opens the door, filling the house with icy air.

It's Isabelle, face distraught, hair tangled.

'Is he here?' she asks.

'Sebastian?' cries Veronica. 'No, he's gone.'

'Shit. Maybe he's still on his way here.' Isabelle shivers on the step.

'I don't understand. On his way *here*?'

Isabelle comes into the house. 'He came back to mine,' she says.

'To yours? When?' Veronica looks outside. 'Where is he? I don't understand.'

'He just left mine. Ran off.' Isabelle pauses. 'He knows.'

Veronica closes the door. The cold stays with them. 'That you love him?'

'Yes. But not just that.'

'What else is there?'

'*He knows.*' Isabelle holds her gaze.

Veronica steps back, hand on chest. She grabs the small hallway table for support. It's like Isabelle has physically punched her. Veronica knows what this means. He knows about the money. But far worse, he knows she lied to him.

'You *told* him?' she cries, angry.

'No.' Isabelle wraps her arms around her body, still shivering. 'He heard.'

'What do you mean he heard?'

'I didn't know he was there. I was telling my dad because he knows I was an escort. And I said that you had paid me to be with Sebastian. I turned around. And he was standing there. His *face*. He heard it all.'

'Where is he now?' Veronica grabs Isabelle's shoulders.

'I don't know.'

'What happened?'

'It was awful. He was hitting himself and thrashing around.' Isabelle shakes her head as though to dislodge the awful scene. 'I tried to calm him, but I didn't know how. Then he ran away.'

'Why the hell didn't you go after him?'

'I tried, but my dad stopped me, said I should let him calm down. I thought he'd come back here. Maybe he will.'

'How did he get to you?' Veronica's brain works overtime.

'In a taxi. But it was gone when he ran off. I don't know where.'

'If he's walking around, he could be anywhere.'

'I know. I'm so sorry. What should we do?'

Veronica runs to the kitchen where her phone is charging for the night. She never keeps it by her bed like most people do – the only person that matters is safe in the house with her each night, so there's no phone call worth having her sleep disturbed by. She finds Sebastian's number and dials. It rings and rings, and eventually goes to voicemail. She dials again. Lets it ring.

'Should we call the police?' Isabelle follows her.

'What the hell will they do that we can't?' Veronica hangs up and rings him again. 'They'll only be worried when it's been twenty-four hours, won't they? And he's a grown man, remember.' Still no answer. She leaves a message. 'Sebastian, it's Mum. Please call me as soon as you hear this. I know I've hurt you and I'm sorry. I'm not mad and you're not in any trouble, I just want to pick you up and bring you home. I love you, darling. Please ring me.'

'I know he's a man, but...' Isabelle doesn't finish.

'Fuck the autism,' cries Veronica, wincing at her own language. 'Fuck it! I can deal with this. I don't want the police interfering and judging. What have any professionals ever done for Sebastian? For me?' She shoves the neat pile of scarves off the worktop with a grunt; she brought them all downstairs earlier to bag some up for charity. They land on the floor in a cloud of colour. 'He's been doing so well. I was just thinking how far he's come. This could set him right back. Do you know what you've done, Isabelle?'

She looks utterly distraught. Veronica knows she isn't being fair. Isabelle didn't start this. But Veronica can't stop. It's much easier to blame this poor girl for the mess they now face. How must Sebastian be feeling? He must be distraught. She knows how wild he can get. They need to find him.

'He can't handle this kind of stress,' she cries. 'He could be in danger.'

'I'm sorry,' sobs Isabelle.

'I told you at the start he could never know.' Veronica tries to breathe slowly. After a moment she says, 'I'm sorry. It isn't your fault. I'm to blame for all of this. Let's be practical. Where would he go?'

'The river,' they both say at the same time.

'His bench,' adds Veronica. 'It'll be freezing. We need to go, right now.'

She grabs her phone and heads for the door. Isabelle follows.

Veronica drives them towards Hessle Foreshore, trying to stick to the speed limit and almost going through a red light. She tells Isabelle to call Sebastian again a few times on her phone, but he still doesn't pick up. It's twelve-twenty-five.

Where has the night gone?

At the foreshore they leave the car at the Country Park Inn and hurry along the muddy path through the tunnel of trees, almost swallowed by the blackness. There are no streetlights down here, only the orange ones on the bridge reflected softly in the water below, a glow that barely reaches the riverbank. As the trees disperse, they run onto the chalky path by the river, the visibility a bit better here. They can't see the two benches until they are upon them; then it's evident Sebastian hasn't come here after all.

'He's not here,' cries Isabelle, over the wind.

'I can see that,' snaps Veronica.

'Maybe he didn't get here yet. He might be on foot remember – though if he called a taxi to come to me, he might call another to come here.'

Veronica kicks the bench on the left. Then kneels and touches it.

'Pete,' she whispers.

Isabelle doesn't speak.

Veronica wishes Pete was here. Decisions are so much harder to make when you're alone. Being a parent is so much tougher when it's just you.

'We should wait here in case he comes,' she says.

'We'll freeze to death,' cries Isabelle.

'He's out in it too.'

'He might not be.'

'What do you mean?'

'He could be with a girl called Norma Jean,' says Isabelle quietly.

'You know about her?' The words come out before Veronica can think.

'You know too?'

'Yes,' admits Veronica.

'Why didn't you tell me when we met?' Even in the darkness, hurt is evident in Isabelle's eyes.

'I wanted to warn you because I wasn't sure how Sebastian would break it you, but I decided it wasn't my place to.'

Isabelle nods, says sadly, 'He could be with the girl he loves.'

'I don't know where she lives.'

'Does he know? Would he have written it down?'

'I don't know. I don't think so. No, he's never been to her house. And trust me, I know how Sebastian thinks. He would never go to a house uninvited.'

'He came to mine tonight.'

Veronica doesn't know what to say.

'Look,' says Isabelle. 'Why don't we go and sit in the car. If he does come down here, we'll see him go past.'

Veronica reluctantly agrees, and they head back along the path, coats tugged by the angry wind. The traffic is almost non-existent on the nearby dual carriageway and this makes the sound of the choppy river all the more turbulent. Once in the car, she rings Sebastian's phone again, knowing he won't answer. It's torture not knowing where he is, not knowing if he has done something stupid.

It's almost one o'clock.

'I can't stand just sitting here,' she cries, reaching for the door.

Isabelle puts a gentle hand on her arm. 'We're in the right place, I'm sure of it,' she says. 'This is where he would come.'

Veronica surrenders. 'You're right.'

'Let's just keep our eyes on the path.'

'OK.'

'And keep ourselves occupied in the meantime.'

'OK.'

Veronica is grateful for Isabelle's calm suggestions. She turns the radio on low. When Billy Ocean's 'Suddenly' comes on, she wants to cry.

'He used to play this over and over,' she says. 'When he was first seeing you.'

'Did he?' Isabelle looks touched.

'Not now though,' says Veronica, before she thinks.

'It's OK. He loves me ninety percent. That will have to be enough.'

'Is that what he said?'

'Yes.'

'Can I ask you something?'

'Yes.'

Veronica looks at Isabelle. 'Do you think you fell in love with Sebastian because you've been in such a dark, difficult place? Because he came into your life at a moment when you needed something?'

Isabelle shakes her head. 'Why can't you just accept that I can love him, regardless? Is it still so hard for you to think an everyday girl like me could care for him like that?'

Veronica tenses. 'That isn't what I meant.'

'I'm in love with him, and he isn't with me.'

'For what it's worth, I wish he was.'

'You do?'

'I do.'

They stare out of the window. An old Madonna song plays, and

Veronica knows Sebastian would be able to name the title and provide the year it was released. The wind occasionally rocks the car as though to lull them into sweet oblivion. Veronica wills him to appear. She calls his phone again and leaves another pleading voice message. Then she and Isabelle stare out of the window, the car clock measuring their slow, agonising wait.

'He's OK,' says Isabelle after a while.

'You can't know that.'

'He has to be.'

'He does.'

They look out of the window again.

'My dad used to own strip clubs,' Isabelle says after a while.

'Oh.' Veronica is surprised by the words but glad of the distraction from desperately scanning the carpark and path until her eyes hurt. 'Is that why you were able to be an escort? You knew he'd accept it because he worked in that industry too?'

'No, I mean I found out tonight. Dad told me because he'd found out I was an escort. His casino manager saw me online. What a night, eh?' Isabelle laughs but it sounds like a croak. 'He's always worked in the entertainment industry, but I didn't know about the other stuff.' She pauses. 'My childhood is a different thing now. The man I adored when I was small isn't who I thought he was. But I'm a hypocrite because I've done what I've done, and I'm the same girl.' Isabelle pauses as though realising something. 'But no, I guess I'm not. I'm not the same girl at all. It's almost destroyed me.'

'Only almost,' says Veronica.

Isabelle nods.

'Maybe your dad was doing it to care for you, just as you cared for him. And that just means that both of you would do anything for the other.'

Isabelle shrugs.

'Do you think I'm terrible for what I did?' asks Veronica. She wants the truth while they are talking about things they're ashamed of. 'When I came to you, I mean. Offering you all that money for my son.'

Isabelle looks her in the eye. 'I don't. You did it because you loved him. You were desperate and felt you had no other option.'

'I only kept it secret from Sebastian so he'd think you had chosen him.'

'And I would have. Now I know him, I would have.'

'I didn't think so.' Veronica stifles a sob. 'What kind of mother am I?'

'A good one. Stop being so harsh on yourself.'

Veronica nods. 'You stop being harsh on yourself too then.'

'No judgement,' says Isabelle.

'No judgement.' After a beat, Veronica cries, 'And now he knows. Where the hell is he? My poor boy. Knowing his own mother didn't even think anyone could want him.' She suddenly thinks of something. 'What if he's gone home?'

'You think he would?' asks Isabelle.

'We're sitting here, but he might have walked home. He'll be mad, upset, but he's so honest he'll want to have it out with me.' She starts the car up. It's two-thirteen. 'He'll be wondering where I am.'

'Wouldn't he have called you?'

Veronica pushes the answer to that away. She drives; she drives hard. Isabelle warns her twice about the speed limit, but she puts her foot down instead. The charcoal trees and hazy lights pass by in a blur. Her boy will be at home. She's sure of it. She doesn't slow down, even at a sharp bend renowned for being a crash hotspot; and as they hurtle into a hedge all Veronica sees is Isabelle's open-mouthed face; all she hears is Duran Duran on the radio; all she does is shout her son's name into the night.

SEBASTIAN KNOWS THE WATER MORE THAN HE KNOWS HIS MUM

It's seven-twenty-five.

Almost time.

I climb over the rocks to get to the water. There are gaps that try and trap me. It's a good job I must keep my shoes on. I'm out of puff when I reach the small beach. The waves lap at my Puma trainers while I catch my breath. They're ruined, which is a shame because they cost fifteen pounds fifty.

I read the rest of my *How To Sink* note. Number three is *Take a Vertical Position In The Water With Your Feet Pointing Down*. I'll do that when I get to the middle. Number four is *Get Into a Tucked Position*. This is because objects sink in water if they take up less space. I know the rest. Just do the opposite of everything I normally do to try and float.

It's seven-thirty now. It's the right time.

It used to be my favourite time when I was with HoneyBee. Now it's my last time. So here I go.

To sink.

ISABELLE REALISES THE TIME

The car is still.

Isabelle looks at Veronica; she looks back, her face bluish in the dashboard lights, her eyes glazed over like a movie zombie. They don't speak. Everything seems quiet despite the wind whistling around them, and the radio still playing. Isabelle can't name the song, though it's familiar. *Sebastian would know*, she thinks with a longing, sad ache.

She and Veronica are both rigid against their seats, the seatbelts having kept them safe, airbags fat to their faces.

'Are we OK?' asks Veronica, voice muffled, clearly dazed.

'I think I am. Are you?'

'The back of my head. I think I banged it. I should have slowed down.' The airbags deflate. Veronica looks around. 'What should we do now?'

'Get out,' suggests Isabelle. She tries to open the door but long grass outside, and the fact that the car is tilted downwards into a ditch, make it tricky. With a lot of shoving, it's wide enough for her to exit. If she is hurt, the adrenaline must be suppressing it; she feels on edge and alert.

Veronica gets out, stiffly stretching and touching her head. 'Oh, my word, the car,' she cries. 'Look at the bonnet – it'll be a write-off.' She glances at Isabelle. 'I'll think about it tomorrow. What should we do now?'

'Your house is just over a mile from here, isn't it?'

Veronica nods. Isabelle is concerned about her. She should check her over but what can she do in a dark, deserted lane at almost quarter to three in the morning.

'We can walk there in twenty minutes,' says Isabelle. 'Are you up for that?'

'I think so.'

'Link arms with me,' suggests Isabelle.

They walk the poorly lit country lane towards Veronica's village, their breaths smoking in unison, icy ground crunching beneath their feet.

'This is what you call street-walking,' jokes Veronica.

Isabelle can feel that her friend is trembling and is sad for her. When they get to the house, she'll make some sugary tea and check her head for injury.

'Not far now.' Isabelle tries to sound encouraging.

Once at the house, Isabelle insists on making a sweet drink and suggests looking at Veronica's head, but she bustles about, ringing Sebastian repeatedly and pacing the length of the kitchen. Despite these circumstances, Isabelle loves being here. She feels close to him. Wants to go to his bedroom and wrap herself in his quilt.

'Still no answer,' says Veronica. 'Should you drive around and look for him in the village while I wait here?'

'Do you really think he'll be there?'

'No,' admits Veronica. 'I can't bear waiting here, but I don't want to go back to the river either. How many hours has it been since he was at your house?'

'I don't know. Just before midnight maybe.'

'It's been over three hours.'

'Would he go to a neighbour?' asks Isabelle. 'A nearby relative?'

'No. And they would call if he had.'

'OK. We should wait here. This is where he'll likely come.' She pauses. 'I do think if we haven't heard by daylight, we should call the police.'

Veronica doesn't respond.

During the darkest hours of night, the two women move around the house like chess pieces on a board, controlled by heavenly hands; one standing by the window, one sitting at the table where Sebastian eats his eggs, one dialling his number over and over despite now getting a 'this phone is switched off' message. Then they swap over and go through the same moves again.

Finally – just after six-fifteen – the lemon fingers of dawn claw at the sky above the trees in Veronica's garden.

'I'm calling Tilly,' she says suddenly.

'Why?' Isabelle was beginning to nod off on the kitchen stool.

'I'll ask her to come early and then we can go out and look again before we...'

'Call the police?'

Veronica nods gravely.

'We'll have to go in my car,' says Isabelle.

Veronica makes the call in the other room and Isabelle just hears the odd word: 'gone ... frantic ... hours ... minutes'. The final word lingers in Isabelle's head: *minutes*. They are ticking by. That's how it feels. Like she can hear them. Is this how Sebastian felt when he monitored the time?

Tilly arrives and hugs Veronica. Isabelle looks at her phone. It's six-fifty-nine. She remembers how Sebastian had to wait until seven-thirty before he'd have sex with her, how one time he told her he needed to prepare for it, and could she not speak until it was that time.

'We have to go right now,' Isabelle cries.

'What?' Veronica frowns.

You are Sebastian's ghost, Isabelle. And you need to catch him before he falls...

The thoughts take her by surprise. Is it exhaustion? Her imagination? 'It's just gone seven. You know how Sebby is about the time. We can't let it get to seven-thirty.'

'Why?'

'Seven-thirty is important to him. If he's going to do anything, it will be then.'

'*Do* anything? You're scaring me.'

Isabelle realises it's part instinct, part logic, the perfect joining of her and Sebastian: the ghost and the scientist; a moment and the exact time.

'Let's go,' she says, without waiting for Veronica.

She looks at the time: seven minutes past seven. Shit. It's about a fifteen-minute drive to the river – less if she's fast – and that only gives them five minutes to run along the path to Sebastian's bench. That's where he'll be at seven-thirty. She knows it. She runs to her car. Veronica follows and jumps into the passenger side.

'What's going on?' she demands.

'We're going to the river.' Isabelle pulls away.

'But I don't th—'

'He'll go there for seven-thirty.'

'Why seven-thirty?'

'It's when we...' Isabelle murmurs. '... you know ... It had to be that time.'

'But you could be wrong,' says Veronica. 'When he was going to tell you about this Norma Jean, I asked when he might do it, and he said he'd decided that that kind of honesty shouldn't have an exact time. He said he'd do it when it felt right.'

The words hurt Isabelle, even though she already knows about Norma Jean.

She looks at the time. Nine minutes past seven. Shit.

'What else can we try?' she asks Veronica.

'You don't think...'

'What?'

They look at one another – the same dark thought is visible in Veronica's eyes.

'Let's just get there,' cries Isabelle.

At seven-twenty-four they dump the car near the Country Park Inn and hurry to the river path. It's a different place this morning, soft and unformed in the dawn light. It curves to the left, following the water. The water flows in the opposite direction to the path, east, swirling and angry. With random bushes dotted along the edge, they can't see the benches at first. Then they do. Isabelle knows Sebby will be there. Despite a bone-aching exhaustion, she runs. Veronica follows.

'Seven-twenty-nine,' she screams as they pound the path.

'I can't keep up,' pants Veronica. 'You go. Leave me and *go*!'

Isabelle runs, faster than she ever has. The two benches come closer. She chances a look at her phone. Seven-thirty-one. She reaches the first bench, heart in her throat, forehead damp.

He isn't there.

Shit, shit, *shit*.

Then she realises he isn't on his bench because he has gone. Into the water. There is a figure, waist-deep, in the river.

'No,' she screams.

She still has to climb over all the rocks to get to him.

'No, no, *no*!' she screams. 'I love you, Sebastian.'

Catch him before he falls...

47

SEBASTIAN IS AN ICICLE

This is cold.

I'm going to freeze before I sink. I didn't have time to follow my *How To Sink* list after all. I'll be a dead icicle instead. Cold, cold, cold, and I'm only up to my waist. The mud at the bottom sucks my Puma trainers down. I should have taken them off at our bench like I did with my dad. They'll be ruined. It's hard to walk. The water is much thicker than at the pool and it's churning around me.

If I fall over, I'm in trouble because I'll get stuck in the slime at the bottom. I shudder at this thought. I don't like this. Too shivery now. My teeth chatter and even the inside of me is cold, like ice cubes are stuck to my heart. I don't want to sink now. I don't want to freeze. And I don't want to fall. But my feet are stuck. I can't turn around. I'm trapped, facing the river forever.

I remember telling my mum there's never a railing or steps from the sea and that's why I had to learn to pull myself out of the pool without them. She said, *But you'll never be alone in any of those places.*

What did she know? She sent me here.

I'm alone.

I used to try so hard to get out of the pool without using the steps or the railing, but I never managed. It was my nemesis. I used to practise my drowning face in front of my mum before doing my rescue certificate. I don't know if my real drowning face will be the same as the one I did then.

I once asked my mum if she would ever rescue me, and she said yes.

Now I don't want her to.

I don't ever want to see her again.

Who can I trust if I can't trust her?

My thoughts are getting blurry now. The cold must be in my brain. Even though my hands are dry inside my gloves, my fingers tingle. The water splashes my chest. I can't feel my legs. Cold, cold, cold. I need to get out. Cold, cold, cold. I'm a Sebastian icicle.

Then I hear a voice.

Faraway.

I love you, Sebastian!

I want to turn and look but I'm scared I'll fall.

Stay there. I'm coming in. Stay there!

Closer now.

It's HoneyBee.

Stay there. Stay there!

What a silly thing to say. I can't go anywhere, can I? I'm stuck here. I don't know if I want her to help me. I'm still mad. But she does love me. She said so.

Don't move. I'm almost with you.

I c-c-can't. I cry. *My feet are s-s-stuck.*

I hear splashing and a huge gasp that I know means she's in the icy river too. Then she's at my side. HoneyBee.

I sh-sh-shouldn't speak to you, I say. *You did me wrong.*

Don't speak then, she says. *Just let me help you get out of here, OK?*

She holds my arm. She is small next to me. She always was.

You're still shivering, she says. *This is a good sign.*

I nod.

Hold on to me and try and pull one of your feet free.

I'm scared I'll pull her over, but she's stronger than she looks. She'll make a good nurse. She'll be able to carry the crippled ones and pull the slow ones. Her body is as strong as her heart.

I've got you, she says. *You won't fall.*

I don't. I pull hard and one of my feet comes out of the mud, leaving my Puma trainer there. We slowly turn together. The water makes it difficult. Then I pull my other foot free, leaving another trainer there. Fifteen pounds fifty wasted. I doubt they are insured. Another slow step, and another. We rise out of the water. We reach the shore. I'm even colder now.

Then I see her.

Mum.

Standing by my dad's bench.

I'm not t-t-talking to her, I yell at Isabelle.

You don't have to. We need to get you straight to the car and out of those wet clothes. Trust me, I'm a nurse.

Not quite, I remind her.

Sebastian, walk with me and walk fast, or you'll end up with hypothermia.

We climb back over the rocks.

Sebastian, darling, my mum cries.

I ignore her and start running up the path. I hear Isabelle tell her that we need to get me home. I run and run and run. Like I did earlier. The wind is painful on my wet legs. The stony ground hurts my feet without the protection of my trainers. I hear Isabelle behind me. I know my mum doesn't do running and I'm glad. Through the trees, I see Isabelle's car. It isn't locked so I climb into the passenger seat. I'm so cold now my breath is stunted. Isabelle gets in and turns the engine on and hot air blasts me.

Take off your jeans, she says.

We're not having s-s-sex now, I say.

I know, she laughs. *They're wet. You won't warm up with them on.*

I peel them off. She's right. The hot air on my legs feels good.

Then Mum opens my door.

You're not coming in here! I yell. *If she does, I'm going back in the river,* I tell Isabelle.

Sebastian, darling, I know how mad you are but just let me—

NO! I can't look at you. You have hurt me.

If I look at her, I might melt. I need to stay as an icicle. I push her hand off the door and slam it shut. Isabelle gets out of the car. I know they are talking about me. I don't care. It's nice and warm in here and my legs tingle and my eyes feel heavy. It has been a long night. I feel cold air again as Isabelle gets back into the car. She puts something over my legs – her coat.

Your mum said you can come to mine for now, and she'll get a taxi home, OK?

I nod. I'm too tired to speak. Isabelle pulls away.

How did you know to come here? I ask before I fall asleep.

I knew because it was almost seven-thirty.

Of course.

Of course.

48

ISABELLE DOESN'T KNOW THE WORDS

Isabelle parks the car on her drive and looks at Sebastian sleeping.

She studies his gorgeous mouth and flushed cheeks and long eyelashes. She leaves the engine running so as not to disturb him. She wants to cherish the moment. He's all hers in his oblivion. But when she opens the door, lets the cold in, and tries to get him inside the house, this will be over. He will never be at her side in the car, quiet, like this again. She knows this like she knew he would go into the river at seven-thirty.

Isabelle remembers the first kindling of her love catching fire.

It was their fifth time together if you included the clinic and their first chat on the river. They were in her car like now, and she was surprised to realise that she was happy; so surprised that she frowned at her reflection in the mirror, looked for a light in her eyes, a relaxation of frown lines. The emotion came pure and gentle. *Happiness*, she had thought, *is right here, in the car beside me, uncomplicated, warm-eyed, and fastening a seatbelt.*

Now he sleeps. He is safe again.

But he's not uncomplicated; he's complex and wilful and strong. He's a man. He's not hers, and he's not responsible for her happiness. She loves him in a way that she would have drowned to rescue him; in a way that she can't bear the thought of a Monday, Wednesday or Friday without seeing him; in a way that she can't imagine waking without his face in her head before anything else.

Her dad appears at the front door.

Isabelle holds a hand up to say that she needs five minutes, and he nods, his face sad, and goes back inside. She realises suddenly that he's had no clue where she's been all night. She didn't even think to let him know what was going on. Was she punishing him the way Sebastian is Veronica? It wasn't intentional; she was wrapped up in finding Sebby. Or was it? She isn't fully sure.

She feels bad for Veronica. Sebastian's rejection of her. She thinks sadly of them outside the car earlier. Isabelle tried to persuade Veronica that she was sure he would see her soon, that he just needed space, and then he would come home. Sebastian doesn't belong to either of them. Isabelle must let him go. She must get him inside, let him sleep, and then let him go.

She switches the engine off.

The car cools.

He stirs.

'Sebby,' she says softly. 'We're at my house now. You need to come inside and have a hot drink, something to eat, and then you can sleep for a few hours.'

He grunts, shakes his head.

'How about a cup of sweet tea?'

'When have you seen me drink tea?' he snaps. 'You know I like hot chocolate.'

'OK, hot chocolate then.'

'And biscuits.'

'Yes.'

Isabelle gets out and goes to help him in case he's weak. She giggles when she remembers he has bare legs. He looks down and then back at the mud-caked jeans on the back seat.

'Are they ruined?' he asks.

'I think so.'

'I'm glad I wasn't wearing my wedding trousers that have never been to a wedding. I want to wear them for my wedding one day.'

Isabelle hurries him inside, trying not to picture his wedding, his bride, a woman who isn't her. The house is deliciously warm. Her dad hovers by the kitchen door, looking first at Sebastian's muddy legs and then at Isabelle. The hallway is no longer scattered with pieces of broken snow globe. He must have cleared it away. She hopes, absentmindedly, that he kept the photo of her and Sebastian.

'I'm sorry I didn't call,' she explains. 'It was a hell of a night, but it's OK now.'

'I didn't sink,' says Sebastian.

'Sink?' Her dad looks worried. 'What happened, lad?'

'I'll tell you later,' says Isabelle. 'Sebastian needs something hot and a good sleep.'

'Why doesn't he go home?'

'Because my mum's there.' Sebastian marches into the kitchen.

'Dad, I'll explain later. Let me rest first.'

He nods. 'Are we OK?' he asks her.

She shrugs and follows Sebby. They take his hot chocolate and a packet of custard creams up to her bedroom. He glugs the drink and devours the biscuits, scattering crumbs among the stars on her duvet cover.

'Can I sleep here?' he asks.

'In my bed?'

'Yes. We can't have sex though.'

'I know,' says Isabelle.

'I did enjoy our sex.' Sebastian climbs under the covers. She doesn't care if he muddies them. 'It was shocking for me to find out my mum had given you thousands of pounds to do it with me though. I'm glad I'm worth more than my Puma trainers, but I wish I had known. I don't think there's anything wrong with paying for it. It's just an exchange of one thing for another. My mum pays Tillda to clean our house. What's the difference? People get very silly about it.' He closes his eyes. 'You can lie next to me if you want, as long as you don't snore.'

'I'll lie on top of the duvet,' says Isabelle.

But he has gone; asleep.

'I love you,' she whispers.

'I know,' he says sleepily, surprising her. 'I love you maybe … ninety-one percent now…'

She smiles, but her heart breaks a little more. She messages Veronica to say he's asleep and that she'll get in touch when he wakes. The phone lights up. Veronica. A short, sad message.

Take care of my beautiful boy.

When Isabelle wakes later, she's momentarily disoriented. Then she remembers why she's sleeping at the opposite side to her pillow, on top of the duvet. She sits up; the goggles hanging on the head-board above Sebastian's wild hair move. She leans over to touch them. Sebby is still asleep. The room is full of his breath and winter sunlight.

What time is it?

Eleven-forty-five.

Isabelle goes downstairs. Her dad is in his chair in the living room, the fire ablaze in the hearth.

'I spend too much time in this chair, lass,' he sighs. 'I've never been so sedentary. I can't stand it.'

'You're still recovering.' Isabelle sits on the sofa opposite.

He holds out the photo of her and Sebby. She takes it, looking at the image with tired eyes.

'I shouldn't have called him *an* autistic,' he says.

'No, you shouldn't.'

'I'm clumsy with my words. You love him. I can see that. Your face lights up at the mention of him. I think I saw it all along – the way you were around him. That's why I thought it was more than tutoring.'

Isabelle can't speak. The magnitude of it overwhelms her: the past few months; the escorting; her dad being ill; loving Sebastian. And now, losing him.

'He doesn't love me though,' she says quietly. 'He loves another girl.'

'Oh. I'm sorry.'

She shrugs. He looks sad.

'What the hell happened tonight?'

Isabelle summarises the whole, crazy night for him.

Her dad comes and sits with her. 'I'm glad you're OK.'

She nods.

'I'm still the same me,' he says.

Isabelle swallows back the sob that begins deep in her chest.

'We're not defined by what we've done,' her dad continues, 'but by what we do *after* that. You accepted money from the lad's mum during a desperate time. When you realised you loved him, you gave it back. And I worked in a job I didn't enjoy, making money to look after us too. But I couldn't do it for long either. In the end it felt ... wrong. For someone else it might be perfectly right, and that's fine too. But we have to do what's right for us, don't we?' He pauses to put a hand over hers. 'But I'm still me. You're still you. We're still *us*.'

Isabelle realises she must accept that her dad is flawed, not a perfect childhood hero, and make it up with him if she is to persuade Sebby to see Veronica again. She must set the example. She must forgive and be forgiven.

'I'm still the dad who missed you on those trips. Maybe not Peter Pan or Santa Claus, but, well...' He smiles. 'And you're still my girl. No matter what.'

Isabelle leans into his shoulder. For a brief moment, she sees Simon, sweating and stammering above her. She pushes it away. There is still a lot to face and it won't be easy. But her dad doesn't need to know about that now. She might tell him one day, when she can put it into words that won't destroy him. Or not. She will decide.

For now, she is his girl again.

☐

After a while she goes to check on Sebastian. Perhaps the opening door disturbs him, for his tousled head pokes up out of the duvet, face perplexed.

'Why am I here?' he demands. 'What day is it?'

'It's Tuesday now.' Isabelle sits on the bed.

'I'm never here on a Tuesday.'

'Well, now you are.'

She longs to kiss him. 'Don't you remember last night?'

'Yes.' He sits up, puts the goggles on. 'Can you make me some eggs?'

'In a minute, yes. First, I reckon you should have a shower and then think about going ho—'

'What did a quarter of a million pounds look like?' he interrupts. 'I tried to imagine it, last night, when I was running. You must have needed a big bag for it.'

'I didn't physically see it,' says Isabelle, embarrassed. 'It was going to be a bank transfer and then it didn't happen. I never liked lying to you about it, Sebby. Your mum only hid it because she wanted to make you happy. Even if she was wrong to pay me like that, her heart was right. You have to talk to her.'

'Don't want to.'

'Now you sound like a child.'

'Well, I'm not.'

'I know that more than anyone.' Isabelle lifts the goggles off his eyes and hangs them back on the bedpost. 'Look, I just talked to my dad. I didn't want to. I was mad at him. But we're OK now. Because we were honest.'

'My mum wasn't honest.'

'No, and neither was my dad about something. Neither was I, both with you and with him. But we have been now. That's what matters.' Isabelle pauses. 'Do you love your mum?'

'Yes. A hundred percent.'

'Then go home and be the man you are and talk to her. She's sad.'

'I would rather stay here and eat more custard creams and listen to music.'

'No, you wouldn't. You want to do the right thing. I know you do.'

'I don't have any trousers.'

'Excuses, excuses.'

'Or shoes. I can't go down the street like this. People will take pictures and laugh at me.'

She shakes her head. 'No, they won't. I'll get some of my dad's for you.'

'Ooo, can I pick for myself?'

'No. You can get a shower.'

When he's clean, Isabelle hands Sebastian a pair of her dad's suit trousers and some overly polished black shoes, realising she may never again see his sturdy, slightly bowed legs bare in all their beauty. He pulls the grey slacks on and fastens them. They are slightly loose. The shoes are tight. He giggles and it melts her heart.

'I look like I'm going to the office,' he says.

'You're not,' she says, 'you're going home.'

'You said you'd make me eggs.'

'You know who makes them best?'

'Mum,' says Sebastian softly.

'Yes.'

'Let's go then.'

'OK, bossy boots.'

Isabelle messages Veronica and says she's bringing her boy home. Then she drives the familiar journey to the house. Sebastian sings along to Spandau Ballet. Isabelle tries not to cry. They pull up on his driveway. She senses it won't be the last time she sees him but knows this is the end of what they shared, the last of their Mondays and Wednesdays and Fridays, the termination of their agreement. Sebby may have written her a new one, agreeing to go swimming on those days instead, but she needs to let him go. Let him see his Norma Jean. Let him live. Let him love.

Veronica opens her front door.

They look at one another.

Isabelle sees a million things in her face.

'I'm sorry about the snow globe, HoneyBee,' says Sebastian, undoing his seatbelt. 'I'll get you another one.'

'Don't worry, Sebby.'

'Shall we go swimming on Wednesday?'

'I think you should see your Norma Jean,' says Isabelle softly.

'On a Wednesday?'

'Why not?'

'I suppose.' He opens the car door. 'Knock, knock,' he says.

'Who's there?'

'HoneyBee.'

She smiles. 'HoneyBee Who?'

'HoneyBee a dear and open the door, please.'

'It already is,' she says quietly.

Cold air fills the car. Then Sebastian gets out and closes it. She watches him go up the drive and push past his mum. Veronica looks at her again, mouths *thank you*, and goes inside. Isabelle turns the radio up on the way home. When Billy Ocean's 'Suddenly' comes on she tries to sing along through her tears, but she doesn't know the words. Without Sebby, she doesn't know the words.

It's time to find her own.

49

VERONICA SPEAKS THE TRUTH

Tilly has been a Godsend.

When Veronica got home from the river, exhausted and tearful, she was waiting with calm kindness, and made fresh coffee and forced her to eat some toast. Until the moment Veronica began sobbing into that coffee, she never realised how much she's come to depend on Tilly over the years. Originally, after Pete died, she kept her out of habit, and because he hired her.

But she's more than a housekeeper; more than paid help.

'Thank you,' Veronica said over and over to her.

'For what, Mrs Murphy? I made toast, that's all.'

'For coming straight away when I called. You have three kids of your own, but you didn't hesitate. And for loving Sebastian like you do. And, Tilly, for God's sake *stop* calling me Mrs Murphy.'

Tilly patted her back and made more toast.

'You must go home to your own family now,' insisted Veronica.

'I'll leave when Sebastian is back, Mrs Mur—' She paused. *'Veronica.'*

Now Veronica is pacing the floor, waiting for her boy to be back in the house. Isabelle messaged ten minutes ago, saying they were on their way. She feels sick. How will Sebastian be? She knows more than anyone how stubborn he is. How absolute he is about things that niggle or annoy him, and she has done more than that.

She sees again his face when he shut the car door on her. It's unbearable. It hurt so much to let him go with Isabelle, to watch her car take him under the bridge and away from her, but she had little choice. He's safe. That's what matters most.

She hears a car on the gravel and rushes to the front door.

The car that took Sebastian away has returned him.

Veronica exchanges a look with Isabelle, one she hopes says *thank you*, over and over, *for everything*.

Sebastian gets out, and after talking to Isabelle – Veronica can't hear what they say – he marches to the house and pushes past her without eye contact or a word. Veronica closes the door and follows him into the kitchen. He's wearing grey slacks that are just too short and a little loose, and some pointed black shoes. If the situation wasn't so desperate, she'd smile at how strange he looks.

'Hi Tillda,' he says.

'Glad to have you back, Sebastian.' Tilly ruffles his hair, which he puts straight as soon as she's done.

'I've had quite the ordeal, Tillda. Can you make me some eggs?'

'Let me make them, darling,' says Veronica.

'I think Tillda should do them.'

Veronica knows he's testing her. 'Tilly has to go now,' she says. 'She has her own children to see today.'

'I know *that*. Tillda, we can resume tomorrow.'

When she has gone, Veronica and Sebastian remain in the kitchen. He stands by the kitchen door, stiff, quiet. She has no idea what to say, and for the first time in her life she can't read him. She suddenly remembers a moment at school, when a careless teacher made an excuse for him to a dinner lady he had insulted, saying Sebastian found it hard to read people's faces. Privately, Veronica took the teacher to task, telling her that he could read faces, perhaps just not those of rude, ignorant canteen staff. Now *she* is the one who has lost that ability. She hardly knows her own boy.

'I'm waiting,' he says.

She panics. For what? Her apology. She's sorry. She opens her mouth to express it.

'We can talk in my room,' he interrupts. 'I want to be on my territory.'

She follows him up the stairs. He opens the door and stands aside to let her in without looking at her. This room evokes so many memories; it's here where she nursed him through the night as a baby, where she held him tightly as a frustrated toddler, where she read stories to him over and over and over as a child. She has always loved how the huge window lets in the most sunlight, how this space contains every precious part of him, from Flip and Scorpion in the bubbling fish tank, to the OCD-tidy books and CDs, to the stars on the ceiling flashing silver as he sleeps.

Veronica doesn't know what to do, where to stand. She loiters, nervous, by the fish tank. Sebastian chooses the opposite corner of the room, facing her, as though ready to fight in a ring.

'You stand there in your corner,' he says, fists tight by his side. 'Like you always have been. Always in your own corner, always in a purple or gold or silver scarf, thinking you know me best.'

'I do know you best,' says Veronica quietly. 'I've known you best since I first held you in my arms and promised to love you forever, more than anyone else in th—'

Sebastian shakes his head. 'No, *I* know me best.'

She nods. Of course. He's right.

'You don't respect me either.'

'I do,' she insists.

'No, you don't.'

'Darling,' she tries, 'haven't I always been the one who stood up for you?'

'You didn't think a girl could love me.'

Veronica feels like she is the one sinking into a muddy river. She wants to argue that she did, but the words stick in her throat. She must say something. She forces them out.

'I did – I *do*!' she cries.

'No. If you had believed a girl could you would never have gone behind my back and given Isabelle a pile of non-physical money to have sex with me.'

What can she say to that?

'You should have *talked* to me,' he cries. 'You know that I think it's fine to pay for sex. I said that way back.'

'Oh, darling, you have to understand that I was just sad to see you longing for sex, and love, saying you wanted a girl. My heart broke for you. I wanted to see you happy.'

'How can I be happy with a mum who doesn't believe a girl could fall in love with me, just by being with me? I was scared it wouldn't happen, but I didn't think *you* were scared too.'

She sobs openly. He remains in his corner. Never has he been so standoffish; her boy can never usually bear to see her upset.

'I was wrong,' she says. 'I don't know what else to say. I'm not perfect or infallible.'

'You were to me, Mum.'

Past tense. 'I'm sorry.'

'You should be.'

'I am. With all my heart.'

'I guess that's a lot then,' he admits.

She pauses. 'Can't we get past it, somehow?'

'Think how big the brain is,' says Sebastian. 'It's like the universe. I read once about how many songs we listen to in our lifetime and how we never forget them once we know them. But you want me to forget what you have done. How can I? You are far harder to forget than Billy Ocean's lyrics.'

'I don't expect you to forget anything, but can you forgive me?'

'I don't know,' he cries, suddenly angry. He paces back and forth. 'I don't *know*. It is hard for me to feel like this.'

'Oh, darling, let me hold you.'

'No. Stay away. You should have talked to me about that money.'

'You're right, I should have asked you.'

'You walked around this house, putting your scarf right and tidying up and going out to meet someone that I know now was Isabelle, and all that time you were lying to me. I can't stand lies. They used to laugh at me at college. Tell me stuff that was lies to trick me. Take pictures of me and share them. Show me rude films on the bus and then hit me when I liked them. But you are worse.'

'They were *college* boys who hurt you on the bus that time?' Veronica is angry again. 'You said you didn't know who they were...'

'Yes, Mum.'

'Why on earth didn't you tell me? I would have had them expelled.'

'Because I don't need you fighting all my battles. Can't you see that?'

Veronica doesn't know what to say.

'I'm not a child!' He hits his head. Kicks the bookshelf.

She tries desperately to find the words to calm him. What does he need to hear? *You know what he wants.* The voice comes to her clearly. It's Pete. *The truth.* Yes, the truth. The very thing she should have started with.

'Shall I be completely honest with you, Sebastian?'

'Yes,' he cries. 'That is all I have ever wanted.'

Veronica braces herself. Sebastian looks at her. Stops pacing.

She speaks.

'I should have talked to you, darling. I was wrong. I've spent all my life arguing for you, putting the do-gooders in their place, speaking on your behalf and standing up for you, so much that I forgot to let you stand up for yourself now you're a man. Because you are. You are my beautiful man. I have no right to make your decisions. No right to think I know what you want. Only *you* know that.'

She pauses. Sebastian is listening intently.

'When I had the idea of paying a ... a ... lady to be with you, I should have talked to you about it. That is a major decision to make for anyone, and I didn't respect you enough to come to you. If I had, I'd have known you might be OK to do it. I kept it from you so you would think Isabelle had chosen you herself. I should have had more faith that a girl *would* eventually choose you.'

She feels Pete beside her.

'I fought all these years against discrimination without realising I've discriminated against you more than anyone. I wanted to smash the limits society set you, but I set limitations for you myself. I pushed for equality without treating you like an equal myself. It has been hard on my own, without your dad. That's no excuse, but a reason. I was blinded by my own fight.' Veronica takes a deep breath. 'I can't undo what I've done, but I admit my errors, and from the bottom of my heart, I'm sorry.'

Sebastian unfurls his fists. There are tears in his eyes. He nods.

Veronica nods too.

Softly, the fish tank bubbles, as always.

'What does a man have to do to get some eggs around here?' he asks after a moment.

It's that simple. Eggs now.

Veronica laughs, relief flooding her body. 'I'll make you some.' She longs to hold him but doesn't want to push it. She goes to the door.

'I would have got there in the end,' he says.

'Where, darling?' She stops.

'Love. Sex. I know I was difficult back then, but I'd have got there in the end.'

'I know it now.'

'I'm hungry,' he snaps to hurry her. 'I *have* been up all night, you know. It's nearly three o'clock and I need to feed Flip and Scorpion. You can make my eggs and I'll be there in two minutes.'

Veronica opens the door. She looks back. In the alien grey trousers and black shoes, Sebastian sprinkles fish food like rainbow hailstones into the tank. Flip and Scorpion gobble hungrily at it. One of the trouser legs is tucked into a striped sock and Veronica wants to tell Sebastian, knowing how smart he likes to be, but she doesn't. He will see for himself. He will right it himself.

She makes Sebastian's eggs exactly as he likes them, flipped over, crispy and almost burnt, three on a plate, no sauce. He devours them, wipes his mouth with his sleeve, thanks her, and goes back upstairs, like none of the last twenty-four hours happened. Isn't that what Veronica wants? Life to resume its pattern. Not perfect, but everyday. Yes. After a while she hears music and goes into the hallway to name the song. Pat Benatar, 'We Belong.' She sits on the bottom step and listens to him heartily singing along, whispering the words she knows too.

They sing together, but he is the loudest.

◻

In the middle of the night, still awake, a thought makes Veronica sit up. She turns on the lamp and scribbles a note for herself on the inside of her latest paperback, so she doesn't forget in the morning.

When she reads it in the early sunlight, she smiles.

You need to give Tilly the £250,000 you were going to give to Isabelle. Give her the freedom to never have to work again and devote her time to her own family. She won't want to take it but you'll find a way.

SEBASTIAN MAKES A NEW LIST

How to Never Sink Again

Number One – Always talk, even when you want to smash a snow globe instead.

Number Two – Respect the river. It is turbulent, cold, and very muddy.

Number Three – Consider seeing HoneyBee on days that are not Monday, Wednesday or Friday.

Number Four – The same as above except with Norma Jean.

Number Five – Consider wearing smart trousers more often. They feel nice.

Number Six – Always talk. This is worth repeating.

Number Seven – Listen to some music from the nineties now and again too. You need to broaden your tastes and consider that this decade produced just as many greats.

Number Eight – Always talk. And be honest too.

Number Nine – Be with Norma Jean as much as you can.

ISABELLE IS HER OWN GHOST

It's late August.

The red-faced day-trippers and holidaymakers, and the dry heat of a long summer, mean Paragon Station is suffocating. Isabelle finds a spot on the cool marble steps, the two bulging cases by her feet, not caring if she's in the way; it's the only place where a dusty breeze occasionally finds a way in through the main entrance. She sips her latte, wishing she had bought a cold drink instead. On the tannoy, an update: twenty minutes until the train departs.

And Sebastian isn't here yet.

Distract yourself, she thinks. *He'll come.*

Isabelle has always had a love/hate relationship with stations. When she was small, she loved that trains could take you anywhere you liked, but that they stole her dad away, she hated. Long ago, she waved him off from here, crying when the carriage door shut and that was it, he'd gone. Now she is the one leaving him. But this is no long-haul getaway; no Hong Kong skyline her dad once described so vividly in his notes, no Golden Gate Bridge appearing out of mist, no New York scattering of lights.

Isabelle finishes her drink, thinks of their goodbye earlier.

Her dad is back at work now. He may never be the robust man he was – the man who walked with vigour – but he's managing the casinos again, just taking a more backseat role, as he assures Isabelle every day, and letting Nick do most of it now. It was awkward the first time Isabelle saw Nick again, after finding out he had seen her page on the website. The anger at him telling her dad had abated by then. Perhaps he had just wanted to get Charles to stop her. Perhaps he was trying to protect her. She may never know now.

Life isn't always neat. We don't always get answers or tidy endings for everything.

'It's only London,' Charles said to her earlier, her luggage by the door.

'A tiny flat in *East* London,' she corrected.

'I mean, it's not far, lass. I'll pop down all the time.'

'You won't,' she said. 'You'll take things easy.'

'Anyway, you'll come home, won't you?'

'Of course.'

He hugged her; she put her cheek to his chest. An engine, outside.

'I think that's your taxi,' he said.

It was. Isabelle reluctantly pulled free.

'Don't forget these,' he added. 'They were in my room.'

He handed her the batch of childhood notes tied with red ribbon. She held the bundle in her lap for the entire car journey to the station. Now, to distract herself from Sebastian still not being here, she reads one of them.

Dad, when the lamp is turned off and you are away, I look up into the night sky and see the moon staring back like you told me to, and I know it's the same moon that you are looking at...

Isabelle is starting a new job as a learning-disability nurse on a London hospital safeguarding team. She managed to scrape a two-two in her degree, quite a miracle after everything she had going on.

When she saw the job advertised in July, it could have been written for her:

> *You will hold an RNLD qualification and have extensive experience working with people with a learning disability and autism. This must be evidenced within your application. Experience of the hospital setting is desirable, but you must be confident in your role, and able to make decisions about complex situations.*

When Isabelle saw that it was in London, she thought, what the hell? It was time she saw another city; for real, not through the glass of a snow globe.

She has left those childhood treasures on her windowsill and desk.

Except for one.

She looks at the time. Fifteen minutes until her train. Where *is* Sebastian? She stands up and surveys the place. She told him she would wait near Starbucks. Has he changed his mind? Is it all too much for him after all? *Don't panic.* He'll come; she knows it. Veronica will make sure he does.

Thinking of her, Isabelle smiles.

They have become close over the last few months. Once there was no money on the table, no agreement in place, they were free to be friends. Isabelle is delighted that Veronica met a man, one she is taking things slowly with, one Sebastian strongly approves of. The two women said goodbye yesterday over coffee, in their usual café overlooking the now scorched, almost-autumn fields. Veronica gave her a beautiful hand-stitched scarf with delicate silver nurse caps scattered across the silk.

'Because you can never have too many,' she said. 'Despite what Sebastian says.'

And they laughed.

Isabelle looks again at the time; just twelve minutes until the train leaves platform two. Sebastian isn't coming. Her heart constricts. A man in a suit pushes past. Sebastian isn't coming. Of *course* he is. He never lets her down. She puts the bundle of notes back in her bag and spots his swimming goggles. She touches the faded strap. Looks up.

He's here.

Out of breath, hair wild, *I AM HUMAN TOO* T-shirt tucked into smart suit trousers; polished shoes on.

'There were too many cars on the road,' he pants. 'I got Bob to drop me near the hospital and ran all the way here.' He bends to catch his breath. 'I ran and ran and ran. It was like that night on the river, except I wasn't running away from you, I was running towards you.'

'You're here,' is all Isabelle can say, looking at the time.

It used to define them: seven o'clock picking him up; seven-thirty for sex. Now it is again – the one-forty-five train will leave in ten minutes.

'I'm glad it was Bob,' pants Sebastian.

'Ah, Bob,' smiles Isabelle.

After Sebastian called a taxi to the river six months ago, he became obsessed with booking them to go places, no matter whether it was the corner shop or into town. And he always asked for the man who had originally dropped him off: Bob Fracklehurst. The taxi firm began to expect his calls. Sebastian and Bob have become firm friends.

Then Veronica joined them on a ride one day.

Since then the two of them have met a handful of times for drinks, much to Sebastian's joy.

'It's about time she got a man,' he said. 'She's nearly fifty-six now. Soon she won't even want sex because she'll be dried up.'

Sebastian looks at the two suitcases and then Isabelle.

'This is it then,' she says.

'Are you ready, HoneyBee?'

'I don't know.'

She loves him. Oh, she *loves* him.

They walk to the platform and find a bench. The train is in. Eight minutes until it leaves. Sebastian picks a wrapper and an empty can up off the bench and puts them in the bin. He won't sit still. Isabelle knows he's anxious. Perhaps this was a bad idea.

'I think I might get my hair cut,' he says.

'Why? I love your hair as it is.'

'You are making changes. I will too.'

She smiles.

Kiss me, she thinks.

Six minutes.

'I don't like saying goodbye,' he says after a while.

'I know,' says Isabelle softly.

'Can we not say it?'

'But I have to go, Sebby.'

'Can we say a different word so it's not like we are.'

Isabelle still loves him. Life is never so kind as to lessen love when the desired person doesn't feel the same. If anything, it only intensifies the feeling. But she loves him enough to let him go. She loves him enough to want his happiness above all else.

And he loves Norma Jean.

They became inseparable over the summer. Sebastian wanted Isabelle to meet her, but she kept making excuses. She was happy he'd found love, but she didn't think she could cope with seeing the young woman who had stolen his heart.

'I wish you'd met Norma Jean,' he says now, as though reading her thoughts.

I can't, thinks Isabelle. *I can't see how you might look at her.*

'The next time I'm home,' she lies.

Four minutes.

'Remember my ghost on the landing,' she says, 'and you said I imagined it, that it was just me. Well, I still think she was there.'

'Good,' says Sebastian. 'I'm not right about everything. I've learned a lot from you. I don't just mean the sex stuff. I mean you have made me think about things I might otherwise not have thought about.'

'Really?'

'Yes.' He pauses. 'HoneyBee?'

'Yes,' she says.

'You know when you're doing your nursing stuff with your autistic patients, it's better that you don't have sex with them.'

'Sebastian,' she cries. 'I *know* that!'

She realises he's grinning; he's joking.

Three minutes.

'There is no shame in it,' he says.

'In what?'

'In exchanging sex for money. I would have been an escort if it had been a way to keep my dad alive.'

'Oh, Sebby.'

'I can't watch the train go.'

'OK.' She nods.

'Can you get on it now and say a word that isn't goodbye?'

'Which word shall we use?'

He thinks, brow furrowed. Isabelle touches his cheek.

'Let's say nothing,' she says.

Two minutes.

'Have you got your snow globe?' he asks.

'Of course.'

Sebastian bought her a replacement for the broken one so she could put the photo of them inside it. It's a cheap, plastic thing, with glitzy gold flakes inside, and she could not love it more.

One and a half minutes.

'I'm going,' she says, the words choked.

'I'm not saying it.'

She grabs the swimming goggles from her bag. 'You should have these. I know you've been swimming a lot.' With Norma Jean.

'I have new ones,' he says. 'You keep them.'

She doesn't speak.

'Keep them,' he repeats. 'Go now.'

She turns and heads for the carriage.

'I'm saying nothing,' he calls after her. '*Nothing!*'

Isabelle wants to look back, but she can't because she might never leave. Choking back tears, she climbs aboard, heaves her luggage into the rack and finds her seat. Has he gone? Is he watching her leave? She can't bear to look out of the window. The train begins to move.

She looks. He's there. He runs alongside the carriage as it departs. She smiles. He waves madly, his T-shirt coming free from his smart suit trousers. When the platform runs out, it is over. He gets smaller and smaller until the train rounds a corner and he is gone. It isn't goodbye. It isn't that word.

But it isn't nothing.

SEBASTIAN TALKS TO HIS DAD

When Isabelle has gone, I call Bob Fracklehurst and he takes me to the river. At first, I'm embarrassed because I'm trying not to cry. Luckily Bob isn't the kind of man you mind being embarrassed in front of. He plays my favourite radio station – Absolute Radio 90s. I've been giving that decade a chance and I have discovered some great songs.

Will you be OK, Sebastian? Bob asks me when we get to the water.

Yes, I say. *This isn't like last time.*

Should I wait?

No. I don't know how long I'll be. I don't want to measure it.

He looks worried, so I tell him I'm sad about Isabelle going, but I don't want to sink this time. I'm sad, but I'm floating. Sad but floating. I like this. I might write another poem. I tell Bob my mum knows I'm here, so he doesn't worry, but he still watches me as I go down the path.

I reach the two benches. I've brought Norma Jean here a few times. Her mum made us a picnic of hard-boiled eggs and vanilla slices the second time, so obviously I asked her again. I always let Norma Jean sit on my dad's bench to eat her lunch. She always takes her shoes off and puts them next to mine. I always think of HoneyBee when she does that and feel bad.

We have kissed here.

She's the only one I ever want to kiss here now.

This is the second time I've ever come here alone. It's a very different alone to the last time though. It's a good alone. A thinking alone. And it's hot. The grass is stiff and dry. The river is still, like a piece of brown glass. I sit on my dad's bench. I look at the water and listen to the cars on the dual carriageway behind me and think about what my dad might be like if he was here.

I talk to him.

Are you happy that Mum has found someone? I say. *I think you will be. She needs to find love, especially since I'll be leaving one day. You would really like Bob.*

But is Dad here?

Can he really hear me?

Is he a ghost?

Is Isabelle right about something lingering when a person has gone?

I've never believed in ghosts because they haven't been scientifically proven to exist. I've researched. Last week I read an article by Professor Brian Cox about the Large Hadron Collider. This is the largest and most powerful particle accelerator that humanity has ever built. It's got a ring sixteen miles long with superconducting magnets built to boost the energy of particles. It picks up even the tiniest burst. Professor Cox said that if there were any ghosts, it would have registered them.

And it hasn't.

But I'm beginning to think that science can't prove everything.

Last night I wondered if you could put love into the Large Hadron Collider, would the magnets pick up its energy? No. They wouldn't. What if a ghost is the remains of love? Love when the person is gone but is still here in your heart.

If so, I say aloud to my dad, *Isabelle is my ghost.*

I hope he can hear me. Just to make sure he does, I look around to check I'm alone, and then I speak more clearly.

Dad, I love you a hundred percent and I love Mum a hundred percent and I love Norma Jean a hundred percent. But some things can't be measured like that. Isabelle can't be measured. I learned from her and she learned from me. This is how we find our place in the world.

Then I whisper the last bit very quietly because it's just between me and him and the river.

This is how we are human.

AUTHOR'S NOTE

Autism spectrum disorder (ASD) is the name for a range of complex conditions. I knew I could never presume or hope to write a book that reflects every aspect of this spectrum, just as in writing a story about one human we are not telling the tale of all humans. To attempt to do so would only weaken Sebastian's voice.

So, I tried to tell one story; a story inspired by Fiona Mills and her beautiful boy, Sean, who is autistic. It is a story that came from her life and his, though of course Veronica is fictional and the path she chose doesn't follow one Fiona took. It's a story Fiona said she would be delighted for me to use as inspiration. I met Fiona and Sean regularly and we 'acted out' and discussed scenes. She guided me through chapters, giving often emotional feedback, much directly from Sean.

#OwnVoices is an incredible movement that encourages authors from marginalised or under-represented groups to write about their experiences, from their own perspective, rather than someone from an outside perspective trying to do so. My experience of autism is as an outsider, and my intention here is not to detract from #OwnVoices. Fiona and Sean told me their story, and I wanted to share it in fictional form because we all felt that it addressed some important issues.

I dedicate this book to Fiona, Sean, Connor, Liam and Pete Mills. You're a special and extraordinary family.

ACKNOWLEDGEMENTS

Thank you to my faithful, early beta readers, as always: Madeleine Black, John Marrs, Joanne Robertson, sisters Claire and Grace, and Fiona Mills, who read it as I went, chapter by chapter, guiding me via her own experience of life with an autistic son.

Also, as always, there are so many writers and bloggers and reviewers who make this journey special: Susie Lynes, Miranda Dickinson, Carol Lovekin, the Motherload group and especially its matriarch, Laura Pearson, plus Claire Allan, Margaret Madden, Nina Pottell, Anne Cater, the great gang of Orenda authors with whom I've travelled and laughed many times, THE Book Club and its matriarch Tracy Fenton, Book Connectors, Janet Harrison, the AMAZING Prime Writers, Carrie Martin, my beautiful WOW girls, Cass, Lynda and Michelle, also Cally Taylor, Nikki Smith, Darren O'Sullivan, Wolfy O'Hare, and Tracey Booth.

Every single time I thank my publisher, Karen Sullivan, for continuing her faith in me, and for giving me the freedom to write the things that I'm compelled to, and here I am again: thank you. Also, to West Camel for his sharp eye and perfectionism.

Thank you to every single blogger who came on the last blog tour, and to those I know will be on future ones. I truly never forget your words and I eternally appreciate your time.

If I've forgotten anyone, forgive me. It's only here, now, writing this, that your names might have slipped my now fifty-year-old brain – but the heart keeps a log.